PRAISE FOR
MIDNIGHT ON JULIA STREET

"Unforgettable entertainment… a spellbinding story… the luscious and culturally flavorful setting of New Orleans, along with a seductive plot. The many novels by Ciji Ware are among the best in the historical fiction genre."

—*Historical Novels Review*

"Entirely unique and exciting… a little historical romance mixed with some urban fantasy and a good dose of mystery and suspense… Being so full of rich history… New Orleans is the perfect setting for Ciji Ware's captivating romance fiction."

—*Romance Fiction Suite 101*

"A historical novel so lively and intriguing, you don't realize you've learnt anything till after you close the book. Exciting, entertaining, and enlightening."

—*Literary Times*

"Intriguing… Ciji Ware's writing is very elegant and rich. Her story lines are complex and inventive. She takes the reader between eras with ease and confidence… She is one of greats in historical fiction and *Midnight on Julia Street* is an example of her writing prowess… Romance readers as well as historical fiction fans will be impressed with this one… It's a must-read!"

—*Debbie's Book Bag*

"Riveting… an exciting, fast-paced story loaded with historic and contemporary detail. Ms. Ware… brings two very different eras to vivid life."

—*Linda Banche and Her Historical Hilarity*

W9-CCD-252

ALSO BY CIJI WARE

Island of the Swans
Wicked Company
A Race to Splendor
A Cottage by the Sea
Midnight on Julia Street

A Light on the Veranda

CIJI WARE

Sexton B. Little Free Library
619 Route 87
Columbia, CT 06237 8/12

sourcebooks
landmark

Copyright © 2001, 2012 by Ciji Ware
Cover and internal design © 2012 by Sourcebooks, Inc.
Cover design by Susan Zucker
Cover images © Susan Fox/Trevillion; Mosaikphotography/iStockphoto.
com

Sourcebooks and the colophon are registered trademarks of Sourcebooks,
Inc.

All rights reserved. No part of this book may be reproduced in any form
or by any electronic or mechanical means including information storage
and retrieval systems—except in the case of brief quotations embodied in
critical articles or reviews—without permission in writing from its publisher, Sourcebooks, Inc.

The characters and events portrayed in this book are fictitious or are used
fictitiously. Any similarity to real persons, living or dead, is purely coinci-
dental and not intended by the author.

Published by Sourcebooks Landmark, an imprint of Sourcebooks, Inc.
P.O. Box 4410, Naperville, Illinois 60567-4410
(630) 961-3900
FAX: (630) 961-2168
www.sourcebooks.com

Originally published in 2001 by the Ballantine Publishing Group

Library of Congress Cataloging-in-Publication Data

Ware, Ciji.
  A light on the veranda / by Ciji Ware.
      p. cm.
  1. Natchez (Miss.)—Fiction. I. Title.
  PS3573.A7435L54 2012
  813'.54—dc23

                            2011050592

          Printed and bound in the United States of America
                  BG 10 9 8 7 6 5 4 3 2 1

This novel is dedicated to

MICHAEL LLEWELLYN, novelist, journalist, and friend beyond price who led me to the Town That Time Forgot in Mississippi and shared all he'd learned,

MARY LOU ENGLAND, book lover, bookseller, and book angel, whose knowledge of Natchez, generosity of spirit, and grace under pressure informed this novel from first page to last,

DEBORAH HENSON-CONANT, brilliant jazz harpist and blithe spirit who could have founded the Aphrodite Jazz Ensemble if she'd wanted to,

RON and LANI RICHES of Monmouth Plantation, and the late ROBERT PULLY, of Governor Holmes House, supporters of the arts and innkeepers *extraordinaires* who helped make Natchez the wonderful place it is.

Everything is vibrational in nature
We respond to things we cannot hear.

—Jim Oliver, composer
Harmonic Resonance

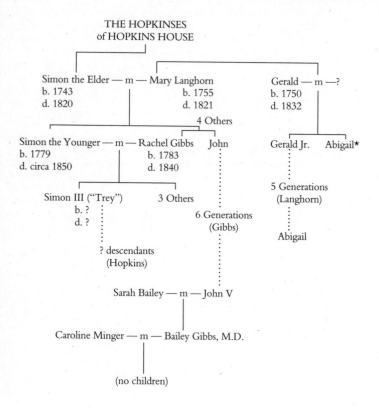

THE HOPKINSES
of HOPKINS HOUSE

Simon the Elder — m — Mary Langhorn   Gerald — m —?
b. 1743   b. 1755   b. 1750
d. 1820   d. 1821   d. 1832

4 Others

Simon the Younger — m — Rachel Gibbs   John   Gerald Jr.   Abigail★
b. 1779   b. 1783
d. circa 1850   d. 1840

Simon III ("Trey")   3 Others   5 Generations
b. ?   (Langhorn)
d. ?   6 Generations
                                 (Gibbs)   Abigail

? descendants
(Hopkins)

Sarah Bailey — m — John V

Caroline Minger — m — Bailey Gibbs, M.D.

(no children)

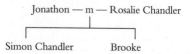

THE HOPKINSES
of SAN FRANCISCO

Jonathon — m — Rosalie Chandler

Simon Chandler   Brooke

★*The Same*

GENEALOGY

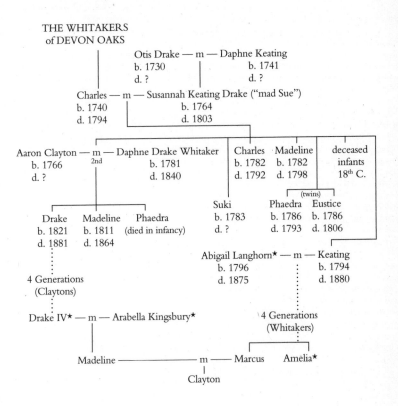

THE WHITAKERS
of DEVON OAKS

Otis Drake — m — Daphne Keating
b. 1730 · b. 1741
d. ? · d. ?

Charles — m — Susannah Keating Drake ("mad Sue")
b. 1740 · b. 1764
d. 1794 · d. 1803

Aaron Clayton — m — Daphne Drake Whitaker · Charles · Madeline · deceased
b. 1766 · 2nd · b. 1781 · b. 1782 · b. 1782 · infants
d. ? · d. 1840 · d. 1792 · d. 1798 · 18th C.

(twins)

Drake · Madeline · Phaedra · Suki · Phaedra · Eustice
b. 1821 · b. 1811 · (died in infancy) · b. 1783 · b. 1786 · b. 1786
d. 1881 · d. 1864 · d. ? · d. 1793 · d. 1806

4 Generations · Abigail Langhorn★ — m — Keating
(Claytons) · b. 1796 · b. 1794
· d. 1875 · d. 1880

Drake IV★ — m — Arabella Kingsbury★ · 4 Generations
· (Whitakers)

Madeline ——————— m —— Marcus · Amelia★
· Clayton

DUVALLONS / WHITAKERS / KINGSBURYS
of NEW ORLEANS

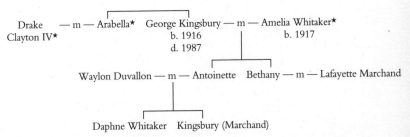

Drake — m — Arabella★ · George Kingsbury — m — Amelia Whitaker★
Clayton IV★ · b. 1916 · b. 1917
· d. 1987

Waylon Duvallon — m — Antoinette · Bethany — m — Lafayette Marchand

Daphne Whitaker · Kingsbury (Marchand)

Chapter 1

March 14

Daphne Whitaker Duvallon always suspected that jilted fiancés could spell trouble, and—in certain circumstances—might even be downright dangerous.

Of course, nobody thought that on the night the classical harpist ditched Jack Ebert *at the altar* in front of five hundred wedding guests at Saint Louis Cathedral in the heart of New Orleans's French Quarter. Most folks thought that Jack took the public humiliation remarkably well. However, from that candlelit evening onwards, any unbiased observer would say that Daphne's life became the female version of Mr. Toad's Wild Ride.

Even so, how could she have known that an entirely *new* path would emerge from the supernova her life had become, or that the orbit of nature photographer Simon Chandler Hopkins was destined to intersect her own? Looking back, she realized that surely the stars must have shifted in the heavens the instant she retrieved that fateful voice mail message one raw, rain-filled night in New York.

"Hey there, Botticelli angel girl! How y'all doing up there in Yankee land?"

Daphne pictured her older brother clasping an amber bottle of Dixie beer in one hand and his cell phone in the other, perfectly at ease chatting to his sister's voice mail in faraway Manhattan.

"It's a lovely spring evening here in New Orleans, and I just wanted you to know that your only sibling's still *very* much a man in love. So guess what, darlin'? Corlis and I are finally going to do the deed! Kingsbury Duvallon is—at last—getting married. Next week, in fact."

Next week?

The mere mention of a wedding—*any* wedding, even her beloved brother's—made Daphne's heart pound erratically and her breath come in short gasps. It had been just over two years since she'd fled back to New York after her eleventh-hour bailout of her own Christmastime marriage extravaganza—a hundred-thousand-dollar event replete with nine bridesmaids; three flower girls; twin-boy ring bearers; acres of roses and pine boughs, supplied at cost from Flowers by Duvallon; seven limousines, supplied gratis from the Ebert-Petrella chain of funeral homes; not to mention sixty-six tall, ivory tapers affixed one to a pew at twenty dollars a pop and the stillborn reception at the posh New Orleans Country Club. And of course, who could forget the television crew in the church balcony sent by WWEZ-TV to cover the "wedding of the season"?

Was it any wonder, Daphne thought, that King's reference to nuptials involving her family in New Orleans made her feel as if she might slip off her kitchen bar stool in a dead faint? She scanned her minuscule, fifth-floor walk-up and wondered if her cordless landline phone would still work if she stuck her head out of the window to get some cool, northeastern air.

"To make up for such short notice," her brother continued carefully, sounding as if he could imagine her discomfort when she heard word of this impending family gathering, "you'll probably be mighty pleased to hear that we're *not* tying the knot in the great state of Louisiana."

"Amen," she murmured, closing her eyes and offering up a prayer of thanks to whatever voodoo gods were handling her case. She leaned her elbows against the kitchen counter for support and held onto the phone receiver like a life preserver. Someone in the next apartment slammed a door and yelled a curse in Spanish that was immediately answered with a string of Anglo-Saxon epithets. Five stories below, car brakes screeched and horns honked furiously. "Manhattan cab drivers," she muttered.

"Corlis and I have decided our little shindig'll work just fine in Natchez, instead of New Orleans, so you have *no* excuse not to be there," King's voice message continued. "We've almost got the church lined up, with the rest of the details—like the reception—to follow. *Y'have* to come, Daph."

King's mellifluous Southern drawl was soothing. Daphne would bet a new set of harp strings that her brother and his fiancée were lounging on King's elegant, fern-strewn gallery overlooking the French Quarter, relaxing after work.

She could imagine her brother's tall, lean figure slouched in a chair, his handsome dark head framed by a fan of white wicker, his feet propped up on the wrought iron railing. Even over the phone line she could hear the sound of a jingling harness, the faint clip-clop of a mule passing by on Dauphine Street below, and the shout of a tourist-carriage driver speeding toward the city's livery stable a few blocks away. According to her kitchen clock, it was still early evening in New Orleans. The gas-lit street lamps would be glowing through a riverine mist obscuring the modern skyscrapers that loomed over the Quarter. Those steel-and-glass monstrosities towering above Canal Street had made King's efforts as an architectural historian to protect the city's remaining store of venerable old buildings a *cause célèbre* in the Big Easy—and justly earned him the title "The Hero of New Orleans" in the *Times-Picayune*. To his younger sister, however, King had been a hero long before that. He'd been her rock. Her bulwark against—

"Guess I'm taking up all the space on the ol' voice mail," her brother said apologetically, jolting her back to reality. "Call us, sugar, ASAP. And don't let any of this wedding stuff freak you out. It'll all turn out just fine. Take good care, y'hear?"

Daphne inhaled shakily, pushed "save," then speed dialed the familiar number in New Orleans. As expected, she got King's voice mail. Daphne knew he routinely screened his calls to avoid any unexpected verbal confrontations with Magnolia Mama, as their mother, Antoinette Kingsbury Duvallon, was known among her intimates.

Daphne's brother concluded his taped greeting with his customary wry dispatch. "Y'all have a decent day, y'hear?"

Before Daphne could leave a congratulatory message, call waiting kicked and King's caller ID appeared.

"Hey! Daphne!" King's deep voice broke in when she clicked the line. "Corlis said it'd be you. Whatcha think, angel girl?"

"I will be forever in your debt for *not* getting married in our hometown."

"Cousin Maddy, up in Natchez, is over the moon 'bout us holding the wedding in the Town That Time Forgot," he replied with deliberate irony. Natchez, Mississippi, and New Orleans, Louisiana, sparred in an age-old rivalry as to which riverside city was held in higher esteem by historians, or possessed the most revered architecture. "She's offered us that tumbling down old mansion of hers, overlooking the river, as Wedding Central."

"You're getting married at Cousin Maddy's *house?*" Daphne asked incredulously. A mental picture of her elderly cousin's chaotic abode materialized in her mind: the lopsided veranda supported by six shaky Corinthian-style front porch pillars, five years of magazines stashed under priceless antique furniture throughout four floors, and a good half inch of cat hair dusting every horizontal surface. Cousin Maddy was a sweetheart and a superb music teacher, but a tidy housekeeper she was not.

"Oh, good Lord, no!" King assured his sister. "Our *very* abbreviated bridal party's just sleeping there 'midst the rubble, since everything in town was booked for Spring Pilgrimage."

"You're getting married during the home tours? You *are* brave."

"The ceremony's planned for First Presbyterian on Pearl Street. We'll know for sure later today if we got the church, but I'm pretty sure we lucked out there."

"Mmmm... it's gorgeous... and a lot *smaller*..." Daphne murmured into the receiver.

"I just don't think any of us could have stomached seeing those same ol' people in that same ol' cathedral on Jackson Square this time 'round."

"I'm afraid my stomach might have made me a no-show," Daphne admitted sheepishly.

"Naturally, Mama's fit to be tied not being able to over decorate

Saint Louis Cathedral with Flowers by Duvallon again, but what else is new?"

"Nothing," Daphne declared, pronouncing the *g* distinctly. She'd worked hard on losing her Southern inflection in a conscious effort to sound like other New Yorkers.

"First Pres being only a third the size of the cathedral means most of Mama's friends will be *highly insulted* not to be invited—as she informed me this morning—but it'll all work out, eventually. I keep telling her the bride gets to pick the church, but you know those magnolias... they think they rule the world."

"You got *that* right," Daphne agreed with more pique than she intended. How could things "work out eventually" when her mother and father had refused to speak or communicate with her in the twenty-seven months since she'd bolted from her wedding at the absolute last second?

"Now, don't you start worrying 'bout Jack getting wind of this. He's moved to Dallas. And besides, everyone on this end's sworn to secrecy—even 'bout the date of this thing. Waylon claims he's goin' fishin' next weekend, so there won't be trouble on *that* score, either," he added with an uncharacteristic edge of bitterness. Daphne's throat tightened at her brother's oblique reference to another family problem.

"Oh, King..." she murmured. "Daddy's so impossible sometimes..."

"You gotta trust me 'bout all of this, Daphne," King insisted. "We've tried to think of everything."

"Of course I trust you," she replied in a rush. "I'm really touched you and Corlis are thinking so much about *me* when—"

"Of course I'm gonna look out for you, darlin'. You're my baby sister, aren't you?" he teased gruffly.

The lump in Daphne's throat swelled to the size of a pecan and she found she didn't dare say another word. At the time of her breakup with Jack, everybody, including her brother and her, had learned that Daphne's father, Waylon Duvallon, was not, in fact, King's biological father. She was still recovering from the shock that she was merely King's half sister, and things within the family would never be the same.

Don't go there. Just don't go there.

In the background, her soon-to-be sister-in-law, Corlis McCullough, was saying something. "Oh, yeah... 'course." King chuckled into the phone. "Here, ask her yourself, California."

Corlis's happy voice interrupted her melancholy musings. "So. Are you surprised we're finally getting hitched, girlfriend?"

"A little," Daphne admitted. "But I'm really thrilled about it, Corlis. I hereby declare you my *real* sister, and not just a sister-in-law. You and I've got to stick together in this clan." Daphne silently thanked the mysterious fates that the Duvallons were acquiring such a welcome addition to their ragtag ranks.

"Count on it, sweetie pie," Corlis said, suddenly sounding solemn.

"And brava for finally saying yes to the poor guy!"

"Oh, I said yes to the guy ages ago. I just didn't have the nerve to say yes to getting *married*. Now, here's the deal, angel," Corlis said, becoming serious again. "We would really love you to play your harp at the ceremony. It'd mean a lot to us both."

"Of *course* I'll play," Daphne assured her, though, privately, she wondered if she could actually make it through a Duvallon family gathering.

"Listen, Daph," Corlis said softly, reading her thoughts, "I know that assembling your clan again for a *wedding* isn't number one on your list of wishes, but King and I have tried to make this pretty much a no-frills event. And if hauling that big harp of yours all the way down here from New York and plucking out 'Here Comes the Bride' sounds too much like work, I'd love you to be one of my bridal attendants. Both Althea LaCroix and Aunt Bethany say they're game to walk down the aisle ahead of me at this little dog and pony show, if *you* are. Want to be an attendant instead?"

"I'm totally up for this, including transporting the harp to Natchez," she replied with more conviction than she felt. "What kind of threads are we talking about for this clambake? Evening gowns? Afternoon garden party stuff?"

"The latter. The wedding's at four... reception starts at five. Everybody's wearing whatever pretty dress they want," Corlis announced breezily. "My great aunt Marge's giving me away in her Hedda Hopper turban. As luck would have it, Hollywood Harry's shooting a game show pilot next week in LaLa Land, and my daffy mother's chanting in a monastery somewhere in Tibet, so…" Corlis paused to catch her breath following her flippant description of divorced parents who had put their small daughter in the care of an aged relation so they could "follow their bliss," as Corlis had once told Daphne privately. "It's the perfect moment to hold this little hoolie, wouldn't you say? As you can see, this is not your average Miss Manners event on *either* side of the aisle."

"Well, as New York's greatest shrink says, we're all grown-ups now, aren't we?" Daphne offered. "We can do what we damn well please, right?"

"That's the spirit," Corlis agreed emphatically. "So it's totally up to you how you want to handle this. We just want you to *be* there, and maybe even have a little fun. Oh! Another call's coming through. Hope it's the minister at First Pres. More details to follow. Love you madly. See you in Natchez on Saturday. Bye."

Click.

Have fun at a wedding?

Not anytime soon.

Then, a giant thunderbolt erased all thoughts about disastrous nuptials, disgusting ex-fiancés, self-centered parents, and trips back home.

See you *Saturday*?

Daphne inhaled a gulp of air and stared, horrified, at the silent phone receiver.

"*Saturday?*" she wailed to her kitchen's four walls, prompting the cockroaches to run for cover. "Oh *no*! Not *this* Saturday!"

The following morning, the skies over Manhattan continued to dump steady March rain on every pedestrian in the plaza fronting Columbus Circle, including the umbrella-less harpist dashing from the subway exit toward the entrance of the Juilliard School adjacent to the Lincoln Center for the Performing Arts. As Daphne ran, she silently practiced her speech to the conductor, Rafe Oberlin, about having to be at her brother's hastily organized nuptials in Natchez on Saturday. Despite her well-rehearsed patter, she knew that the thirty-five-year-old musical *wunderkind* was bound to make the next half hour of her life an absolute misery.

But he can't forbid me to go, she tried to assure herself. *This sort of thing falls into the category of "family emergency," right? It's covered in our union contract.*

Maybe so, but March 20 at eight p.m. marked the fledgling Oberlin Chamber Orchestra's debut concert at Lincoln Center, and contract or no contract, Daphne steeled herself for trouble.

"So? You wanted to see me?" Rafe waved her into his office deep in the bowels of the Juilliard School, where he continued to teach conducting while his star rose steadily in the musical firmament. "You have exactly seven minutes to tell me what this is about before I start a master class next door," he announced, gesturing toward a chair. "Next time, I suggest you phone for an appointment."

"This will just take a minute."

The dashing blond impresario wore knife-pleated gray flannels and a turquoise polo shirt that complemented a physique more suited to the winner of the *Tour de France* than a classical music conductor. Rafe leafed through a mammoth score on a desk large enough to accommodate architectural blueprints for a skyscraper. He made no attempt to disguise his annoyance occasioned by Daphne's unexpected arrival.

"By the way," he said, staring down at his score, "you were late coming in on bar thirty-two at rehearsal yesterday. Make sure that doesn't happen on Saturday, will you please?"

Daphne found it bitterly ironic that she remained under the baton of the man whose abject betrayal had thrown her directly into harm's way in the first place. If she hadn't been so dazzled by the maestro's magnetic personality, she might have seen a lot sooner what an absolute rat he was underneath all his celebrated charisma and might also have avoided a classic rebound romance with Jack back home.

Good Lord, Daphne thought, cringing at the memory. She'd

certainly been naive when she arrived at Juilliard. Rafe had swiftly wooed and won the virginal heart of the younger, more impressionable Ms. Duvallon, late of New Orleans, failing to mention in the white heat of their mad affair what everyone else in New York already knew: that he was married to a British ballerina who was away on a year's tour of Commonwealth countries.

"But you weren't wearing a ring," she'd wailed when she'd confronted him in a storm of grief and chagrin that swept over her like straight-line winds down the Mississippi Delta—and immediately felt like an even greater fool.

Her hasty exit from Rafe's magnificent Westside apartment was even more mortifying because it had left her feeling like an idiot *and* a trollop. Far from taking time to lick her wounds and consider the genesis of her folly, she'd crawled home at Christmastime to the social whirl of New Orleans. Shell-shocked from Rafe's betrayal, she allowed herself to be flattered, wined, and dined by the son of her parents' business partners, Alice and René Ebert, co-owners of a chain of funeral homes in Louisiana that—along with the proprietors of Flowers by Duvallon—had a virtual lock on the lucrative business of being laid to rest in the Big Easy.

Daphne briefly lowered her eyes to stare at the musical score on the conductor's desk, angry all over again at herself and everything that had happened since her double-barreled debacle with Jack and the almighty maestro Oberlin. She attempted to gather her thoughts and continue with the matter at hand.

"Rafe, I know how important Saturday's concert is, and I realize—"

She hesitated, as unhappy images skittered through her head, erasing the carefully prepared words she'd hoped would soften the news of her untimely departure.

Rafe waited an instant, then said with rising irritation, "Well, what is it? I'm five days away from the most important night of my life, Daphne. I don't have time for chitchat."

Daphne inhaled swiftly and spoke before her voice froze. "I'm very sorry, Rafe, but I can't play the concert on Saturday. My brother is getting married in Natchez on the same day and I have to be there."

Rafe shot her a look of disbelief, and snapped, "It's a joke, right? People plan weddings *months* in advance."

"No. They just decided yesterday and called me last night."

"They're eloping," he said flatly. "Nobody wants a lot of family around when they elope. They're just being polite."

"They're not just being polite and they're not eloping," she replied doggedly. "It's a full-on church ceremony in Natchez, Mississippi, and it's my *brother's* wedding, Rafe. Remember him?" she added, unable to keep the sarcasm out of her voice. "The man who contributed ten thousand bucks to your orchestra?"

"You signed a contract with *me* to play the harp Saturday night, remember?" Rafe replied coolly. "If you don't show up, you're in violation. You know the rules. You're going to have to tell him to get somebody else to play at his wedding."

"Our contract allows for family emergencies," Daphne began.

"This doesn't qualify as one," Rafe shot back.

"That's not how I read the contract, but I'm certainly willing to pay for my replacement," she promptly volunteered, hoping she didn't sound as desperate as she felt.

"That's hardly the point," Rafe retorted caustically. "I can't believe you'd be so idiotic as to miss your chance to solo at the most significant concert date you've ever played in your life." Rafe's lips had compressed into a straight line and his eyes narrowed dangerously. "Now, listen, Daphne, if you were a true professional—"

Ignoring these warning signs, she jumped from her chair, her heart pounding and repressed humiliation simmering just below her ladylike smile. "No! It's your turn to listen to me," she interrupted. "I showed up at every single rehearsal and performance even after I found out you were two-timing me *and*—as it turned out—your *wife* with another woman. And I never missed any planning meetings, either, when you were barely paying your musicians minimum wage, before we unionized!"

Rafe eyes were practically slits now. He wagged a cautionary finger in her direction. "There are hundreds of harpists just as well trained and just as talented as you are. You're lucky to be working for any wage, and *I'm* the one who made that possible. I strongly advise you to show up Saturday night or, believe me, Daphne, you will regret it."

Daphne took a step forward and put both hands on his desk so she could stare directly into his turquoise eyes. "I'm flying home this week," she said softly. "I'm going to play in my brother's wedding on Saturday. Evelyn Farnsworth can easily move up to principal harpist for this one performance. She's played at my side every rehearsal and knows the solo as well as I do."

"Good!" he snapped. "She can move right into your slot—permanently."

How could she ever have thought this man was a grown-up?

"Look, Rafe." She switched to a conciliatory tone she hoped would bring them both back from the brink. "I'm rooting for all of us to succeed like gangbusters Saturday night. Our Lincoln Center debut marks a watershed for our group." She softened her next remark with a crooked smile. "And I truly believe you'd regret firing me because I'm the best damn harpist in New York who ever played for union scale."

"Then show me how good you think you are on Saturday, or you're out."

Daphne tried not to let a sense of panic take hold. "C'mon, Maestro," she cajoled. "You know I have the highest professional regard for this organization you've created, and I very much want to continue as principal harpist. Why don't we call a time-out for now and we'll talk it over when I get back from Natchez?"

"I know what my decision is right *now*," Rafe retorted, glowering like a small boy who'd just lost a game of marbles. "You're history, Ms. Duvallon. Excuse me, won't you? I have a class to teach."

Unable to disguise her shock, she cocked her head to one side, and asked slowly, "You're actually letting me go?"

"I actually am," he replied smugly, lifting his baton off the desk. "For cause. Play or pay. Just the reason I was looking for. I've been thinking for quite a while that you really don't have what it takes to be first rank."

"That's crap and you know it!" she cried in an uncharacteristic show of vulgarity.

"It's my well-considered opinion," he said as if he were enjoying this exchange.

"I'll file a grievance," she countered, while disjointed images of monthly bills, stomach-churning auditions, and the shame of actually being canned by a man with whom she'd been intimate collided in her brain.

"If you do, other colleagues in our business will hear my side of the story. Face it, Daphne, it was consensual sex."

"I don't mean that," she said sharply. "I'm talking about *this*." She pointed at him and then at herself. "You're trying to intimidate me right now to prevent my exercising my rights under our union contract."

"You'll be known around town as capital-*T* trouble, and you know what that means."

She certainly did. There were too many talented musicians chasing too few top-echelon jobs in New York. The last thing a harpist wanted to be dubbed was "trouble."

"I'm willing to give you one more chance," Rafe said with a calculating air, "but you have to tell me right now you'll play the Lincoln Center concert—or you're through."

Daphne pictured her brother, King, swiftly stepping out of the line of tail-coated ushers and whisking her away from her philandering groom, down the aisle of Saint Louis Cathedral, and out the arched doors to freedom.

"I love my brother very much," she said quietly. "I can't let him down and miss his wedding. He saved me from mine."

"Yeah, yeah… well, we all have problems. Mine is to fill your chair before our final rehearsal tomorrow." He punched his intercom. "Helen? Get Evelyn Farnsworth on the phone."

For a split second, Daphne nearly fell on her knees and begged him to reconsider. A boss who wished her well could easily have interpreted the family emergency clause in her favor. But by now she should know that Rafe Oberlin cared about the advancement of Rafe Oberlin, period. She regarded the handsome young conductor for a long moment as silence filled the room.

I will not cry, she scolded herself.

She breathed deeply and nodded in acquiescence. Then she summoned her sweetest magnolia smile and bid farewell in a deliberately exaggerated drawl. "You take good care, now, Rafe. And, all the best on Saturday, y'hear? Ah mean it sincerely…"

⤜⤏

Hundreds of travelers, anxious to begin their revels on Bourbon Street, surged toward the Delta Airlines baggage carousels. Daphne, however, hardly noticed them. She pointed to her claim check and then gazed, incensed, at the lost-and-found clerk standing behind the Formica counter.

"I watched them load the harp on board the plane in New York *myself*," she said with growing desperation. "It's six feet tall and weighs at least a hundred and fifty pounds. Not an easy item to misplace."

"Perhaps it's comin' on another flight, miss," the woman offered hopefully.

"Oh, please," Daphne said, her exhaustion and stress level zooming into the stratosphere. "It's got to be here somewhere!"

First I lose my job. Now I lose my harp. What else can happen?

"I'll contact New York and call you when we locate it," the clerk said, with a shrug. "That's all I can do."

"You need to know that this little problem will cost forty thousand dollars to solve, so I suggest you—"

"Daphne!" King hissed. "Look over there. Quick!"

Startled, Daphne turned to stare in the direction her brother indicated. A slender, sandy-haired man standing twenty-five feet away was in the act of handing a fistful of bills to a grinning skycap.

"Jack?" Daphne whispered, dumbfounded to see the very person she never wanted to lay eyes on again.

Jack Ebert.

Her almost husband.

A man she had known since they shared a playpen set up in the Ebert or Duvallon back parlors by their mamas—two women engaged in endless competition, yet who claimed to be *best* best friends. There stood the person with whom she'd gone to grade school, high school, and college for sixteen years—but had ignored as best she could for most of that time, until later when, unbelievably, he became her short-term fiancé.

Daphne's unhappy musings were cut short by the sight of Jack's dark blond head bobbing toward the pneumatic doors that led to the bus and taxi stands. In that same instant, she knew that it was no coincidence that her jilted fiancé should have suddenly materialized at the Delta baggage claim just as she was attempting to find an industrial-size harp that had somehow gone astray. She took off at a dead run.

"Hey, Daphne! Wait!" King called. "Let *me* deal with it!"

She ignored her brother's urgent command. Instead, she bolted toward the skycap, who was smiling to himself as he stowed the wad of cash in his back pocket. She arrived at his side out of breath.

"Don't you *move*," she shouted, assuming her most abrasive New York persona. "You can keep the cash," she announced, pointing to the skycap's pants pocket. "But I'll give you exactly *two minutes* to go wherever the hell you stashed my forty-thousand-dollar concert harp and deliver it to me *here*. Otherwise," she said, pulling out her cell phone, "I'm calling the N.O.P.D. right now and having you and my former fiancé—who I saw give you money to hide my harp—*arrested* as an accessory to grand theft!"

By this time, King was at her side. The baggage handler stared at Daphne for a moment and then, with a shrug, sidled off toward a door marked "Employees Only." Within minutes, he reappeared pushing a handcart through the crowds. The instrument loomed even larger than its six feet, shrouded in a form-fitting, ink-black fiberglass case that weighed more than the harp itself.

"Think that's it?" King asked, deadpan.

Before Daphne could deliver a retort, the skycap asked nonchalantly, "Is this what y'all are lookin' for? It was in the locked room. For safekeepin'," he added baldly.

"Yeah. Sure," Daphne scoffed. The skycap lingered, his hand resting on the retrieved harp.

"Forget it," King snapped. "You already got your tip." The

man shrugged again and slunk off in the direction of a flustered elderly woman surrounded by suitcases.

"You told me that Jack had moved to Dallas," Daphne said, her breath ragged. Her heart was still pounding, and she could actually feel adrenaline thundering through her limbic system like the crescendo of the "William Tell Overture."

"He lives there, all right," King said grimly. "Works as a public relations flak for some oil company. Someone obviously tipped him off as to exactly when you were expected to arrive in New Orleans, en route to the wedding."

"Gee... who could *that be*?"

Brother and sister exchanged knowing looks.

"Had to be our sainted mama," King said, with a resigned shake of his head. "She left me a voice mail late this morning saying she wouldn't be coming to the wedding without a down-on-your-knees apology from both of us for the way we humiliated the entire family at Saint Louis Cathedral—and for everything since."

"What a surprise," Daphne replied, unable to keep the bitterness out of her voice. "You support me when I refuse to marry a total jerk and Mama hates us for life."

"*And* I invited Lafayette Marchand to be my best man on Saturday."

Daphne gazed at her brother in wide-eyed wonder. "Your father? Oh, boy." She rested her head against the harp case and heaved a sigh. "Jack must be jumping for joy about all of this." She affected a shrug. "So Mama's not coming to Natchez. Okay. Maybe it's for the best." She patted her harp. "At least we rescued this baby so I'll still be able to play at your wedding."

"Too bad you didn't take up the piccolo, or something sugar," King noted dryly. "Even on a *good* day, traveling with a harp must be as easy as transporting a howitzer." Daphne, long the recipient of such attempts at wit, didn't respond to his quip. "I'm going to take you and your harp in the Ford Explorer we rented in your honor, okay?" he proposed. "We'll meet up with Corlis and her aunt and they'll follow us in the Jag. I figured the drive to Natchez'll probably give you and me our only chance to catch up before wedding madness takes over."

"Sounds like a plan," she agreed, nodding. She'd already decided not to mention she'd been kicked out of the orchestra because of her decision to come to the wedding. She didn't want to put a pall over the proceedings or burden King and Corlis in any way. Instead, they could talk about how pleased she was to have checkmated Jack—and the son-of-a-gun didn't even know it. She pointed to the harp. "Just let me attach these two little wheels to the bottom of the harp case, here, and away we go."

As any refugee from a hurricane watch knows, the escape route out of New Orleans is due west and then north on an interstate highway that eventually leaves the bayous behind and joins a two-lane road that meanders along the Mississippi through plantation country. Within the hour, the two vehicles were whizzing by grand, pillared mansions glimpsed through verdant arched canopies formed by two-hundred-year-old trees.

"Oh, King… look… there's Oak Alley." Daphne glanced in the rearview mirror to make sure Corlis, in the Jaguar behind them, was pointing out the landmark to her elderly relative. "Doesn't it always knock your socks off?" she murmured, gazing at the double row of ancient oaks that lined the approach to a splendid Greek Revival house with its celebrated twenty-eight columns, fan-lighted doorways, and wide, welcoming verandas.

"Always," replied King reverentially.

Farther down the road, another stand of massive oaks displayed branches laden with cascades of gossamer gray-green moss. "We couldn't be anywhere but Louisiana, could we?" Daphne sighed contentedly and settled into the passenger seat. She lowered her window a few inches and inhaled the velvety March air laden with the scents of dogwood and pink jasmine. A mere hint of humidity foretold a stiflingly hot summer a few months away.

By one o'clock, the Jaguar and the Explorer had nosed into the parking lot of a restaurant called South of the Border, located just before the Mississippi state line and renowned for its ten-alarm Bloody Marys, fried green tomatoes smothered with crawfish rémoulade sauce, and drop-dead coconut cake. Arm in arm, Daphne, King, Corlis, and a turban-clad Margery McCullough strolled toward the entrance in the warm noonday sun.

"Daphne, dear," Corlis's great aunt said, giving the younger woman's elbow a gentle squeeze. "I'm so looking forward to hearing you play your harp at the wedding. Corlis tells me you are superb." The celebrated retired journalist, who looked like a stand-in for the forties gossip columnist, Hedda Hopper, beamed in the direction of her great-niece, and declared, "You know, Corlis? Except for you and me, the family you're marrying into is a damned sight more talented and accomplished than ours, don't you agree?"

"You've got *that* right, Aunt Marge," Corlis replied, feigning a long face. Tanned and smiling, WJAZ's star television reporter wore only light makeup and had pulled her shoulder-length brown hair into a ponytail that made her appear a decade younger than her thirty-five years. "Not a game show host in their entire family tree, lucky them!"

Everybody laughed, and Daphne realized that the stomach knot she lived with full-time in New York had begun to untie.

Two hours later, the foursome emerged from the roadhouse after a feast of "fried everything," as Marge McCullough described their crunchy, corn-battered oysters, crispy fried catfish, and green tomatoes topped with Vidalia onion rings—all lightly dusted in flour, cooked to a spectacular golden brown, and washed down with frosted pitchers of sweetened tea. Groaning in mock misery, Corlis pretended to stagger across the parking lot, beckoning Daphne toward the Explorer.

"Now, it's my turn to get you to myself," Corlis said affectionately, patting the passenger seat. "Climb in, girlfriend." King and Marge McCullough drove ahead in his midnight-blue Jaguar—a reward from his savvy investments in information technology stocks in the mid-nineties.

The bride-to-be looked relaxed and happy, not the ball of nerves Daphne had been on the eve of her ill-fated wedding. Daphne flipped down the visor and peered into the mirror, taking in her shoulder-length, curly blond hair and dark brown eyes with dark smudges beneath the lower lids. Publicity photos showing her with full makeup and good lighting produced a much more dazzling effect. However, at the moment, she looked a far cry from that, she thought, gazing at her New York pallor. Swiftly, she retrieved the lipstick from her purse and applied it generously, rubbing a small amount into her cheekbones in an effort to revive them.

"Let's spend the next sixty miles debating the merits of 'Amazing Grace' versus 'Jesu, Joy of Man's Desiring,'" Daphne joked, snapping the visor in place. They had settled on the order of music for the ceremony by the time Corlis turned off the main highway and headed toward the wide expanse of river seen in the distance.

"What do you say we take the scenic route through town?" Corlis asked. "I'd love to see a bit of Natchez before it gets dark."

"Then go straight ahead and turn right on Canal Street," Daphne directed, and soon they caught sight of the silver-painted bridge that connected Natchez, Mississippi, to the communities of Vidalia and Ferriday on the Louisiana side.

It was nearly four thirty. The sun slanted off the water, turning the Mississippi molten gold. *Lady Luck*, a paddle-wheeled gambling boat, rested in her permanent berth at the foot of a cliff on whose lofty palisades early settlers found relief from swarming mosquitoes and the heavy, sultry temperatures along the water's edge. The vessel's pilothouse glittered with white tracer lights that beckoned gullible tourists, down-on-their-luck Natchezians, and citizens out for a night on the town to try their fortune. A hundred seventy-five years earlier, Natchez-Under-the-Hill, as the streets flanking the waterfront were called, had been a red-light district, full of raucous bars and boarding houses for gamblers, thieves, and ladies of easy virtue. On the bluff above, block after block of pillared, antebellum mansions and splendid churches bore witness to a city "built so the eighteenth and nineteenth-century cotton planters from around these parts could come to town and show off their wealth and piety," Daphne told Corlis. "In a city of about twenty thousand people, there are still at least sixty antebellum mansions offering house tours around here. Before the War Between the

States, there were more millionaires in Natchez than there were in New York City."

"No wonder King wanted to get married in this place. What a Shangri-La for an architectural historian."

They turned right off Canal Street onto Franklin. Daphne pointed through the windshield as they passed the intersection at Wall Street. "Right over there stood the old Mansion House Hotel where—supposedly—the duc d'Orléans's son, Louis-Philippe, danced at a ball in 1798."

"No kidding? French aristocrats?"

"Yup," Daphne said with a grin. "That was after he'd hot-footed it out of Europe during the French Revolution follow-ing his father's encounter with *Madame Guillotine*. Eventually, Robespierre and his cronies were kicked out of power and young Louis-Philippe was invited back to Paris and became the Citizen King in 1830."

"Man oh man," Corlis murmured with admiration. "You're just like your brother. You really know all this stuff."

Daphne shrugged. "Local lore, drummed into me by my Natchez cousins. Other folks around here insist the young duke wasn't entertained at the hotel, but at Concord, a big house on the other side of town that burned down. We know, for sure, though, that Louis-Philippe and his entourage reviewed the local garrison while they were here, over near what was once Fort Rosalie."

"Really? So he and his courtiers hung out in the South till things cooled down in France?"

"Something like that."

"What happened to the hotel? Urban renewal?"

"No, the Tornado of 1840. It blew away half the town, but, luckily, it only flattened a few of the big plantation houses in the outlying areas."

"If I weren't getting married tomorrow," Corlis said wistfully as they passed Stanton Hall, another magnificent pillared home on their left, "I'd love to tour every one of these places. They're gorgeous."

"Wait till you see where your reception's being held," Daphne replied smugly.

"As a matter of fact, we'd better head over to Monmouth Plantation right now. I need to check out a few things."

"King told me, driving up today, that you booked it at the last minute. Do you know what a miracle that is? Around here, Monmouth's reserved for weddings when a girl child is *born*."

"Some poor guy just died—ten days before he could celebrate his ninety-fifth birthday. We took over his spot."

"This wedding is meant to be." Daphne laughed happily, her spirits rising each mile they got closer to Monmouth.

A few minutes later, they steered the Explorer into a sweeping drive that led to a magnificent white mansion with imposing square pillars. The plantation house, now a hotel, perched on a lawn-cloaked hill dotted with magnolia trees and giant, moss-hung oaks. A gargantuan tour bus was just pulling away from the front door. Their timing was perfect, Daphne thought.

"Oh... my stars..." Corlis said softly. "What a wonderful place for a wedding reception."

"Out back is a huge courtyard and a gorgeous garden beyond, plus a pond and vine-covered trellises, azalea and camellia bushes, not to mention a gazebo—which are very big items around here, by the way," she confided with a grin. "And statues all over the place. The acres of old orchards and cotton fields have been sold off over the years and turned into Greater Natchez."

Corlis drove the car to an area marked by a discreet sign indicating visitors' parking. Stepping onto the gravel, she pronounced happily, "It's perfect! Trust King to get the architecture right."

Within minutes, they were greeted by the lady of the manor, Lani Riches, a warm, welcoming woman dressed in trim lime linen slacks and a silk blouse. Ushering them into the front hall, she explained that she and her husband Ron, a California developer, had fallen in love with the derelict mansion twenty years earlier on their first trip to Natchez.

"Ron's the history buff, and I love the decorative arts. We became obsessed with the idea of restoring this pre-Civil War white elephant to its original splendor." She led them beyond the magnificent delft-blue foyer into a high-ceilinged double parlor festooned with pale blue silk draperies and matching upholstery. "We've been so grateful to King for all the good advice he's given us over the years," she said. Daphne's gaze was immediately drawn to the rear of the large room, which boasted two fireplaces separated by an arch with a fanlight window overhead. Among a scattering of magnificent period mahogany furniture, a small harp of the sort that well-brought-up young ladies played for gentlemen callers stood beside a grand piano.

"This entire place just bowls me over," Corlis breathed.

"Let me show you the plans we've made for your wedding reception," Lani replied, all business now. "And don't worry. People on the Pilgrimage tour will be long gone from here tomorrow evening." Then she addressed Daphne. "Your brother told me you'll be playing your harp at the church, but you might want to see if you'd like to play ours at the reception. That way, you won't have to transport yours from First Presbyterian. This one is an antique, but we keep it tuned."

Corlis said quickly, "You're a guest, Daphne. Only play at the reception if you feel like it."

Daphne smiled gratefully at Corlis, then said to their hostess, "Do you mind if I have a closer look?"

"No, of course not. Please do."

"My cousin Madeline Whitaker, at Bluff House, also has a very old one—which is probably why I never considered taking up the tuba," Daphne volunteered with a wry smile.

"As I'm sure you know," Lani said, laughing, "Natchez is a town where there's a harp in practically every parlor. Feel free to try it out."

Corlis and Lani headed for the back courtyard to confer on canapés and the merits of various champagnes. Meanwhile, Daphne sat down on a round, pale blue, velvet-covered stool next to the antique instrument. She hiked up her black gored traveling skirt and drew the harp between her legs, briefly considering the sensuousness of such a motion while she nestled the sound box gently against the top of her breast and her right shoulder. Compared to her massive concert harp, this one felt almost cozy. She strummed the opening chords of the teatime favorite "Greensleeves," then halted abruptly. Resting the palms of her hands to quiet the vibrating strings, she heaved a sigh. The harp was, indeed, in tune. That wasn't the problem. The trouble was, she honestly didn't think she could stand to play that boring old chestnut one more time.

A Bach cantata?

The mere thought of a classical piece of music reminded her of the concert taking place without her at Lincoln Center and the memory of Rafe Oberlin angrily gesturing for her to leave his office. Suddenly, she experienced an avalanche of anxiety she had previously managed to keep in check. She forced herself to take a cleansing breath to fight a deepening sense of depression. Then she sat bolt upright on the stool and tilted her chin skyward. She lifted her fingers from the strings and brought them down again, stroking the notes of a blues favorite, "Georgia on My Mind," to calm her nerves. The music resonated from the harp and filled her chest in mellow waves as she began to sing in her husky lower register.

"Geor-gia… Geor-gia… the who-ole da-ay long…"

Man, she thought, did it improve her outlook to sing like this and pull funky jazz chords from an antique harp. It was during moments like these that she realized how thoroughly bored she'd become with most popular classical music. She was also tired of her "angelic harp persona" and the halo of shoulder-length curly blond hair that served to reinforce it. Occasionally, she imagined herself playing her gilded instrument while wearing a leather miniskirt and a chain bustier like Madonna in her bad-girl days—just for the shock value. When she'd once told King about her musical daydream, he'd laughed and challenged her, saying "Why don't you try it sometime?"

She never would, of course. It was just a fantasy she conjured on days when she wearied of playing too many crowd-pleasers. Even so, her brother's words echoed in her head as she launched into the second chorus of the sultry tune.

She heard a door open, and footsteps. Then a tall figure loomed in the wide entrance dividing the hotel's foyer from the double parlors. The thirtysomething man wore a forest-green polo shirt under a khaki vest studded with half a dozen bulging pockets, along with khaki slacks, leather hiking boots, and two professional-looking cameras slung around his neck. He was holding a collapsed tripod in one hand and had just deposited a duffel bag at his feet, as if he had appeared straight out of an L.L. Bean catalogue. His features wore a look of expectancy. He smiled slightly and nodded encouragement for her to keep playing as he settled himself comfortably against the doorjamb.

She felt like smiling at the stranger and did, thereby gaining a closer look at his handsome, strongly defined nose, chiseled cheekbones, and a chin that suggested one of those brooding models with a five o'clock shadow in the Calvin Klein ads—except that the friendly intruder appeared to be in a very good mood. For some reason, she wasn't embarrassed to be discovered singing a provocative blues number at the top of her lungs. She returned her gaze to the harp's strings and her full attention to the tune's mesmerizing cadences and slow, languid rhythms.

Like Lot's wife, she couldn't resist another surreptitious peek at the visitor. However, at that instant, her vision unaccountably began to gray around the edges. The handsome photographer in khaki slacks and vest leaning against the entrance to the parlor at Monmouth Plantation had subtly been transformed into a young man from some other century who appeared to have recently dismounted a horse. Now, he was wearing a dark green, swallow-tailed riding jacket with a fountain of lace-edged linen at his throat. His knee-high riding boots and the thighs of his buff-colored breeches were caked with Mississippi mud. His dark hair glistened with sweat and he clutched a riding crop, which he beat repeatedly against the palm of his other hand, as if he were trying to make some sort of momentous decision.

What in the world?

Daphne was thoroughly rattled by the photographer's inexplicable metamorphosis and wondered suddenly if Rafe's dismissal and seeing Jack Ebert again, so unexpectedly, had sent her way, way over the edge.

Chapter 2

As swiftly as the misty vision of a dismounted horseman appeared before Daphne's eyes, it vanished, and the tall photographer reappeared, smiling appreciatively from across the parlor at Monmouth Plantation. Bewildered, Daphne threw her head back, closed her eyes, and continued singing, segueing into the musical bridge of "Georgia on My Mind."

"Other arms reach out to me... other eyes smile tenderly..."

When, finally, she finished the song, she rested her hands on her thighs and allowed the harp's last notes to linger in the air. Absolute quiet descended upon the old house. Slowly, she turned her head and experienced enormous relief to see that the photographer was still standing there. From all indications, the absurdly good-looking figure was as real as the Canon and Nikon cameras he now removed and set carefully on top of his small duffel bag. He regarded her as if they were old friends.

"Thank you for not stopping when you saw me."

Her breath caught when he pushed his shoulder away from the door frame and took a step toward the harp. She glanced self-consciously at her callused fingertips and her blunt, unvarnished nails and curled them into her palms.

"Well..." she said slowly, shaken by the distinct feeling that she had somehow fallen in and out of some crazy time warp, "'Greensleeves' it ain't!"

The stranger laughed at her joke, which pleased her immensely somehow.

"I've never heard a harp played like that before," the man said. "Like a blues guitar... or a bass fiddle."

"I rarely play jazz on the harp—or sing, either—that's for sure," Daphne admitted ruefully, suddenly embarrassed by her flamboyant exhibition. "Not in public, at least. Only as backup a couple of times at a blues club owned by a friend's family in New Orleans," she amended, feeling more foolish by the second. "I was just testing out this old harp."

He advanced a few more steps into the parlor where he towered over the Victorian furniture. Extending his hand, he volunteered, "Hello. I'm Sim Hopkins."

"Sim?"

"Short for Simon. If you heard my triple-barreled name, you'd understand why I go by Sim."

"I know the feeling. I'm Daphne Whitaker Duvallon," she said with a laugh, shaking hands.

"Will you be playing here later?"

"At my brother's wedding at First Presbyterian Church tomorrow, and maybe at the reception here."

"Oh. A private party."

There was a pause, and then she surprised herself by asking, "Are… ah… you staying here at Monmouth?"

"I'm *sleeping* here, at least," he answered with a faint grimace. "Most of the time I'm either on my belly in the woods or hip-deep in some swamp. I've taken a room here for a week or two, using this place as a base while I work on a book."

"Oh, really? What's it about?" she asked, filled with curiosity.

"It's going to photographically document the series of birds painted by John James Audubon in this area some… oh… hundred and eighty years ago. At least the ones that aren't extinct."

"No kidding? The naturalist?" Daphne said, impressed. "A coffee table book?"

He laughed. "I guess that's what everybody calls them. And a calendar, too. I sold the idea to a publisher that specializes in nature books and related products."

She pushed the harp away from her shoulder and stood up. "What a great assignment. Then, you must know that Audubon lived in Natchez for a while, and taught painting to the daughter of the owners of Oakley Plantation, down toward St. Francisville."

"That's right," Sim said, smiling broadly as if she were a kindred spirit. "I was shooting there just last week."

"And have you been over yet to the house on Washington Street, here in Natchez? I can't remember who told me that Audubon supposedly rented a room there when he did his famous drawing of the town."

"I *didn't* know that," he said admiringly. "You live here, yes?"

"I grew up in New Orleans but have relatives in Natchez. Actually, I live in New York. Believe it or not," she added, laughing at herself, "despite what you just heard, I make my living as a classical musician. Where do *you* live?"

"San Francisco... when I live anywhere," he said, making his nomadic wanderings sound glamorous, indeed. No, she thought, except for his amazing good looks, he didn't seem the moody, handsome model sort at all. "I've been reading all the biographies about Audubon's life I can get my hands on," he continued, "but I hadn't come across the reference to Washington Street. So thanks. I'll check it out."

"You're welcome," she said, pleased she was able to enlighten him in his own area of expertise. "I imagine that you know a lot about botany and zoology, since Audubon depicted the birds in their natural habitat."

"Exactly," he acknowledged. "But the natural science is the easy part of the job. I'm a science writer, too."

"Really? How'd you end up combining the two careers?"

"In college, I majored in science, like my parents wanted me to, but I spent most of my time as photography editor of the yearbook. When I got out of grad school, I was torn between the two, so I found a way to do both."

"That's pretty impressive." She recalled the endless wrangles with her parents—even as a college student—whenever she went with Althea to listen to jazz in the French Quarter. Like a good little magnolia-in-training, she'd never dared perform anything but pieces like "Greensleeves" and "Claire de Lune" for her mother's parties. Wouldn't Antoinette Kingsbury Duvallon have thrown a fit if her daughter had launched into a sultry rendition of "Georgia on My Mind" in front of her Garden District friends?

"Well, thanks for the compliment," he replied, interrupting her thoughts. "Combining both careers turned out to be a happy compromise. And I still like my work," he added with an engaging grin, "so it must have been an okay decision."

And he's *very* charming, she thought.

Just then, Corlis and Lani Riches entered the parlor through the open door from the courtyard.

"I never heard you sing on your own before," Corlis exclaimed, gesturing toward an open window. "Maybe you'd consider doing a few songs like *that* at the reception, to give us all a break from the 'Oh Promise Me' stuff—" The bride-to-be halted in her tracks at the sight of Sim Hopkins. "Oh... sorry. I didn't mean to interrupt."

"Hello, Mr. Hopkins," Lani said, also advancing into the room. She introduced Corlis to the photographer, and then asked, "Did you have a successful day scouting birds?"

"I was a success at sitting in the bushes in your back acreage for three hours, waiting for a yellow-rumped warbler to show up," he replied, shaking his head with mild annoyance, "but I definitely was *not* a success getting the rascal to perch anywhere for more than a second. It'll be interesting to see what I finally got on my camera."

Turning to Daphne, Lani inquired, "And how did the harp sound to you?"

"It's lovely. You've kept it in wonderful shape, considering how old it is."

"Coming from you, I consider that a high compliment."

"Well," Corlis said with a smile of satisfaction, "Lani and I just nailed the menu, figured out the wines, and approved the flowers she ordered. And even though King has spent the college fund of our firstborn on the champagne, I think this reception is ready to launch."

Daphne was acutely aware of the highly masculine presence of Sim Hopkins standing among three women engaging in "boring gal talk"—as her father Waylon was wont to describe such female exchanges. However, Sim appeared intrigued by their conversation.

"You've just decided all that and you're getting married *tomorrow*? I'm impressed. The lead-up to *my* wedding felt like the Bataan Death March."

Daphne felt a jolt of disappointment at this last revelation.

I should know by now that every man I'm even remotely attracted to is either nuptialized—or certifiable!

Corlis laughed, and said, "With Lani's help, fast as the speed of sound is the only way to go with an event like this." She put her arm around Daphne's shoulders. "And now, on to Cousin Maddy's. Ready for that, my almost-sis?"

"If you can organize Madeline Whitaker as you have your wedding, you *are* Wonder Woman," Daphne said, unable to resist a sidelong glance at Sim's left ring finger. It was a large hand, as he was a large man—but it was bereft of jewelry.

Probably just another guy who refuses to wear his wedding band!

She could just hear him tell people that wearing a ring interfered with squeezing off camera shots, or something. Even so, there was no denying the currents of electricity that had hummed between them when she was playing the harp. However, in the world of professional performers, Daphne had met scores of traveling Lotharios in the mold of the dashing Mr. Hopkins. These were men vaguely dissatisfied with their marriages, but who always opted for the homecoming at the end of a tour. They easily found willing females on the road who provided them with just enough emotional intimacy to ensure that these seductive characters retained permanent membership in the "Have-Their-Cake-and-Eat-It-Too Club," as one cynic in Daphne's circle of New York musician-friends put it. Maybe they were great lovers, but rotten prospects for committed relationships. And even if Sim Hopkins was now single, Daphne thought, she'd sworn off traveling men for good.

"Well, are we off?" she asked Corlis brightly. She offered a stiff smile to the photographer, shook hands with Lani Riches, and led the way to their car parked out back.

"I'll drive," she announced.

"Great." Once in the car, Corlis asked slyly, "You think that guy's still married? With looks like his, he should be in *front* of the camera."

"He lives in San Francisco and travels for a living, so it's a non-starter as far as I'm concerned," Daphne replied tersely.

"Got it," Corlis said, with a regretful shrug.

As dusk appeared, Daphne steered the car down the hotel drive, cruised back through the heart of Natchez and out along the bluff, heading upriver. She was doing her best to put the arresting Simon Hopkins and the strange, sudden appearance of his tail-coated mirror image out of her thoughts.

"Where's Cousin Maddy's place?" Corlis asked.

"Surely King has warned you about her... ah... shall we say... slightly bizarre abode?"

"He told me that there's a race as to whether her house or the cliff will collapse into the river first."

Up ahead, at a bend in the Mississippi, half a bright orange sun hung on the horizon, poised to plunge into the river. "Some years back, the Army Corps of Engineers decided to take out a loop... right over there"—Daphne gestured through the windshield—"to speed up river traffic, they said, claiming the river was rerouting itself anyway. The result of the government's fooling with Mother Nature is that megatons of water slam against the bluff each year and eat away at the earth on the bottom. Not a cool thing, since ninety-five percent of the city *rests* on the top."

Corlis peered through the gloom of early evening. "Oh, my God! You weren't exaggerating. Tell me *that's* not her house."

A hundred yards distant, a great, hulking mansion with patches of missing wooden siding and roof shingles perched at the very edge of the bluff. Daphne parked and locked the car next to King's Jaguar in the Whitaker driveway to the rear. The two women strode toward the large, once-graceful structure whose front porch tilted alarmingly.

"This place may be crumbling around her ears, but Cousin Maddy always leaves a light on the veranda," Daphne said happily as they walked up the front steps in the lengthening darkness.

Propping up the second story—barely—were towering Grecian-style columns whose peeling white paint curled like the skin from a banana. Not five feet from the outer edge of the ground-floor veranda that encircled most of the house, the front lawn halted abruptly and a sheer precipice plunged toward the riverbed five hundred yards below.

"Is it safe for anyone to *occupy* this place?" Corlis gasped, paling at the sight in front of them. "Half the cliff must have eroded," she marveled, peering apprehensively over the edge into the void.

"It's safe enough," Daphne allowed. "At the moment, at least—while we taxpayers foot the bill to shore up the base of the promontory and keep historic houses like Maddy's from careening down the slope. No one will buy her place, of course. She can't get a bank to loan on it, and she can't afford to sink money into maintaining it anymore—since it may well tumble down the bluff in the end."

"What happens now?" the television reporter queried, concern creasing her forehead. "How does the poor woman make ends meet? King told me that there's no Mr. Whitaker, right?"

"Sadly, not anymore. Maddy was my first music teacher and has taught harp to half the females in Natchez. As you will soon see, Madeline Clayton Whitaker's a remarkable woman."

However, Corlis and Daphne were forced to postpone their first encounter with their hostess. Cousin Maddy, King explained upon greeting them at the sagging front door, had gone off on an important errand having to do with last-minute floral arrangements for the church. Upon his arrival he had found a hastily scribbled note directing them to eat heartily of the red beans and rice she'd left warming on the stove. Three cats swirled around three pairs of ankles as the trio made its way through a darkened front foyer toward the lighted kitchen.

"Meet Harpo, Chico, and Groucho," King announced for Corlis's benefit. "Don't let 'em fool you, though. I just fed the beasts, so ignore their pathetic mewing." He pointed to a black cat with a white tuxedo front. "Watch out for that one… Groucho. He does this little bitey thing when he gets annoyed."

Daphne set her suitcase on the floor's wide cypress planking and gazed into a kitchen whose sink was piled high with unwashed dishes. In the hallway, she glanced at a sideboard littered with a hodgepodge of two months' worth of half-opened mail, a cut-crystal ashtray heaped with paper clips, and a priceless Fabergé egg on a gold stand. A brief survey of the front parlor revealed Maddy's antique harp cheek by jowl with a larger modern one, and both surrounded by a jumble of exquisite old furniture and piles of musical scores. Newspapers and magazines were scattered everywhere. The mere sight of such chaos exhausted her.

"Would y'all be insulted if I just fell into bed?" Daphne asked, feeling suddenly depleted. "I'm still stuffed from lunch and I can hardly keep my eyes open."

"Must be too much fresh air, Ms. New Yorker," King teased. "Sure, honey. Hit the sack. I've assigned you the bedroom next to the sleeping porch. You remember, turn right at the top of the stairs."

Suitcase in hand, Daphne headed straight up the staircase, passing family portraits that stared down on her from high on the walls. A sketch of a sinister-looking hawk—*Falco Peregrinus*—purportedly by John James Audubon, hung crookedly at the top of the stairs. The drawing had been given to some member of the family when Audubon briefly lived in Natchez, and its presence suddenly made Daphne think of the handsome photographer again.

Heading down the shadowy hall, she studiously avoided peeking through open doors at bedrooms she knew to be chockablock with upholstery sorely in need of refurbishment, rain-stained wall coverings, and threadbare draperies. She quickly got ready for bed, doing her level best to avoid any mental review of Cousin Maddy's disordered lifestyle.

What was there to say? The woman tolerated clutter. Feng shui and simplicity were definitely not part of her lexicon. Who could be critical when they knew about the life-and-death issues this wise and wonderful woman contended with the last four years? End of story.

Madeline Whitaker was one of the dearest, kindest people in the entire world, and that was all that mattered, Daphne considered sleepily, sinking between clean but wrinkled sheets. Her thoughts drifted as she closed her eyes and heaved a grateful sigh that she and her harp had arrived safely. Good thing she could store it in the locked Explorer, for there didn't seem an inch of space left in Maddy's front parlor. For some reason, a French nursery song sprang to mind. It was one that Maddy used to sing to her when she was a child visiting during the summer and first learning to play the harp. She softly sang the words to the familiar melody as she snuggled into a comfortable position beneath the ancient satin coverlet.

> *Frè-re Jac-ques… Frè-re Jac-ques…*
> *Dormez vous? Dormez vous?*
> *Sonnez les mat-in-es… sonnez les mat-in-es*
> *Ding, dang, dong… ding, dang, dong…*

And despite the French rhyme's message to wake up, she slept.

A grandfather clock downstairs tolled three chimes, its lingering tones echoed by two French timepieces sounding the hour—one of which had apparently decided it was four o'clock. Daphne swam to the surface of consciousness but somehow couldn't force herself to open her eyes. Disoriented by the unfamiliar night sounds, she tried to remember where she was.

Her apartment in New York? Juilliard? Her parents' house in the Lower Garden District?

Somewhere, she could hear a harp being played faintly, as if someone was practicing in a far-off rehearsal room in Lincoln Center. No, she thought groggily, she was in Natchez. At Bluff House. Was Cousin Maddy having a sleepless night?

The delicate staccato roused her to a more conscious state and she sat bolt upright. The harp was playing the same French nursery song that she'd been remembering right before she fell asleep. She could hear the strings being plucked with precision, just as if accompanying a chorus of little children in ages past… just as *she* had heard it played and sung by Madeline Whitaker some twenty-five years earlier, in an antebellum mansion on the edge of a bluff overlooking the mighty river.

Frè-re Jac-ques… Frè-re Jac-ques…

Daphne grabbed her robe, crept toward the stair landing, and looked down. Cousin Maddy's antique instrument was usually woefully out of tune, she remembered suddenly. But not *this* night.

Slowly, she advanced down several stairs until she had a clearer view through the front foyer and into the sitting room. Moonlight streamed through the windows that faced the river, illuminating with remarkable clarity the parlor and its peeling wallpaper. Daphne caught sight of the first harp she had ever touched. The antique instrument had fewer strings than its neighboring modern version, and had never produced a very robust sound. In fact, when it was properly in tune, as it obviously was this night, Daphne would have recognized its tinkling, music-box quality blindfolded.

Arriving at the foot of the stairs, the classically trained harpist grabbed the newel post and simply stared, awestruck, at a harp whose strings were vibrating—all by themselves.

In the Lovell Room at Monmouth Plantation, Sim Hopkins awoke slowly, realizing in some distant sector of his brain that it was far too early even to stalk Audubon's blasted birds. After a few moments, he realized what had caused him to stir. He could distinctly hear the sound of harp music tinkling through the planks of the thick cypress door to his elegant rented bedroom. He glanced at the coral-colored silk canopy engulfing his massive four-poster plantation bed and listened intently. These were not the earthy, bluesy chords that that angelic-looking young woman had played in Monmouth's double parlor the previous afternoon, but rather, a child's lullaby plucked on an instrument known for making listeners think they'd died and gone to heaven. Surely, the harpist with a set of legs that just didn't quit couldn't possibly be rehearsing for her brother's wedding at the ungodly hour of—

Sim glanced at his watch, the only item he wore to bed. Its luminous dial told him it was ten minutes past three. He reached for the velour robe draped over the bottom of the mattress and swiftly padded to the door. Oddly, the music didn't grow louder when he crossed the threshold and moved toward the hotel stairwell. He descended the carpeted steps to the front hall and stood at the wide entrance to the parlor where he had leaned against the door frame and listened to Daphne Duvallon's sensuous rendition of "Georgia on My Mind."

A shaft of moonlight slanted through a window, illuminating one corner of the Empire-period sitting room. Sim's breath caught when he saw that the harp's strings were still vibrating as the haunting melody faded into silence. What surprised him even more, however, was that the stool next to the harp was vacant, and there was not another soul to be seen in the room.

The following morning, Daphne sat alone in the cluttered kitchen at Bluff House, sipping a steaming cup of chicory coffee laced with hot milk and trying her best not to think about the odd scene she'd witnessed in Cousin Maddy's parlor at three in the morning.

Or had she? she wondered. Maybe all the stress lately had suddenly caused her to sleepwalk? Perhaps she'd merely had one of those dreams that seem *so* real the next day?

Groucho, belying his name, was peacefully curled up on a nearby kitchen chair, snoozing in the morning sunshine that filtered through the dusty window above the sink. Earlier, in response to the cat's plaintive meows, Daphne had fed him a few morsels of chicken she'd filched from a half-eaten sandwich found in Maddy's nearly empty refrigerator. While she was musing about the previous night's events, the kitchen door opened.

"Mornin', darlin' girl! I cannot tell you how *wonderful* it is to have y'all under my dilapidated roof." Madeline Clayton Whitaker burst into the room, her arms full of groceries. "Just dashed out to the Piggly Wiggly, since all I had 'round here were those ol' red beans and rice and half a chicken sandwich. Not exactly fancy fare to serve the bride and groom on the mornin' of their weddin', do you think?" She set the bulging grocery bags on the kitchen table and bent to engulf Daphne in an enormous hug. "Now stand up, and let me look at you!"

Daphne rose and embraced her cousin heartily in return. "Oh. Maddy! It's great to see you too!" She nodded in Groucho's direction, and said solemnly, "The chicken sandwich is history."

Daphne gave her sixty-seven-year-old cousin an indulgent once-over, noting her faded denim skirt and flowered blouse. Untidy wisps of dark hair threaded with silver drifted alongside her lined cheeks. Maddy looked as if she'd set out for the Piggly Wiggly without once glancing into a mirror.

Despite Madeline Whitaker's disheveled appearance, however, the tall, erect woman exuded a wonderful *presence*, Daphne thought, smiling into her cousin's warm, amber-colored eyes. Maddy radiated an aura that said here was a person who had known better days, when life was not burdened with cares and tragedy. Yet, she carried all that had befallen her with remarkable dignity and grace.

"Look how absolutely gorgeous you are!" Daphne's first harp teacher crowed, extending hands that sported fingertip calluses that were equally as thick as Daphne's. "I'll just bet people in New York mistake you for... you know! That fabulous actress with the halo of blond curls who looks and talks like an *angel*..." She shook her head in frustration. "*You* know the one I'm talkin' about... Michelle somebody."

"Michelle Pfeiffer?" Daphne offered obligingly, thinking to herself that it had been a long time since Maddy had been to the movies.

"*Yes!* Exactly. You've heard people say that to you before, haven't you, darlin'? She's an *angel* on screen—and so are *you!* Now, what can I get you for breakfast? Bacon? Eggs? *Pain perdu?*" she offered, referring to a wonderful Southern version of French toast.

"No thanks, Maddy. I've had your delicious coffee and some toast. But let me help you put all this away before I head for First Pres. I have a ten o'clock rehearsal with the organist."

"Don't be silly," Maddy said, with an airy wave of her arm. "I'll do it later. Let's get you a second cup of coffee and sit down a spell. How was your trip down from New York?"

Daphne thought briefly of the career disaster awaiting her return to Manhattan, as well as of the unwelcome sight of Jack Ebert at the New Orleans airport and the near mishap with her harp, but decided not to mention either disturbing event. Instead she said, "As you probably noticed when you got home last night, I was totally pooped after I got here and went straight up to bed."

"Well, *good*. You deserve it, workin' as hard as you do up there. Was your bed all right, sugar?" Maddy asked, suddenly anxious.

"I slept like a stone most of the night," Daphne reassured her quickly, adding, "But you know... the oddest thing happened." She hesitated, and then continued. "About three o'clock in the morning, I could have sworn I heard a harp playing. It wasn't you, was it?"

Madeline, coffeepot in hand, paused midway to Daphne's cup and gazed at her houseguest speculatively, but all she said was "Really?"

"At least that's what I *thought* I heard. I came downstairs, but... well... no one was in the parlor." She held out her coffee cup. "It must have been some wacky dream."

"Maybe you heard the family ghost playin' the harp," Maddy said matter-of-factly, pouring a dark brown stream of coffee from the spout of the chipped, enamelware pot.

"Oh, c'mon." Daphne laughed. "I'm not a tourist, remember, and you're not on house tour duty this morning."

"Tease 'bout it, if you want to, but surely I told you, when you were a little girl, 'bout my family's harp-playin' specter? You never heard the story when you were stayin' here?"

"No, never. Who's it supposed to be?" Daphne said, taking a sip from her cup.

"Well," Maddy said with enthusiasm, seating herself across the kitchen table from her younger cousin, "according to family lore, your namesake—"

"*My* namesake! I thought you said this was a Clayton family deal."

"Daphne Drake *Whitaker* Clayton. You'd have to look at the family genealogy chart to keep it all straight 'cause we've had cousins marryin' cousins and I don't rightly know *what* all. But way, way back in the mists of time, Daphne Drake Whitaker—later she married a Clayton, which is *my* maiden name—fell in love with a real *cad*."

"Sounds kinda familiar," Daphne joked ruefully.

Maddy smiled in sympathy and continued with her story. "He was a French aristocrat, or something, tagging along with the duc d'Orléans who'd been exiled, for a time, to America in the aftermath of the French Revolution." She paused for breath and then waved at Daphne. "Well, *you* know all this history stuff, but, anyway—"

"Wait a minute," Daphne interrupted. The hair on her arms was standing on end. "You were born a *Clayton*. How could this Daphne also be a Whitaker like Cousin Marcus and Grandmother Kingsbury?" And how strange, she mused, that she had just been telling Corlis yesterday about the young duc d'Orléans's celebrated visit to Natchez.

"The ghost on my direct side of the family is also considered a Whitaker because, like I said, my husband Marcus and I were *cousins* several generations back—like half the folks in Natchez," Maddy said with amused exasperation.

"Oh," Daphne said in a small voice.

Warming to her tale, Maddy continued, "Your namesake, the other Daphne, met this Frenchman when she was an impressionable girl and was totally smitten by the scoundrel. He promised to return from New Orleans to marry her, and she reportedly pined away for the bounder till her dyin' day, playin' the harp and waitin' for her faithless lover to return. Such a waste."

"And did he ever come back to Natchez?" Daphne asked, unwilling to admit, even to herself, that her heart was pounding erratically and her pulse was racing.

"Well, I don't rightly know," Maddy said thoughtfully. "Clearly, she finally married someone else... but apparently she's still playin' her harp in the parlor in the middle of the night!" she pronounced triumphantly.

"Do you know who she married?"

"Oh, of course I do, 'cause it caused a lot of talk at the time. Daphne Drake Whitaker eventually married Aaron Clayton—a Yankee, my great-grandmother said he was—and musta had children by him, 'cause that's where my daddy got his name, Drake Clayton the Fourth."

"Now, tell me the truth," Daphne demanded. "You *live* in Bluff House. Have you ever heard your harp playing by itself in the middle of the night?"

"I thought I heard it once," Madeline said with a pensive, far-away look. "Right after Marcus and Clayton passed on… but, of course, I was not myself much durin' that time…"

"Oh… sweetie." Daphne was suddenly contrite that their bantering conversation had led to this subject. Maddy's grief over the double tragedy of losing a husband and a son in the same year had thrown her into a serious bout of depression requiring medication and a brief period of hospitalization. "What person *wouldn't* have thought she heard—"

"But a tour guide over at Rosalie *swears* she's heard Daphne Whitaker playin' her ghostly harp in the parlor there," Maddy rushed on, obviously not upset by their discussion of ghostly matters. "And believe me, she's a prominent member of the D.A.R. The tour guide, I mean… not the ghost!" Maddy laughed at her own joke, which completely assured Daphne that her adored cousin's spirits were fully restored.

"Have other people seen this supposed ghost?" Daphne asked skeptically.

"Oh, lots. The cleaning woman at Monmouth says she heard a harp playin' by itself a while back, and one of the gardeners at another plantation house upriver, that has a harp in the upstairs music room, vows on a stack of Bibles he hears it through the open windows every spring—"

Daphne stood abruptly, carried her coffee cup to the sink, and rinsed it out. "Well, this flesh-and-blood harpist better skedaddle out of here," she announced firmly. She'd been overtired and overwrought from the accumulation of stress in her life these days. Proof? The brief but bizarre moment at Monmouth Plantation when Simon Hopkins seemed to morph into a high-booted horseman. She'd seriously begun to wonder if long-term anxiety and sleep deprivation weren't playing very strange tricks on her.

Smiling to Maddy in farewell, she silently vowed to get lots of rest and plenty of fresh air during her visit to Natchez.

"Well, I'm outta here," Daphne declared with as much good cheer as she could muster.

"Don't forget, angel girl, you and Corlis have beauty parlor appointments at Anruss Salon at one o'clock," Maddy reminded her.

"*You're* the angel," Daphne pronounced, kissing her older cousin on the top of her untidy head.

Within minutes, she had pointed the Ford Explorer down Clifton Avenue and headed for Pearl Street in downtown Natchez and the magnificent, pillared First Presbyterian Church. A janitor kindly helped her extricate the bulky harp from the car, transport it upstairs to the balcony overlooking the sanctuary of the Federal-style church, and position it next to the organ.

It took Daphne some fifty minutes to tune the harp strings, by which time Avery Johns, the octogenarian organist, arrived. Then the two musicians swiftly ran through the wedding program before the floral designer arrived to decorate the church.

Later at the nearby Anruss Salon, Daphne and Corlis happily submitted to having their hair done, along with manicures and pedicures. At three fifteen in the back room, Daphne donned a sage-green silk dress with a flowing skirt and matching silk shoes. She swiftly touched up her makeup, and emerged to wish Corlis good luck.

"Same to you, sweetie pie," Corlis said, swathed in a black cotton dressing gown. "You look drop-dead fabulous! Was everything okay with your harp? King told me about Ebert trying to hijack it at the airport yesterday."

"The harp loves being back where it's warm," Daphne said, her banter belying the tension that gripped her stomach whenever she thought about Jack Ebert's sudden appearance.

"Well, I love you for schlepping that mammoth thing all the way down here," Corlis pronounced, kissing Daphne lightly on the cheek. "And I can't tell you how much it means to me to become your sister-in-law today—not to mention King's wife."

"Me too, you," Daphne murmured. She hugged Corlis and grazed her cheek against a gigantic hair roller. By this time, both women had tears welling at the rims of their eyes. "Now can I claim your Aunt Marge as kin?" Daphne asked with a watery smile. "She and Cousin Maddy are the greatest, aren't they?"

"Since it would appear neither one of us did too well in the parental department," Corlis said, wiping a tear from the corner of her eye with a freshly manicured forefinger, "I'll share one Marge McCullough with you for one Madeline Whitaker—what do you say?"

"It's a done deal!" Daphne replied, sniffing inelegantly as she reached for a tissue from a nearby dispenser. The women gazed quietly at each other for a long moment.

"I'd say we are two lucky *mademoiselles*," Corlis said softly, "even if my mother is a wilted flower child, and yours is a no-show."

"I'm really sorry Antoinette's playing the major magnolia," Daphne said, and gently squeezed Corlis's arm. "She's still steamed at me—and King, by association. Please don't take it personally, 'cause it's definitely not."

"I'm trying not to," Corlis said. "I mostly feel terrible for you and King."

"Thanks," Daphne replied quietly. "You okay if I leave now? No last-minute jitters? I'm an expert on those, you know."

Corlis smiled, her eyes taking on a joyful shine. "Maddy and Marge have made a blood pact to get me to the church on time." She added with a hint of embarrassment, "After all my neurotic flip-flops over the *idea* of marriage, I actually can't wait to say 'I *definitely do*!' to that brother of yours."

It was nearly three twenty-five by the time Daphne entered the back of the church.

"Your harp's downstairs now," Miss Carrington announced brightly. The church wedding supervisor was a sixtyish woman, dressed in a fluttery, flowered organza ensemble and a straw picture hat with pink and coral roses clustered around its brim. She pointed to the narrow stairway that led from the balcony to the side entrance foyer where they were standing. "I had two of our men bring it down from the balcony. I hope that was all right?" she asked with a kind of wide-eyed innocence inappropriate for a woman of her maturity—and all too familiar to Daphne. "I just thought you'd look so *pretty* sittin' up front, near the pulpit."

Daphne was thrust into a mild panic to discover that her harp was no longer beside the organ where she'd carefully positioned it that morning. "Will I be able to see the organist from down here?" she asked worriedly.

There was no point in telling Miss Carrington that hauling a harp down a set of stairs and then dragging it fifty feet into the church sanctuary meant that it would have to be retuned, top string to bottom. Daphne knew that her preferences didn't matter a whit to this officious woman. She had dealt with bossy belles a million times before.

"Oh my, yes," Miss Carrington assured her with a coquettish smile, "you'll have *perfect* lines of sight. All the harpists play down front near the pulpit. They just love it there!"

"Well, here's hoping I do, too. When given a choice," she added pointedly, "I vastly prefer to be near the organist."

Miss Carrington appeared startled. Clearly she wasn't accustomed to having her decisions questioned.

Daphne cocked an ear, and exclaimed, "Goodness! It sounds as if people are being seated. I'd better get settled and retune."

"Close the door when you enter the sanctuary, won't you please?" Miss Carrington directed archly, lips pursed in a faintly triumphant smile. No New York harpist with a master's degree from Juilliard would be allowed to hide up in the balcony.

Daphne's large, gilded harp had been placed forward and to the left of the pulpit. She slipped onto the stool and surveyed the scene. Nearby, two waist-high plaster columns supported magnificent sprays of spring flowers that Cousin Maddy had gathered from friends with private gardens all over Natchez. Attached to each pew were smaller, professionally made bouquets of dainty Queen Anne's lace anchored with fragrant gardenias and ivory silk ribbons. Daphne was forced to admit that the bride czarina and the floral designers she'd recommended certainly knew their stuff. She cast a measured glance around the interior of the gleaming white church with an eye to the volume she would be required to produce on her harp in order to be heard over the organ.

She began the process of fine-tuning her harp's forty-seven strings. Mellow organ music muffled the repetitive twangs she produced as she swiftly worked her way up to middle C. Fortunately, most notes had remained in tune despite the harp's last minute journey from the balcony.

Meanwhile, a platoon of wedding guests took seats in the forward pews. Daphne's aunt, Bethany Kingsbury Marchand—a recent bride herself—offered a gentle assist to Grandmother Kingsbury, who reluctantly relinquished her aluminum walker to the care of her gray-haired daughter and sank, with great effort, into her seat on the aisle in the first row. Aunt Bethany had dutifully volunteered to sit next to her aged mother at the ceremony instead of serving as matron of honor when her sister, the mother of the groom, made her dramatic proclamation that she wouldn't be coming to the wedding.

"Hello, darlin'," Bethany said to Daphne in a hushed voice. "Mother... there's Daphne. All the way from New York! Doesn't she look pretty sittin' at the harp?"

"Hello, hello," Daphne whispered back. "See y'all later at the reception."

She lightly ran her fingers over the strings while she nodded at several other members of the Kingsbury clan from Baton Rouge, who were entering the center aisle just as members of the celebrated LaCroix family of musicians made their appearance. Earlier, Daphne had scarcely had time to say hello to Corlis's solitary bridal attendant, Althea LaCroix, a friend since Daphne's grammar school days—and the only black student in her class. Now Althea was a close friend of Corlis's as well.

Daphne glanced at the rear door just in time to see Cousin Madeline coming down another aisle. She was dressed in a wide-brimmed straw hat and flowered frock similar to the one worn by the wedding organizer. The principal difference was that Madeline's outfit looked as if it had come straight out of the clothes dryer with no detour to an ironing board. Maddy's black handbag was at odds with her beige shoes, and both accessories battled the Kelly-green leather belt encircling her thin waist. All in all, Madeline Clayton Whitaker's ensemble would make a New York clothes designer run screaming into the night.

As Daphne continued quietly tuning the rest of the harp strings, a side door opened. Her breath caught at the sight of her lanky, exceedingly handsome brother striding into the church. He was followed by an older, silver-haired version of himself—Lafayette Marchand, Aunt Bethany's new husband.

Father and son wore impeccable Brooks Brothers attire. They stood side by side in front of the pulpit, both smiling broadly at the assembled guests. Daphne felt a lump rise in her throat. How had half of New Orleans not guessed that the two were related by blood? she wondered. Why hadn't her own father, Waylon, figured out the truth ages ago, despite her mother's carefully nurtured fiction that Lafayette Marchand was just an old family friend?

Just at that moment, the church organist pointed discreetly at his watch. Without further warning, Avery Johns commenced the musical introduction to the first of two pieces that he and Daphne were to play: Mozart's Concerto in C Major, composed originally for flute and harp. She prayed that the strings ascending from middle C to the harp's arch, the ones she hadn't had time to retune, hadn't gotten fried in transit from the balcony and worriedly cast a quick glance at them. As she joined in with the organ music, wedding guests began turning in their seats to gaze at someone sailing down the center aisle with the confidence of a diva making a grand entrance in *Aida*.

The woman who had captured their attention had shapely ankles, an ample bosom, and a waistline a mere inch and a half larger than the eighteen inches it had been thirty-seven years earlier when she'd donned her magnificent ball gown and ermine cape as queen of the New Orleans Mardi Gras. Today she was dressed in a Donna Karan sheath and matching coat in a sophisticated shade of dusty teal.

The mother of the groom—Mrs. Waylon Duvallon, née Antoinette Whitaker Kingsbury—had, indeed, made an appearance at Natchez's First Presbyterian Church.

CHAPTER 3

WHAT WE'RE SEEING HERE is vintage *Antoinette*, Jack Ebert mused, lingering in the back of the church as his mother's best friend strode regally down the center aisle toward the front pew. Jack figured that the woman's ability to upstage virtually anyone was probably stamped into the strands of her DNA. Try as Alice Ebert might, Jack's mother would never even come close to Mrs. Waylon Duvallon in the magnolia department.

Jack noticed, of course, that Daphne had finished the Mozart without mishap—although nobody else seemed to be listening to her play. Her mother's dramatic entrance had captured everyone's attention. In fact, it appeared that the entire congregation couldn't take its eyes off Antoinette Kingsbury Duvallon in her high-fashion attire, gold and diamond jewelry, bouffant black hair, and the unmistakable aura that proclaimed, "Stand back world, here I come, and I'm *a lot* more important than *you* are!"

"She's just one of those people who sucks all the air out of the room," Jack remembered Daphne telling him not long after they got engaged. That was at a time when he was making every effort to be witty and charming—and she was making every effort not to cry over that asshole, Rafe What's-his-name, who'd popped her cherry in New York, the lucky bastard.

Much to his surprise, that Christmas the ice princess had seemed grateful for the attention he'd paid her at her parents' annual holiday party. Before that, she'd always been Miss High-and-Mighty-Sorry-I'm-Busy. Not that he'd ever really wanted to date Daphne Duvallon, despite his mother's unrelenting prompting over the years. Daphne's ethereal act never really turned him on. Later, he'd taunted her that the calluses on her fingertips from playing the harp were bigger than her boobs. It wasn't true, but people always laughed when he said it.

There was one night, though, when she looked like such a class act, playing "Greensleeves," or something, on that old harp in the parlor on Orange Street in the Lower Garden District. Her parents' place had been done up with pine swags, holly boughs, and gold French ribbon everywhere. Candlelight glinted off Daphne's blond hair, and she seemed genuinely interested when he described the juicy, off-the-record details of the symphony's bankruptcy that had just hit the papers that week. He'd had a field day with that story on TV and in *Arts This Week*, and it had finally earned him some goddamned recognition as a force in New Orleans media. Jack had thought that, for once, the snooty Miss D. had actually considered him witty and charming. How was he supposed to know that her rapt silence merely reflected her state of shock at having just found out that the conductor who'd deflowered her was a married man, for Christ's sake! He should have known never to trust a woman without major hooters. Cindy Lou, on the other hand, had one great pair of ta-tas.

Jack's gaze drifted away from the woman who'd been within minutes of being his wife. Then, suddenly, he wasn't even thinking about Daphne Duvallon or even Cindy Lou Mallory and the night they'd—

As often happened when he thought about sex, the memory of another woman—lifeless, naked, and laid out on a stainless steel gurney—rose unbidden before his eyes. That day, decades ago, his thirteen-year-old cousin Victor had dragged him into the embalming room at the back of Ebert-Petrella's and gleefully whipped off the sheet. Vic laughed harshly and pointed at the corpse, rigid as the slab of cold metal that lay beneath her, shoving his younger cousin forward with a hard push.

The dead woman was minus one breast. There she lay... one huge knocker on the right side of her chest, and on the other side—*nothing*. Only a big old scar. She'd had cancer, or something, Vic had said—and then the creep fondled the breast she had left and dared Jack to touch her.

How old had he been then? Five? Six? He'd freaked out, started to cry, and peed in his pants. He'd run screaming and sobbing into the back parking lot, straight into his father's legs as his old man was climbing out of the hearse. His father smelled of whiskey, because he'd probably stopped off somewhere for a snort or two on the way back from Metairie Cemetery. The bastard gave him hell for wetting himself and then joined Vic's taunts for being such a "fucking baby."

Man, he *hated* women with no tits, that was for sure! That was probably why Cindy Lou could make ol' Pete come to attention with a flick of her—

Jack silently ordered himself to stop obsessing about that red-headed hellcat and pay attention to what was about to happen to Daphne. From behind the pillar, he still had a direct view of his ex-fiancée and that shitty harp that everyone thought was so frigging beautiful. Thanks to the printed program he'd secured earlier when the florists were decorating the church, he knew she'd be playing "Amazing Grace" before the ceremony began, accompanied by the organ. It was perfect. Just perfect.

Wouldn't Miss Priss be surprised to know who'd served as her mother's chauffeur from New Orleans to Natchez? As soon as he'd dropped off Antoinette at the front steps, he'd parked the big old limo right outside the church on Pearl Street. What a joke it all was!

Much to Jack's surprise, King, who was standing in front of the pulpit next to Lafayette Marchand, brought his left hand from behind his back and took several steps forward, leaving his father to gaze bemusedly at the unfolding scene. With great flourish, the groom presented his mother with a corsage of dainty white roses. Antoinette's jaw appeared to clench while she allowed her son to pin the flowers on the lapel of her ensemble. Next, King bent forward, brushing his mother's cheek with a light kiss, and whispered something into Antoinette's ear while the bastard stared right at him.

Okay. So King had spotted him. Jack figured he'd just been officially *un*invited to the reception.

So what? He'd already done what he came here to do.

With a renewed sense of purpose, Jack left the cover of the church pillar and slipped into a pew toward the back of the church. Now he was in the perfect spot to see the disaster unfold before his very eyes.

⤨

Out of the corner of her eye, Daphne spotted the slender, sandy-haired latecomer sliding into a seat toward the rear of the sanctuary. She was halfway through a dramatic glissando when her fingers nearly froze and her brain finally registered that she was staring, for the second time in as many days, at the person she prayed she would never see again as long as she lived.

Jack? Jack's here? At King's wedding?

Just at that moment, a dissonant *twang* resounded loudly. One of the higher-register strings near the harp's graceful harmonic curve painfully lashed her wrist.

"Ow!" she exclaimed under her breath, startled by its sting. She was dismayed to see that a second string had just snapped and was dangling, useless, above the soundboard. The wedding guests sitting closest to her shifted uneasily in their pews.

As her fingers inexorably swept again in a repeat *glissando*, a third string emitted a startling, popping sound. Before she knew it, the last and shortest string on the instrument gave way with a loud ping the instant she touched it.

Four broken strings?

Never, in her twenty years of playing the harp, had she ever broken *four* strings! She pulled her hands away from the instrument as if it would scorch her fingers and allowed the organist to carry on playing the melody.

The organist's back was to the congregation and Daphne doubted that the musician's rearview mirror, which offered a reverse view of the sanctuary, would take in what had just transpired. Frantically, Daphne wondered what she would do when her solo began.

By this time, her palms were sweating and her heart had begun to pound. She silently called upon every ounce of training and experience she possessed. The face of her teacher at Juilliard, Eleanor Beale, swam before her mind's eye.

"Change keys!" a voice barked in her head. "If you possibly can, whenever you break a string, just *change keys* and keep playing!"

With sudden inspiration, she raised her right hand, formed a C with her thumb and forefinger, and prayed that the organist would see her discreet sign in his small, rearview mirror. Luckily, he did, for he emphatically nodded his balding pate in a show of understanding. At the next opportunity, Mr. Johns remained silent and allowed Daphne to begin her solo, subtly shifting into the key of C in a maneuver calculated to avoid the missing strings and a host of others that might snap at any moment in the path of the key of G. Fortunately, there was only one remaining glissando during which her hands would be forced to play adjacent to the four empty spaces.

I will get through this, she lectured herself fiercely. *Somehow, I will do this for King and Corlis. Screw Jack Ebert!*

For she knew, instantly, that her former fiancé was the cause of this musical near-catastrophe. Defiantly, she glared in the direction of her nemesis seated at the back of the church. While Daphne gingerly plucked her harp strings, the mortician's son, unwilling heir to the Ebert-Petrella chain of funeral homes, stared at her with unwavering hostility.

He can't believe I'm pulling this off, she thought, willing her hands to find their way to the end of the music.

Ignoring him now, Daphne braced for the final trill, her callused thumbs skimming over the thicker bass strings toward the short, thin ones near her right shoulder. She pulled up an octave short of the broken strings, making a reasonable finish to the familiar piece while trying not to wince when another filament suddenly gave way.

The remainder of the wedding ceremony whirled past in a complete blur. Somewhere between the "I do's" and the exchange of rings, Jack Ebert slipped out of the church. If it hadn't been for the five damaged harp strings, Daphne might have thought she'd hallucinated the entire scene—not unlike her bizarre encounters with the handsome morphing photographer at Monmouth and the auto-playing harp in Cousin Maddy's parlor.

Her mind reeled with other questions. Had Jack and her mother driven up to Natchez together—even though King had specifically asked Antoinette not to mention the wedding to any of the Eberts or Petrellas? Surely she wouldn't condone his plan to damage her harp?

Such speculation was fruitless, she thought, attempting to regain her composure. The only thing that mattered was the cold, hard fact that Jack Ebert had reappeared in Natchez—clearly with mischief in mind. He'd popped through that church door…

Like a jack-in-the box…

Daphne stared with unseeing eyes at the empty seat in the back pew as the bride and groom turned to face each other, both smiling joyfully. Her brooding reverie was brought to an abrupt halt by the sight of King reaching for Corlis and kissing her lingeringly on the mouth. Marge McCullough, her turban slightly askew, looked on benevolently as moisture rimmed her eyes. The minister was beaming as he pronounced the couple husband and wife. Daphne automatically swung into the age-old recessional music, allowing the mellow sounds of the organ to fill in for her missing harp strings.

She was startled to feel a flood of tears course down her cheeks. Helpless to wipe them away as she played the harp, she hastily lowered her eyes. A sudden recollection of the engaging young man with two cameras hung around his neck filled her with poignant, piercing regret.

Daphne watched her mother rise from the front pew and grandly lead the wedding guests out of the church in the wake of the bride and groom without the slightest glance in her daughter's direction. First Presbyterian's sanctuary slowly emptied. With a weary sigh, Daphne retreated to a side room and fetched her harp's carrying case. She wondered morosely if any attempt she might make to forge a new life was simply doomed to failure.

❧

The parking lot at Monmouth was nearly full. Daphne drove past a black limousine stationed at the grand entrance and finally found a space for the Explorer at the opposite side near some hedges. As soon as she switched off the engine, she heard a familiar voice hailing her from across the graveled drive.

"Hey, girl! You want some help with that harp, sugar?"

Daphne emerged from the driver's side and stood in the warm March sunshine, her spirits reviving slightly at the sight of her childhood friend, teetering on wickedly high heels, moving in her direction.

Althea LaCroix's ample figure was clothed in a salmon pink silk outfit that the thirty-year-old black woman had probably last donned for the confirmation ceremony of one of her numerous younger brothers. Her normal wardrobe consisted of dark slacks and T-shirts printed with faded New Orleans Jazz Fest logos, which she also wore when she played in her family's celebrated band at their own Cafe LaCroix on Decatur Street in the musical heart of the French Quarter.

"Thanks," Daphne replied, "but there's a harp in the parlor I can play, so, for once, I don't have to lug this thing to hell and gone."

Althea scrutinized her closely, her dark eyes bordering on coal black. "You all right? You look kinda woebegone, honey."

"Did you see Jack Ebert sitting in church?" she blurted. She and Althea had been friends so long, there was no need to beat around the bush.

"No," Althea exclaimed. "Sweet Jesus, was *he* there? I was so nervous 'bout walkin' in these high heels down that long aisle, I never looked beyond m' feet!"

"He sat in a back pew and split before the ceremony was over."

"Then why did he bother to come?"

"He wasn't *invited*," Daphne retorted with frustration. "He just showed up."

She was about to tell her friend about the severed harp strings when Althea said apprehensively, "He's gone now, right?" She surveyed the parking lot. "Personally, he's always given me the creeps. 'Member how mean he was when I first got my scholarship to Newman School?" Then she shrugged, and added with a sly smile, "I just thought he held some fatal charm for you white girls. C'mon, darlin', forget him. Let's go in and get us a glass of that expensive champagne."

"You go ahead," Daphne said. "I'm trying to find the music from *Phantom*... I know it's in here someplace."

"Okay," Althea agreed doubtfully. "But 'member what Corlis tol' you: you're a *guest* at this shindig."

Daphne smiled and threw her arms around her friend. "I am *so* glad to see you, Alth! I've missed you like mad."

"When ya'll goin' come down to Cafe LaCroix and play some jazz with us again?" Althea cajoled. "Now that you're a full-fledged graduate of Juilliard and payin' your own bills, your mama can't give you grief 'bout that anymore."

"Don't think I wouldn't love it," Daphne replied, happily recalling the two times she'd played jazz harp as a backup musician at Cafe LaCroix. Then she smiled. "Why don't you come up to New York and I'll show you all the hot spots? I've heard some *great* jazz there." Should she tell Althea, now, about Rafe's firing her?

Her best friend gave her shoulders a squeeze. "I jus' might take you up on that sometime, angel girl." She pointed to the house. "Gotta get in there. See you in five," she added, and wobbled in her high heels across the gravel drive and down the brick path to the wide, white-columned veranda and the mansion's front door.

Daphne rifled through a pile of music charts in search of the misplaced music. She located the cheat sheets in question and was about to file them in her briefcase when she heard someone say, "Need a hand with that?"

Her fingers tightened on the handle of her case as she looked over her shoulder to confirm that it was, indeed, Jack Ebert's voice. He was lounging against the Explorer's front fender, standing not two feet away.

Where in the world had he come from?

She regarded his slight frame that was just this side of skinny. No doubt about it, her brief attraction to the man had never been about his looks. His facile mind, however, was something else.

Clever. Witty, at times—but invariably at others' expense. *Evil genius* were the words Althea had used to describe him when they were in college. At Tulane, his scathing reviews of cultural events around campus published in the student newspaper had been legendary. His cutthroat reputation had grown when he worked for *Arts This Week* in New Orleans and reviewed books, concerts, opera, and films on-air for WWEZ-TV, where Corlis McCullough had worked when she first came to New Orleans, fresh from a job in Los Angeles.

True, Jack Ebert could actually be charming on occasion, but she'd learned to her sorrow that he also employed vitriol more effectively than almost anyone she'd ever known.

Face it, Daphne, he is and always was a skunk. You have lousy taste in men.

"Jack," she acknowledged with a degree of calm she didn't feel. "Don't need any help, thank you. I'm not using this harp." Jack's gloating expression said it all. A wave of anger surged over her and it was all she could do not to haul off and hit him for injuring her beautiful harp. However, allowing him to see how much his actions upset her just encouraged his cat-and-mouse games. "You're not welcome here, you know," she said in a low voice, marveling at her blunt words as soon as they'd escaped from her lips. "Even if you did come with my mother."

"Last I heard, Monmouth Plantation is a public accommodation," he replied coolly. "And First Presbyterian welcomes all worshipers. It said so in the flyer I found on the hall table when I checked into my hotel."

"How did you know the details about this wedding?" she demanded, feeling her blood pressure soar. She had already guessed the answer he would give.

"You know how," he said with a short laugh. "Your mama told my mama. Some mutual client of theirs kicked the bucket last week, and while they were coordinatin' the flowers and the funeral arrangements, Antoinette let it slip. Complainin' to Mama 'bout you and King, of course. She was thinkin' then she wouldn't even come to the weddin'. I called her up late yesterday, though, and tol' her I'd be happy to drive her up here today—if she decided to attend at the last minute—since I was comin' to Natchez on business anyway, and there's no other sensible way to get here."

"Yeah... sure. Look Jack," Daphne said, trying desperately to keep her cool, "you know what the deal was. You keep your distance from my brother, Corlis, and me, and we'll do the same. So far, it's worked out just fine and—"

"Don't flatter yourself, Daphne," he interrupted rudely. "Like I said, I'm in town on business."

"What business?" she scoffed.

"I'm workin' for Able Petroleum now... out of Dallas." He beamed a smug smile. "I'm their chief information officer. Petrochemicals are a big part of the cotton growin' process these days," he explained as if she were a first grader. "The pesticides we make keep the bugs off, and the defoliants strip off the cotton plants' leaves so the pickin' machines can go through the fields like a hot knife through butter."

Jack's imagery made Daphne shudder. He probably wrote the copy in those glossy brochures that told the public what a friend to nature the petroleum industry was.

"And now it turns out I've got another reason to come to Natchez."

She raised a questioning eyebrow, not really wanting to know.

Jack frowned faintly and said, "My parents and the Petrellas have bought one of those old funeral homes here in town. Part of their plan to expand the chain into Mississippi."

"Ah. And this means what to you? I thought you hated the family business."

"I *do* hate it, but I said, seein' as I was heading up here anyway, I'd get the new signs put up, file the name change to Ebert-Petrella, and check out how the staff's doing under the new management. My daddy's gettin' a bit long in the tooth to crack the whip, like the old days."

I'll just bet. I've heard he did more than crack a whip with his employees...

However, all she wanted to do at this particular juncture was to get as far away from Jack Ebert as she could.

"Well. I wish you all the best in Texas, Jack... really, I do."

Magnolia Manners Rule One: Always be polite, no matter how disgusting the situation.

Just then, she glanced at her briefcase that rested on the car seat. The sheet music to *Phantom of the Opera* beckoned. Swiftly, she snapped shut her case. She didn't owe Jack Ebert even courtesy, so why was she being so nice?

"Wait, Daphne!" he said loudly, his words having a strange power to halt her in the act of extracting her car keys from the car door. She turned her head to look at his pinched face. "I've given... what happened two years ago... a lot of thought," he said with only the faintest hint of condescension. "Even you have to admit that everythin' got blown way out of proportion, and it wasn't *all* my fault." Daphne stared at him, speechless. "After all, I was hurt, just as much as you were when—"

"Oh, please!" she exploded, a rush of ire shooting through her entire body like a burst of adrenaline. "Screwing my brother's girlfriend *for months* before our wedding wasn't such a bad thing?"

"Oh, for Christ's sake, Daphne. All you can do is bring up old—"

"And what about blabbing all over town that Lafayette Marchand was King's real father?"

"You have no proof I did that!" he spat. "My cousin Vic—"

"Oh... but that whisper campaign had your forked tongue all over it," she interrupted. "Just like I know you hacked partway through those harp strings this morning!" She grabbed her briefcase off the seat and slammed the car door. "And, surely, you haven't forgotten when you and your gooney cousin, Vic, *kidnapped* my brother before the city council demolition hearing and locked King in a cemetery crypt in hundred degree *heat*."

"He had air and water—"

"You could have *killed* him, you moron!" She was almost shouting now. "You were lucky King didn't press charges and have you arrested and sent to federal prison for the rest of your *un*natural life! Now, just get out of here, or—"

"Or what?" He glanced around the parking lot, and they both noted that all the guests had made their way inside to the reception. "The Hero of New Orleans is gonna beat me up? You're gonna hit me with your music stand? If I were you, Daphne," he said, looking through the car window to where her harp lay on its side in its black fiberglass case, "I'd be much more watchful 'bout leavin' things you care 'bout where they can get hurt."

"Get lost, Jack," she said, making no more attempts to keep her composure. "Go back to Texas and your slime ball job shilling for some polluting oil company, and leave me alone, or I'll—"

"You'll what, exactly?"

She had scored a hit, she knew, because Jack took a menacing step closer, cocking his head to one side in a fashion that reminded her of nothing so much as a coiled snake, ready to strike.

"Or I swear. Jack Ebert, you'll become a six-part series on Corlis's TV station, that's what!" she hissed, wondering at her bravado. "Everybody in New Orleans is on to you, you creep. Go back into your viper's nest before someone you *least* suspect chops your goddamned head off!"

"No wonder your mama hasn't spoken to you in two years," he said, shaking his head in mock disapproval. "You've got the manners of a Yankee, young lady."

Rigid with pent-up fury, Daphne whirled in place and clicked the key lock device, her hands shaking as she secured the car. Eyes blazing, she turned abruptly to face him once again. "If you don't leave me alone, I'll make sure your *new* employer and anyone who counts in your life in Texas learn about every rotten thing you've ever done, starting with kindergarten. And this time, your crooked pals in the construction business, or your uncle, or your crazy cousin Vic won't be able to cover it up!"

Without another word, she stalked toward the plantation house, turned the corner on the veranda, and collided with a tall, dark-haired man with two cameras slung around his neck and an aluminum tripod in his hand.

"Oh, sorry," Sim Hopkins apologized. Then he gazed at her with a look of concern. "Are you okay? Did that guy in the parking lot finally leave?"

"Sweet Jesus," she exclaimed, sinking weakly into a white wicker porch chair. "How much of that did you hear?"

"Quite a bit," he admitted, setting the tripod on the veranda's decking. "I was sitting behind a hedge over there, waiting for a warbler to show up." A vulgar black stretch limousine—no doubt with Jack Ebert at the wheel—was just nosing into traffic on the parkway. The photographer lightly touched Daphne's sleeve, and asked, "Aren't you supposed to be in a receiving line, or something?"

"Yes," she murmured, too exhausted either to speak further or to rise from the chair.

A paused stretched into ten seconds. "Actually," Sim offered by way of conversation, "I stayed at Monmouth today hoping to hear you play again. I love your voice. You're really quite a remarkable musician."

Daphne was mortified to feel sudden moisture fill her eyes for the third time in one day. "That's very sweet of you to say so…" she managed, bowing her head. A moment later, she was aware that Sim had knelt on the porch beside her.

"Hey… that guy really upset you, didn't he?" He cupped his large left hand over her smaller one resting limply on the arm of the chair.

"Yes… yes, he did," she whispered brokenly.

Daphne looked up to meet his eyes through her tears. His simple act of kindness nearly unhinged her in the wake of Jack's baffling and contemptible assault.

"And no," she added, bowing her head and gazing at his fingers, bereft of any gold jewelry. "I'm not okay. Not by a long shot."

CHAPTER 4

Simon Chandler Hopkins watched the distraught young woman bury her face in her hands as she began to weep in earnest.

"My b-beautiful h-harp…" Daphne sobbed. "He c-cut the s-strings…"

A jilted fiancé—and mortician's son to boot—could cause such grief? he thought. *Figures.*

He'd barely restrained himself from leaping over the hedge and strangling the guy. Now, kneeling next to Daphne's chair, he easily placed his right arm around her shoulder. Without thinking, he pulled her against his khaki vest as a wave of crying wracked her body. Her chin bumped against his wide-angle camera lens.

"This isn't working very well," Sim declared, rising to his feet. "C'mon. My room's just upstairs off the foyer. You can cry there."

He gently helped her out of the chair and guided her swiftly and discreetly up the front staircase past a few guests so intent on finding their way to the bar they didn't seem to notice the incongruous pair.

Daphne nearly stumbled when they passed the threshold of a door with a white enameled plaque that read *#23—Lovell.* She took no notice of the large, high-ceilinged room, with its massive plantation bed festooned with coral-and-cream striped silk hangings, antique upholstered furniture, gigantic mahogany armoire, and floor-to-ceiling windows covered with matching yards of cascading coral draperies. She also appeared oblivious to the open aluminum cases stuffed with lenses of all sizes and miscellaneous photographic paraphernalia littering a hotel boudoir elegant enough for Marie Antoinette.

"Sit there," he directed, pointing to a brocade chaise nestled into one corner. "I'll be right back."

Stemming a hiccup, Daphne obediently did as she was told while Sim disappeared into the marble bathroom. He soon reappeared with a damp washcloth and a bottle of Evian water. "First aid for weeping harpists."

"This place… has… e-everything," she said between sobs.

"My mom sure would like those silk swags," he joked, nodding at the ruffled drapes. She smiled wanly at his attempt at humor and reached for the washcloth to wipe her streaming eyes. "Do you really think Jack what's-his-name is responsible for those harp strings breaking today?" he asked, taking a seat beside her on the chaise.

"They didn't break," she protested. "They were cut." She appeared to be struggling to overcome another wave of emotion. "Oh, God… I haven't cried like this in two years. H-how much did you h-hear?"

"I discreetly took leave of the hedge at the point when you predicted that someone that Jack character least expected might chop off his head," his disclosed wryly.

"Well, it's… a long story," she said with a sigh, using the washcloth to make another swipe across her eyes, "and I don't even know you."

"After what I saw in the wee hours when that harp you played yesterday decided to do another little number on its own," he said quietly, "I'd say we might have some strange sort of connection."

Daphne stared at her rescuer with a shocked expression. "You heard a harp playing *here*… after I left Monmouth, Friday?" she murmured.

"We can talk about that later," he replied, sensing she was far too upset to delve into things that went bump in the night. In the cold light of day, merely mentioning his decidedly eerie experience at three a.m. made him doubt it had ever happened.

For his part, Sim congratulated himself that his latest attempt to track the elusive warbler in the back garden had resulted in this fortuitous meeting. This angelic-looking woman had been the very person he had been thinking about as he unplugged the chargers on his two digital cameras less than twenty minutes earlier. He'd been astonished to recognize her voice on the other side of the hedge, and in fact, was guilty of eavesdropping for much longer than he should have.

Meanwhile, he watched her eyes fill again with tears and her face crumple at the onset of another bout of deep, wrenching sobs that she did her heroic best to muffle with the monogrammed washcloth.

"I-I can't believe what that bastard did to my harp! I thought that Jack Ebert was finally out of my life!"

Sim gave her shoulders another comforting squeeze, enjoying his proximity to her halo of wonderful, curly blond hair. It wasn't excessively blond, he mused, but a light amber hue, more like organic honey, or the bronzed summer hills north of San Francisco. He usually didn't like curly hair on women. However, the caramel-colored nimbus that framed her expressive brown eyes and golden skin—along with the silky sage-green dress she was wearing—transformed her into a kind of seductive celestial spirit. She wasn't particularly tall, but she had remarkably long legs, and when she'd nestled that handsome harp between her thighs, well—

He pulled himself up short. His imagination was heading in directions that weren't very gentlemanly, given the fact he had ushered the poor woman into his hotel bedroom on a mission of mercy.

"Let me get you some more Kleenex," he said suddenly, rising to his feet and heading for the bathroom once again. How in the world, he wondered, had this gorgeous creature gotten herself engaged to that Jack clown? He hoped she wasn't another of those wounded birds he'd encountered in recent years in a conscious effort to find the diametric opposite of Francesca Hayes. At least Daphne hadn't allowed her ex-fiancé to roll over her out there in the parking lot, that was for sure.

In the bathroom he grabbed an entire box of tissues and returned to her side. He handed her a wad, which she accepted appreciatively, and watched her blow her nose. He realized, suddenly, that he'd been mulling over every aspect of his encounter with this woman, even before he'd stumbled downstairs in the middle of the night and beheld the amazing sight of a harp playing on its own.

I was probably still jet-lagged...

"Thanks," she said bleakly. "I'm so sorry. Really."

"Don't be. This is rough stuff."

Her low speaking voice reminded him of the way she'd sung in a husky contralto as sensual as a siren's song. The minute he'd heard her friend Althea call her name in the parking lot, he'd felt an uncensored jolt of anticipation. For the truth was, he reflected, handing her another tissue, he'd changed his entire day around, hoping to catch sight of her again. He'd been about to reveal his presence on the other side of the hedge when that vicious idiot accosted her and launched into his nasty exchange. Sim had learned more about their unhappy history than a stranger ought to know, and yet he was unabashedly curious to discover even more about the harpist crying in his hotel bedroom.

As for Daphne's graphic accusations against her former fiancé—it certainly put into perspective the disastrous end to his own marriage. Who knew better than he that there's no nice way to end intimate relationships? Everybody gets hurt.

"I'm feeling better now," Daphne volunteered with a sniff, but Sim didn't really believe her.

Feeling better takes a very long time, sweetheart.

However, he said, "Good. Glad to hear it."

"Thanks... again," she said, balling a tissue into her palm.

"You're welcome," he replied, retreating once again into the bathroom, where he draped the damp washcloth over the edge of the tub. Turning, he stared briefly at himself in the mirror above the sink. Granted, the lady was highly intriguing. She sang jazz tunes like a vamp and looked great even when she cried. But she also had said yesterday that she lived in New York. His base was San Francisco. They were both just passing through Natchez, and she was probably too much of a Southern lady to consider a simple—

"I-I think I'd better go downstairs," he heard her say from the next room.

"Yeah… you probably should," he agreed, returning to the bedroom. "The bride and groom must be wondering where you are. Do they know this Jack guy showed up? That he cut your harp strings?"

"I don't know… I-I don't think so."

Surprisingly, she had remained on the chaise. Her head was bent forward and her gaze rested on her lap, a crumpled tissue still clutched in each hand. She looked so bereft that he suddenly felt the urge to sit down beside her and pull her hard against his chest again.

Instead, he asked without preamble, "Would you consider having dinner with me later?"

She tilted her head back and gazed at him as if she hadn't heard him correctly.

"Dinner?" she murmured, puzzled.

"Yes, dinner. When all the hoopla is over. There's something I'd like to talk to you about."

Her brow furrowed. "What is it?"

He paused, labeled himself a fool, and then decided against his better judgment to say what he'd wanted to ask her all along. "Have you ever seen… or heard of a harp that… can play by itself? Maybe like one of those old-fashioned player pianos?"

She looked at him wide-eyed, as if he'd just scared the living daylights out of her.

"By *itself*?" she echoed. Before he could respond she said, "Yes."

"Yes, you've heard of such a bizarre thing? Or, yes, you'll have dinner with me?"

"Are you married?"

He was taken aback by the bluntness of her question. "No…" he replied slowly, "I'm not married. Haven't been for… some years now. So, will you?"

She abruptly rose from the chaise, dropped the Kleenex in a nearby wastebasket, and extended her hand in a farewell. "Give me a while to collect myself, will you? I'll tell you if I'm up to having dinner with you after the reception is over."

And without another word, she walked out of the room.

❧

Downstairs in the magnificent blue sitting room, Daphne headed directly for the antique harp next to the baby grand piano and sat down. The reception line was history, and she was grateful for an excuse not to mingle. On top of everything else that had happened, Sim Hopkins's strange question about self-playing harps, along with his dinner invitation, had completely unnerved her, and she needed time to think.

A harp that can play by itself...

She cast a wary eye at Monmouth Plantation's antique instrument and wagered it was nearly a twin to the one sitting in Cousin Maddy's parlor at Bluff House. Gingerly, she began to pluck its strings to judge how well it had held its tune since she'd played it the day before. Then, with brief nods to some familiar faces milling about the wedding reception, she immediately launched into a series of romantic standards without even opening her briefcase to extract any sheet music. Through the parlor door she had a good view into the large foyer and out to a brick courtyard where an open-sided tent had been pitched. Soon, she had a small group of wedding guests, champagne glasses in hand, standing nearby, listening to her play.

While she offered up "We've Only Just Begun," she kept her head down and her eyes half shut in an effort to discourage anyone from attempting to start a conversation. She just wasn't up to idle chitchat. Most of all, she needed some time to reflect upon whether it was a good or bad idea to have dinner with the intriguing man upstairs who'd just helped her dry her eyes.

She segued into "That's All I Ask of You" from *Phantom of the Opera* and caught a glimpse of her mother prancing through the foyer. Without a glance toward the source of the music, Antoinette paused at the wide entrance to the parlor, surrounded by several pot-bellied men she had known since her childhood—and still referred to as her beaux.

The raven-haired mother of the groom certainly wasn't making any effort to connect with her daughter after all these months of hostile silence. She and her admirers engaged in boisterous, champagne-fueled small talk for several minutes. And despite Daphne's carefully lowered expectations, she felt cut to the quick when her mother finally gazed into the sitting room—and then coolly looked away. Daphne closed her eyes again and tried to concentrate solely on her playing.

A quarter of an hour later, her new sister-in-law suddenly appeared next to the harp, her smart ivory silk suit giving her the appearance of a very chic guest, rather than the bride herself.

"C'mon, Daphne! Stop hiding behind your harp! You were smart enough to deep-six the reception line, but we definitely want you to sit with us for the toasts."

Daphne wound up the tune she was playing and allowed Corlis to lead her to the courtyard. The tent's stanchions had been swathed in gossamer white tulle with bouquets of pink azaleas. Small china teapots filled with spring flowers adorned round tables cloaked in snowy linen. A rectangular table positioned to one side was also draped with a white embroidered cloth. On it stood a three-tiered wedding cake and a spectacular display of cream and blush roses, lavender delphiniums, purple gladiola, and pale peach snapdragons.

A table near the fountain had been set aside for the bride and groom and other members of the official wedding party. In one corner of the tent sat the entire LaCroix family trading jokes with Corlis's camera and sound operators and the rest of the staff from her TV station, WJAZ. At another table, King's teaching assistant at the university's school of architecture whooped it up with a troop of foot soldiers from the New Orleans historic preservation community. It was a tribute to the bride and groom that they'd all gathered in Natchez on such short notice.

Before Daphne could sit down, her mother appeared suddenly not ten feet from where she stood. Antoinette intercepted a waiter carrying a full tray of champagne glasses and exchanged her empty flute for a full one as mother and daughter locked glances. Daphne found herself unable to move from her spot beside the splashing fountain. It was as if the entire wedding scene had faded into the background and she and Antoinette Kingsbury Duvallon were alone on a stage.

"Hello, Mama," Daphne said after a long pause. Corlis discreetly stepped away. Antoinette closed the short gap between them. Daphne absently noticed that she had removed the corsage from her coat's lapel, as if to say "These sweetheart roses aren't quite up to the standards of Flowers by Duvallon." Her mother gave her the once-over, leaving Daphne with the distinct impression that she was a contestant in a beauty pageant at which Antoinette had already been declared the winner.

"You look very... nice, dear."

Well, at least it was a decent beginning after more than two years of stony silence, Daphne thought hopefully.

"So do you," she replied promptly.

"I 'spose you always have to wear those shapeless skirts 'cause of playin' your harp, and all."

It certainly hadn't taken Magnolia Mama long to lob a zinger. Daphne forced herself not to rise to the bait.

"I love that shade of teal on you, Mama. It looks gorgeous with your hair."

Why did she always try to appease this woman? she wondered.

"Did y'all see Jack?" Antoinette asked, as if she were casually inquiring about a second cousin, twice removed.

"I thought King asked you not to tell the Eberts *anything* about this wedding."

"Oh, for heaven's sake," Antoinette exclaimed airily, taking a sip of her champagne. "You can't keep somethin' like this a secret in New Orleans!"

"Not if you tell the Eberts *personally*, you can't."

"I've done business with René and Alice Ebert for thirty-five years," her mother retorted. "Alice is a dear, dear friend. We were in the same Mardi Gras court, for pity's sake. Of course, we talk. You're just tryin' to make me feel bad."

Oh, God... here we go...

Daphne knew she was heading down an old, familiar road, but couldn't seem to help herself. "Just now, Jack told me quite a bit about that conversation between you and his mother."

"Oh?" Antoinette said warily. Then she switched tactics with lightening speed. "Well, then, you *did* deign to talk to that poor boy today," she declared triumphantly. "So why're you makin' such a big fuss over whether or not he knew 'bout King's weddin'? You're just tryin' to turn him into some kind of villain 'cause you embarrassed your whole family in front of the entire city of New Orleans two years ago. Alice's been worried *sick* 'bout him livin' in Texas."

Daphne glanced around at the other guests and gestured toward the entrance to the tent. "Let's go outside, okay?" she suggested tersely. "There's no point in refighting this battle in front of an audience."

Amazingly, Antoinette followed in her wake. "Well, at least you have the sense not to be rude to me in front of all these people," her mother said. Meanwhile, the guests were wolfing down hors d'oeuvres under the canvas a few yards away. "I certainly can't blame Jack for being upset," she declared, switching tactics once again. It was a method of arguing that had driven Daphne nearly insane over the years. "You keep accusin' him of all those terrible things with Cindy Lou, which *both* of them will deny to their dyin' day, and now, you attack the poor man by—"

"I *saw* him with Cindy Lou, Mama." Daphne lowered her voice, and added, "When I dumped Jack at the altar, *you* were the one who was embarrassed, weren't you? It was more important to you and Daddy to look good in front of all your fancy Garden District friends than to face the truth that your best friend's boy had been cheating on your daughter with your son's girlfriend for *months*."

"Alice says that you'd been ignorin' Jack when you were up in New York at Juilliard," Antoinette replied reproachfully. "She says that all along you probably were still seein' that conductor you'd been—"

"Oh, for God's sake!" Daphne exploded. "Rafe Oberlin wasn't the reason I left Jack at the altar—and you know it."

Thirty feet away, a trio of musicians were setting up their instruments near a dance floor erected on the lawn beside a bed of white and yellow tulips. Fifty yards beyond, a graceful arbor sparkled with crystal lights.

"Well, there was certainly no need for y'all to make such a *public* fuss about everything," Antoinette declared. "The mess you created by runnin' out of that church—right in front of the *priest*—caused such awful talk, Flowers by Duvallon is still recoverin' from it all."

"Even though I've paid you and Daddy back the money, you still have to make me wrong, don't you?" Daphne asked quietly in rising frustration and sadness. Antoinette glared at her daughter, refusing to speak. "Convince me, Mama, that you don't really care more about your business relationships with the Eberts and the Petrellas than about my almost marrying a two-timing, double-crossing pathological *liar* who could've killed your *son!*"

"You're just twistin' everything all 'round," Antoinette cried shrilly, and then glanced toward the tent to see if they were attracting unwanted attention. "Just like you always do!" she whispered harshly. Her vermilion lips had bloomed into a full-blown pout.

"I'm not twisting one single thing," Daphne retorted, starting to tremble. "You've got to stop making things *up!*" Pushed to the limit by her mother's persistent refusal to face reality, she raised both hands and sketched imaginary headlines in the air. "Dateline: Mardi Gras. Back in the day. You had drunken sex with Lafayette Marchand, betrayed your own sister, and married Daddy to cover it up. Dateline: Christmas. Two years ago. Jack had drunken sex with Cindy Lou Mallory the night before my wedding, betraying King and me at the same time. See any parallels?"

Antoinette's air of injured innocence had transformed itself into righteous indignation. Daphne ignored this, however, adding, "If the fallout from all that was humiliating to you, I'm sorry. But that's the way it *happened.* Don't you take *any* goddamned responsibility for the way things turned out?"

"Don't you *dare* talk to me like that, young lady!" Antoinette hissed.

It was always like this between her mother and her, Daphne thought distractedly, wondering if Antoinette's glare had the power to vaporize her, right on the spot. She glanced into the tent. If she didn't extricate herself from this situation soon, both of them would begin to behave even more appallingly.

Just accept the way she is, she lectured herself ferociously. She had no power to alter her mother's compulsive need to dispute hard facts—a habit ingrained since her girlhood. For a brief moment, Daphne studied the fine lines around Antoinette's lips and at the corners of her eyes. In the full light of day, even the most carefully applied makeup couldn't camouflage these telltale signs of aging. She knew, suddenly, that it was up to her to make different choices in the way she responded to the woman's lunatic behavior.

"You know, Mama…" she said slowly, hardly believing what she was about to say, "I'm glad to see you looking so pretty today." Her mother blinked, as if she were dumbfounded by her daughter's abrupt change of demeanor. "And I'm glad you came to the wedding, for King's sake. I know it couldn't have been easy for you, considering everything that's happened. Now, please excuse me, will you? Corlis is waving at me."

Antoinette was clearly mystified by Daphne's conciliatory tone. The younger woman briefly rested her hand on her mother's coat sleeve. Then, she turned and reentered the tent. King called out to her just as the musical trio began to play softly in the background.

"Hey, Sister Woman! Sit right here, darlin'." He pointed to a chair beside him. His bride was already seated to his right. Daphne inhaled deeply and sat down.

"Are you all right?" Corlis whispered. "I was about to send out the search-and-rescue squad."

"I'm… okay," Daphne confirmed. "At least I'm still breathing."

"King told me Jack made a brief appearance at the church, the scum. Fortunately, I never saw him or you might have witnessed the lovely bride decking an uninvited guest."

Daphne couldn't help but laugh at Corlis's wisecrack. She was surprised, herself, to discover that she'd regained most of her composure. In fact, she felt pretty great. She had faced the snake and the tigress—and survived with dignity. This time, at least. She glanced surreptitiously in her mother's direction in time to see her wander over to the table where some Kingsbury cousins from Baton Rouge had gathered.

"Since we thought your mother wasn't coming," Corlis said,

nodding in the direction of her new mother-in-law, "Lani Riches squeezed her in where I thought she'd do the least damage."

King nodded agreement and then leaned forward and kissed his bride lightly on the forehead. "Bless you, O wife of mine."

Daphne quickly filled them in on Jack's latest untoward behavior in church and in the parking lot and, briefly, about the photographer coming to her rescue.

"Just watch your back while we're on our honeymoon, okay, sugar?" King urged. "Hopefully Jack's bosses in Texas will keep him too busy to mess with you anymore. But, good for you for givin' the guy what for."

From that moment on, the joy in the room became palpable. A series of raucous, ribald toasts were offered by friends and relations honoring Corlis and King; Great Aunt Marge; King's newly acknowledged father, Lafayette Marchand; and the rest of the bridal party. King then raised a glass to Daphne's harp playing "under duress," as he obliquely put it. The jazz trio began to play again, and soon, everybody paired off.

Through the open-sided tent, Daphne caught sight of Sim Hopkins walking out the mansion's back door with his ubiquitous cameras looped around his neck. He turned toward the rear garden near the arbor, as if prepared to take off in pursuit of the elusive yellow-rumped warbler once again. Impulsively, Daphne rose from her chair, dashed down a brick path flanked by neatly sculptured, knee-high hedges, and hailed him just as he was descending the stone steps near the rose beds aflame with pink, blush, and peach-colored flowers.

"Sim! Hey, Sim!" she called, wondering if two glasses of vintage champagne provided the impetus that drove her to take this wholly uncharacteristic action. "Hi, there!"

"Well... hi," he said, smiling as he turned to her. "You obviously feel a lot better."

"A lot," she pronounced, suppressing a champagne-induced giggle. She was slightly breathless by the time she arrived at his side. "Sim... won't you come have a glass of the bubbly and meet my brother and new sister-in-law? I told them what a lifesaver you were today, and they said they'd love it if you'd join us for a bit. Will you?"

He pointed to his khaki pants. "I'm not exactly dressed for a wedding."

"Oh, that doesn't matter," she declared, waving her hand dismissively. "Plus, if you have a drink with us, then you can also dance with me," she added, smiling up at him in a deliberately flirtatious fashion that even Magnolia Mama might admire.

Oh, puh-leeze, she thought, chagrined.

Then she almost laughed aloud. Maybe there were some things she'd learned from Antoinette Kingsbury Duvallon that might actually prove useful.

CHAPTER 5

SIM DIDN'T RESPOND IMMEDIATELY to Daphne's invitation to join her family's wedding celebration inside the tent.

"It's absolutely fabulous champagne," she assured him in a rush. "My favorite… Veuve Clicquot." When he didn't reply, she suddenly felt inane. "Oh. Well…" she added uncertainly, "I can see you're just on your way out…"

He glanced up at the sky and then at his watch. "Sure, why not?" He flashed a grin, and then added more graciously, "I'd be delighted to raise a glass to the happy couple."

Daphne eyed the mellow shafts of light pouring through the moss-covered branches of the large oak tree that Jack had probably hidden behind earlier. "It's the perfect time of day for shooting pictures, isn't it?" she asked with a guilty expression.

"Golden time," he acknowledged with a shrug.

"I'm sorry. I didn't stop to think about the job you're here to do."

Sim gazed pensively toward the rear of the garden. "That little sucker in those hedges out there has dodged me for two days now," he declared, as if he'd reached an important decision. "Why should I let him deprive me of a glass of fine champagne and a dance with a beautiful woman—not to mention getting to meet the famous Kingsbury Duvallon?"

"You know about my brother King?" she asked, startled.

Daphne did her best to ignore the fact he'd called her beautiful. After all—in the words of her cynical female musician friends—he was a "travelin' man," and they tended to say those sorts of things to women they met along the way.

"He's an architectural historian, right?" Sim asked. "Mrs.

Riches told me all about the 'Hero of New Orleans' and your brother's fight in Natchez, too, to keep people from demolishing some great, old places around here."

"That's right," she said proudly. "The guy lies down in front of bulldozers for a living. One of the last real crusaders around, and I adore him for it."

Daphne was inordinately pleased that Simon had been asking the owner of Monmouth Plantation about the Duvallons. Well, she amended silently, he'd been asking about her *brother*, at least.

She waited in the front foyer while Sim took his camera equipment upstairs to his room. When he reappeared, he'd shed his khakis for a pair of gray slacks, a blue blazer, a pale-blue collared shirt, and regimental striped tie.

And looks terrific, Daphne thought.

The jazz trio was well into a romantic bossa nova by the time they returned to the tent. She made introductions on the dance floor while Corlis and King moved gracefully to the sensuous Latin music. The musicians then swung into a set of rock and roll tunes, which left Daphne mildly disappointed that Sim and she were consigned to dancing like planets orbiting in different galaxies. However, she liked watching the supple way he moved and wondered what it would be like to tango with him.

At the end of the set, as guests gathered around, the bride and groom cut the cake, and immediately waiters delivered snowy wedges on gold-rimmed dessert plates, along with coffee, to the assembled guests. Eventually, the wedding party returned to the head table, where everybody made room for Sim's added chair, and King signaled the waiters for more champagne.

"Thanks for letting me gate-crash," Sim said, pointing apologetically to his more casual attire.

"Thanks for being there for my sister earlier today," King countered. His eyes rested briefly on Daphne with a look of concern. "The last thing any of us wanted was for Jack Ebert to show up in Natchez. We've all learned to stay on our guard 'round that guy."

Just then, two members of the hotel staff entered the tent pushing a dolly. The antique harp that Daphne had been playing earlier in the sitting room glided by their table on its way toward the band.

"What—" Daphne said, gaping at the instrument as it was placed next to the bass fiddle.

"Do you mind?" Corlis asked with a mischievous expression. "I know I told you that you weren't expected to work at our wedding reception, but would you be willing to do that song I heard you sing yesterday in the parlor?" She turned to address her new husband. "Do you have *any* idea what a foxy little songstress your sister is?"

Daphne's brother smiled faintly. "Not really," he replied, "but I'd consider it a mighty fine weddin' present if she'd show me." He rose from his chair and tapped his knife against an empty glass. "Hey, everybody!" he shouted over the din. "Y'all already know that my sister is a very accomplished classical harpist. Just now, I'm told by my new wife, here, that Daphne's been holdin' out on us. What's the tune you're gonna sing for us, sugar?"

Daphne rose from her chair, and loudly announced, "'Greensleeves.'" At her brother's look of confusion, she shook her head, laughing, and said, "Just kidding… just kidding! I think y'all will recognize the song right away." She crossed to the dance floor and took a seat upon the silk-covered stool that had been placed next to the harp. She pulled the instrument against her shoulder and smiled at the leader of the jazz trio. "How's 'Georgia on My Mind'?" she said in a low voice. "Is the key of F all right?"

The musician nodded doubtfully. He was a man who looked to be in his midfifties, with thick, black-rimmed glasses, patches of gray, curly, close-cropped hair, and coffee-colored skin. "I never played with no harp before," he whispered.

"I've never played jazz with a trio before, either," she said with a grin, "except as backup for the Cafe LaCroix band, in New Orleans."

This last statement appeared to bolster the bandleader's confidence. "Well, me and the boys'll play real soft, and you play real loud, and we'll probably do just fine. You can use that mike right there to sing into, okay?" He directed his next words to his compatriots. "Ready, fellas? Key of F, And a one... and two, and..."

The foursome easily slid into the opening bars and played through an entire chorus before Daphne began to sing the familiar refrain.

"Georgia... Georgia... the who-le da-ay through..."

As the rich, velvety musical tones filled the tent, Daphne closed her eyes and gave herself over to the song's wonderful rhythms and haunting sentiments. All her cares and worries and frustrations fell away like autumn leaves off a tree, and she reveled in the hush that descended upon the boisterous crowd. The tune she sang was one that male singers performed, mostly, but Daphne never cared about that. She abandoned herself to the nostalgia expressed by the timeless lyrics and the layers of meaning that also conveyed her own longing for a certain style of life she'd grown up with in the South.

"Other arms reach out to me... other eyes smile ten-der-ly..."

At this moment, she opened her eyes and observed King and Corlis staring at her with both pride and amazement. Her gaze slid left, and her heart took an extra beat at the sight of Sim Hopkins watching her intently over the rim of his champagne glass. It was a strangely intimate moment, as if they were still in his bedroom upstairs, or alone in a romantic restaurant in the French Quarter. He held her gaze, and she found herself unable to look away.

"...still in peaceful dreams I see... the road... leads back... to you..."

A rush of sensuality held her in its grip. For several more bars she sang *to* Sim, communicating to this virtual stranger the longing she felt for some mythical man who could touch her soul with recognition of her own, best self.

When the last notes of harp and voice hung in the air and then faded, there was utter silence in the tent. Then a storm of clapping and wolf whistles ensued, and Daphne felt herself turning scarlet to the roots of her blond curls. She refused all pleas for an encore. Instead, she made a mock curtsy and collapsed into the chair next to Sim.

Althea leaned across the table and declared, "Well, that's *it*, girl!

You are comin' down to New Orleans, and playin' with us 'fore you head back to the Big Apple—as a *solo* act. Only, you gotta get yourself some sexier clothes that show off those legs of yours."

"Amen," Sim mumbled into her ear.

Daphne cast him a look of mock reproof as King poured her a glass of iced water from a crystal pitcher. She smiled happily and took a large swallow, basking in the glow of praise from all sides of the table.

Then, out of the corner of her eye, she saw her mother marching across the dance floor, the coat over her matching sheath snapping like a flag in a storm, heading directly for the bridal party. When she arrived at their table, Antoinette addressed her daughter in a tone laced with anger and bitterness.

"Well, Daphne Duvallon! Once *again*... you certainly made a spectacle of yourself... singin' like some floozy on a riverboat... *defilin'* that wonderful old harp with such vulgar music! And you, King, eggin' her on. Isn't your bride 'sposed to be the focus of attention, here? Isn't this 'sposed to be *Corlis's* big day?"

For a fraction of a second, everyone around the table gaped in stunned silence. Corlis's great-aunt Marge raised an eyebrow beneath her pink silk turban. Aunt Bethany leaned closer to Lafayette Marchand, as if her husband would shield her from her sister's fury. Daphne stared at her mother in bewilderment, followed by anger, followed by an avalanche of doubt that she'd unwittingly done something absolutely awful to ruin another family wedding.

"Mama—" King warned, but he was interrupted by his bride of two hours.

"Mrs. Duvallon," Corlis said, her eyes flashing as she stood abruptly and leaned across the pristine linen tablecloth. "This *is* my big day," she announced with pointed emphasis. "Mine and King's and Daphne's and Althea's and my Aunt Marge's and Bethany's and Lafayette's, and especially our hostess, Mrs. Whitaker. *All* the people you see sitting here who've been so kind and loving to us. No one, that I've noticed, has made a spectacle of herself at this wedding—except, perhaps, *you*!"

Antoinette's jaw visibly dropped. Fortunately, the jazz trio had begun to play again, and most guests were already on the dance floor. Corlis inhaled deeply, turned away from the outraged intruder, and addressed the others at her table.

"Well… babycakes," she said in an exaggerated Southern drawl. "Any of y'all feel like cuttin' a rug?"

"Like the great wife you are, you're readin' m'mind, darlin'," King declared. He glanced at his mother calmly, and added, "You take care, now, Mama, y'hear?"

Instantly, Sim seized Daphne's hand and pulled her to her feet. Everyone else quickly followed suit and either headed for the dance floor or the bar. Antoinette Kingsbury Duvallon was left standing alone.

Daphne had no sensation that she was even on the dance floor, let alone held in the sheltering arms of Simon Hopkins. She hadn't the faintest notion what music they were moving to, other than that it was mercifully slow.

"I take it that was your mother?"

Daphne remained silent for a few seconds. Then she sighed, her lips close to his ear. "That is correct."

"Well… you Southerners sure know how to throw an exciting party."

She heaved another sigh, and asked, "Do you feel as if you've suddenly been dropped into a Tennessee Williams play, or something?"

"Or something," Sim agreed. "How long before the bride and groom take off?"

Daphne surveyed the dance floor. Corlis and King were nowhere to be seen.

"Soon, I think. They must be upstairs, changing. They're going to Venice, Florence, Siena, and Rome," she said wistfully. "King loves architecture, as you know. Corlis says she just wants to sleep for three weeks, order room service, and be fed pasta in bed."

"Sounds like the perfect honeymoon."

"Believe me, with those two, it will be."

"I liked them both… a lot."

A moment of awkwardness bloomed suddenly between them.

They had known each other less than twenty-four hours, and yet Sim had been privy to Daphne's most intimate family secrets. Three tables away, Antoinette angrily gathered up her clutch purse and sailed past them on the dance floor without another word.

Sim leaned forward, and spoke softly, "Look, Daphne, you've had a pretty rugged day. You haven't even said if you'll go to dinner with me tonight, but maybe you'd like to take a rain check…" He allowed his statement to hang in the air.

Daphne wondered if the family dramas had proved too much for the poor guy. Suddenly, fatigue invaded her every pore. "Maybe you're right…"

"How long are you staying in Natchez?" Sim asked. "We could make it later in the week, if you like."

So he actually *was* thinking of her welfare, she marveled. She didn't have a job to go home to. She might as well stay the week.

"Any yellow-rumped warblers in your future tomorrow night?" she inquired, smiling and casting him a sidelong glance. Once again, a slightly Southern inflection had mysteriously crept into her speech, and Daphne began to wonder if she was starting to sound and act like her mother, Queen of Flirts?

"Not after sundown. I'll find out from Lani Riches how to get to where you're staying and pick you up about seven, okay?"

"Perfect."

"Got any restaurant suggestions?"

The music had stopped, and the guests had begun to migrate back into the plantation house. A knot of partygoers congregated in the parlor and front foyer, waiting for the bride and groom to descend the stairs en route to a flower-decked horse and carriage waiting in the circular drive. Daphne knew King's Jaguar was parked out of sight down the street.

"Well, there's always the Magnolia Grill…" she ventured. "It's down by the river and serves every kind of catfish known to man. And then there's Biscuits and Blues, or the Under-the-Hill Saloon. They play terrific jazz, blues, and Dixieland at both places, though I don't know what kind of food Biscuits and Blues serves these days. Around here, it's very Miss-Lou-funky, if you know what I mean."

"Miss-Lou what?"

"Mississippi-Louisiana. Gumbo and catfish and deb gowns and bib overalls—all mixed up! You're in border country, boy!"

"How about we eat at the first place you mentioned and catch the music at the other two?"

"Perfect." She nodded happily and held out her hand to Sim in a gesture of farewell. "Thanks for being such a pal today," she said sincerely. "And tomorrow night, I'd really like to hear what you have to say about harps that play themselves in the middle of the night."

Sim gazed at her thoughtfully. "Okay…" he agreed. "But the same goes for me." He wagged a finger at her. "I want to hear what *you* have to say on that subject as well. You know a lot more about harps than I do."

Just then, Lani Riches approached holding a beribboned straw basket over one arm. Smiling broadly, she bestowed upon each of them a small pouch of birdseed tied in fine, pastel netting and a silk ribbon. "Everyone out on the veranda, please," she directed gaily. "The bride and groom are about to leave!"

Daphne pointed to Sim's sachet of birdseed. "Hey, Flash," she teased, "maybe if you throw a bunch of this stuff out in the woods, you'll finally get that warbler to pay some attention to you."

Daphne drove the Explorer through the deserted streets of Natchez while Cousin Maddy silently gazed out the passenger seat window. Behind them, in the vehicle's cargo area, mounds of wedding presents wrapped in silver and white were wedged around the black case containing Daphne's wounded harp.

"Such a beautiful ceremony…" murmured the older woman. She turned to look at Daphne. "How you ever continued to play with those broken harp strings I never will know, darlin'."

"You noticed." Daphne kept her eyes on the road as she drove down Jefferson Street and made her way through a maze of one-way thoroughfares toward Clifton Avenue.

"Oh, *I* noticed," Madeline Whitaker confirmed. "Right after

I saw Jack Ebert come into the church." She paused, and then added, "He cut them, didn't he? He did this terrible thing to your harp."

Startled, Daphne took her eyes off the road for an instant to glance at her companion. "You think so too, huh? I can't prove it, of course, but somebody sure filed them halfway through so they'd break at some point during the ceremony."

"I'm sure it was Jack." Cousin Maddy said the words with absolute conviction, as if she had been shown proof from a higher authority. Then she reached across the car. "You must be extremely careful when it comes to that young man," she cautioned, lightly patting Daphne on the shoulder. "I don't like him. Never have. I was so relieved that night when you obeyed your instincts and called off that wedding, even if it was at the very last minute."

"You're a member of a very exclusive club that feels that way," Daphne said dryly. She drove in silence for a few moments, then added "You know, Maddy? The minute we got engaged, this horrible sense of doom came over me. But the next day, Mama had ordered the monogrammed silverware, and I just didn't have the guts to call a halt." Then she wondered aloud, "Do you think 'bride's nerves' is really a code for 'I shouldn't be marrying this person'?"

"Sometimes," Maddy agreed. "I know that with Marcus, I never had a moment's doubt that he was the man I wanted to spend the rest of my life with. He told me he felt the same way."

"Really?" Daphne said, awed by her cousin's certainty. "After what I went through with Jack... and Rafe Oberlin, before *that*... when it comes to the opposite gender, I don't have much faith in my own judgment anymore."

"Don't be too hard on yourself," Madeline assured her kindly. "After all, you never had a very good example set for you by your mama and daddy... and now, we all know why. Let your brother be your touchstone from now on. I think he's made a wonderful choice in a life partner."

"Me too," Daphne said softly. "And he had to work through much more emotional garbage than I did, that's for sure."

"We all have things to face in life, no matter who we are, darlin'," Maddy replied, and fell silent again.

At length, Daphne asked gently, "You miss them terribly, don't you?"

Madeline nodded. "Every day. Every single day. I suppose Marcus's death is easier to accept because he was sixty years old. But when your child dies before you do—" Her cousin's voice cracked, and Daphne felt dreadful that she'd asked such a direct question.

"Oh, Cousin Maddy, I'm so sorry if I—"

"And the worse part, of course," she continued as if Daphne hadn't spoken, "is my not understandin' how such a thing could happen. How could both my husband *and* my son die of the same form of cancer?"

"Did Clayton ever smoke?"

"No, never once! And that's what got the doctors so mystified. How could the linin' of the lungs of a twenty-seven-year-old be riddled with that damned disease, same as his cigar-smokin' papa?"

"Secondhand smoke?" Daphne ventured.

"Marcus always smoked out on the veranda, *never* in the house or the car."

"Oh, Maddy... it's so awful," Daphne blurted. "Between losing them and, then, your house practically falling down the bluff... you've had a really awful time of it, haven't you? I'm sorry I've made you sad."

"No... *no*, darlin'," Maddy protested as Daphne nosed the car into the driveway and parked behind the dilapidated mansion. "You can't imagine what a relief it is to have someone to talk to 'bout Marcus and Clay. Everyone else tiptoes 'round the subject as if my husband and son never existed. I think I've gone slightly mad not bein' able to speak openly with folks about them these last three years." She pointed at the roof where broken shingles dangled over rusted rain gutters. "I got to the point where I just didn't care about anything, even if the house were eventually to fall off the bluff and crash into the river—with me in it."

"You don't feel like that now, do you?" Daphne asked, alarmed and wondering if Maddy should still be taking antidepressant drugs.

"I cannot lie, darlin' girl," Cousin Maddy admitted. "Some days those Whitaker blue devils get ahold of me so bad, I don't even want to get out of bed." She patted one of Daphne's hands that rested on the steering wheel. "But not today. Today was good. Wonderful, in fact."

"Even my playing that 'vulgar music,' as my mother called it?"

"You were absolutely enchantin' at the reception and she's a jealous fool," Cousin Maddy replied tartly.

"Jealous?" Daphne echoed, shocked by Madeline's blunt pronouncements.

"Always has been," she said flatly. "She always gave Marcus the once-over whenever she came to Natchez to visit her Whitaker cousins."

"*No!*" Daphne said, giggling.

"Truth, I swear," Maddy said, putting her hand over her heart. "And just look how she behaved toward her own sister—playin' the Jezebel to Lafayette like that when she was a girl. Thank God those two finally got together again," she sighed, referring to Aunt Bethany and King's biological father. She reached for Daphne's hand and cast her a level gaze. "Don't you realize something, darlin'? Antoinette wants to be the star! That's why she never lets anybody forget that she was Mardi Gras queen, way back in the mists of time. And that's why she couldn't stand you bein' the center of attention for a few moments at King's weddin'." Maddy shook her head emphatically, chiding them both. "But let's not turn into chattering ol' gossips! The main thing I wanted to say was that I've been playing a harp all my life and *never* imagined a person could play jazz on it like that."

"It was fun," Daphne replied with a sidelong smile.

"Well, that young man who came in late and sat with you certainly seemed to be enjoying your performance."

Daphne rolled her eyes and gave a self-deprecating laugh. "Well, he *is* taking me to dinner tomorrow night. That is, if you don't mind my staying with you a while longer?"

"You're welcome to stay as long as you like. You know that, dear."

"How's two weeks?" she asked impulsively, hoping during that time that Maddy might be able to offer some sound career advice regarding her options in New York. "You'd tell me, wouldn't you, Maddy, if my staying that long isn't convenient?"

"Two weeks is barely enough," Maddy chided. She leaned across the car's seat and chucked her chauffeur gently under her chin. "Daphne, darlin'—you can have the whole top floor of this mausoleum to yourself for as long as I'm on this earth, if you want it," she insisted vehemently. "I was starting to feel sad that all of you had to leave so soon. I'll sleep better, just knowing you're under the roof a while longer—leaky ol' thing that it is." She opened the car door and ushered Daphne across the rear veranda and into the kitchen, flicking on a light and pointing to the door that led to the foyer. "Now, be a darlin' and go right into the front parlor. If you'll play me that pretty song again that you sang at the wedding, I'll make us a nice hot pot of tea. I tuned both harps just this morning, and you know what? That ancient ol' thing hardly needed it at all."

Two empty teacups, one with a tiny chip on its gilded lip, sat on the book-laden coffee table next to a massive horsehair sofa whose plum velvet upholstery had seen far better days. The silhouettes of both harps cast graceful shadows on the wall. Madeline began putting the crockery on a black toile tray in preparation for returning the tea things to the kitchen.

"I'll do that, Maddy," Daphne offered quickly. "Just leave everything and toddle off to bed. You must be exhausted."

"What about you?" her cousin asked, and yawned agreement.

"I always get jazzed when I've played," she said, laughing. "I need a few more minutes to get sleepy again."

"Well, I loved my private concert tonight. I had no idea you knew all those numbers and could sing 'em so well. You get such great bluesy sounds out of that big ol' harp. You're quite amazing, my dear."

"This kind of music has become a hobby of mine." She gave Maddy's concert harp a fond pat. "I have a couple of friends in

New York who love jazz tunes, too, and we go to the clubs all the time. It gives me a break from a life of *Swan Lake*, if you know what I mean."

"I can only imagine." Daphne was tempted to bring up the subject of Rafe's firing her, when Maddy added, "Well, sugar, your ol' cousin's going to go rest her weary bones." Madeline bent and kissed Daphne on the top of her head. "I had a lovely day, and much of the credit goes to you, darlin'. Nighty-night."

Daphne watched as her cousin turned off a sequence of hall lights en route to the back parlor that she had converted into a bedroom suite following the deaths of her husband and son. Daphne called after her, "Are you okay? Can you see all right?"

"Made it back here just fine, thank you," her cousin answered. "G'night, again."

And then Daphne heard the thick cypress door close, and absolute quiet descended upon the house. She carried the tray into the large, cluttered kitchen and began to rinse out the cups and saucers, placing them on the wooden drain board to dry. Overhead, huge metal cooking pots hung from a wrought iron rack attached to a beam in the ceiling. Nearby stood an outsized stove that contained two ovens, a warming cabinet, six burners, and a large griddle carbonized from long use. Stored on open shelves over the kitchen counters were several patterns of chinaware, each of which would provide service for at least twenty-four guests. Through the open pantry door, Daphne spied a forest of crystal glasses in every conceivable size, holdovers from an era when mint juleps and old-fashioneds were regularly dispensed on the wide veranda overlooking the river.

It had all been so grand, once, she thought sadly. Now, an entire style of life was close to tumbling over a bluff… into oblivion.

A piercing melancholy descended upon Daphne as she returned to the front sitting room. One by one, she began to switch off the lights. In the shadows, the huge horsehair Victorian sofa looked like a large jungle cat, curled up asleep for the night. Maddy's two harps stood in a pool of light cast by a last, solitary lamp that glowed in the gloom. For some reason, Daphne was drawn to sit on the padded stool next to Maddy's antique instrument and pull the harp against her shoulder.

Instead of fingering a modern tune, as she had done all evening, she began softly to play Bach's Prelude and Fugue in C Major written for harpsichord. She strummed the strings lightly, fearful that she would awaken Maddy or make her think that the so-called ghost was making an appearance.

The music began to have a strange effect on Daphne. As she played, she seemed to be descending toward a dark, sorrow-filled place, a place where there was only suffering of a kind no human should ever have to endure. The familiar and haunting pattern of notes became steps spiraling down, down to the disconsolate depths of an emotional gloom she had never experienced, even in her darkest days after her aborted wedding.

As the music unfolded into minor chords, the notes reverberated in the marrow of her bones, intensifying the anguish that now held her in its grip. She plucked the strings as one possessed, seeking from each its deepest, most pensive tone, calling forth the sadness of a tortured soul, pushed to the breaking point. The lamp on the mahogany table nearby began eerily to glow. A glimmering and luminescent play of light and shadow danced upon the walls.

Candlelight…

In an unfathomable convergence of time and space, the figure of a teenage girl, long, coiling, caramel tresses cascading down the back of her ruffled bed gown, sat at a small harp. All was darkness, except for the gilded instrument that shone like a specter in the flickering candlelight. The mournful music the girl played muffled the sound of her weeping as an avalanche of tears streamed from her amber eyes.

CHAPTER 6

"MIZ DAPHNE, YOU'VE BEEN playin' that harp long enuf, y'hear? You stop that nonsense right now!" Mammy scolded in a low but insistent voice.

Her admonishments had begun at the archway leading to the front parlor and continued, without interruption, until the tall, slender black woman stood beside the thirteen-year-old daughter of the house, who had been playing the harp in the near dark at high volume for more than an hour.

Mammy put her hands on her hips, and declared in a harsh whisper, "Now, don't *you* be cryin'! You jus' makin' things worse than they already *is*! Hush, now!"

Daphne Drake Whitaker, clad only in her nightdress, her pale cheeks wet with tears, stonily continued to play as if she were alone in the shadowy chamber. She utterly ignored the entreaties of the woman who had virtually raised her from babyhood, and continued to pluck the strings of her instrument like someone possessed. And though her fingers ached, in some perverse way the pain and the loudness of the music almost obliterated the crushing heat and keening cries emanating from her mother's upstairs boudoir.

For at least two hours, now, Susannah Whitaker's unrelenting sobs had rent the oppressive air inside Devon Oaks plantation house. Her daughter could think of nothing to dull the sound save for the resonant tones of Bach's Prelude and Fugue in C Major. Daphne hadn't mastered it in its entirety, but that didn't matter.

The first section mesmerized her like a carriage wheel that went round and round until everything became a blur. The young girl had resorted to playing her harp whenever her mother erupted into these explosions of rage and anguish. This was an almost daily occurrence since the afternoon a month earlier when Mammy had carried a small, blue-tinged body shrouded in a blanket down the broad staircase and out the back door to the wood shop. There, a minuscule coffin had been hastily constructed while Daphne's mother howled to the heavens that God in his cruelty had taken her fifth child in as many years.

Daphne's father, tall and grim-faced, had seen to the brief burial of yet another son in the family graveyard that perched on the rise overlooking Whitaker Creek—and, in the distance, the broad and muddy Mississippi. The grassy plot was enclosed in wrought iron fashioned by the plantation's blacksmith, Willis, Mammy's husband. The hallowed ground already had provided eternal sanctuary to Daphne's little sister Phaedra, felled the previous summer by the fever that spared Phaedra's twin, Eustice, but left him a sickly child. Beside Phaedra lay poor Charlie Boy, whose chronic respiratory ailments had choked the life from him by age ten. Next to him were two small plots with miniature tombstones marking the brief existence of stillborn infants born within eight months of each other.

And now the little baby boy with no name had been laid to rest. On the day of his birth, Daphne had heard him mewling for a brief while… then silence. Immediately, her mother's wails had begun. That same dreadful afternoon, Susannah's eldest surviving child had stood beside her father, Charles Whitaker Sr., while he tossed a mound of dirt on the newest grave, then ordered one of the slaves to saddle his gelding. Drinking deeply from a silver flask he kept inside his frock coat, he didn't even bid Daphne farewell, but rather rode off to inspect the tobacco fields that barely fetched enough money to pay for the seed and the clothing and feeding of the fifty-three slaves who tended them.

A few hours later, the front door had been flung open, loudly banging against the wall. Daphne's father burst into the front hallway and halted at the foot of the sweeping staircase. He stared into the parlor at his daughter while his wife's incessant weeping pierced the air. Charles remained rooted to the garnet-and-sapphire Persian carpet, as if absorbing his wife's cries into the pores of his skin. Then he had spun on his boot heels and, striding into his study, slammed the door, and vanished from sight until the next morning.

From that day to this, Daphne's mother had suffered unremitting bouts of anguish. As for the young girl's father, he'd kept to his inner sanctum, sleeping on the burgundy leather couch all night. The frightened youngster's only relief from the misery engulfing Devon Oaks had been to play, play, *play* her harp till her fingers and mind were numb. Then, exhausted, she would go to her room and sleep with a pile of pillows on her head to shut out the continuing cries.

"I said, time for you to go to *bed*, missy," Mammy insisted, rousing Daphne from her melancholy reverie. "And tomorrow, no more of this, y'hear, or you'll be just as crazy-sick as your poor mama. Can't play this ol' harp all day and night!"

In response, Daphne merely gave a vehement shake of her dark blond head and continued to pluck the strings with even greater force, taking no overt notice of the fact that her father, at long last, had emerged from his study. Out of the corner of her eye, she saw his figure walk unsteadily past the parlor's open doorway toward the graceful staircase.

Mammy's large, angular features registered surprise as she and Daphne watched the master of Devon Oaks heavily mount the stairs to the second-floor landing, turn the corner into the hallway, and disappear. The servant shook her head woefully.

"Well, suit y'selves, then," she grunted loudly above the rolling swell of Daphne's music. "I's goin' to bed! But jus' remember, if you keep actin' so crazy, then Miz Madeline, Miz Suki, and Masta Eustice won't have nothin' to do with a sister like you when they gets back from Grandmother Drake's in Natchez. They *never'll* want to come home from Bluff House with you carryin' on like this. Mark my words, chile!" The head house servant glanced around the parlor, which was plunged into gloom except for a lone candle burning in its brass holder. "You 'sposed to be the big, brave one, stayin' at the plantation to help take care of your mama, and jus' look how you actin'! Now you take that candle up with you to bed, and be sure you blow it out, y'hear me?"

Heaving a sigh of frustration, Mammy swept out of the parlor and through the house, and disappeared down the back stairs. Without looking back, she strode into the shadows between the big house and the scattering of slave cabins that dotted an acre adjacent to the tobacco fields bordering Whitaker Creek.

Daphne barely heard the clock on the mantel strike nine. However, the door to her mother's bedchamber must have been left ajar, for suddenly a new sound cascaded down the stairwell, piercing the protective wall of music she'd created around herself. And though Daphne played the chords with all her might, there was no way to escape the strident argument that had begun to rage between her parents.

"You are my wife!" Charles shouted, his words slurring slightly. "I have every right to enter this chamber."

"You're *drunk*!"

"And what if I am? 'Tis the only amusement left to me."

"Have you no decency?" her mother cried brokenly. "Our baby barely three weeks in his grave, and you barge in here—"

"He was my son, too!" exploded Charles. "They *all* were my sons, and my daughters, and now they're all *dead*. But can I allow myself to lie on a faintin' couch, howlin' to the moon and carryin' on as if I were the only one who suffered?"

"You simply don't understand!" her mother cried. "I carried that child in my body. He was alive and then God—"

"*God!*" Her father spat the word as if it were poison. "You think God bothers 'bout one more mewlin' infant in this world? You're just a poor breeder, that's all. Sickly, like the children you produce. Show some spine, woman! Devon Oaks is on the edge of catastrophe. Pull yourself together!"

By this time, Daphne had ceased playing, mesmerized by the bitterness that had transformed her father's voice into a cruel weapon.

"A king has lost his head in Paris, Susannah! Britain and France are at war, and those damnable blockades make my tobacco virtually worthless, even if the land it's growin' on wasn't dyin' out. Can you think of nothin' but your own woes?"

"That's right!" her mother screamed. "Weep your crocodile tears over money, Charles Whitaker! I merely ask for a little compassion—and for you to satisfy your carnal desires someplace else. I suggest the brothels Under-the-Hill!"

"I weep that you cannot bear a male child with any spirit to live," he retorted viciously.

"Do you care so little for the one son you *do* have that you doom Eustice to the grave as well? You terrify him, making him ride that big horse."

"Eustice is the sissy that you have made him. He clings to your skirts and takes after your snivelin' brother, Drake."

"Eustice is easily frightened by bullies like you," Susannah retorted, "and who wouldn't be? But, surely, you cannot blame *me* for his delicate constitution. Your own father wheezed around animals as well, and—"

The report of a palm against flesh and her mother's scream pierced the heavy night air.

"Silence, woman!" Charles growled. "'Tis your family, not mine, that brings me grief."

Downstairs, Daphne sat frozen on the padded stool, her narrow chest slumped against the harp, the callused tips of her fingers clinging to the strings like a prisoner holding onto the bars of a jailhouse window. Her father must be seriously in his cups to slap her mother's face and shout such abominable things to a woman barely risen from childbed, Daphne thought.

"*Grief?*" Susannah Whitaker shrieked. "You dare speak to *me* of grief?"

"You cannot… refuse me a healthy son," Charles roared. "My slaves obey me… and so must you, Susannah!"

"Charles, you can't be thinking—"

Her mother's protests were abruptly cut off. Daphne's heart hammered in her chest and she renewed her efforts to blot out the horror of her parents' exchange by attacking the harp strings with renewed vigor. Nonetheless, the first few bars of the fugue were not nearly loud enough to drown out her mother's hysterical protests.

An extended, bloodcurdling scream raised the hair on the nape of Daphne's neck. Her fingers on the strings froze in place. An unearthly, low keening floated down the stairwell.

"No... no... oh, God... noooo!"

It was her mother's voice, muffled. And then silence. What was happening? Daphne wondered with alarm. Had her father completely lost his temper and seriously injured poor Mama? She rose from her music stool and swiftly mounted the stairs. Devon Oaks was deadly quiet for the first time in weeks.

Well... almost quiet, Daphne considered, tiptoeing toward her parents' bedchamber. The moans commenced again, only this time they were much softer and prolonged, with an accompanying change in pitch and timbre. There was another sound as well, deeper, more guttural, as if a racehorse had just been reined in, heaving hollow, rasping breaths.

Worried and confused, Daphne pushed against the half-opened door and peered into the bedchamber. Her eyes soon grew accustomed to the gloom lit only by a solitary candle affixed in a cut-crystal holder on the bedside table. A pair of breeches, a linen shirt, and a pair of riding boots lay strewn on the floor A figure hovered like an attacking vulture over her mother's inert form. And then her naked father grunted and fell on his wife's chest where her nightdress bunched around her neck.

Neither Charles nor Susannah Whitaker saw their young daughter standing, stunned, in the doorway. Reeling from shock, she retreated, leaving the door ajar. In the hallway, her entire body was overtaken with trembling as if in the grip of a deadly ague. She sped down the stairs and pounced on the harp strings with all her strength.

I won't listen... I won't listen... I won't listen...

Her mind whirled in a litany of denial as she plucked each note of the Prelude with a vengeance. She began to sing loudly.

"Da-da-da... da-da-da-da..."

Concentrate on the notes... play them as loud as you can... and those other sounds will fade away. Sing... sing... sing!

The terrified thirteen-year-old crooned in time to the music as she banged her blond head against the harp's polished wood sounding board. She had no notion how long she'd attempted to blot out what she'd witnessed on the second floor. Mammy's daughter, Kendra, appeared silently in the hallway that opened into the foyer. Before Daphne could react, she was startled into silence by the thud of heavy footsteps overhead and the appearance of her father on the landing above. He pounded his fist on the banister.

"Cease that noise *at once*," Charles thundered. He was bare-chested, dressed only in breeches, and carried his boots in one hand. "I will not have *two* females in this household screechin' like banshees. Go to bed, girl, and not another *sound!*"

He turned on his heel and stalked in the direction of the guest wing. Kendra McGee had remained still as a statue, unseen by her master. The young black slave stared at Daphne for a long moment as silence descended upon the house. The fourteen-year-old glided noiselessly across the Persian carpet to stand by Daphne's side.

"Mammy worried you'd forget to snuff the candle," she whispered, nodding in the direction of the brass holder perched on top of the pianoforte nearby. "She say for you to come wid me." Her dark, expressive eyes peered compassionately at her playmate. Then she laid a sympathetic hand on the sleeve of Daphne's dimity nightdress. "Mammy say, it's all right for you to sleep wid us out back tonight."

A black cat, resplendent with a white bibbed tuxedo chest and matching ivory paws that gleamed in the light of the lamp in Maddy's parlor, rubbed its furry flank sensuously against Daphne's leg, startling her nearly witless. The feline delicately nibbled the harpist's anklebone.

"Groucho! Ow! Bad kitty!" Daphne cried, startled into present reality. Groucho appeared oblivious to the reprimand, changed directions, and rubbed his opposite flank against Daphne's calf while she attempted to catch her breath.

Whoa, there! What was that?

Where in the world had she been just now? One minute she'd been sitting in Maddy's cluttered parlor, idly fingering Bach's Prelude and Fugue in C Major on her cousin's antique harp, and the next, she was observing a family drama of Wagnerian proportions in some place called Devon Oaks Plantation!

But it wasn't just *any* plantation house, was it? she reminded herself, her heart pounding in her chest. Devon Oaks had once belonged to the family of Maddy's husband, the late Marcus Whitaker. She'd seen a picture of it somewhere in Bluff House and remembered Cousin Marcus speaking of it fondly.

Apprehensively, she glanced around the shadowed parlor, noting that Groucho had abandoned her legs and was pacing in a circle on the seat of the horsehair settee. After a few moments, he nestled comfortably in a corner and languidly closed his eyes.

Easy for you to do!

Daphne wondered, after tonight's bizarre episode, if she'd ever be able to sleep a wink in this house—or any other old mansion, for that matter. The unrelenting wails were of a woman obviously suffering from acute postpartum depression after the death of her child—an infant that was one in a string of closely spaced pregnancies that had probably caused poor Susannah Whitaker's hormones to yo-yo.

If ever there were a Susannah Whitaker!

She tried to recall any talk about mental illness in the Whitaker, Duvallon, or Kingsbury family lines. As far as she'd observed, her mother merely exhibited the average neurotic, narcissistic behavior of a female trained since babyhood to be a "magnolia." Her father's borderline alcoholism came with the territory for all those "good ol' boys" in the great state of Louisiana, as King would say. Maddy admitted to suffering from depression, but who wouldn't, losing two close family members in the same year? As for herself, the report to her insurance company when she'd gone to visit Dr. Yankowitz in New York after her aborted wedding had labeled their work together "life adjustment after loss of a significant other." Surely, Dr. Y. would have told her if he thought she had a screw loose?

With a wary eye on the sleeping cat, Daphne stood and stretched her arms over her head. Numbing fatigue invaded every sinew and corpuscle. She reached for the solitary light and switched it off.

It was a dream... she fretted silently. *It felt real, but it couldn't be...*

Strangely, Daphne experienced no fear or dread as she climbed the broad staircase to her room. There had to be a logical explanation, she insisted to herself, remembering the restless nights she had in New York prior to flying south. And then she'd been awakened by the sound of harp music that first night at Bluff House. Perhaps tonight, she'd merely nodded off—which she had done once or twice when practicing late into the night at Juilliard—and the scenes she'd witnessed were merely dreamscapes.

As if to prove a point, she slipped beneath the bedcovers and fell into a dreamless sleep the instant her head touched the pillow. Much to her surprise, when she awoke she found Groucho curled up on the foot of her bed. Apparently, whether she wished to or not, she'd made a new friend.

That morning, Daphne was determined to put all thoughts of the previous night's unsettling events out of her mind, chalking up the experience to the hugely stressful day she'd spent warding off both Jack and her mother's punishing anger.

For most of the day, she read and rested on Maddy's wide veranda with its spectacular view of the river. In the late afternoon, she spent a leisurely forty-five minutes choosing clothes to wear on her date with Simon Hopkins. The evening was slated to include both dinner at an upscale restaurant and dancing at a couple of funky blues bars.

"Not so easy to figure out, is it, Groucho?" she declared aloud, scanning the limited wardrobe she'd brought from New York and hung amid a raft of garment storage bags in the closet. Ultimately, she selected a pair of trim, lightweight black twill slacks, a black cotton tee with spaghetti straps, a collar-less red linen jacket, and a pair of comfortable, black sling-back Chanel pumps that were great for dancing. She donned her one good pair of plain gold earrings and the eighteen-carat gold Tiffany pin in the shape of a harp that King and Corlis had given her when she'd earned her master's degree. Dressed and made up a little before seven o'clock, she filed the essential lipstick, mirror, comb, and credit card into a black crochet handbag the size of a small envelope.

"Dr. Hopkins is here, darlin'," Cousin Maddy called up the stairwell, "and he's brought us a big ol' batch of gorgeous roses that Lani sent with him from Monmouth! Now, isn't that just dear of her?"

Doctor Hopkins? Maddy, of course, would ask what Sim's proper title was. Daphne descended the steps wondering how a man with a PhD would react to the creative chaos that reigned in Madeline Whitaker's household? She found visitor and hostess in the kitchen debating the virtues of a tin bucket to serve as a vase for the roses, versus a dented, tarnished silver trophy that Cousin Marcus had won in a croquet match as a Rhodes scholar at Oxford.

"Let me just find us some silver polish," Maddy declared, and began to root among the clutter of cleaning gear and washday products under her kitchen sink.

Daphne smiled self-consciously at Sim as she felt his gaze meander from her face to the tips of her sling-back pumps. He smiled a warm welcome, then bent to seize a large bucket from a cupboard to the left of the sink. He had on the navy blazer he'd worn at her brother's wedding and a sage-colored polo shirt that intensified the gray-green of his eyes. Trim beige pleated slacks and a pair of loafers made him quite the *GQ* cover model, indeed.

"I liked your first idea, Mrs. Whitaker. Let's do a Martha Stewart and use this wonderful old bucket," Sim proposed. "We can fill it with these long stem beauties and set them right here in the middle of your kitchen table."

"Why, I think you're absolutely right, dear boy," Madeline declared delightedly, shoving the silver polish back into the crowded cupboard under the sink. "An easy, sensible solution. What do you think, Daphne?"

"Perfecto," Daphne agreed, and exchanged smiles with Sim.

He swiftly unwrapped a copy of the *Natchez Democrat*, freeing at least two dozen roses in shades of pink, peach, and vibrant coral, and handed them to his hostess.

"And champagne!" Maddy exclaimed. "He brought two gorgeous bottles."

Sim grinned at Daphne and shrugged. "From the wedding. Mrs. Riches thought you two were the proper recipients of such leftover largesse of Veuve Clicquot."

Daphne put a hand over her heart, and said with mock solemnity, "King and Corlis would definitely want these committed to our care, and I'm sure as shootin' going to drink some before I go back home. But, let's save the other bottle for their first anniversary, shall we, Maddy?"

"How about having a glass, now, with these?" Sim said, revealing a dish of cold, baby artichokes sitting on the kitchen table next to the champagne. "My mother, believe it or not, FedEx-ed them to me at Monmouth, and the chef there was kind enough to steam them." He laughed with an edge of embarrassment. "Apparently, she didn't think a California guy could survive without my monthly bounty from Castroville, the Artichoke Capital of the World."

"That's south of San Francisco, isn't it?" Daphne said, staring at vegetables that looked to be a cross between a thistle and a cactus.

"Way back when, my family grew them as a business. Then, my grandfather used to grow them as a hobby. Now, half the land the family owned is covered with mini-malls and tract housing, but we still have a small interest in a couple of artichoke farms and my mother gets paid in produce from time to time."

"Doesn't your father like artichokes?" Daphne inquired with a smile, "or do you and your mother have some sort of side deal?"

Sim paused, and said lightly, "My father died last year, but, yes... he was crazy about them. It's in the blood, my mother says."

"Oh!" Daphne said, embarrassed. "I'm so sorry—"

"You couldn't have known."

Madeline carefully set the bucket of roses on the kitchen table. "Was it sudden, dear?" she asked sympathetically. "He must have been relatively young—that is, when you look at life from *my* vantage point."

"Sixty-two. From prostate cancer. He'd ignored the symptoms for quite a while, it turned out."

"That's *terribly* young," Maddy said, distressed. She turned to Daphne. "It almost seems as if we're in the middle of an epidemic, doesn't it, dear?" She switched her attention back to her guest. "I lost my husband *and* my twenty-seven-year-old son to cancer several years ago. I know what a blow that must have been to you and your mother, and I'm so sorry you had to go through such an awful thing."

Sim nodded almost imperceptibly. "It was pretty rough, but the one good thing was that my father and I—" He paused, gazed out the kitchen window for a moment, and then started his sentence again. "In the last three months of his life, we really came to know one another... maybe for the first time. If he hadn't gotten sick, I sometimes wonder if that would ever have happened." He picked up a bottle of champagne. "Well, now. Mrs. Whitaker, shall we—"

"*Maddy*, please," Madeline insisted. "Let me just get a clean tea towel from the drawer there so you can work out the cork."

Daphne shot Sim a conspiratorial look and crossed the kitchen to assist her cousin in the search. Maddy had opened a drawer filled to overflowing with piles of wrinkled tea towels, crumpled cloth napkins, and wads of cheesecloth from her previous cooking projects.

"Ah! There it is!" Maddy exclaimed triumphantly, seizing the needed towel and waving it in the air.

The threesome soon moved out onto the veranda and gathered together several serviceable wicker chairs from a variety of furniture in various states of disrepair. By the time they settled down with their artichokes and champagne, the sun was slanting off the bend in the river directly opposite Bluff House and a shimmering twilight silently enfolded the scene.

"What a magnificent view," Sim murmured. "Kinda makes me want to burst out singing 'Old Man River.'" Daphne and Maddy chuckled as Sim pointed straight ahead, adding, "Look at those vast tracts of land across the river on the Louisiana side. In California, it would be so built up, it'd probably look like Silicon Valley by now."

"My husband's family once had big cotton fields over there," Maddy said, "and upriver, they had a magnificent house and a plantation on the Mississippi side called Devon Oaks that first produced tobacco, and later, cotton, when the land played out."

Daphne felt her heart begin to race at the mention of the mansion that had so unexpectedly appeared the previous night in her—what? Vision? Apparition? Full-blown hallucination?

"Does the house still exist?" Sim asked.

"It's a country inn these days," Maddy answered, "A gay couple from Atlanta turned it into a B and B, like so many of the old places. The Tornado of 1840 didn't blow it down, as it did some neighbors' houses up there—or some big ol' developer bulldoze it to the ground to build one of those ugly mini-malls. The new owners did a beautiful job restorin' it and makin' it a mighty pretty place."

Sim raised his glass and tipped it first in Maddy's direction, and then, with a smile, toward Daphne. "Amen to saving pretty places."

Half an hour later, Daphne and Simon stood up, bid Maddy farewell, and walked toward Sim's dusty white Range Rover, a recreational vehicle that easily accommodated a large amount of photographic gear and could transport it to any sort of terrain where rare birds might be found. In less than two minutes, they had driven down the hill to the restaurant. Someone was just pulling out of the parking lot next to the Magnolia Grill on Silver Street, a narrow thoroughfare that wound its way to the mooring where the *Lady Luck* lured gamblers aboard her decks, and where the touring paddle wheel boats tied up when they called at Natchez.

The evening had grown cool, now that darkness had descended. On the Mississippi a hundred yards away, tiny crystal lights outlining the riverboat's pilothouse reflected like dancing gems off the water, and the smell of dogwood floated in the air. Sim locked the car, and he and Daphne headed toward a red brick building nestled into the base of the bluff that towered overhead.

"There used to be a couple more streets down here, once upon a time," Daphne explained, "but the river washed them away over the years. Silver Street is basically all that's left."

Sim pointed at the two-story structures that lined the cliff side of the street. "You know, they *look* as if they were all once boarding houses and dance halls, don't they?"

"Not to mention a bordello or two," she said, pointing to a building with a freshly painted wooden sign reading *Magnolia Grill*. "This place claims to be the oldest, continuously operating eatery in Natchez, but this building was constructed about twenty years ago to look like the falling-down saloon that used to be on this spot." Sim clasped Daphne's arm as they strolled past the restaurant's enclosed porch and made their way to the entrance.

Inside the restaurant, Daphne surveyed the bare, wooden floor and plank tables and wondered if Simon Hopkins might find the spot a little too "down home" for his refined tastes. Meanwhile, he calmly surveyed the wine list and, after consulting with her about her entree, selected a California Pinot Noir that would go nicely with both the duck breast she'd ordered—topped with toasted pecans and a sugar-bourbon demi-glace—and his own fresh Gulf redfish smothered in crabmeat and a Creole meunière sauce.

"As you might have guessed by now, the Magnolia Grill serves a sort of soul food with attitude. Not bad for lil' ol' Natchez, wouldn't you say, though I might like it better if they changed the restaurant's name," Daphne joked, glancing around the packed dining room.

"Thank God I know an almost-native," Sim replied, smiling. "I was afraid that my eating would be confined to the Pig Out Inn."

"I *love* the Pig Out Inn!" she protested, then realized Sim was teasing. "You haven't even been there, have you?" she demanded accusingly.

"No… just noticed it as I drove by. Mostly, I've grabbed a hamburger somewhere on my way out to the wilds."

"The Pig Out has *the* best barbecued pork sandwiches you ever tasted in your life."

"Sounds like you could get us a good table there, too," he replied, poker-faced.

After that, they fell into a comfortable discussion of Sim's pursuit of the yellow-rumped warbler and other elusive photographic prey. When the conversation shifted to the subject of Daphne's life as a classical harpist in New York, Daphne regaled Sim with amusing backstage anecdotes and avoided recounting the unhappy saga of the professional price she'd paid for attending her brother's nuptials. Their easy exchange of banter made it hard to imagine that only yesterday she had been sobbing her heart out over Jack Ebert's treachery in Sim's stunning bedroom on the second floor of Monmouth Plantation. Sim obliquely reminded her of that fact over coffee and their order of caramel bread pudding.

"So…" he said, taking a sip from his demitasse, "any more sightings of your jilted fiancé?"

"No, thank heavens," Daphne replied. "Let's hope he checked out the financials at the Natchez funeral home that his parents bought, and hightailed it back to Texas." She kept her words light. Even so, she suppressed a shudder, wishing Sim hadn't allowed the unpleasant subject to intrude upon their enjoyable evening.

Daphne was suddenly conscious of Sim gazing at her intently above the burning candle in its glass holder that cast a warm glow over their table. Light and shadow played across his striking features, reminding her of Maddy's parlor last night, just before—

"And your mother?" Sim was asking. Daphne returned her full attention to her dinner companion. "Did she get in touch before she left Natchez?"

"No… and I didn't expect her to." Daphne felt her chest tighten as it always did when the subject of mother-daughter relationships was broached. She studied Sim's expression, trying to read the thrust of his rather personal questions.

He arched an eyebrow. "I was hoping maybe that she'd… thought about some of the things she'd said and would—"

"Apologize?" Daphne interjected softly. She pointed to the silhouetted flower etched into the restaurant's wine list resting on a corner of their table and gave a small, defeated shake of her head. "Magnolias never say they're sorry. They just change the subject." She toyed with her coffee cup. Finally, she said, "I was so touched when you mentioned earlier to Maddy that in the last three months of your father's life, you... you were able truly to get to know him... and... to settle any issues that existed between you." She turned to gaze out the window at the lights dancing on the water near the *Lady Luck*. "I envy you that." She turned back and looked directly at Sim. "But, isn't it sad that it took his illness to bring you both to that point?"

"Yes, it is," Sim agreed soberly, "but sometimes, that's what it takes to make people... strip the mask off, you know what I mean?" He reached across the table and gently encased her fingers, curled around the stem of her wineglass. Daphne lowered her eyes to take in the sight of their joined hands. "From what I saw of your mother yesterday, I'm not sure that can happen with certain people. Both sides have to be willing to be honest about the good *and* the bad things they bring to the party, don't you think?"

"Is that what happened with you and your dad?" she asked, fighting back a lump in her throat.

"Oh... yes," Sim said with a pained smile. "We were both definitely ready and willing to clear up a lot of misunderstandings." He withdrew his hand from Daphne's to take another sip of his coffee and she felt bereft at the sudden loss. "I had been on the road so much, I'd used it as an excuse to avoid talking about stuff that had built up. I'd say to myself, 'Gotta catch a plane, so there isn't time.'"

"Did he disapprove of your being a photographer?"

"Not really. Of course, early on, he and my mother assumed I'd be a doctor, like he was—"

"Your father was a *doctor* and ignored cancer symptoms?" she asked, astonished.

"He was a dermatologist," Sim replied, with a sad shrug. "You know the old saying, 'a cobbler's children have no shoes'? He could spot a melanoma on someone's face across the room, but he was frightened of getting sick himself, just like the rest of us. And too busy, like we all are sometimes, to take proper care of himself."

"Had you considered being a doctor?"

"I liked science a lot, and I took all the premed courses at

Stanford. Like most kids, I knew my parents would be pleased if I carried on the family tradition, since my mother's family also had its fair share of medicos—as well as newspaper types. The majority of my dad's family had been farmers down in the valley, with the big shots in the family in the railroad business. But no, when push-came-to-medical-school, I got my advance science degrees in botany and ornithology, and took a fellowship at the Brooks Institute of Photography, in Santa Barbara—and they were okay with that."

"And then Bird Man hit the road," Daphne said, smiling as the waiter poured a second round of espresso.

Sim remained silent for a long moment, and repeated softly, "And then Bird Man hit the road."

Suddenly, Daphne grew wide-eyed. "Oh, m'God," she exclaimed. "Sim, I just got it! Railroads, hotels, newspapers. *San Francisco?*"

"Top of the Mark, and all that?" he admitted with a crooked grin. "We're only distant kin to Mark Hopkins—one of the Big Four who brought the railroad out west and got a hotel named after him on Nob Hill—but my grandfather on my mother's side was a Chandler."

"The *Los Angeles Times* Chandlers, right?" Daphne said, identifying the flagship publication of the Times Mirror Company founded by the Chandler family in the nineteenth century and sold for millions at the beginning of the twenty-first century.

Sim pantomimed taking a picture of her across the table. "I guess it pays to get there early in a gold rush," he said modestly. "As for me, after grad school, I was working steadily in my chosen field. All my parents' friends in San Francisco suitably admired the nature books I wrote and gave my full-color calendars to each other for Christmas. My profession wasn't the problem."

"So, why the estrangement with your family?" Daphne asked, and then added with a pinch of embarrassment, "If you don't mind my asking?"

Sim grew silent once again. Finally he said, "After I got married and started flying all over the place… my parents and I just sort of… drifted in different directions."

"What about sisters and brothers?" she asked sympathetically.

"My sister Brooke and I've done better keeping in touch, especially now."

Daphne fiddled with her napkin in her lap. "And how did your wife deal with your traveling so much of the time?"

An uncomfortable silence grew between them.

"Not well."

He pronounced the words as if they were two distinct sentences and with a finality that indicated, in no uncertain terms, that the subject was one he preferred closed. The growing sense of intimacy that Daphne had felt taking hold had been erased in an instant by her question concerning the breakup with his wife.

Sim glanced at his watch and signaled for the waiter to bring the check.

He's gone absolutely cold, she realized, bewildered. Why would he do such an about-face at the mere mention of a wife from whom he'd been divorced for nearly a decade?

Battle scars still festering, Flash? she asked him silently.

Simon took a final sip of coffee. "Interviewing subjects is supposed to be my line of work, isn't it?" he asked in a tone only slightly warmer. "How about we head a few doors up from here and go dancing?"

Sim's sudden withdrawal left Daphne feeling utterly deflated. Magnolia Mama had nothing on him when it came to changing the subject. Clearly, the evening had taken an unhappy turn into no-man's-land, and all because she'd brought up the subject of Sim's ex-wife.

Obviously, time had not healed all wounds.

CHAPTER 7

SIM SEIZED THE PEN left by the waiter and signed his name with a vengeance, wondering why he'd cut off Daphne so abruptly. Considering all the personal questions he'd asked *her* these last twenty-four hours, she'd inquired in a perfectly reasonable fashion about his relationship with Francesca, and he'd stifled her.

"Back in just a sec," his dinner companion said tersely, rising from the table and effecting a strategic retreat toward the ladies' room. She strode purposefully toward the rear of the restaurant, providing Sim a chance to admire her slim figure and the chic, understated clothes that marked her for the New Yorker she had become. With a defeated sigh, he marveled at how an extremely enjoyable evening had suddenly taken a sharp turn south.

Angry with himself, he added a generous tip, and handed it to the appreciative waiter. Even after all these years, the subject of Francesca Hayes still caused consternation in his solar plexus. As usual, he had simply ended all discussion when it came time to assess blame for the ultimate explosion that ended his marriage. The jury was in... and had been for nearly a decade. He'd gone AWOL when his wife was pregnant, as Francesca had declared to all their friends and family.

Simon Chandler Hopkins: guilty as charged.

His marriage had died the day he'd been photographing ducks in a remote rice paddy outside Sacramento, for God's sake. It was so unbelievably prosaic.

"A flock of fucking mallards is more important to you, you bastard, than your wife at the worst moment of her life!"

And then Francesca had turned her back on him to face the

hospital wall. The irony of it all was perfect. He'd ducked his responsibility, and couldn't be located for three days. At least, those were the scathing words Francesca had used in her last note to him, the one she'd attached to the crib's bare mattress with a diaper pin.

He looked up just as Daphne returned to their table with her generous mouth now set in a tight smile.

"Ready?"

"Ready," he echoed, rising from his chair.

She merely nodded, and marched silently by his side out of the restaurant and up the street toward the Under-the-Hill Saloon. He gently took her arm as they walked, his thoughts a million miles from Natchez, Mississippi.

Give up hoping for a better past, pal You can't rewrite history. Concentrate on the future...

"Daphne?"

When she turned to look at him, the old-fashioned streetlight cast a golden nimbus around her glorious caramel-colored hair as if it were spun sugar, good enough to eat.

"What?" she asked coolly.

He could read the new wariness in her dark eyes. In the distance, the sounds of a Dixieland band playing on board the *Lady Luck* drifted across the water. He gazed beyond the guard railing at the river's edge, wondering if he would ever be free of the ache in his gut whenever he pictured that note pinned to the crib mattress.

"I'm very sorry I was so... curt... when you asked how Francesca—that's my former wife's name—how Francesca felt about my traveling so much."

Daphne affected a shrug. "Maybe I was being nosy."

"No. That wasn't it. I've asked you plenty of personal questions in the last twenty-four hours, so I owed you an answer." She looked surprised by his words, but remained silent. "To tell you the truth, my traveling to here-and-gone became a major bone of contention when my wife became pregnant. It's what ultimately caused our split."

That, and a few other things that are far too complex to sort out, even now...

"So you have a child," she murmured.

"No. The baby died."

Her startled expression was immediately transformed into one of compassion.

"Oh, Sim… I'm so sorry," she said, touching his sleeve. "I can't imagine how hard that must have been. For both of you."

Now this is a kind woman, he thought gratefully. Despite all the knocks she's taken in the romance department, she doesn't automatically assume that only Francesca suffered.

She doesn't know the half of it…

Daphne turned to face the river, a light breeze lifting her hair off the shoulders of her linen jacket. "You know," she mused, "in my world, the principal thing that breaks up couples—even if only one spouse is a professional musician—is just that: the horrendous amount of travel required if you want to be a soloist at the top of your field." She turned and looked him squarely in the eye. "It's pretty hard to maintain any sort of intimacy when only one person is ever around."

"Do you mean physically, or emotionally, or both?"

"Well," Daphne replied slowly, "if one person isn't there phys-ically, it's tough staying emotionally connected, wouldn't you say? Too many distractions."

"That was pretty much Francesca's opinion ten years ago."

"And yet, you remain a travelin' man." She drawled the words, giving them a slight edge that he'd heard from other women of his acquaintance in the years since his divorce. Instead of bristling—as he usually did—he paused a moment, allowing her words to sink in. Here was someone who understood the demands of a profes-sion that required travel in order to succeed at the job. She just didn't like what she'd seen it do to couples. Well, at this stage, neither did he.

Even so, he felt slightly on the defensive, and so he said, "I'm not ready quite yet to trade in my passport for some studio job photographing babies for grandma's wallet."

Daphne laughed. "Wait a minute, Sim. Isn't there a middle ground between living in airports and taking baby portraits all day long?"

"Maybe so," Sim acknowledged. "I just haven't figured out what that is."

"How hard have you tried?" she asked bluntly. "Traveling constantly is a choice, too, it seems to me."

Ouch. This woman was definitely not a ships-that-pass-in-the-night type, he thought regretfully. "You may be right about that," he murmured. Then she surprised him a second time.

"I think I gave you a shot in the chops just now—instead of the guy who deserved it," she said, grimacing faintly. "Sorry."

"Black Jack?"

Daphne flushed. "No, the Travelin' Man Sweepstakes goes to a musical conductor in New York who shall remain nameless, but easily falls into the 'astonishingly unfaithful' category."

"Ah… one of those," he said, nodding. He gazed directly into her brown eyes. "Not that you probably care, but infidelity wasn't my sin. Francesca and I had plenty of *other* sources of strife to derail us."

Her eyes widened in surprise, and then she said, "Well… anyway… thanks for apologizing. I felt sort of blindsided over dessert, you know what I mean?"

"I could see that."

"And by the way," she added, "I want you to know that I *do* realize it's not easy to make your living photographing and writing about wildlife if you stay in one location."

"In a word, no," he replied. "And thanks for that."

"You're welcome. Have you noticed that things seem to get a lot more complicated as we get older?" she declared in a tone of voice that indicated they were becoming friends again.

"Believe me, I've noticed."

They both stared contemplatively across the Mississippi at the bridge spanning its sluggish depths. Then Daphne abruptly placed her back against the guardrail and pointed up the street in the direction of a brick building with the sound of a hard-driving blues band pouring out of the door and windows. "Behold the Under-the-Hill Saloon!"

He took her arm again and they walked another fifty yards,

entering a shadowy room where fewer than a dozen patrons sat at the bar and the few small tables scattered around the club. Daphne nodded in the direction of the band.

"Miss-Lou funky," she pronounced with obvious pleasure. She cocked her head and listened for a few moments to a riveting back-beat. Then she grinned, and her broad smile infused Sim with a sense of impending fun and adventure. "Hey… let's forget the last fifteen minutes—and the last ten years—and just have a good time, okay?" she said. By now, he could swear she was batting her sable eyelashes at him. "Wanna jitterbug, shutterbug?"

"Yeah, baby, yeah," he deadpanned.

"There's no dance floor here, so we'll have to go to Biscuits and Blues for that," she pronounced.

As a matter of fact, he couldn't wait to get his arms around this woman, but first he wanted to talk to her about another thorny subject.

"Great, but how about we have a drink here," he suggested over the din of the three-piece band, "and then head on up the hill?" He guided her to a table that another couple had just vacated and placed an order for two stingers. "Maybe this is my chance to ask you about harps that… uh… how shall I put it?"

"Why don't you just tell me what happened at Monmouth the other night?" she asked, her eyes suddenly wary once more.

Just then, the music ended and the band took a break. Now that the joint had grown considerably quieter, Sim felt self-conscious and more than a little foolish. Despite this, he plunged ahead, relating the sequence of events that had brought him to the entrance of the ornate Victorian parlor at his hotel at three o'clock in the morning.

"The room was full of moonlight, but even so, the harp was sitting in the corner where there were mostly shadows. No one was in the room," he said, shaking his head, "but I swear to God I heard harp music!"

"Do you remember what it sounded like? Classical?" She bit her lip. "Maybe you were just dreaming 'cause you'd heard me playing earlier that day?" she suggested.

But Sim was trying to recall exactly what he'd heard that night. "No… it wasn't classical music I heard, and… it wasn't blues, or anything." He snapped his fingers excitedly. "It was a nursery tune… a lullaby, or something. French! You know…" He began to hum softly and then stopped. "I can't remember the words that go with it, but—*you* know!" And he resumed humming the familiar tune.

"'Frère Jacques.'"

She pronounced the name with no excitement whatsoever, but rather with an odd air of resignation.

"'Frère Jacques'! That's *it*!" He congratulated her. "I can't sing worth a damn, but you figured it out. But, then, you're a musician, aren't you?" he said, laughing.

But Daphne wasn't even smiling. She looked disconcerted, in fact. Just then, a waitress appeared with their drinks, and she took a long draft of her stinger.

"I think you've seen the town ghost."

"The what?"

"You *really* are going to be a welcome addition as far as the Natchez Chamber of Commerce is concerned," she teased, but her smile stopped short of her eyes. And then she proceeded to tell him about a forsaken young woman two centuries earlier who'd played the harp and had fallen in love with a French cavalier passing through Natchez. "Apparently, the poor girl has spent her afterlife waiting for the cad's return and has been seen or heard playing harps in parlors all over town by everyone from a Grand Dame of the Daughters of the American Revolution to a local gardener. So, congratulations for having made a sighting!" she finished, her demeanor now thoroughly tongue-in-cheek.

Sim raised an eyebrow and shrugged at Daphne's fanciful tale, sensing she wasn't telling him what she truly thought about the bizarre incident. Well, he didn't know what to make of it himself. He finished his drink, thinking that the entire evening had been a bit bizarre. He'd enjoyed Daphne Duvallon's company. In fact, he'd enjoyed it very much, but he also felt as if he'd been navigating minefields—both his and hers. He glanced around the barroom. The band seemed on a permanent break.

Daphne stole a peek at her watch, and said, "It's Sunday night. Maybe they just play one set." It appeared she was about to call a halt to the evening—and that felt disappointing, somehow.

Hurriedly he asked, "Well… are you still up to seeing what's going on at Biscuits and Blues on *top* of the bluff?" He signaled the waitress to bring their check.

She gave him a curious look, and then replied, "I can take it, if you can." She almost seemed relieved to change not only the subject, but the scene as well.

∼≈∽

The minute Daphne and Sim walked into the blues club, Daphne recognized the bandleader, Willis McGee, who'd played at her brother's wedding. The bar was half full, and Willis and his group were doing their utmost to liven up the place with an up-tempo rendition of "Summertime." He'd added a new member to his group, a young black woman who played bass guitar, freeing up Willis to wail on a tenor saxophone. Sim and Daphne sat down at a small table near the front, and as soon as the tune ended, she waved to the musicians.

"Hey, Willis! Y'all sound great!" she called.

Willis peered through the thick lenses of his black-rimmed spectacles and did a double take.

"Well, hey there yourself, Miz Daphne!" He turned to the members of his group. "Hey, guys… remember her? Did that down-home version of 'Georgia On My Mind' at the weddin' over at Monmouth yesterday." His fellow musicians nodded and smiled in greeting. He introduced the woman bass guitarist. "This here's m' daughter, Kendra. Kendra, meet Daphne Duvallon, and—" The gray-haired bandleader looked apologetically at Sim.

"Hi, Kendra… Willis. I'm Sim Hopkins. Please. Play some more."

Willis and his daughter nodded amicably. "Anything you folks wanna hear tonight?" Willis asked, looking at Sim and Daphne expectantly.

Daphne, who couldn't take her eyes off Kendra McGee, was virtually struck dumb and deferred to Sim, who swiftly suggested "'I'll Be Seeing You'?"

Kendra? Kendra McGee?

"The old Billie Holiday tune? Cool, man," Willis was saying. "You got it!" He turned to the band, and called, "And a one… and two…" and the musicians swung into the familiar standard.

As for Daphne, she could only force a smile and nod. This Kendra looked nothing like the young house servant who had kindly told another Daphne in another life that she was welcome to spend the night in the safety of her family's slave cabin behind the Devon Oaks Plantation house.

This is just too damn weird!

Daphne stilled her pounding pulse with the thought that local families in a small town like Natchez—population eighteen thousand—went back for generations. Names, such as hers, and perhaps Willis and Kendra McGee's, were handed down for so long, no one even remembered who the original ancestor might be. Meanwhile, she attempted to shake off her bewilderment that both a Willis *and* a Kendra were playing at Biscuit and Blues the night after she encountered their namesakes in some inexplicable "flashback." Instead, she focused her attention on Sim.

"Have you heard Etta James do 'I'll Be Seeing You' on her *Mystery Lady* CD?" she asked.

"Yeah, but I'm a loyalist," Sim replied emphatically. "I think I own every Billie Holiday tune ever recorded. If I have a song by Miss Billie, I don't buy it by anybody else."

"Wow… you're tough!" she teased. "I can't remember if Billie Holiday ever recorded 'Georgia on My Mind'—but I *hope* not!"

He reached across their table and tapped his forefinger on the end of her nose. "For *you*, I'd make an exception."

It was a simple, playful gesture, but Daphne felt as if it were as intimate as a kiss. The Willis McGee quartet languidly swung into the second chorus of the old World War II tune, galvanizing Sim to rise from his chair and ask Daphne to dance. The rest of the bar's patrons, it seemed, were bent on consuming more alcohol, and except for Daphne and Sim, the dance floor was deserted.

"Just us?" Daphne asked, suddenly feeling self-conscious. She was accustomed to playing music, not dancing to it.

"Just us," Sim confirmed, and drew her into the circle of his arms.

He was the perfect height for her, and Daphne felt as if a key had fit effortlessly into a lock somewhere in the cosmos. The few moments that she'd slow danced with Simon Hopkins at her brother's wedding had been an altogether different experience. After her mother's flame-throwing episode, when she called her daughter a "dance hall floozy" in front of fifty guests, Daphne had simply gone numb, remembering the subsequent fox-trot only as a near out-of-body experience.

Now they were standing shoulder to waist to thigh, and Daphne wondered how a perfect stranger's body could feel so right, his six-feet-two so exquisitely proportioned to her five-feet-four. The room's walls and the bar's patrons seemed to recede, and Daphne's entire world became the curve of Sim's navy-clad shoulder and the warmth of his left hand holding her right.

The words of the song drifted through her head.

I'll be seeing you... in all the old, familiar places...

It *felt* so familiar, one part of her brain insisted, but a warning voice rang a clarion call: Sim Hopkins was a travelin' man who was still deeply troubled by the end of a marriage that had been officially DOA for a decade.

Sim's arm tightened around her waist, and she fought a desire to fit the top of her head under his chin. It felt wonderful. It felt dangerous. It felt—

Oh, shut up, and just dance!

And dance they did. To a moody rendition of "Skylark," and then to a sultry, down-to-the-bone version of "Embraceable You," another Billie Holiday tune that Willis called for with a mischievous wink in Sim's direction.

Daphne gazed briefly at Sim from beneath her eyelashes and felt a bolt of electricity when their glances met. They moved across the dance floor as one, or as if they were Ginger and Fred, or Gene and Cyd, two dancing fools who magically knew *exactly* where to put a foot, make a turn, or change directions.

"Hey..." Sim whispered against her ear. "You're some dancer, you know that? When do you practice? Three a.m.?"

"I hardly ever dance," she said in a small voice. "I—"

Sim pulled her closer and exhaled softly against her ear. He appeared unabashed by his state of arousal that bloomed against her thigh. It was as if she'd been dancing with him her entire life. In *another* life.

Now, stop that! Thank your lucky stars no Sim Hopkins has appeared in any of these wacky visitations…

She ceased thinking then, and allowed herself to be swept up in the rhythm and the melody.

When the quartet swung into "I Don't Stand a Ghost of a Chance with You," Daphne stiffened within the circle of Sim's arms. Sim held her even closer and amazingly, she felt her entire body relax.

Somebody, somewhere has a wicked sense of humor, she thought dreamily, the crown of her head now firmly tucked under Sim's chin.

By the time the music concluded, Daphne had fallen into a kind of a contented daze and wished they could dance like this all night. Long after the last note faded and polite applause rippled around the room, she and Sim remained motionless in the center of the parquet floor.

"Thank you," he said quietly, touching his forefinger to the tip of her nose for the second time that evening. "I loved every step."

"Me too," she said, making no attempt to disguise the closeness she felt. She found that she was unable to pull her gaze from his, so she grinned crookedly, and added, "The band quit on us, so I guess we have to go home." She forced herself to turn away and walked over to Willis McGee. "You guys were just wonderful. Thanks for such great tunes."

"You two looked mighty pretty out there," Willis said genially when Sim appeared by Daphne's side. The bandleader officially introduced them by name to the male members of his band. "And you met Kendra earlier—my eldest girl." Willis addressed his daughter. "Kendra? Daphne, here, has played jazz harp with Althea LaCroix in New Orleans."

"Only backup a time or two," Daphne hastened to add, enjoying the feel of Sim's hand resting lightly on her shoulder.

"And she sings like somethin' else, don't she?" Willis said admiringly.

"Why doesn't she sing with us sometime, Daddy?" Kendra asked. She glanced around the deserted club. "Natchez nightlife sure could use a goose."

Willis gazed inquiringly at Daphne, who shook her head. "I'm only in Natchez for another week or so," she explained regretfully.

"Well... you could do a few oldies with us next Saturday... couldn't you? We'll be at the Under-the-Hill Saloon."

"We just came from there," Daphne exclaimed.

"So you know the place. Great. Be easy on yourself and just do a couple of numbers like 'Georgia,' that you know real well."

"Daphne, what a great idea!" Sim grinned broadly and said to the group, "I'll be front row, center, and bring some other people I've met." He squeezed Daphne's shoulders encouragingly. "What about it, Ms. Harpist? Have a little fun before you get swallowed up forever by the likes of *Swan Lake!*"

Daphne turned to stare at Sim. How could he know that was exactly what she'd been thinking—and dreading? The mere thought of those intimidating auditions played behind a screen so the judges wouldn't be swayed by anything but the music they heard made her stomach churn like a Waring blender. She wanted to have some *fun* before she plunged back into a world where ambitious classical musicians would eat their own young if it meant they'd succeed in their demanding art.

"I'll do it," she announced, and the small group gave a spontaneous cheer. "Do you want the harp, too?"

"Yeah!" Willis said enthusiastically. "It'll make people in the audience sit up and take notice. We'll bring you on 'round ten o'clock... and I'll put a notice in the *Natchez Democrat*," the bandleader promised. He glanced around the bar, whose last patrons were making their way out the door. "Here," he directed, "write down your number on this piece of sheet music—and can you email me a picture of yourself we can use in the newspaper? I'll call you 'bout a rehearsal 'fore next weekend." He turned to his daughter, and said, "Kendra... you're right, girl. We definitely need to jazz up our act."

They said their good nights and returned to the Range Rover parked a block away. Sim drove toward Bluff House down deserted streets with pillared houses shuttered for the night. Daphne couldn't believe that she had agreed to play jazz harp and *sing* in a real club!

Absorbed in these thoughts, she was suddenly aware that Sim was gazing at her across the car. Then he said, "Would you like to drive out to the Natchez Trace with me tomorrow?" referring to a four-hundred-fifty-mile stretch of woods that ran northeast from Natchez to Nashville, Tennessee.

"Oh, Sim… I don't know…"

But he continued without pause. "Everyone tells me it's the area where I'll have the best chance of finding surviving species of the birds Audubon painted."

"You'll be working," Daphne protested mildly. "Wouldn't I slow you down or get in the way?"

"I'm not shooting tomorrow," he replied. "I'm just going out to meet an elderly doctor who's established a private bird sanctuary on his property that borders the Natchez Trace Parkway. Hopefully, he'll let me photograph on his forty acres, but he wants to meet me first. My friends Liz and Otis Keating have set up the introduction, but Dr. Gibbs has to give it his official okay." He addressed her in a tone of mock supplication. "And besides, I might get lost. I need a local guide to get me out there, plus all the personal references I can get."

"A man who's traveled up the Amazon?" she queried, skeptically. "I'm sure you can find your way up the lil' ol' Mississippi River Valley."

"Oh, I've come to the conclusion recently that the Mississippi region could be much more dangerous than I thought," he replied with a wry smile. He was gazing at her steadily when he asked "Please spend the day with me."

One more slow dance with a man of Sim Hopkins's charm and good looks and she knew she'd be in big trouble. However, a mere hike in the woods…

"If my cousin Maddy doesn't have anything planned," she said after a long pause, "I'd love to."

Now, why did she say yes? The electricity between them on the dance floor had been the product of the sexy music—hadn't it? Or perhaps mere lust on her part, she thought with some chagrin. After all, how long had she been celibate since bolting from Saint Louis Cathedral? Two years, plus?

"I'll call you—what? About nine tomorrow morning?" he proposed. "I'd like to get started by nine thirty, if that works for you."

The truth was, she'd love to see some backwoods country after all this time living among the concrete monoliths of Manhattan. She reached back with both hands and lifted her hair off the nape of her neck, allowing the soft, fragrant night air to cool her skin. She'd be returning to New York in a little more than a week. She was on *vacation*, after all… her only respite before the grim task of finding a steady job with another orchestra. Surely she was entitled to enjoy the company of an attractive man without making a fool of herself, wasn't she? It would be a good exercise in self-restraint.

At least, she hoped so.

❧

The drive out to the Natchez Trace past the historic red brick Jefferson Military College, founded in 1802 when Mississippi was still a territory, took less than twenty minutes. The Monday traffic on the divided parkway was light, and Daphne settled back in the leather seats of Sim's car, sighing contentedly as emerald woods of oaks, dogwood, and sweet gum trees streamed by on both sides of the vehicle.

"Not a billboard in sight! I'd forgotten how absolutely gorgeous Mississippi can be," she murmured.

"It's bucolic, all right," Sim agreed. "Hard to believe that in the last century or so, a lot of folks were robbed and killed among the wild orchids along the trail."

"That's probably why the survivors coming down from Nashville called the Trace 'The Devil's Backbone.' Did anybody tell you you'll need leather boots and snake leggings if you go very far off the trail?"

Sim nodded and gestured over his shoulder in the direction of a pile of gear in the rear. "Left over from the Amazon," he said with a laugh. "If it worked with the exotica there, it should protect me against copperheads and water moccasins on the Trace."

"Let us pray…" Daphne said, shuddering.

Sim took a left-hand turn down a dirt road. "First stop is Liz and Otis Keating's," he announced. "Liz is the floral designer at Monmouth. She offered to show me her new house and point out where the old Trace parallels the roadway. She's also going to give us directions to Dr. Gibbs's place because it turns out she can't join us. A landscaping client called this morning and wants to talk to her about a job and her husband Otis will still be at church this morning."

The Range Rover bumped along a gravel driveway up a small rise where, through the thick foliage, Daphne caught sight of a low-lying, broad-roofed house flanked on all sides by a veranda that was supported by widely spaced pillars.

"It looks straight out of the West Indies, doesn't it?" Sim remarked.

"That's because it is," Daphne replied, surveying the newly built structure whose freshly stuccoed walls were not yet white-washed. "The style, at least. A lot of colonists from the Caribbean came to Louisiana and Mississippi, during the slave revolts in the seventeen hundreds, and brought their architecture with them."

Sim's car rolled to a stop, and he put on the emergency brake. "Well, it's a perfect design for the climate, I'd say."

Inside the Keating house, the ceiling fans and tall windows opening onto the veranda also reflected the West Indian flavor of the place.

"Oh… isn't it lovely and cool," Daphne remarked approvingly.

Liz Keating, a pleasant, round-faced woman in her late thirties, held out her hand in welcome. "I think I'm related by marriage to that wonderful cousin of yours, Madeline Whitaker. At least, that's what Otis tells me. She taught me the harp when I was a little girl."

Daphne looked around the living room. "No sign of a harp," she said, laughing. "You were one of the lucky ones. I see you avoided the dreaded disease."

Liz smiled, pointing to an easel in the corner. "I liked art classes better, and gardening even better than that. Didn't Maddy ever twist your arm about becoming a member of one of the rival gardening clubs?"

"I only spent vacations in Natchez." Daphne turned to Sim, explaining, "The town is famous for its two competing garden organizations—the Natchez Garden Club and the Pilgrimage Garden Club. For a time, there were what's fondly referred to as the Petticoat Wars when the leaders weren't speaking to one another."

"Now the Petticoat Mafia cooperates beautifully," Liz said dryly. "Tourism is Natchez's main product, so everybody finally buried the hatchet in an effort to make a success of the twice-a-year home tours."

Daphne liked the woman's sense of humor and no-nonsense approach. Liz poured them each a glass of lemonade and, following a brief interval on the veranda, led the way down a grassy path that veered away from the house.

"Any snakes 'round here shouldn't be out and about much this time of year, but just keep an eye out," Liz warned. She halted on the path and pointed to a narrow lane branching out from the one on which they were standing. "We're nearly at a linkup with the trail."

Sunlight filtered through a thick stand of black willows, casting dark shadows and creating a cocoon of cool air as they trod down a steep, four-foot rise into a peaceful forest track.

"Down the rabbit hole," Sim murmured as they found themselves in a green tunnel of trees. The vaulted, verdant ceiling sprouted bright, new spring leaves.

"Isn't it just?" Liz said proudly. Braids of dangling vines added to their sense of being inside a leafy cathedral. An eerie hush descended, and their guide spoke in a low, reverential voice. "Thousands of travelers risked their lives over hundreds of years tramping this old Indian trail into a sylvan burrow that runs on for miles like this."

"*Sh*, listen," Sim said urgently. The women halted in their tracks and concentrated on faint, rustling sounds on either side of the lane. Occasionally a solitary birdcall was answered in the distance. "How far are we from the Mississippi River?"

"Oh, 'bout twenty miles, as the crow flies, I 'spect," Liz replied.

"That's why we can hear more bird sounds," Sim declared. "There are fewer pollutants in a national parkland, so their eggshells aren't thin and the young survive at a higher rate."

Liz nodded grimly. "You'll hear all about that from Dr. Gibbs." She glanced at her watch. "Speaking of which, we'd better get you on the road. I've written down the directions for you back at the house. He's expectin' you at ten thirty, sharp. And as you'll discover, he's a very punctual man."

CHAPTER 8

S IM AND DAPHNE LEFT Liz Keating's place and returned briefly to the parkway, heading back in the direction of Natchez. Less than two miles down the road, they made a sharp turn left and bumped along a dirt driveway reminiscent of the tunnel-like Trace itself. Dappled sunlight streamed in silver shafts through thick stands of oaks and flowering dogwoods that arched overhead. Myriad shades of budding green foliage lined the lane leading to a tall, wrought iron gate hung between thick brick posts painted white and topped by cast concrete finials shaped like pineapples. A sign on the left declared "Gibbs Hall—Private Drive."

"The gates are open," Daphne said. "That's a good sign."

Nodding agreement, Sim sped forward past a large pond with graceful willows ringing its shore and trailing apple-green tendrils into the pellucid water.

A rolling lawn dotted with tall pecan trees surrounded a pristine white, two-story antebellum mansion. Doric columns graced a veranda on the first floor and supported a wraparound gallery on the second. A pair of massive oaks, perhaps one hundred feet tall, stood sentinel beside steps leading to the front door where a pair of smaller fluted columns framed the entrance.

Sim and Daphne gazed admiringly at the row of paned glass windows that stretched along the veranda—each window taller than a man and set off by shutters painted high gloss black.

"Isn't it just about the loveliest thing you've ever seen in your life?" Daphne breathed.

"This place definitely gets the Gorgeous Award," he agreed softly.

Sim parked his car toward the rear of the house near several outbuildings that appeared to serve as garage and wood shop. Daphne stood and stretched, absorbed in the rustle of new leaves as a soft, fragrant breeze blew across the open lawn.

"I looked up the house in my Natchez guidebook," Sim said. "The core of Gibbs Hall existed as far back as seventeen eighty-one."

Daphne shaded her eyes with her hand. "Really? Well, I'd say that the current structure looks to have been built in the early to mid-nineteenth century. It's classic antebellum, isn't it, with those columns and the double gallery."

They walked across the lawn and followed a slate path to the front door. They hadn't reached the welcome mat when the door was slowly opened by an elderly, rotund gentleman wearing khaki pants, khaki vest, and knee-high leather boots. Daphne gave a side-long glance at Sim's identical attire and nearly burst out laughing.

They look like an L.L. Bean father and son ad!

On the short drive to Gibbs Hall, Sim had given Daphne a thumbnail biography of Bailey Gibbs, a retired general practitioner and former president of the local Audubon Society. He had long been a passionate bird watcher and founded one of the finest private bird sanctuaries in the country on the remaining forty acres of his family's former plantation.

"Ah… Doctor Hopkins. Right on the dot," their host said, holding out his hand. Then the plumpish gentleman, who looked to be in his seventies, removed a pocket watch from one of the many pouches sewn into his khaki vest. "I may be Southern, but I'm mighty pleased when guests show up when they say they will. We've about fifteen minutes for a glass of iced tea, and then it's bird feeding time."

"Doctor Gibbs," Sim replied, beaming, "it is a pleasure and an honor to meet you at last."

"Likewise." He shifted his gaze to Daphne. "And Miz Duvallon! Liz told me to expect you, too. Glad your pretty face didn't slow him down this mornin'—not that I would have been surprised if it had! You're as lovely as your Cousin Madeline Whitaker was when she was a girl," he said, winking slyly. "I was a second-tier contender for her hand, until I met my Caroline, but Maddy and I have remained friends ever since. Come in, come in!"

Daphne was ushered in ahead of the men. "Thank you so much, Doctor Gibbs, for letting me tag along today," she said over her shoulder. "The grounds and your home are magnificent."

"I'm sure, by now, you've seen scores of old places like this," he declared modestly, as he led the way directly to the back veranda. Daphne barely had time to take note of the elegant foyer blanketed in handsome Persian carpets and distinguished by a mahogany grandfather's clock and a carved sideboard with graceful curved legs that ended in fanciful ball-and-claw feet.

An elderly black woman, introduced as Leila Washington, awaited them with a pitcher of iced tea. She greeted the visitors with a friendly smile and then returned to the kitchen while Dr. Gibbs indicated that they should take seats on the white, bent willow chairs lined up on the wooden veranda. Handing out the tall, frosted glasses, he gazed at Daphne intently, and said, "You're a Whitaker, aren't you? On Marcus Whitaker's side?"

Startled by his direct question, she nodded. "He was my great-uncle. Marcus and my Grandmother Amelia were brother and sister, so that when Marcus married Maddy, she and my grandmother became sisters-in-law."

"Then Maddy is really your great-aunt," Dr. Gibbs interjected.

"Correct," Daphne said, "but since she's a generation younger than my grandmother, we always called her Cousin Maddy."

Dr. Gibbs nodded sagely, while Sim looked faintly confused.

"Grandmother Amelia married George Kingsbury and had two daughters: my mother, Antoinette Kingsbury Duvallon, and my aunt, Bethany. Maddy descended from *another* Whitaker on her father's side—my namesake, Daphne Whitaker Clayton." Daphne cast a sympathetic glance in Sim's direction. "I don't know how much sense any of that makes to an outsider—or even to me, sometimes," Daphne concluded with a laugh.

Dr. Gibbs chuckled. "Around these parts, those danged Whitakers are allied through a confounded web of family affiliations to the Claytons, the Drakes, and even the Gibbses, but nobody remembers exactly who's kin to whom anymore. Most of 'em can be found in the Natchez Cemetery in little vainglorious, fenced-off sections loaded with marble angels and headstones with fancy carvings telling the world how great they are. Me?" he said with a pixieish grin, patting his generous midsection. "Just plant this Gibbs in the ground under a bird feeder on the rise this side of Whitaker Creek." He pointed vaguely toward a stand of trees at the far end of the lawn. "You know, don't you, Daphne, that Devon Oaks, a mile or so from here, once belonged to Marcus Whitaker's family? That graceful old relic suffered mighty heavy damage in the terrible Tornado of 1840, but like we did here at Gibbs Hall, thank God, the old place survived. Some others in these parts weren't so lucky."

Daphne took in her host's recitation of family lore in shocked silence. The old photograph Marcus had pointed out to her once, so long ago, showed cotton fields stretching practically to the front door. Until Maddy had told Sim where it was, Daphne had assumed the place was across the river in Louisiana, like so many other plantations in the area. Instead, Devon Oaks was practically next door to Gibbs Hall.

She smiled weakly and allowed her eager companion to quiz his fellow ornithologist about which surviving species of birds, painted by Audubon nearly two centuries ago, he was likely to encounter in the region. Meanwhile, Daphne couldn't help but recall her distraught thirteen-year-old namesake ferociously playing her harp to drown the sounds of a terrible family trauma taking place under the Whitaker roof, apparently not far from the very spot where she was calmly sipping iced tea.

"Well," Dr. Gibbs said decisively, setting down his glass with a thump on a whitewashed willow-reed table beside his chair. He pulled out his pocket watch once more, and proposed, "What do you say I show you my back forty, m'boy? You too, Daphne, if you're game."

"I'm longing to see it, Doctor Gibbs."

They rose from their chairs and followed their host down a few stairs to the lawn. "I admit it," he said, walking gingerly toward a dirt path marked by two miniature versions of the gateposts that had greeted them on their way in. "What I'm about to show you is my pride and joy. It's been mighty hard, at times, to keep the bird sanctuary going, now that my Caroline is gone, but whenever I get lazy, or feel like chucking the whole thing, I hear her voice saying 'Now, Bailey Gibbs, don't you dare! Get out there with your birdseed. We don't want our friends to eat poison!'"

With Dr. Gibbs as Pied Piper, Sim and Daphne wound through a dense wood not unlike the Natchez Trace itself. A hundred yards along the footpath a large clearing suddenly materialized. In its center stood a charming, hexagonal white cottage surrounded by bird feeders of all descriptions dotting the nearby landscape. The enclosed, gazebo-like structure looked a bit larger than a child's playhouse. It was encircled by a small porch, and fresh white curtains hung in each window.

Their guide pointed overhead to a miniature version of Gibbs Hall itself, secured to a pole at least ten feet tall. Five or six birds fluttered in and out of the small-scale windows to feed on birdseed that Dr. Gibbs and his helpers restocked every few days from atop ladders specially designed for that purpose, he explained proudly.

"Those are just chickadees," he noted for Daphne's benefit, "but we love all birds the same 'round here… scarce and common alike."

A few minutes into the tour, the old man halted and peered at Sim to assess his reaction to the unique collection of bird houses.

"I know, I know, Doctor Hopkins. It's not your classic bird sanctuary where our feathered friends are safe on the land and living off local flora, but Caroline and I began as your average bird lovers who simply fed birds outside our windows for our own enjoyment."

"The urban environment encroaches everywhere, these days," Sim said diplomatically. "I'm sure the feeders attract and sustain the local birds, but the rest of your land probably does an important job of supporting migratory types as well."

"Oh, Sim." Daphne interrupted excitedly, pointing to a bird feeder that could only be a replica of Cousin Maddy's house. "Look! How wonderful!" She turned to Dr. Gibbs and smiled wistfully. "I hate to say it, but *your* Bluff House looks in far better condition than the genuine article on Cliff Avenue."

"Your poor, dear cousin has had her share of troubles these last years, that's for danged sure," Dr. Gibbs said softly. "These old places cost a fortune to keep up."

Daphne turned in place, and as she gazed around the wooded glade, it became obvious that over the years, Dr. Gibbs and his wife had built models of all the well-known houses in and around Natchez.

"We've created our very own Pilgrimage Tour here, you see?" Gibbs said with a pleased smile. "Here's Linden…" he said, pointing. "And over there is Rosalie. And that's The Elms."

"And isn't that Monmouth Plantation?" Daphne asked, gesturing toward a minuscule white mansion with square pillars. "That's where Sim is staying."

"You must be enjoying a royal visit here in Natchez, m'boy." Gibbs chuckled and gestured expansively. "You see, as we educated ourselves over the years about the plight of the birds, it became Caroline's fondest dream to turn what was left of our land into a bird sanctuary and to build these reproductions to guarantee we'd always have these creatures to delight us."

"The scale and design…" Daphne murmured. "They're *perfect*!"

"Caroline's family is related to practically everybody 'round here, and she loved all the houses in these parts," Gibbs confided, "so, once I retired, we started buildin' 'em in our wood shop, house by house." He pointed to the cottage. "Just after the birdhouses were built, she got sick. So, I built her her own little gazebo to watch the birds from."

The elderly doctor's expression grew solemn as he invited them to have a seat on a pair of rocking chairs on the diminutive porch with its panoramic view of the clearing in the woods.

"Last year, she begged me to enclose the gazebo and turn it into a cottage so she could stay inside, rain or shine, and watch through those big windows, there," he explained, gesturing in the direction of the squares of plate glass fitted into each of the house's six sides. "Just before she died, I installed a shower and a toilet, and we both camped here for several weeks, with just Leila kindly bringing us our meals on a tray."

He paused, and when he spoke again, his voice was husky with emotion.

"My Caroline looked like a little bird herself, at the end. One sunny afternoon, she passed away in my arms right here, while we sat in this very rockin' chair, her on my lap, light as a feather... peacefully, to the sound of birdsong."

Daphne felt her eyes grow moist.

"You and your wife created a magical place, Doctor Gibbs," Sim said quietly. He reached for one of a matching pair of binoculars resting on the nearby railing and lifted them to his eyes. "A sanctuary, indeed..." he murmured.

"M'boy, all you have to do is just sit in that chair, and Audubon's birds will come to *you*," he said with obvious pride. Then he added, "That is, what's left of 'em. Between the drilling for oil up and down the Mississippi Valley and the pesticides and the defoliants used on the cotton 'round here, we'll be lucky if the birds in these parts will last another fifty years."

"No," Daphne protested, awestruck by the chattering sounds of birds everywhere.

"It's true," Simon confirmed, nodding. "That's one of the reasons I came to Natchez on this photography project. The Mississippi Flyway from Canada to South America is in real trouble, thanks to us humans."

"And as the birds go... so go the humans," Dr. Gibbs predicted fiercely. "Ask Maddy," he said, addressing Daphne. "Ask half the folks in Natchez who've had relatives die of cancer." He made a helpless gesture toward the cottage. "Ask me."

"I take it, then, that your wife died of cancer, too?" Daphne inquired softly.

"A different kind from Marcus and Clay—who were both my patients, by the way. Caroline's was strange, too, in its own fashion. She had a relatively rare brain tumor. Deadly. Untreatable. It's called GBM, for glioblastoma multiforme. Never saw one in thirty years of my practice, and then saw a swarm of 'em in the last ten years. The medical literature has finally confirmed that a swath of it, these days, runs from Houston to New Orleans and points north." He laughed harshly. "I guess Natchez is 'points north.'"

"Well, I'm sure you also know, Doctor Gibbs—"

"Call me Bailey," Gibbs interrupted. "I'll call you Sim so's I can call this pretty lady here Daphne, which is *such* a lovely name," he added with a generous dash of courtliness that made Daphne smile. "But, you were sayin', Sim?"

"I was about to say that you've probably seen the growing body of evidence that air borne pesticides and defoliants can also work their way into the water table, and have been linked to all sorts of human cancers. The good news, though," he continued, "is that the deadliest ones used in modern agriculture have finally been banned or severely curtailed."

"Well, those recent bans didn't come soon enough to save entire species of birds that are now close to extinction," Gibbs retorted. "And they weren't put in soon enough to save Caroline—or Madeline Whitaker's husband and son, or the scores of people I've treated in this town." Dr. Gibbs banged his palm on the nearby railing. "And guess what *else* those jackasses want to do now? There's some danged fool legislative plan brewing up in Jackson and Washington, D.C., to put a bunch of toxic dump sites 'round poor states like Mississippi and Louisiana and New Mexico in order to dispose of the chemicals that those yahoos finally were forced to get rid of by rabble-rousers like Caroline and me. And you know what?"

Sim and Daphne merely shook their heads questioningly.

"One of those dumps is slated to be put right here in Adams County—*next door* to my bird sanctuary on land owned by that pirate neighbor of mine," he declared, pointing through the woods.

"You're kidding," Sim said, incredulous. "Do the politicos realize the sanctuary is located right here?"

"Sure they know!" The old doctor's face had grown flushed, and Daphne estimated his blood pressure had risen twenty points by now. He rubbed the tips of his fingers together as if he were a bank teller. "I think it's payback time for all the trouble Caroline and I caused agitating against chemical and oil companies all these years."

"So, you think people are getting paid off?" Daphne asked, dismayed.

Dr. Gibbs gave a shrug. "Cyrus, my greedy neighbor up the Trace, was once a big wheel in politics around here. Believe me, he has nothing good to say 'bout *me* since I stole my sweet Caroline right out from under his thumb a million years ago. I 'spect he still can play a few of his ol' chips up in the capital. These days, though, he's pretty broke." Then he narrowed his eyes. "Maybe he'd like to unload that derelict old place next door and go into a nursing home. I bet he hasn't got any relatives that'll speak to him anymore, he's so cantankerous."

"Have you stated your case yet to the state officials?" Sim asked, his concern evident.

"No legislative hearings have started yet. Just backroom stuff and rumors, you know. That's what's got me worried." He banged his fist again. "Those policy wonks'll probably just say this is another case of not-in-my-neighborhood-you-don't! Well, maybe it is, but we've got a precious sanctuary here, and besides, I'm willin' to fight *any* dump site anywhere near folks that might get sick because of it."

"We're poisoning the planet," Daphne said softly.

Bailey nodded emphatically. "That's right, little lady. Who knows if those toxic dumps don't leech into the groundwater, endangering people and animals alike—just as if those rotten so-and-so's were still spraying that poison on everything in sight."

"No wonder all these cancer spikes are starting to show up everywhere," Daphne declared.

"That's just what Caroline kept sayin' till the day she died."

"I'm so sorry, Bailey," Sim said soberly. "This must make the loss of your wife that much harder." He looked into the distance, as if his thoughts were far afield. "My father died of cancer last year, and every time I fly into San Francisco or L.A. and see that crud in the air, I want to commit a felony."

"What'd your daddy die of, son?" Dr. Gibbs asked quickly.

"Prostate."

"That's what I've got."

"Oh, no," Daphne cried before she could help herself. She glanced at Sim sitting in the chair beside her. He wore a stricken expression that he didn't attempt to hide.

However, Dr. Gibbs merely shrugged. "I've lived with it for eight years, now. Run-of-the-mill deal. Probably fifty percent or more of men my age have it. Mine's pretty slow growing. Old coots like me usually die of somethin' else before this kind of cancer gets to 'em. I caught it early, and got the best treatment money can buy—and now, I eat organic," he added proudly. His expression grew grave once more. "With Caroline there wasn't a thing we could do. She started having headaches, and speech loss, and died within months."

"But what a wonderful tribute this place is to her," Sim said quietly.

Bailey Gibbs put a hand on his visitor's shoulder. "I feel that way too, son, and I'm sorry 'bout your daddy. I know how much it hurts when it's one of your own."

Daphne watched a series of emotions play across Sim's sober features. He'd lost a baby, too, she reminded herself. And a wife through divorce. She'd read somewhere that marriages often didn't survive the death of a child. Suddenly, she had an over-powering urge to touch his sleeve in sympathy—yet, she resisted, bewildered to be feeling such closeness with a man she'd known only four days.

"My father ignored all the warning signs of cancer," Sim disclosed.

Dr. Gibbs nodded sadly. "I don't know much 'bout the environment where y'all live out west, but the problem 'round here is, it's almost impossible to prove that *any* of these illnesses are due to the stuff in the air or the groundwater. So the damned polluters get away with it over and over."

"Well..." Sim said, with a determined look, "I work the problem from the other end... taking photographs that might make people appreciate the wildlife that still exists, and maybe even inspire them to join the fight to save what's left." He laughed mirthlessly. "That's what keeps me going these days when I'm hip-deep in some tropical river, praying the piranha won't get me before I squeeze off a close-up of an endangered parrot!"

"And thank God you do," the doctor said gruffly. He glanced at a busy bird feeder that was a dead ringer for Stanton Hall, the magnificent mansion in the heart of downtown Natchez that Daphne had pointed out to Corlis the day before her wedding. "Seein' those little fellas inspires me to live a good while longer," he announced. "And besides, Caroline left a lot on my to-do list. Now, why don't I show you the rest of the three-ring circus I've got going here?"

Bailey Gibbs forged ahead, leading his guests to the bank of a burbling creek where foliage grew even thicker than at Liz Keating's house, and horsetail rushes made the going considerably rougher.

"You know, gentlemen," Daphne declared after forging ahead a few more yards, "I'm not properly equipped in terms of footgear, should some lil' ol' snake-in-the-grass cross my path. Why don't you two continue on your tour, and I'll wander back to the cottage in a few minutes and wait for you there, okay? And take your time."

Dr. Gibbs inspected his visitor's feet and nodded. "Wise woman. Obviously knows her way 'round this neck of the woods. Caroline loved birds, but she hated snakes. She always said, *she* was in charge of the glade... but the back forty was a hundred percent my bailiwick." He looked at Sim. "Okay with you, son, if we press on?"

Sim glanced questioningly at Daphne, who smiled and waved them ahead. "I'm fine. I'd love just to sit on this log over here and listen to the creek for a while." She walked around her proposed resting place making a mock inspection, and declared, "No snakes and no weeds. It's perfect! See you later."

She took a seat and listened contentedly to the sound of twigs snapping as Sim and Dr. Gibbs's footsteps faded into the distance. A shaft of sunlight shone down through the canopy of trees, warming her face and making her sleepy. She closed her eyes and absorbed the gurgling sounds of water flowing by a few feet away. A frog croaked and crickets chirped nearby.

A bird called *Ca-coooo… ca-coooo…* and Daphne wondered if it were a spoonbill or a wood stork en route north.

Another bird cawed… and then another, and suddenly the surrounding woods were alive with birdsong, hoots, and trilling noises. Her eyes flew open, and she stared, amazed, at the flutter of wings overhead. In fact, wherever Daphne gazed, birds abounded on branches and were silhouetted in the air. A flock of small creatures flew over the brook fifty yards upcreek from the grassy footpath nearby. Soon, woodcocks were screeching and a buzzard circled over head.

Suddenly, the woods were alive with fowl. Daphne began to experience vertigo, as if the sounds in her ears were pulling her into a vortex of another time, a time when millions of birds filled the trees, and their musical notes were as common as human speech. A time when another Daphne, in a place very close to where she sat overlooking the burbling play of water in Whitaker Creek, gazed through a window and watched a flock of sparrows circle and swoop… circle and swoop… warbling their delight at a simpler world—that turned out to be not so simple, after all.

CHAPTER 9

JANUARY 29, 1794

DAPHNE WHITAKER GAZED MOODILY through her bedchamber window, idly noticing that Mammy's daughter was emptying the bread crumbs gathered in her apron onto the ground outside the cookhouse. A flock of brown sparrows fluttered at Kendra's feet and greedily gobbled the unexpected bounty on this unusually cold, January morning. Even through the wavy glass windowpanes Daphne could hear the birds twitter excitedly, but she paid little heed.

It will start all over again. Mama'll shriek and shriek and shriek, and I shall go mad.

Daphne heard the rustle of starched cotton skirts advancing down the hallway, and suddenly Mammy stood in the door frame, a cautious smile illuminating her dark brown features.

"Chile, you have a new baby brother. He's mighty small, but his color's good. Your mama wants you to come say hello."

"Don't want to," Daphne said shortly.

"Now, Daphne," Mammy reproved.

"He'll die."

"He might not," Mammy said in a hopeful tone. "That's up to the Lord to decide, not young'uns like you."

The faint cries of the newborn drifted down the carpeted upstairs hall from Susannah Whitaker's bedchamber.

"He sounds puny," Daphne declared. "Has Daddy seen him?"

"Yes, and now your daddy's out with the men in the fields, plannin' the sowin' for next year."

"I don't believe you," Daphne said sullenly. "Daddy won't even look at him, will he, 'cause he thinks he'll die, same as the others."

"Now you stop that, y'hear?" Mammy scolded. "They've given him a name. Keating, after your mama's grandma, so you be a nice chile and tell your mama you're happy for her."

After a few moments of silence, Daphne rose from her chair by the window and walked halfheartedly toward the door. Mammy stepped aside to let her pass.

"She didn't want this baby," the girl announced flatly. "Daddy made her have it and hurt her to do it, and now the baby'll die."

"What you talkin' 'bout?" Mammy demanded with a shocked expression.

Daphne refused to respond. Instead, the Whitaker household's eldest child walked swiftly past her mother's door and down the stairs to the parlor. Soon, the house was filled with the sound of a single passage of music, played stridently on the harp.

By the time Charles Whitaker flung open the front door, Daphne's fingers were aching from repeating the same section of the Bach cantata a dozen times or more.

"What's the point?" he shouted to no one in particular as he tramped into the foyer. "What's the whole, damnable *point* to any of it?"

Her father's boots were muddy and his frock coat wrinkled from shoulder to hem. Given his foul temper, Daphne quickly surmised that he must have received even more bad news on his latest inspection of his tobacco fields. She'd heard the conversations behind the half-closed doors of her father's study. It had become widely known that Devon Oaks Plantation was threatened with foreclosure due to the steady fall of tobacco prices in recent years. In the months following the ghastly night Daphne had watched her father storm into her mother's bedchamber, the king and queen of France had lost their heads to the guillotine, and tobacco shipments from America were still blockaded by hostile French and British forces. For the third year in a row, the money loaned to a host of planters for the purchase of seed and supplies was now past due. Everyone around Natchez was feeling the pinch, including the bankers who had granted Charles Whitaker another round of credit.

Daphne gazed into her father's library. This chilly morn, he hadn't even bothered to close his study doors. The harp fell silent and she watched, mesmerized, while her father poured himself a full glass of spirits and downed it in a few gulps. He opened a drawer to his desk, took out a pistol, cocked the hammer and then set about pouring lead powder into a piece of cloth and wadding it into the short barrel of the gun. He served himself another half glass of spirits, drank that down like the first, and strode out of the room and through the foyer without even a glance into the parlor where Daphne sat transfixed beside her harp. She heard the back door slam, and with the sound, an overwhelming sense of foreboding overtook her.

Through the parlor window she watched her father bend into the stiff January wind as he headed toward the stable yard. She sat on the harp stool, frozen with apprehension, and then slowly lifted her hands and continued—midbar—with the Bach cantata.

The tall clock in the foyer suddenly struck the hour of eleven. Its tolling sound rose above her mindless music-making and roused Daphne from her stupor. She jumped up from her padded perch, convinced that she must follow her father, despite the likely chance he would be terribly cross with her. When he was in these awful tempers, he shunned all company—in contrast to her mother, who cried out for Daphne's presence when she fell into dark despair.

The youngster made a dash up the staircase and down the hallway. The newborn wasn't crying as she ran past her mother's bedchamber. All was silent in the house.

He's probably already dead. How stupid of her to give him a name! He's bound to end up buried next to all the other Whitaker babies.

A faint voice called out. "Daphne?"

Her mother sounded feeble and weary. She ignored Susannah Whitaker's summons and rushed into her own bedchamber, flinging open the armoire. She seized her red woolen cloak and ran out again, not casting so much as a glance in her mother's direction as she sped by her open door, down the broad staircase, and out through the scullery leading to the mansion's rear door.

The air outside was unusually frigid for the Natchez Territories and the limbs of the leafless trees were etched against clear skies. She saw the flash of a figure on horseback two hundred yards ahead, moving through the underbrush. On foot, she picked up her pace, but horse and rider outdistanced her with every step and soon she couldn't see anything but trees and birds flitting from branch to branch.

She trudged along the path through the woods until her lungs began to ache and her legs grew weary. Why was she doing this? she asked herself haplessly as tears welled in her eyes, obscuring her vision. She halted and leaned, gasping, against a tree. As her father had said, what was the point?

Everyone's so sad at Devon Oaks... Angry and sad.

And no one but Mammy and Kendra even seemed to notice that she, Daphne, was alive and sad, too. Suki and Maddy and Eustice had been shipped off to Natchez once again during their mother's latest confinement, and Daphne was alone, cut off, certain that as far as her parents were concerned, she might as well not be there either.

The first sob escaped her lips, and slowly her back slid down the length of the tree trunk. Months of loneliness and fear poured out of her like the rush of the river during spring thaw. She wept for all the dead babies; for life as it had become on the plantation; for a future devoid of laughter or joy.

She had no idea how long she'd been crying when, suddenly, she heard the sounds of twigs snapping and branches moving.

"Well... look what we have here!" exclaimed a deep voice.

Daphne, her breath visible in the chilly air, raised her head from the cradle of her arms and felt a wave of embarrassment prompt a deep flush. Two men on horseback called out to her, not fifty feet from where she sat crumpled on the hard earth within the folds of her cloak. She swiftly wiped each eye with an edge of the fabric and saw the red wool darken with moisture.

"Daphne," the younger man exclaimed, "what are you doing

out here, sitting under a tree in the cold? You'll catch your death! C'mon, girl, give me your hand."

By this time, Simon Hopkins the Younger and his roan gelding were by her side. Daphne gazed up at the fifteen-year-old with dark hair and kind eyes. He leaned over his saddle and held out his hand, but Daphne just stared at father and son as if they were apparitions risen from the mist.

"My father..." she began brokenly. "Have you seen him? He looked so angry. I... I tried to follow him, and—" Daphne felt another sob swell in her throat and choked it back.

The Hopkins men exchanged glances. Simon's father cleared his throat and looked at her kindly from the majesty of his sixteen-hands-high gray stallion.

"Your father's upset, and surely he has cause to be," he said compassionately, "as we all have during these difficult times. Simon and I saw him by the creek a bit ago. We were heading to your house to call on your mother. My Mary wants to come by in a day or two to see if Susannah and the new babe will be needing anything—"

"The baby's dead... or he will be," Daphne intervened in a dull voice.

"Now, there! That's not true," the elder Simon admonished. "Your father just told us the little mite is holdin' his own, despite his size."

"Then why is Daddy's acting so... so..."

Before she could finish describing her father's earlier whiskey-swilling behavior, her glance fell on young Simon's waistline. Just visible where his riding habit fell open to reveal a ruffled shirt, her father's distinctive pearl-handled pistol was jammed into the young man's belt.

She stared with mounting apprehension and blurted, "That's Daddy's gun! Why do *you* have it?"

"Not to worry, my girl," the elder Simon said briskly. "Your father seemed... a bit out of sorts just now, 'tis all. Feeling the pinch of the creditors, I suspect. Every planter in the Territories feels the same."

"But you took his gun?" Daphne asked, incredulous.

"Just for a while," young Simon said soothingly, smiling at her from atop his horse. "We said we'd lock it in the cabinet in his study for him, and he agreed that was the proper place for it."

Daphne's gaze drifted from Simon's face to that of his father, who hadn't time to disguise the worry that creased his brow. She stared in the direction whence they'd ridden.

"Where is he now?" Daphne demanded. "Why didn't he come back with you?"

"He said he wants to check the fish trap in the eddy near Big Rock."

Daphne stared while a thousand thoughts skittered through her brain.

"Oh, no," she whispered. She jumped to her feet, shouting, "Daddy! Daddy... please don't! Please! Please! *Please!*" Her last words rose to a shriek.

"Daphne, wait!" Simon cried. "What's wrong?"

Ignoring him, she set off at a dead run toward Whitaker Creek, her cloak and dark blond hair streaming behind her.

"Daphne!" Simon's father shouted in alarm, her name echoing in the misty air.

Daphne raced down the footpath toward the creek whose rushing water could just be heard in the distance. Behind her, the Hopkins men spurred their horses in pursuit. On and on she ran, as terrible images stalked her like the goblins Mammy said would get her if she didn't behave like a lady.

She reached the creekside location at the spot where she, Maddy, and Suki swam in the summertime. Eustice was afraid of the water, she remembered. Her timid little brother wouldn't even dip a toe in the stream.

Her father's horse was calmly grazing in a patch of grass that had survived the unexpected frost. Daphne frantically surveyed the undulating water where a large rock rising near the riverbank had created a pool large enough to accommodate several bathers at once. There, about a foot below the aqueous surface, she saw her father, facedown, his arms drifting out like Christ on the cross.

"Jesu! I can't believe he—" Simon's father shouted, bolting from his mount.

"Stay there, Father!" his son cried, leaping from his horse. "I'll get him. He can't have been in there long!"

"Daaaa-ddy!" Daphne screamed in a keening cry. "No... nooooo," and as her wails reverberated in her own ears, she realized she sounded just like her mother had when the last baby had died.

Sim waded into the icy water up to his waist, grabbed one of Charles's boots around the ankle, and slowly tugged his body toward the creek bank. Daphne gaped in horror as they rolled her father onto his back, his glassy eyes staring up at nothing.

"Oh, my God!" the senior Simon exclaimed, pointing to Charles's bulging pockets. "The damnable fool's stuffed rocks in his coat!"

His son rested a forefinger on Charles's neck and then sadly shook his head. "He's dead."

"Like Eboli," Daphne whispered, staring wide-eyed at Sim who now stood several paces from her with water streaming down his breeches into puddles around his boots.

"Who?" Simon senior demanded roughly.

"Eboli," Daphne repeated in a small voice. "A slave we owned, who tried to run away. Daddy beat him for it. He ran away again, but Daddy and his men caught him and... beat him again." She pointed at the collection of rocks spilling from the pockets of her father's frock coat. "Eboli put stones in *his* pockets and threw himself into Whitaker Creek. That's why he sank nearly to the bottom of the stream and drowned."

"Ah... Eboli," Sim's father murmured, nodding. "A most unfortunate matter."

Tears were streaming silently down Daphne's cheeks as she pointed toward the stand of trees at their backs. "Daddy said Eboli couldn't be buried in the family plot... in consecrated ground... so he's buried somewhere here in the woods," she said, barely above a whisper. "Daddy never would tell Ellie where it was—and said he'd beat the slaves who helped him bury Eboli if they ever told her, or the other women."

"Ellie?"

"Eboli's wife. Mammy's sister."

Ignoring his own sodden state, the younger Simon walked slowly toward Daphne and enfolded the young girl in his arms. Sobs had begun to wrack her chest, and together they sank upon the damp grass while Daphne wept as if she were the last person on earth.

The older man's voice intruded. "No need for anyone to know Charles has done this damn, fool thing," he declared. "He was checking the fish trap in the pool, 'tis all. He was alone out here... checking on the trap. He slipped on an icy rock and fell in by mistake, didn't he, now? Unusual to have ice in these parts. Must have hit his head, and knocked himself unconscious."

Daphne raised her head from Sim's chest where her tears had melted into his damp linen shirt. "But the stones in his pockets—" she protested shrilly.

"No one knows he committed this sin but Sim, you, and I, Daphne," the elder Simon insisted. He stared intently at the two young people, and added, "There's no point in distressing poor, benighted Susannah Whitaker more than she already is by letting some damned vicar say Charles can't be buried in sacred ground. I *hate* that sort of nonsense!"

"But, surely, Father—"

"And killing himself isn't exactly the news the other hard-pressed planters around here need to hear right now," Simon Hopkins declared, raising his voice to smother his son's objections.

Daphne gazed at her father's body. Tiny ice crystals clung to his drenched clothes. His skin had taken on the same blue tinge as Mama's dead babies when they were put into their tiny coffins before the lids were nailed shut.

Simon's father bent down and extracted several stones from the drowned man's pockets.

"Father... I really... I don't think—" his son ventured.

"You will both do as I say, do you hear me?" the Hopkins patriarch bellowed. "Tis for the best, I tell you!"

The younger Simon's lips settled into a thin line as his father angrily began tossing the stones, one by one, into the brook. Each time he heaved a rock into the water, he punctuated his action with a solitary word.

"It... never... happened—do you hear me?"

Splash. Splash. Splash.

"Father," Simon demanded sharply. "Are you asking Daphne and me to *lie* to everyone about this?"

His sire, panting now from exertion, merely pulled more rocks out of Charles's coat pockets and tossed them into Whitaker Creek.

"It... never... happened... at... all!"

Daphne had ceased to listen to the man's words. All she could hear was the sound of rushing water and, intermittently, the impact of stones landing in the creek and the shrill call of startled birds rustling in the trees that lined the stream.

Splash. Splash. Splash. Splash... Splash!

CHAPTER 10

WATER FROM WHITAKER CREEK splashed over the bank, drenching Daphne Duvallon's tennis shoes.

"Daphne? Daphne!" a voice rang out.

A peculiar mental fog clogged Daphne's conscious mind until, finally, she was alert enough to realize she was slumped against the trunk of a willow tree, on the very edge of the creek. Oddly, she was now several yards farther downstream from the pool of deeper water that swirled gently around a large rock and rippled out from the base of the boulder.

"Daphne! Where *are* you?" Sim called, concern evident in the raised timbre of his voice.

"Maybe she got tired of waitin' for us, son, and went back to the house? Didn't she say she might?" Bailey Gibbs suggested.

Daphne struggled to stand up, her head throbbing with the beginning of a headache. Her legs felt like pins and needles, and she wondered how long she'd been—what? Dreaming? Seeing visions of the past like some deranged person?

Her heart pounded at the sight of Sim appearing through the trees in exactly the same fashion that another Simon Hopkins had materialized on horseback in these very woods. It was just like the first day they had met, when the photographer, dressed in khaki slacks and a vest, mysteriously morphed into a man wearing eighteenth-century riding attire.

"Here!" she cried, startled by how weak her voice sounded. Her gaze was drawn back to the water splashing against the rock upstream, and for an instant, she imagined she saw a body in a frock coat floating facedown in the stream. Startled, she turned abruptly and saw Sim and Dr. Gibbs standing near the log where they had left her—how many minutes ago? she wondered. Both wore perplexed expressions.

"Here I am!" she shouted in a stronger voice. "Down here! Hold on… I-I'll be right there!"

She made her way through the horsetail rushes to the spot where the two men stood. Sim took in the sight of her muddy tennis shoes, and said mildly, "You were definitely the one who needed boots. Look at your shoes!"

Daphne flushed and glanced from Sim to Dr. Gibbs. "I-I wanted to see if there were any fish downstream," she fibbed. "I thought it might be interesting if any had gotten past the old trap."

Dr. Gibbs looked at her strangely. "How did you know about those traps?" He turned to Sim, and explained, "Generations of folks from these parts have been setting underwater traps to catch bass and catfish in that hole, but Caroline demanded I take them out a while back. Said fish had as much right as birds to move freely on the earth." He smiled mistily. "She became a complete vegetarian at the end." He gave a guilty grimace. "I've been a backslider since she passed. Can't resist a piece of Leila's wonderful fried chicken once in a while." Then Dr. Gibbs stared, gimlet-eyed, at Daphne. "But seriously, young lady… who told you about those fish traps?"

Daphne felt another flush of color fan up her throat. "I-I… I think Cousin Marcus might have mentioned them… when he talked about his family's old place at Devon Oaks," she ventured lamely.

"Daphne?" Sim asked, gazing at her intently. "Are you sure you're all right? You look…"

"I'm fine," she protested. "I think the sunshine made me sleepy." She looked from Sim to her host and offered brightly, "Well! What's the word from the back forty?"

❧

Leila had mint juleps waiting for them on the rear veranda when they returned to the house.

"The sun's well over the yardarm," Dr. Gibbs declared firmly, "and this blessed woman knows to have these at-the-ready when I come in each afternoon."

"Oh, Lord, Doctor G.," Leila declared, waving a tea towel with a pleased smile for her employer of thirty years. "If you think flattery'll get me to make you a second julep, you sure are in for a mighty big disappointment. *One* a day for you, sir... just like your vitamins." Then she turned on her heel and marched inside the house.

The rims of their tulip-shaped glasses were encrusted with sugar crystals and a large stem of tangy mint nestled among the ice cubes. Immediately, Daphne excused herself and retired to the powder room to splash water on her face. When she returned, some of the ice had melted and she sipped just enough julep to be polite. In her queasy state, she didn't trust herself to imbibe an ounce of hard liquor.

"Look what Bailey just dug out of an old file," Sim exclaimed.

Dr. Gibbs and Sim had resumed their places in the white chairs overlooking the wide expanse of lawn leading toward the bird sanctuary. The elderly physician handed Daphne a yellowed, late-1920s newspaper clipping with a drawing that depicted a series of plantation houses, including one whose caption read "Hopkins House." The story headline proclaimed "Ghosts Along the Mississippi."

She took the article from Bailey, and as she skimmed the newsprint, her hand began to tremble. The body of the piece described the now-demolished structures in more detail, lamenting their loss to the architectural landscape of the Natchez region.

"It was bothering me all the time we were on our walk," Gibbs declared, excitement evident in his voice. "Hopkins... Hopkins... I kept saying to m'self down there in the woods. And now, look at *this*." He smiled slyly at Sim. "Are you sure, son, you don't have Southern roots? Obviously a family named Hopkins once lived in Adams County—right down the Trace from the old Whitaker place and all the rest of us."

Daphne remembered the Hopkins men—in frock coats with linen at their throats—riding through the woods on a cold January day.

Okay, she lectured herself sternly. *So a family named Hopkins once had a plantation around here.*

Hopkins was a fairly common name. This article wasn't proof-positive that she was turning into some lunatic-fringe psychic medium, was it?

Daphne struggled to regain her composure while Sim and Dr. Gibbs made plans for Sim to return to the bird sanctuary to photograph later that week. Then the two visitors thanked the doctor and said good-bye. Within minutes, Sim was steering his car down the wooded drive and onto the Natchez Trace Parkway, heading for town.

"You're awfully quiet," Sim said, breaking a few moments' silence. Daphne turned to study his handsome profile as the heavy foliage whizzed by the driver's side window. "I hope all our tramping around in the woods didn't seem as if we'd abandoned you to the wilds."

"Oh, no. Absolutely not," Daphne hastened to assure him. In fact, she'd loved the afternoon, except for the disturbing interlude by the side of Whitaker Creek. "I adored visiting this part of the Trace. After all, maybe we *both* have roots here."

Sim glanced across the car's interior and smiled, shaking his head. "Well, if we do, nobody in California ever told me about it. If there's any connection, it must be way, way back. My father told me once that some ancestor of ours followed Lewis and Clark's trail to Jackson Hole, Wyoming, but no one's ever said anything about any Hopkins having lived in the Deep South, sorry to say." He chuckled and turned up the air-conditioning a notch. "I'd sure like to lay claim to that beautiful old house Bailey showed us in the clipping, wouldn't you? Too bad it got flattened by a tornado." Then he laughed. "Lucky you, though. You can stake a claim to— what house was it?"

"Devon Oaks Plantation," Daphne said quietly.

"That's right… Devon Oaks. And don't forget Bluff House," he said, a ghost of a smile turning up the corners of his mouth.

Sim left the parkway and wound his way on a smaller two-way street toward Monmouth. He glanced at her, and said suddenly, "Would you ever be interested in seeing a portfolio of my work?"

Sim almost seemed diffident about his offer. This quite pleased and amazed Daphne as she figured Simon Chandler Hopkins was considered tops in his field of nature writing and photography.

"I'd love to see the kinds of images you capture, sometime."

"Great! How about right now? And then I can take you to dinner. The Monmouth chef is doing crawfish soup and some fabulous catfish with mango chutney—according to the menu they slipped under my door this morning."

Oh, boy. What did she do now?

Daphne was wildly curious to see Sim's work. Furthermore, there was no denying that attraction was pulling them together like a pair of fifty-ton magnets. But was it such a good idea for her to spend another evening in the company of the compelling Dr. H.?

Oh hell… the guy's only asking me to have dinner. Chill out, Daphne!

"Sure," she said finally. "I'd love to see your photographs. But after supper, I've got to get back to Maddy's and find out which days Willis McGee wants to rehearse this week."

"Deal," Sim said, making a turn into the hotel's sweeping driveway.

On this, Daphne's third visit to Monmouth, she was in a far more cheerful frame of mind to appreciate the magnificence of Sim's accommodations. The massive four-poster bed and the dark mahogany dresser and armoire made her feel as if she'd landed in a remake of *Gone with the Wind*. Simon shrugged off his khaki vest and poured her a glass of water from the bottle of Evian on a silver tray placed on the coffee table.

"Cheers," he said, clinking cut-crystal glasses. "You know," he added, casting a penetrating glance in her direction, "you still look a little pale. Truly, are you feeling okay?"

"I look pale? I'm fine," she insisted, taking a sip. "Honestly." Feeling suddenly self-conscious to be in a man's hotel room, Daphne avoided the big bed and sat on the settee. "Now… let's have a look at those photographs," she requested brightly.

Sim opened the armoire and withdrew a black leather portfolio the size of a film poster. He swiftly unzipped the case and removed

several large-format books—one with a majestic bald eagle gracing
the cover, another with a flamboyant parrot perched amid thick,
green jungle foliage, and a third with a fierce-looking owl deep in
its lair, glaring into Sim's camera lens.

The photographer then reached back inside the portfolio and
withdrew two large pieces of museum-quality white mounting
board, between which lay a series of photographic enlargements
separated by thin sheets of archival paper. He sat down next to her
on the settee and handed her the top image.

"These are from my book on the world's waterfowl," he said
with quiet pride. "We still have the captions to write and the edit-
ing to do, but with any luck, it will come out in time for the
Christmas season."

"I'm taking a wild stab at this," she said, laughing, as he held up
the first photograph. "Puffins?"

"Good! Puffins they are, photographed on the coast of
Cornwall, England. And these?" he queried with a roguish smile.

"Easy. Penguins. In the Antarctic?"

"Clever lass. And what about this one?"

"Ducks, of course. Mallards. Am I right?"

Sim cocked his head and held the photograph at arm's length.
"Mallards," he confirmed, his playful mood shifting slightly.
"I hadn't photographed them for ten years, but my publisher
wanted them in the book, so last autumn I went to an area around
Sacramento I know and sat in a duck blind in the cold rain for
about four days."

"Yikes!" Daphne said. "And I think it's hard practicing a Bach
cantata for a few hours straight."

One by one, Sim displayed his latest prints that captured creatures in their nests, in the air, and roaming their habitats. When
Daphne had thoroughly examined the last photograph, she said
quietly, "These are absolutely wonderful, Sim. You have a marvelous eye." She pointed to the books that lay on the coffee table.
"And you wrote the text as well," she marveled. "You must be
one of those amazing right brain/left brain people."

"Oh, I don't know about that," Sim said modestly, and then

they lapsed into companionable silence while Daphne picked up the picture of the puffin and studied it closely. Meanwhile, Sim refilled her water glass. After a moment he asked, "Tell me more about how harps came into your life. Did your cousin Madeline launch you on your career as a musician?"

"That she did, but it was my mother who cracked the whip," Daphne said ruefully, continuing to stare at Sim's photograph. "Not that she could read a note of music herself, of course, but for some reason she felt I should." She glanced at Sim. "According to her, 'there's nothin' prettier than a young lady sittin' at a harp playin' *Swan Lake*,'" she pronounced in her best approximation of her mother's heavy Southern accent.

"And now you're a rising young star," Sim offered gallantly.

"Oh... not quite that," Daphne replied, with a modest shake of her head.

"That's what Lani Riches told me. She said you play with the Oberlin Chamber Orchestra."

Daphne merely nodded, tempted to blurt out the professional dilemma facing her when she returned to New York. The mere thought of Manhattan and all the problems awaiting her there suddenly threw a pall on their conversation.

"Actually, I'm thinking about options other than the Oberlin," she said carefully, "and I'm glad I have some time off to figure it all out."

Sim began to wag a finger, musing, "You know something? I actually think I *attended* a concert of yours once. In Boston... about a year ago."

"I played that concert," she confirmed, startled by the thought that the two of them had inhabited the same space before, "I was the harpist you couldn't see because they stuck me in the back next to the timpanists."

"Well, I wish I'd known. Might have kept me awake... Though, don't get me wrong," he hastened to add. "You all were great. It was just that I was jet-lagged and, well... I'm more a jazz and blues buff, myself."

"So *that's* why you were so up for going to all these funky little spots around here," Daphne said, pleased. "Have you been to New Orleans much? Or New York?" Sim nodded. "Then you know what great music you can hear in those towns."

"And don't forget the San Francisco Bay Area," he said loyally. "There's a vibrant club scene in Fog City and over in Oakland that won't quit. We even have a couple of jazz festivals. You've got to come out and let me show you what *we've* got."

"If you're ever there," Daphne commented, pointing at his photographs.

An awkward pause caught them both off guard. Sim's faintly guilty expression confirmed that he was rarely in his hometown. In fact, she wondered if they would ever see each other again when her visit was over. She considered the truth revealed in Sim's portfolio. The man's life was about traveling to the next location. She suddenly had a feeling that she'd fallen for the oldest ploy in the world. Didn't the old saw go "Come up and see my etchings, my dear?"

She set her glass of water on the coffee table. "You know, Sim," she said firmly, "on second thought, I think I'd better pass on dinner."

"Why?" he demanded, concerned, and she knew her abrupt shift in demeanor had been obvious.

She paused for a long moment and then surprised even herself. "Look," she began earnestly, "I've really enjoyed getting to know you these last three days, and I'm a huge fan of what you're doing and what your life is about, but—"

"But what?" He shifted on the small couch so that he could gaze directly into her eyes.

"It's *me*," she insisted. "I've just come off two years that would kill an alligator, and I've learned a few things about myself along the way."

"You mean, blowing off your wedding? That must have been horrendous, but what's that got to do with having crawfish soup?" he asked with an encouraging smile.

"It's more than that," she replied doggedly. "It's a rather long, embarrassingly clichéd story. I won't bore you with the details."

"Try me, Daphne," Sim said with an intensity that startled her. "I want to know how a knockout like you could ever have considered saying 'I do' to a jerk like Jack Ebert."

"You should have seen Rafe Oberlin's act," she retorted, and then immediately regretted mentioning his name.

"Ah... the *rest* of the story. As you said the other day, life gets complicated sometimes, doesn't it?"

"It does. And I don't want it to get more complicated."

"You mean... by me?"

She looked at him sharply. "Why are you asking about all this personal stuff?"

And why am I longing to tell you about the whole, sorry mess?

"Because I really want to know," he said simply, then added, "And because I don't want you to leave till we've had another dinner together."

They both appeared startled by his declaration.

"But I *am* leaving," Daphne said in a low voice. "One week from today, I'll be back in New York, and frankly, I'm just not into brief encounters these days—should that possibly have been what you had in mind."

"Well, I wouldn't expect you to be."

"Because you see, that's what it turned out to be with maestro Rafe Oberlin. Chump that I was, I allowed myself to listen to the flattery of a sweet-talkin' travelin' man," she said mockingly, "and foolishly thought he meant what he said—and got my heart handed to me, big time." Sim's expression revealed that he didn't fully understand her. "Rafe was *married*, but didn't deign to wear a ring," she explained. "His wife was a ballet dancer touring the world at the time the chamber orchestra was also on the road. When I found all this out, I of course felt like a colossal fool." She laughed shortly. "I *was* a fool on several counts to have gotten involved with Rafe, since I already knew firsthand the crazy life of even an unmarried musician who was always on the road."

"But wasn't that more than two years ago?" Sim asked. "Before Jack?"

"But I was forced by my contract to continue to play in his

chamber orchestra until—" Daphne hesitated and then made an impulsive decision. "Well, just last week, Rafe fired me for choosing to play at my brother's wedding instead of our debut concert at Lincoln Center on Saturday."

"Wow," Sim said with gentle humor, "you certainly *did* have a tough week."

"No kidding," she replied, appreciating both his empathy and his effort to lighten the atmosphere.

"But with your talent, you'll be able to sign on with another orchestra, won't you?" he asked encouragingly.

"My tax accountant certainly hopes so," she replied with a smile. "It takes a lot of teatime gigs to pay the rent in Manhattan."

Sim nodded knowingly. "Ah… the freelance life."

"Amen."

He regarded her for a moment, and then brought the conversation back to a previous topic. "I would imagine that the miserable experience with Oberlin made you pretty vulnerable to Jack Ebert's brand of persuasion."

Daphne agreed glumly. "I was fairly clueless not to recognize instantly that I was desperately on the rebound when I got involved with Jack."

"Probably everyone on the planet has made some foolish rebound play at one time or another," Sim said charitably. "However, I admit that I *am* curious to know what finally made you call off the wedding at the last minute."

"At the *altar*," Daphne reminded him. "In front of the priest and five hundred guests," she added. She paused, feeling her heart speed up at the memory of what she'd seen in the cloakroom at Antoine's during the groom's dinner. "It took something monumental to make me recognize the idiotic thing I was about to do, but I finally did… at ten thirty-five the night before the wedding, to be precise."

"What happened?" he asked, incredulous.

Daphne stared at her glass of water, not seeing it at all, but rather the darkened cloakroom that led to the restaurant's powder room farther down the hallway.

"The groom's dinner was hosted by Jack's parents for all the out-of-town guests," she began. "The raucous toasts were over with. The dancing had begun in the private dining room hired for the occasion. I could tell Jack was pretty drunk because his toast to me had been less than heartfelt," she continued, tracing her forefinger around the circumference of her glass. "Right afterward, he disappeared from the room, which created a fairly mortifying scene. About fifteen minutes later, I slipped out of the party in search of some quiet place where I could regroup, you know?" She looked up, finally meeting Sim's steady gaze.

"And?" he prompted.

"This part's almost funny," she confided, though, in truth it wasn't amusing in the slightest. "I was heading for the restrooms when, *ta-da*! There was my almost-husband facing away from the cloakroom door with his trousers around his ankles and his bare backside mooning me, his bride-to-be. And there was flame-haired Cindy Lou Mallory—my brother King's *girlfriend* then, mind you— with her short, tight-fitting black cocktail dress unzipped to her fanny." Daphne couldn't bring herself to describe the woman's bra bunched around her minuscule waistline, or the moaning encouragement she had been giving the incipient groom—who had ready access to Ms. Mallory's ample mammaries.

"Oh, God, Daphne... I'm so sorry." Sim covered her hand with his as he had done on the porch at King's reception.

"Later, of course," she said, her voice tight, "my brother and I discovered that they'd been having a torrid affair all the time *I* was in New York, finishing my master's at Juilliard. Cindy Lou was just doing one of her prima magnolia maneuvers, trying to get King to ask her to marry him by making him jealous."

"I see her ploy didn't work," Sim remarked, deadpan.

"Obviously no. Corlis came along a bit later—and theirs was definitely *not* a rebound bounce," she added emphatically. "Even so, my new sister-in-law waited two years to marry King, just to make damn sure. As for Jack's motives?" She shrugged. "Too much family pressure? Boob fetish? Insanity? Who the hell knows?"

"What did you do when you saw Jack and Cindy... uh..."

"In flagrante delicto?" she interrupted sarcastically. "I was literally speechless with shock. I backed out of the cloakroom, raced through the public dining rooms and out of the restaurant onto St. Louis Street, where I promptly lost my eighty-six dollar dinner—including wine—into the gutter."

"What in the world did you do between then and the wedding the next day?" he asked, shaking his head in wonder.

"I think I was in a state of emotional paralysis." She rose from the settee and walked toward the elaborately carved, white marble fireplace. "I felt sort of like a Stepford wife in training, you know? I just allowed myself to drift from moment to moment. The next day I got into my wedding dress. I got into the limousine. And I let myself be driven to the church."

"Never telling anybody what you'd seen?"

"Not till I got to the cathedral. When I saw King in the vestibule, I burst into tears and dragged him into the men's room and locked the door. I told him what happened and just kept sobbing hysterically into his starched shirt and tail coat."

"That must have been some conversation," Sim commented dryly. "It had to be a tough blow to your brother as well."

"It was *horrible*," Daphne said emphatically. "King had been betrayed just like I had. But you know something, Sim? He never hesitated for an instant. He just said 'Darlin'... whatever you want to do, I'm right there with you.' We found Althea LaCroix—my friend who was scheduled to play the organ during the ceremony—and told her what had happened and warned her to be ready for *anything*."

"So you hadn't made a decision what to do even by the time your father walked you down the aisle?" Sim asked, astonished.

"Call me crazy," she replied grimly, "but I honestly didn't know if I had it in me to say 'I *don't!*' at the eleventh hour like that. By that time, remember, nine bridesmaids, including Cindy Lou, were lined up, ready to start the show. My mother had about twenty thousand dollars' worth of wholesale flowers plastered all over Saint Louis Cathedral, along with five hundred of the Ebert and Duvallon's nearest and dearest packed into the pews. They'd hired the New Orleans Country Club for the reception, which included a seated dinner, and a full twenty-piece dance orchestra— the whole nine yards."

"What a nightmare," Sim said sympathetically. "What finally made you run out on all of it?"

Daphne slowly shook her head in remembrance.

"The pain etched on my brother's face when I saw him watch Daddy walking me down the aisle," she declared without hesitation. "I suddenly imagined future Christmases and Thanksgiving holidays... what it would be like for King and me, knowing what we knew? Then I looked at Jack standing beside the priest and suddenly saw him as he was. A snake and a liar and the last person on earth that I wanted to be married to. I just blurted out everything to the wedding guests and took off down that aisle, heading for freedom from the whole, hideous thing." Daphne turned her back to the fireplace. "Of course, my mother and father wanted to kill me."

"Weren't they upset by what *Jack* had done?"

"Honestly? I think they were more upset by what their friends would say. What upset them the *most* was that my bolting out of the church hurt their flower business." She shook her head once more, unable to keep the bitterness out of her voice. "What you need to understand is that my mother and father were never what you'd call a love match." She looked at her watch. "But that's another story, and I don't really have the energy to describe the rest of my Faulknerian family history tonight." A feeling of acute embarrassment suddenly swept over her. "Lord, Sim... why did I go on like this? You already knew the bare bones of the story. You heard it behind a hedge in the parking lot."

"You filled in the details just now because I asked you to."

"So tell me, sir," Daphne said, attempting to lighten the atmosphere by speaking in an ersatz Southern drawl, "why would a gentleman like you be interested in such a sorry tale?"

Sim's interest and sympathy seemed genuine enough, but Daphne wondered if such sentiments were merely the laying of groundwork for luring her into his gorgeous canopied plantation bed later this evening. His next words even gave credence to this disturbing theory.

"Because, frankly, Scarlett," he said, rising from the couch, "I've mightily enjoyed these last three days in Natchez." He took a few steps closer, his steady gaze belying his teasing words and then, losing the drawl, he confessed, "I'm drawn to this part of the world... to the music we both enjoy... to a lot of things that I haven't felt for... for quite a while." He reached up and grazed the back of his hand against her cheek. "And, I'm drawn to *you*, Daphne, in case you hadn't noticed. As you've clearly noted, I've been on the road a long time. For almost a decade, in fact." His hand now gently cupped her chin. "Don't you think I should pay attention when something tells me, 'Hey, Hopkins! This feels better than good'?"

Daphne stood transfixed, her face only inches from Sim's, surrounded by one of the most romantically appointed hotel suites she'd ever seen. Try as she might to fight it, she was forced to admit that she felt exactly the same way. Everything about Sim felt good. Felt right.

Yeah, sure. Until the next time his publisher sends him to Antarctica for six months to photograph a bunch of penguins.

Daphne swallowed hard, and replied, "The problem is... I can't trust what *I* feel at the moment. Between Rafe Oberlin drawing me into his tangled web and then canning me last week, and Jack Ebert, whom I should have known better than to get involved with—I'm pretty tapped out."

Sim's next move proved he hadn't been listening to a word she said.

"So I take it that the groom never got to kiss the bride?" he murmured, bending closer. "What an idiot."

And before Daphne knew what was happening, he framed her face in his large, slender hands, and kissed her tenderly and thoroughly on the lips. It was a long kiss, one with fire and compassion, and full of promise.

Then Sim took a step backward, as if to survey his handiwork.

"Why did you do that?" she asked in a low voice.

"Pure naked impulse," he said, watching her intently. "Did you like it?" Daphne felt totally off balance and merely stared at him, speechless. "Well, did you?"

"Don't they *all*, Mr. Inquiring Photographer?" she snapped, finding her voice in a rush of anger for all the slick lines that the Rafe Oberlins of the world had ever delivered to the unsuspecting women of their acquaintance. "I just told you, Sim, that I'm tapped out emotionally, so I'm no real judge of kissing prowess these days."

Sim looked startled by the passion and hostility of her tone.

"Daphne... it was just a simple question. Did you like it when I kissed you?"

"Yes," she said in a small voice. How could she bring herself to tell him that she was mortally afraid he was cranking up the razzle-dazzle, only to land her in his four-poster before he moved on down the road?

Sim seized her hand and held its palm flat against his heart. It was beating faster than normal—just as hers was.

"I can only imagine what you've been through, and it's obvious to me now, that there were a lot of complicating factors," Sim said, his gaze still locked onto hers. "But, believe me, I've had some pretty crazy bounces myself over the years."

"Like?"

Sim released her hand and returned to the coffee table where he refilled his glass of water. "I did the opposite of what you did," he said in a bantering tone. "You've had the courage to return to the scene of the train wreck and come home to the South. Me? After my divorce, I took to the woods for ten years and refused to venture out of my duck blind, so to speak. As you've pointed out, I made a choice to stay on the road so I wouldn't have to deal with... with all that went before."

"Which was?" Daphne pressed. When he hesitated she said, "After all, Sim, it's only fair that you play *This Is Your Life*, since I have—at your request, remember?"

Sim looked at her for a long moment, and then glanced down at his watch.

"That, too, is another story for another time," he announced evenly. "How 'bout I take you downstairs for some of that crawfish soup?"

The man just ducked a direct question, didn't he? she asked herself, feeling blindsided again. *Seeks intimacy. Doesn't offer it. Not a good sign.*

Daphne hesitated, squared her shoulders, then looked Sim in the eye. "You're really nice to ask me to stay to supper, but I've decided that I'd better get back to Cousin Maddy's in case I have an early rehearsal tomorrow with Willis."

Even if Sim Hopkins wasn't traveling the globe—and he *was*—he had a bad habit of shutting down whenever certain questions came his way. As far as Daphne was concerned, she'd learned enough about the hopeless pursuit of unavailable men to last a lifetime.

Sim hesitated and then seemed to think better of trying to persuade her to stay.

"Can you give me a lift back to Bluff House?" she asked pleasantly.

"Sure," he said coolly. He began to collect the large photographs scattered around the settee. "Just give me a sec to put these back into my portfolio, and we'll be off."

CHAPTER 11

A KIND OF FREE-FLOATING awkwardness developed between Sim and Daphne during the short drive from Monmouth. As they approached the entrance to Bluff House, a pickup truck with "U.S. Army Corps of Engineers" stenciled on its door nosed out of the driveway.

"Oh boy…" Daphne murmured, watching it drive past. "Hope poor Maddy didn't get any more bad news about the condition of the bluff." When the Range Rover rolled to a halt, Daphne resignedly reached for her door handle and made her farewells as brief as possible.

"Thanks for sharing Doctor Gibbs with me." She summoned a smile as she stepped out of the car. "All the best on your bird sanctuary safari this week. Have fun. Bye." She kept her tone light and her movements swift. She had advanced a few feet down the path to Maddy's back door when Sim called out.

"Hey, Daphne! Wait! You haven't told me what day you leave for New York."

She hesitated and glanced into the rear compartment of her rented Ford Explorer parked near the spot Sim had halted the Range Rover. Her harp lay on its side, protected within its hulking traveling case. She hadn't even looked at the instrument, much less tackled its re-stringing since the near-debacle with Jack at King's wedding.

"I'm leaving next Sunday to drive down to New Orleans and catch my plane from there," she disclosed, reluctant to think about the difficulties that awaited her in Manhattan. At least in the Big Apple, she'd surely elude any more bizarre mental flip-backs of the sort that had plagued her regularly since her arrival in Natchez, she thought, searching for something to be cheerful about.

"So, you're heading straight home after you play at the Under-the-Hill Saloon Saturday night?"

Home? Hardly.

"Yes, I'm heading back to reality," she said, forcing a smile.

"I'll be back from the Trace by Friday night," he volunteered. "Okay with you if I escort your cousin Madeline on Saturday so we can cheer you on from the front row?"

Daphne took a step in the direction of the Range Rover. "That is really nice of you," she replied, touched by such glimpses of kindness that Sim had shown her these last few days. "I'm sure she'd love it. I'll tell her to expect you... what? Around nine thirty Saturday night? Things probably won't get under way much before ten."

"You musicians are regular night owls," he said, flashing a grin.

"And you photographers have to get up at the crack of dawn," she reminded him with an ironic shrug.

See? It would never work, even if we lived in the same town...

"Please don't tell me that my next line is 'Let's call the whole thing off'?" He opened the car door and got out. "Look, Daphne," he said, walking toward her. "Just so you know, *I* liked kissing *you* very much."

Startled by this declaration, Daphne could only gaze at Sim, feeling too foolish and conflicted to admit again she'd had the same reaction.

Finally she said, "I did... I mean... thank you."

Sim waited an instant longer for her to elaborate. When she didn't, he arched an eyebrow and then ambled back to his car without further conversation. Daphne watched until his car's taillights disappeared down Clifton Avenue. Then she slowly walked toward the house that clung precariously on the edge of the bluff. Maddy, as she always did, had left a welcoming light on the veranda.

"You're not asking Sim in?" Maddy asked when Daphne came alone through the back door into the kitchen. The older woman was drying her hands on a dishcloth that she then tossed over a straight-backed wooden chair near the kitchen table. Several coffee cups sat on the drain board next to the sink—and would likely remain there until the next person used them, Daphne thought, hiding a smile.

"No... he's off to the wilds of the Trace to photograph Audubon's birds all next week."

"Oh. Now, that's disappointing. I was going to invite him to supper just now. It was so sweet of him bringing those lovely artichokes yesterday. I thought I'd return the favor." Maddy peered curiously at her younger cousin. "Did you two have a nice day together, dear?"

"Uh huh. And by the way, Sim would like to be your date for Saturday night when I play at the Under-the-Hill Saloon. Unless you have other plans, he'll pick you up at nine thirty."

"Other plans?" She laughed. "Not likely... and I'd *love* to be escorted to your concert by such a good-looking young gentleman."

"It's not going to be a concert, Maddy," Daphne warned. "More like a jam session, since I've played with Willis McGee and his trio exactly *once*."

"Oh! That reminds me. Mr. McGee called while you were out. Wants you to come to a rehearsal... now *where* did I put my note?" she said with exasperation, rooting among a collection of bills, magazines, and third-class mail cluttering every available inch of countertop. She sighed. "Oh, well. I remember what he said, thank heavens. Meet him at the club tomorrow at eleven in the morning. I told him I was sure you'd be there. Was that all right?"

"Perfect," Daphne assured her. She pointed out the kitchen window. "What's the latest from the almighty Army Corps of Engineers?"

Maddy rolled her eyes. "They came by to deliver the news that nothing more will be done about shorin' up that crumbling ol' cliff beyond sporadic 'erosion abatement.'"

"That's all?"

"Well, at least they *did* say that, for the moment, the bluff appears stabilized, and I'll finally be able to renew my insurance policy—though how I'll pay the premium I don't rightly know. I'll be an 'assigned risk,' they tell me. Very costly, I hear."

"Are you saying, Maddy, that there's no insurance on this house at the moment?" Daphne asked, dismayed.

"Nobody'd issue it, darlin'. And given the way I was feeling after Marcus and Clayton died, I didn't care much 'bout it anyway, to tell you the truth."

"But, Maddy… you live in Tornado Alley," Daphne protested, recalling Dr. Gibbs's tales of the killer Tornado of 1840. "Now that you can finally *get* insurance, you can't afford *not* to carry a homeowners policy, sweetie."

Maddy heaved a sigh. "I know… I know. I'll figure out what to do, eventually," she muttered. Then she brightened. "Did you have any supper yet?" Daphne shook her head. "Well then, you just sit right down here and let me heat up some of my red beans and rice I keep going in the pot all the time."

"Sounds wonderful," Daphne agreed gratefully.

"And you can tell me all 'bout that charming Doctor Hopkins," she said with a twinkle.

"Not much to tell. He's off to the woods and I'm off to rehearsal," she said, sounding a great deal more nonchalant than she felt. "He's looking forward to taking you to the Under-the-Hill Saloon Saturday, though. I think he considers you a hot date."

"Noooo, no, my dear," Cousin Maddy retorted. "I think that's exactly what the gentleman considers *you*."

❧

"Leila's packed you a lunch, son," Bailey Gibbs declared, handing Sim a brown paper bag, while cocking his head and surveying the large pack that the photographer had strapped to his back. "Hope you've got room for it with all that gear you're toting."

"Just unzip the top and jam it in there, if you can." Sim chuckled as he bent his knees so Dr. Gibbs could stow the lunch in his backpack, along with the rest of his photographic equipment.

"When the sun's over the yardarm, head on back and we'll have mint juleps waiting for you on the veranda."

"What an incentive," Sim replied. "But starting Wednesday, I'll be camping at night, if that's all right with you. There are a few species I'm more likely to spot after dark."

"Absolutely, m'boy," Gibbs agreed heartily. "If I weren't such a gimpy old fool, I'd go with you. 'Mi back forty *es su* back forty,' as they say in ol' May-hee-co. I'll look forward to a complete report." And with that, the old doctor waved Sim on his way.

In the woodlands, the temperature was at least ten degrees hotter than the previous day—a hint of the scorching summer yet to come. Sim retraced the path that wound past the charming white cottage and through the village of birdhouses. Soon he was headed down the grassy lane that led to Whitaker Creek.

By noon, he figured he'd covered about a third of the forty acres that made up the remaining lands belonging to Gibbs Hall. He'd sketched a rough map and squeezed off a few good shots, taking notes in a spiral-bound journal about the birds sighted. Sim imagined that—despite his modern equipment—his actions were very likely similar to the routine John James Audubon had followed when he foraged in these very woods for fowl to paint for his monumental *Birds of America* color portfolio.

Only I shoot our feathered friends with a camera, he thought.

He relished the irony that Audubon, considered now to be the first genuine American naturalist, shot his prey with a gun, or bow and arrow, so that he would have motionless subjects he could replicate on canvas or paper. Sometimes the painter would kill several birds of the same species over a few weeks' time so that he could finish a work and not be sickened by the smell of a rotting carcass. A conservationist he was not, Sim thought.

As the day wore on and hunger pangs began to gnaw in his stomach, Sim circled back in the direction of Whitaker Creek to find a pleasant spot for lunch. All morning he had remained on the side of the stream closest to the pillared mansion, so in a matter of minutes, he caught sight of the fallen log where he and Bailey had left Daphne to sit in the sun.

Ah… Daphne… the beautiful, hugely talented wounded bird…

Sim pulled out his sandwich and began munching on it thoughtfully.

Daphne Whitaker Duvallon was definitely a woman on the mend, and certainly one who had learned through painful experience to look out for herself. The rigorous, sometimes ruthless world of professional music had apparently taught her to keep her guard up. New York also had probably toughened her. Made her a bit cynical, and properly so, Sim judged, considering her treatment by that Oberlin character. And the unhappy business with her former fiancé had also left her with a fairly negative view of men in general—which was probably a good thing too, he thought, grimacing slightly as he took another bite out of his sandwich.

I'd have taken her straight to bed, if she'd let me...

Sim settled his back against the log and idly mused over the fact that the stunning Ms. Duvallon had reclined on the very spot where he was currently sitting. The mere thought conjured up a variety of randy images.

The lady from Louisiana was something, all right. A seductive combination of vulnerability and moxie, so different from the women he had dated in the years since his divorce, and certainly a far cry from Francesca Hayes, formerly Hopkins. He finished off his sandwich, willing his thoughts not to veer in *that* dangerous direction, but preferring to remain on the subject of the intriguing young harpist whose music had even played in his dreams.

Or was it a dream? The sound of harp music wafting upstairs at three a.m. at Monmouth Plantation had a piercing sense of reality. Even now, the lullaby floated in his head in a singsong rhythm not unlike the gentle lapping of the water in Whitaker Creek next to where he sat relaxing in the sun.

He gazed into the gurgling brook past a large rock that dammed the water into a pool large enough for a man to swim in. He wondered, briefly, if water moccasins frequented this spot, for the temperature had notched up another degree or two, and if it weren't so risky, he would strip off his clothes and dunk his naked body into the cool, inviting depths.

The buzz of cicadas and the rustle of leaves lulled Sim into drowsiness. He turned his head, and through half-lidded eyes, stared into the center of the pool. The water there appeared dark and fairly deep. Its surface rippled in gentle, hypnotic waves outward from the large boulder at the stream's edge. The sound of slowly advancing water slap-slapping gently against the rock was mesmerizing.

With no warning, a ghostly image slowly came into focus within the pool's shadowy depths. A body could be seen a foot or so beneath the caliginous surface, then it bobbed closer... closer... arms outstretched... a halo of sparse gray hair drifting around the submerged head.

Drowned... drowned by his own hand...

Somehow, Sim knew this, though he was at a loss to explain how. An overpowering repugnance assaulted him—not so much for the startling sight of a dead man in riding attire and boots drifting facedown in a creek—but for the heartache such an act of self-destruction was sure to cause those close to the stranger.

Sim wondered, suddenly, why he should even be *thinking* such thoughts. And then, in the same slow fashion that it had appeared, the specter in Whitaker Creek faded into nothingness, leaving the waters of the narrow stream to meander as always past the large rock and around the next curve in the landscape.

Sim shook himself awake from a strange sort of slumber that left him feeling as though he were in a jet-lagged daze. Who was that drowned man? What had transpired that would make the fellow wish to end his life? Scores of questions swirled in Sim's head like the creek's eddies. Who really knew another man's secrets, he mused? Everyone kept some things hidden. God knew that was true for him.

Simon mopped his face with his paisley neck scarf and sat back on his haunches, both shaken and baffled by what he'd just seen... or dreamed. Wasn't it true, he asked himself, that *he* was the one with secrets he hadn't disclosed to anyone but his dying father—for they were too shameful even to contemplate? Perhaps, just now, he'd merely drifted off, a soporific effect of Leila's delicious chicken salad sandwich and the midday heat. More likely, some deep corner of his brain had taken over, flying like a homing pigeon to the gray matter where he stored his guilt about what had happened with Francesca.

And then he began to wonder who, indeed, was the wounded bird.

❧

"Hey, Daphne! I just got a *great* idea," Willis McGee announced, and then fell into a paroxysm of coughing. He pounded his chest and tried to catch his breath.

"Gosh, Daddy, you sound awful," his daughter Kendra declared. "Don't you think that cough's getting serious?" she asked Daphne, looking for support from the newest member of Willis McGee's group.

"Maybe we should take a break?" Daphne suggested, glancing around the Under-the-Hill Saloon at brick walls studded with Rubenesque nudes, historic photos of old Natchez, and antique posters that urged local citizens to "Vote Dry!" Overhead, ceiling fans droned, creating drafts that were probably aggravating Willis's ailments.

"Just… a little spring… cold," the bandleader insisted between efforts to blow his nose with a cloth handkerchief that he kept stuffed in his belt. "That, and the danged smoke that people have blown in my face for years in places like this." As if to emphasize his self-diagnosis, Willis succumbed to another spasm.

"Man oh man, sometimes I wish we could take this gig to California," the drummer, Ebner Stimpson, said. "I hear from my buddies there ain't no secondhand smoke allowed out there in public places *anywhere*—even in the nightclubs or on public party boats."

Willis, recovered now, nodded at Ebner, the long-haired, forty-ish son of a local black judge. A majority of his family members frowned upon his choice of a career—a fact he'd disclosed earlier with a kind of rakish pride when he'd been reintroduced to Daphne at rehearsal.

"Now here's my idea," Willis said, tucking his handkerchief into his belt. "We're not hearing the harp enough so why don't we put a microphone inside that thing, Daphne? You know… electrify it… like Kendra's guitar or my electronic keyboard over there? I've even got a plug for my saxophone nowadays."

"You think it would work?" Daphne replied, intrigued by his suggestion.

"Well, let's try it and hear how it sounds," Willis proposed.

Daphne grinned at Kendra, with whom she'd felt rapport the moment they'd swung into the first tune on their list of possibles. "It'll be a war-of-the-strings," Kendra warned, laughing.

"And wouldn't it just be something if a harp could drown *you* out on the guitar?" Daphne teased while Willis rummaged through an aluminum case lined with black foam that cushioned a series of mikes in various sizes. "It'll have to be awfully small, though, Willis," she warned. "The holes in the sound board at the back of the harp are only about a half inch in diameter."

"Got just the thing," the bandleader exclaimed, holding a minuscule microphone over his head in triumph. "Now give me a moment to rig this baby up."

Daphne and Kendra headed for the ladies' room at the rear of the club. Daphne retrieved a lipstick from her purse and applied more coral to the remains of color she'd put on earlier at Maddy's.

"Daddy was right," Kendra said, pulling out a large, needle-like comb from her shoulder bag and poking it through her close-cropped Afro. "You sing real good, for a white girl," she joked.

"I'm a rank amateur," Daphne said, pleased to get a good review from a first-rate jazz guitarist, "but man… it sure is fun to play with you guys. Now, if I can just remember the *words* to half the songs we're doing on Saturday."

"Oh, you'll remember 'em," Kendra assured her. "I'm pretty blown away by what you can make that harp of yours do, lady. So, as far as the lyrics go, just close your eyes and think what the words really *mean*… and it'll come to you nice and natural-like, y'know?"

"Hmmm." Daphne nodded, pulling a small brush through her mass of unruly curls. She had been worried that Kendra McGee might resent her added presence in her father's band—even if it were only temporary. To the contrary, the bandleader's twenty-two-year-old daughter had been enthusiastic, as well as wonderfully intuitive when it came to blending her bass guitar with the lighter notes from the harp.

"Well, girl… we'd better git," Kendra said, glancing at her watch with its two-inch, Day-Glo green plastic wristband.

The novelty watch was merely one aspect of Kendra's startling ensemble. The shapely musician was wearing a tight cotton top in a color just short of psychedelic pink, and a pair of cut-off shorts that left nothing to the imagination. Daphne, on the other hand, had donned her pleated beige gabardine slacks and matching blouse and felt ridiculously conservative.

"I have a serious problem about what to wear Saturday night," she confessed. "I came down here from New York for my brother's wedding with very few clothes. What in the world am I going to put on? Jeans, probably." She held open the door to the ladies' room allowing Kendra to pass through.

"I don't know, sugar pie. You'll look good in anything. I kinda get the feeling nobody in the audience's gonna care what you got on, once you open that mouth of yours."

"Thank you for saying that, Kendra. You're bolstering my courage."

Kendra waved the arm sporting the outsized watchband. "Ah... don't worry. You'll do just fine."

Willis was still battling his hacking cough, but his eyes danced with excitement when the two women returned to the bandstand. He pointed to Daphne's tall, imposing instrument—all of its forty-seven strings now intact—and declared, "Now you just try that."

The foursome swung into the first verse of the slow, languid tune "Embraceable You," and as the melody unfolded, Daphne's heart began to pound with excitement. The harp sounded ten times louder than usual and twice as mellow. It now produced a sustained, liquid quality, making it possible to attain emotional phrasing that was thrilling to her ear.

However, when the quartet tried out another tune, with Willis on his saxophone instead of his electronic keyboard, they immediately ran into problems.

"Hey, Daddy," Kendra protested, "we *still* need a keyboard to hear the melody's through-line, or everything's gonna sound mighty muddy, seems to me."

"I agree," Daphne seconded her, wrinkling her nose in dismay. She looked at Ebner. "What's your verdict? Maybe electrifying my harp won't work for a lot of the pieces I planned to sing."

Willis put down his sax and asked them to try the same tune while he played his electronic keyboard.

"It sounds better, but what a shame to lose the sax in this piece," Kendra declared.

"I've got an idea!" Daphne said excitedly. "How about turning ourselves into the Willis McGee *quintet* for just one night? What would you say if I called my friend in New Orleans who plays keyboard? That way, Willis can play the sax, or keyboard as he pleases."

"Who're you thinking of?" Willis asked dubiously.

"The musician I told you about. She plays keyboard at her family's place—Cafe LaCroix—in New Orleans. Althea LaCroix."

"Wow..." breathed Kendra. "I'd be playing bass guitar with Althea LaCroix?" She looked at her father and grinned. "Daddy, you've gone and done a genius thing, getting this harpist lady to play with us, especially if she can get Althea LaCroix up here." She turned back to Daphne, and said earnestly, "That sister is my idol... I mean, my absolute *idol!*" Then her face fell. "Do you think she'd do it? Come all the way up here for a gig at this ol' place?" she added, gazing around the room, which looked as if it would seat a mere fifty patrons, tops.

"Well... it won't hurt to find out." Daphne pulled out her cell phone and direct dialed Cafe LaCroix on Decatur Street. "Since this is turning out to be kind of a jam session anyway—Oh! Hey, Alth?" she said, amazed that her friend had answered the phone. "You're not gonna believe where I am." She grinned at the members of the Willis McGee band who stared at her with varying degrees of astonishment and admiration. "And you're not gonna believe what I've done to my harp!"

❧

Daphne, Kendra, and Althea stood in front of the mirror in Cousin Maddy's big bedroom at the top of the stairs.

"I can't wear *this!*" Daphne glared at her childhood friend indignantly. "Just look! This leather miniskirt barely covers my crotch!"

"That's right," Althea said smugly. "That's the point." She

reached into a shopping bag and pulled out a pair of black, high-cut bikini underwear and sheer black stockings. "You wear these with it."

"*Those?*" Daphne replied, scandalized. "You expect me to go on that stage—having to sing *and* play an electric harp for the first time in my life—dressed like some floozy on Esplanade Avenue? Are you *crazy?*"

Althea pointed to the black leather miniskirts she and Kendra had just donned. "We're in 'em too, girl," she reminded Daphne sharply. "And besides, I paid a lot of money for these and the chain-mail bustiers."

Kendra preened in front of the mirror, the tops of her voluptuous breasts swelling above the bustier's curved edge, creating a sight that was downright arresting. "I just *love* 'em!"

"Fine," Daphne declared. "Y'all wear all this stuff, then. I'll pay you back for mine, but I can't go on stage with my boobs *and* my rear end hanging out, all at the same time."

"Why not?" Althea demanded. "You're gonna look great. After all, you told King you'd always fantasized wearing sexy duds like these playing your harp. Least that's what he told *me* at the weddin'."

"But that's just it," Daphne said, gazing at Kendra with an expression that begged her support, even though she knew the younger girl was thrilled with the red-hot outfits her idol had brought from New Orleans. "It was a *fantasy*. I was joking! I was never serious about something as crazy as this."

"What you 'fraid of, Daphne Duvallon?" Althea demanded.

"That's not the point," Daphne replied defensively. "It's just that... this look definitely isn't *me*."

"You think all those high-and-mighty ancestors of yours will come back to haunt you if you don't wear buttons and bows on stage tonight?"

If only you knew...

"If I wear this, I'll die of embarrassment, right on the bandstand." She could just imagine Sim Hopkins sitting in the audience with her wearing this streetwalker getup. It didn't exactly jibe with her well-articulated, keep-your-hands-off-the-merchandise policy.

"I just don't see what your problem is, Daph," Althea said crossly.

Daphne pleaded for her friend's understanding. "You two are used to showing your legs in public, but remember, I've been wearing long, shapeless skirts all my life when I play music."

"Don't you think your ol' angel act is a bit over-the-hill for an Under-the-Hill joint like this?" Althea stated bluntly with all the candor contained in their years of friendship. "At least for one night of your life, maybe it's time you started acting like the woman you obviously want to *be*? You've been handed the perfect chance to be a jazz singer tonight. If you don't go for it, what's this exercise in Natchez all about, huh?"

"It's not about going on stage looking like a slut," Daphne retorted. "The audience'll just think we're a bunch of working girls."

Althea's eyes narrowed dangerously. "What is it with you, Daphne?" she snapped. "You just slummin' with the black folks while you're visitin' down South?"

Stunned by the hostility in Althea's voice, Daphne's mouth parted slightly as she stared at the friend she'd known since her first year in high school. Race had never come between them—ever. Somehow, they'd made their way through that particular minefield early on and had been loyal friends for more than a decade, respectful of their differences and appreciative of the many points where their interests and intellects intersected.

"This is not about 'slumming' with the *black folks*, Althea," Daphne said, keeping her voice low and attempting to hide the hurt. She noticed that Kendra had retreated to the corner of the bedroom and slid into a shabby, upholstered chair. "This is about how scared I am to be doing what I'm about to do. What are you playing the race card for?"

A painful silence ensued. Then Althea said softly, "I'm sorry, Daph. I was out of line."

Daphne put her arm around her childhood friend and said, "Thank you."

"I guess my feelings were hurt when you didn't like all this stuff I bought, when it was 'specially for you 'cause of what you said to your brother that time."

"I'm really grateful for all the trouble you went to, getting it and bringing it up from New Orleans. And I'm sorry I said it made us look like working girls, but, jeeze, Althea... have a little pity. These clothes are so... revealing."

Althea gave Daphne's shoulder a squeeze to show she'd forgiven her. "I know it takes guts to put it all out there," she replied slowly, "and I don't just mean putting on a short skirt. But anybody who had the courage to run out of Saint Louis Cathedral like you did can suck it up enough to wear a lil' ol' miniskirt. C'mon!" she said encouragingly. "I think that underneath all that Miz Magnolia stuff your mama's laid on you since you were in kindergarten is a real *bombshell*, waiting to make her wild woman debut."

For several long moments, Daphne stared at her reflection in Maddy's mirror while Kendra and Althea looked on. Her legs seemed ten yards long.

"Oh... what the hell," she said finally. "I'll wear it."

"You *will*?" Althea asked in a startled voice.

"I will." Daphne repeated firmly. "I will wear it and you will *weep*, Althea LaCroix!" The tops of her breasts bulging above the strapless bronze bustier could have passed for a pair of Triple A League softballs. Worse still, her miniskirt left her even more exposed. How in the world would it look to have a harp nestled between thighs clad only in see-through, come-hither black net opera hose, she worried, cringing at the thought?

"*Ta-daaaaa*," Althea crooned into a make-believe microphone. "I give you the one... the only... 'Harp Honey'!"

"Turn 'round." Kendra giggled softly. "Well... smack my mama! Every guy in that bar's gonna think you look good 'nuf to eat!" She glanced at her plastic watch. "I told Daddy we'd meet Ebner and him by nine thirty at the bar. He was gonna take a little nap, so's to help his cold, you know?"

"C'mon," Daphne groaned, "Let's get out of here before Maddy sees us or someone calls the fashion police."

❦

The three musicians needn't have worried that the Natchez authorities had the Under-the-Hill Saloon under surveillance. The place was nearly deserted at the worrisome hour of nine thirty. In addition, the women had another problem. Two big problems, in fact.

"That was Mama," Kendra said, tucking her cell phone back into her purse as the threesome huddled in the restroom at the back of the club. "Daddy's been coughing something fierce all day and Mama called the doctor late this afternoon. The doc says no way can he play tonight. He might have walking pneumonia, or something! Mama's really worried. He's starting to take antibiotics, she says."

"Pneumonia," Daphne gasped. "Oh, no!"

"It's okay... it's okay," Althea assured her. "Willis just needs some rest, and I'm here, remember? We'll miss the sax, but I'll play solo keyboard and it'll sound fine."

"Ah... something else bad's happened, Mama said," Kendra said, glancing nervously between Daphne and her idol. "Ebner's car done broke down. In Baton Rouge. Even if he gets it fixed, he told Mama that he can't get here by ten o'clock."

"Oh... m'God," Daphne said, horrified. "No drummer? How am I going to sing in time to the music? I'll be terrible without a drummer."

"You're a graduate of *Juilliard*, for God's sake," Althea scolded. "Kendra plays her bass hot and heavy, and just listen to me for a downbeat."

Daphne gulped air and tried to calm the square dance in her stomach. "We can't call ourselves the Willis McGee Quintet," she pointed out, "if we aren't *five* members, and Willis isn't here. Oh, Jesus! This is horrible!"

The women exchanged worried looks.

"Hmmm... the name's definitely a problem," Althea agreed.

"How 'bout calling ourselves the Real Bad Girls?" Kendra proposed.

"Naw..." Althea replied, shaking her head. "Too obvious."

Daphne brightened and snapped her fingers. "I've got it! We're an all-women band tonight, right? How about calling ourselves the Aphrodite Jazz Ensemble?"

"We're only three people, for God's sake!" Althea groused.

"Who's Aphro-whatsit?" Kendra asked meekly.

"Aphrodite. The goddess of love," Althea said briskly.

"*And* beauty!" Daphne said.

"Greek stuff," Althea informed Kendra. She turned to her childhood friend, and added dryly, "Very classy, Daphne. Typical." Then she grinned. "Oh, what the hell. We're desperate. Hardly anyone's out front, anyway. Let's just have some fun, okay?" She slapped her musical partners gently on their backsides and then glanced at the clock hanging crookedly on the wail above the paper towel dispenser.

"Well... y'all get ready," Althea declared, all business now. "It's just 'bout show time, ladies."

"Oh, m'God," Daphne groaned, reality returning with a thud. She winced at the thought of Simon Hopkins and Cousin Maddy sitting among the deserted tables and chairs out front while she sang, half naked, with an electrified concert harp nestled between her exposed thighs.

At least if Magnolia Mama ever gets wind of this little caper, Daphne thought gratefully, *I'll be safely back in New York.*

Meanwhile, Althea, hidden off stage, approached a standing microphone and announced with professional panache, "Ladies and Gentleman... five minutes to show time! Y'all get your drinks and come right down front for a ringside seat. Get ready to give a big, warm round of applause to... *the Aphrodite Jazz Ensemble!*"

CHAPTER 12

MARCH 27

S IM COULD SMELL STALE smoke outside on the sidewalk even before he and Madeline Whitaker entered the Under-the-Hill Saloon.

"Oh, dear," the older woman exclaimed. "I just *knew* I'd be overdressed." She fretted self-consciously, referring to the black cocktail sheath she'd donned for the occasion.

"It's so dark in here," he reassured her, "nobody will notice what *either* of us is wearing." He guided his companion toward a raft of empty tables and chairs positioned near the raised bandstand.

"I haven't been down here since I was a girl," Madeline disclosed, glancing around the room curiously, "and even then, I had to sneak in behind my mama's back. She called the predecessor to the Under-the-Hill Saloon 'that bucket of blood,' and forbade my sister and me from setting foot in the place." She gave a girlish laugh, and then added conspiratorially, "We did come here with our beaux, of course, and loved it." Again she surveyed the dark den and sighed. "Oh, my. There doesn't seem to be much of an audience tonight, does there? Poor Daphne."

Sim spotted one table, however, where three patrons were sitting sipping their drinks. He waved and escorted the harpist's cousin across the room to greet Bailey Gibbs and Otis and Liz Keating.

"I understand you all already know Madeline Whitaker?" Sim said.

"Know her," Bailey Gibbs exclaimed delightedly as he promptly rose to his feet and made a courtly bow. "We're kissing cousins, aren't we, Maddy, dear? Come here, darlin', and give me a peck on the cheek. It's been too long."

Maddy roundly bussed Dr. Gibbs on his proffered cheek and hugged the Keatings as well. "Why, what serendipity. All our families go way, way back," she disclosed for Sim's benefit, "but since I haven't been out in so long, I haven't seen these wonderful folks for ages. What a treat to be with y'all tonight."

"Likewise, Maddy girl," Bailey said, patting the seat beside him. "Now, you just sit right down here and tell me all about yourself lately. Your note about my darlin' Caroline was most appreciated, and thank you again for those lovely flowers you brought to the church."

"Has it been that long since we've seen each other?" Madeline asked with a look of chagrin. "I do apologize to all of you. With Daphne here in Natchez, I seem to be getting a bit of my ol' zest back."

Dr. Gibbs sobered and patted the hand of the widow and mother of his former patients. "We understand completely, darlin', what you've been through. No one more than I."

Sim ordered drinks from an emaciated young man with stringy hair and dirty blue jeans, and wondered if their small party would be the only ones out front for Daphne's big night. He knew all too well what it felt like to throw a party to which nobody came.

At the opening of the first one-man show of his pictures held in a San Francisco gallery, the only attendees at the opening were his mother and father, his sister Brooke, and a few fraternity brothers from his Stanford days. Francesca—then his girlfriend—had shown up late, explaining that she'd been stuck researching a brief for a senior partner at her law firm. Afterward, one of his college buddies took him aside and said that on his way to the gallery he'd stopped off for a drink at the Boulevard Bar—a see-and-be-seen watering hole near the financial district. Less than an hour earlier, he'd spotted Francesca shooting the breeze over beers with a bunch of colleagues.

Upon reflection, Sim wished he'd paid more attention to that little white lie of Francesca's. Even in her early twenties, she'd a bad habit of shading the truth just enough to give everyone else the feeling that *they'd* done something wrong.

Sim heard a burst of laughter and turned around. He was relieved to see that a few patrons had ambled over from the bar and taken seats at the next table. Another explosion of raucous mirth erupted from the back of the room as several couples walked through the front door and ordered a round of tequila shooters. Daphne's audience tonight was sure different from the attendees of Oberlin Chamber Orchestra concerts, he thought worriedly. He wondered how she was feeling right about now.

Scared witless, probably. She was a gutsy lady to try something like this, he thought admiringly, even if it was only a lark. She was gutsy *and* beautiful *and* talented *and*… geographically unsuitable.

Or am I the one who's geographically unsuitable?

True, sometimes he left a place with mild regret, but more often than not, it was with profound relief. There were always new landscapes to photograph and elusive birds to track. Both these distractions kept him from thinking too much about the past or the sadness he always connected with the fabled City by the Bay. One thing he knew for sure. If he and Daphne Duvallon remained in *this* place for much longer, the chameleonlike harpist would have to use those long legs of hers to run very fast, indeed, to avoid his proposal that they head straight for his suite in the Monmouth Hotel and—

"Ladies and gentlemen…"

Sim's thoughts were interrupted by a sultry voice making an announcement over the public address system. Suddenly, three good-looking young women in micro miniskirts, stop-the-presses strapless tops, and wickedly high heels burst on stage wearing the kind of headsets preferred by call-center switchboard operators. With campy abandon, the trio slithered toward their musical instruments and immediately struck up the Paul Desmond instrumental "Take Five"—with Daphne performing a dazzling jazz solo on her harp.

"Oh, my land…" Madeline Whitaker murmured, leaning toward Sim's ear. "No *wonder* the girls said they wanted their outfits to be a surprise and wouldn't let me come upstairs."

"*That's* Daphne Whitaker Duvallon?" Bailey Gibbs whispered with astonishment as he gaped in the direction of the leggy blonde with a halo of golden hair cascading fetchingly to her shoulders.

Sim might well have asked the same question himself. He could hardly believe the arresting sight of the scantily clad woman who sat beside an incongruously formal gilded concert harp. Her cheeks were faintly flushed as she played the tune with lowered eyes glued to the harp strings as if her life depended on them.

At the end of the opening number, Althea LaCroix greeted the scattered applause with a broad smile and stepped up to the standing mike. "So glad y'all came to be with us tonight," she purred to the crowd as if the place were packed to the rafters. "We hope to make it worth your while…"

One or two wolf whistles filled the air, while the group quaffing tequila shooters back at the bar stamped their feet in appreciation and began to seek seats nearer the small stage. Daphne righted her harp and briefly rubbed the palms of her hands on the seat cushion. Althea nodded her thanks to the small crowd and smoothly introduced her compatriots. "For our second tune," she announced, oozing confidence, "we'd like to do an old standard… but do it *our* way, right, ladies?"

Kendra and Daphne nodded, and Sim was relieved to note that a mischievous smile tugged at the corners of Daphne's mouth. Maybe he was more nervous than she was! Where in the world was the long-haired drummer, not to mention Willis McGee? he wondered.

Meanwhile, Daphne gracefully tipped the golden instrument against her bare shoulder again and pulled the soundboard between long legs encased in the sheerest of black net stockings. It was a gesture so casual, yet so sensual, that Sim felt an unanticipated jolt of desire. Like some college freshman watching a wet T-shirt contest, he was helpless to prevent his gaze from zeroing in on the amazing article of clothing gracing Daphne's torso.

It was strapless. It glittered. And it nearly put him in cardiac arrest!

His gaze was drawn inexorably to where her breasts spilled over the top of a—what the hell were those tight-fitting things called? he wondered.

Good Christ! Dressed like that, the woman was a lethal weapon, he thought. *And get a load of Althea LaCroix and Willis McGee's daughter!*

He was amazed that the bandleader hadn't vetoed an ensemble so provocative that any responsible parent would have dug a moat between the stage and the audience and filled it with alligators.

As the trio smoothly swung into "The Very Thought of You," Sim craned his neck to see if Willis McGee would make an appearance anytime soon. Maybe he and the drummer had passed out backstage from shock. He glanced around the club and saw a few folks had entered from the street and were headed for the empty tables down front.

"Oh, my land…" Daphne's cousin exclaimed for the second time, observing the males in the group shoulder each other in an attempt to claim seats closest to the bandstand. Sim noticed that the slightest hint of a smile now creased Maddy's lips.

"Daphne's a knockout in that outfit, don't you think?" Sim whispered loudly over the music.

"If you *didn't* think that, I'd figure you're unconscious," Maddy replied, her head nodding in time to the rhythm. "One thing is for sure… I'm very glad her mama's nowhere in the vicinity."

Sim silently seconded the motion.

The first musical set offered by the Aphrodite Jazz Ensemble ran the gamut of his favorite Billie Holiday blues songs, along with several jazz standards, and eventually, a couple of rollicking numbers in which Daphne's harp and husky solos sounded as if they belonged to a rock 'n' roll band.

Sim looked on with astonishment as the Juilliard-trained musician and her club-singing friend, Althea LaCroix, embarked on a rompin', stompin' duet, a signature tune often performed by the legendary Etta James, called "I've Got the Will."

Halfway through the number, Althea took off on a solo keyboard riff while Daphne stood up from her harp stool and commenced a highly suggestive—but somehow ladylike—bump-and-grind while thumping the harp strings like a bass player. Her performance was an intoxicating mix of blatant sexuality with a dash of the girl-next-door, and for Sim, it prompted a rush of heat that could prove embarrassing.

Daphne's provocative display incited hoots and hollers from the small group of men at the next table. Several couples leapt to their feet and started dancing around the tables. Sim felt an almost uncontrollable urge to start dancing himself. Instead, he glanced over his shoulder at the sound of a swarm of people, curious to see what all the excitement was about, coming through the open door from Silver Street.

Near the end of the tune, another group of tourists who had been strolling toward the gambling boat *Lady Luck* were diverted into the Under-the-Hill Saloon by the seductive sounds of the trio roaring toward the conclusion of the Otis Redding number as if they'd been performing it together all their lives.

"If there's a will, girl… there's got to be a way, now!" Althea sang in a powerful, throaty voice while looking steadily at Daphne, as if her words were aimed directly at her friend and musical colleague.

For her part, the harpist had closed her eyes, singing and swaying to the song's pounding rhythm, as if every note moved her down to her toes.

By this time, the club was more than half full. When Althea, Kendra, and Daphne stomped their feet during the final notes of *"I got the will now, but I can't find my way…"* the thunderous applause was nearly drowned out by piercing whistles and cheers that bounced off the club's brick walls.

Once the clapping finally subsided, the trio smoothly segued into a slow, sultry rendition of "Body and Soul," followed by the old standard "I'll Be Seeing You," and finally a moody, heart-tugging rendition of Gershwin's "Summertime."

"Do you suppose Daphne's stuck a microphone somewhere in that thing?" Sim hissed into Maddy's ear. He was astounded by the vibrant, mellow sounds of an instrument that had proved tonight that it could hold its own against Kendra's emphatic bass guitar and Althea's hard-charging keyboard.

"She must have…" Maddy murmured. She turned to Sim with eyes that almost appeared sad. "You know, don't you," she said, cupping her hand near his ear, "if she's *this* good singing and playing jazz and blues, and heaven knows what all… she's gonna face a lot of hard decisions when she goes back to New York tomorrow."

New York? *Tomorrow?*

Until that very moment, Simon Hopkins hadn't allowed himself to acknowledge that the sexiest, most intriguing woman he'd ever met was about to fly out of his life.

❧

Daphne could feel perspiration trickling between her breasts and shoulder blades. It was only March, but under the hot lights, it felt as if she were swimming in a bayou in July. The audience had kept them on stage for so long, she prayed that the batteries in her headset mike would last the night.

A sea of smiling faces beamed at her from all sides, but there were two people she hadn't dared to look at even once during the evening: Cousin Maddy and Sim. A signal rang in her brain, warning her to focus only on the music, the beat, and the mysterious river of sound that had carried her successfully, thus far, through the miraculous performance, even if there was no drummer keeping time, nor the comforting presence of Willis McGee. She marveled, in fact, at the mystifying musical telepathy that had allowed Althea, Kendra, and her to play and sing all night as one instrument. Now, however, something else was called for, and she was scared to death.

She felt as if she were looking through one of Sim's telephoto lenses when Althea began to thank the audience for their wonderful reception and introduce their last number for the night. She realized with a jolt that the group's concluding song wouldn't have as great an impact unless it was sung to a solitary male. The tune worked like gangbusters if the guy was good-looking and sexy as hell, and there was only one candidate in the room who fit that description.

In for a penny, in for a pound, she thought, silently quoting Cousin Maddy's advice from years before when Daphne worried her about signing the loan for her forty-thousand-dollar harp.

"And so, ladies and gentlemen," Althea announced with a wink, "we'll let Daphne here take the lead in our final number. It's by that genius songwriter, David Fishberg... and all you guys out there—I strongly advise you to listen up!"

Laughter masked the first four bars of the vamp. By the last count of the intro, Daphne finally summoned the guts to flick the air with one stiletto heel and cast a shameless come-hither look at Simon Hopkins that could have waylaid a humvee.

> Peel me a grape...
> Crush me some ice...
> Skin me a peach... save the fuzz for my pillow...
> Talk to me nice... talk to me nice...
> You've got to wine me and dine me...

A flicker of a smile pulled at one corner of Sim's mouth when Daphne arched an eyebrow and wagged her finger at him across the footlights.

> Don't try to fool me...
> Be-jewel me,
> Either amuse me... or lose me.
> I'm gettin' hungry...
> Peel me a grape!

Appreciative chuckles rippled through the audience. Sim, however, held her gaze with such intensity that the four walls of the club seemed to vanish. It was as if there were just the two of them, as if they were alone in the Lovell Room, each wondering who would be the first to make a dive toward the towering plantation bed that dominated the room.

Daphne abandoned her harp during the musical bridge and began to prowl around the small stage area like a restless tigress, always keeping her eyes riveted on the good-looking man at the front-row table—much to the delight of everyone in the room. Daringly she broke the "fourth wall" and ventured into the sea of small tables, illuminated only by candles in cheap red glass containers, while Althea and Kendra pounded out the melody.

Daphne's progress was tracked by the single spotlight to which the scruffy-looking assistant bartender was assigned when he wasn't pouring tequila shooters. Enveloped in a glittering shaft of light, she made her way to Sim's table and brought her face eye-level with his while running her fingers through his generous head of dark brown hair.

> Pop me a cork…
> French me a… fry…

She felt the thrill of the blatant seductress and knew, suddenly, absolutely, how drawn she was to this man she had met barely a week ago. She reveled in her power to beguile him with song, with her sexy attire, with all the feminine wiles she possessed, yet without feeling one whit like a magnolia!

> Entertain me…
> Champagne me…
> Show me you love me…
> Kid glove me…

She gently touched a forefinger to the tip of his nose and felt—bizarrely—honest!

Whatever this night might hold, she knew with certainty that this moment was authentic. Even so, she would proceed only if she could ask for what she wanted and have a better-than-even chance of getting it. And since she was returning to New York in precisely twelve hours, their relationship was unlikely to progress beyond the pure enjoyment of revealing to Sim what might have been. With a flick of an eyelash, a sultry, searchlight stare, she joyously indulged in the freedom the music afforded to put her metaphoric cards on the table.

> When I say "do it"…
> Hop to it!

By the last chorus, she had worked her way back, step by slinky step, to her harp. She took great pleasure in slowly, sensuously,

drawing the instrument toward her body and finishing the song
with a staccato flick of a string.

>*I'm getting hungry…*
>*Peel me… a grape!*

A moment of rapt silence hung in the air like secondhand
smoke. Then someone near the back gave a piercing wolf whistle
soon followed by others, as well as by shouts, foot-stomping, and
thunderous applause. Daphne's gaze swept the room. People were
waving empty glasses over their heads. Others were clapping their
hands and putting their fingers between their lips and whistling like
New Yorkers in search of a cab.

At Sim's table, everyone was laughing and hugging each other
and clapping wildly as if they'd just won the lottery. Sim, however, sat motionless in his seat with a stunned expression on his face.
Finally, he broke into a broad grin and, looking only at Daphne, patted his chest just over his heart. Althea then grabbed Kendra's right
hand and Daphne's left and dragged them forward to take a bow.

"No encores!" she commanded her troops over the continuing
uproar. "Let's beat feet outta here while we're still ahead!"

Daphne squeezed Althea's hand in a signal of agreement, and
the three members of the ad hoc Aphrodite Jazz Ensemble took
one last bow, then made a dash for the exit with the sound of the
audience demanding just one more song ringing in their ears.

Jack Ebert leaned against the bar for support. The sound of applause
reverberated on all sides of the room while he tried to regain his
equilibrium. This was not exactly what he'd expected when he'd
read the brief announcement in the *Natchez Democrat*.

>*Saturday evening, classically trained harpist*
>*Daphne Duvallon will be joining Willis McGee's*
>*group for a one-night-only performance at the*
>*Under-the-Hill Saloon.*

There had been no Willis McGee on the bandstand tonight, and what in the world was that black bitch, Althea LaCroix, doing on stage posing as the leader of the pack? Daphne had acted like a whore up there dressed in that miniskirt and that thing that pushed up her tits till they were practically under her chin. *Yes... a whore!* Jack thought, resentful of the faint throbbing between his legs. He *hated* having a physical response to a woman he loathed, especially when she'd flaunted her hooters in the face of that goddamned photographer tonight.

"Peel me a grape!"

Yeah, sure, Jack thought. *I'd like to peel her—*

Jack reminded himself that he had another agenda. He'd figured that Simon Hopkins might show up for this gig. Antoinette Duvallon had told Alice Ebert—and his mother, of course, had told *him*—that the pair had hung out together all during King's wedding reception and obviously had something going between them.

Briefly, Jack wondered if they'd slept together yet. Probably not, he concluded, his eyes narrowing as he stared at the back of Hopkins's head. Daphne might flaunt her ass in public like she did tonight—little cock teaser—but she'd sure been slow to come across with the goods during their engagement.

Jack would just as soon forget the night he'd finally got into her pants—and then couldn't do anything about it. She'd been silent and accepting of his failure to get it up that first time, and that made it even worse. He liked it hot. He liked it dangerous. Daphne had wanted moonlight and magnolias, and he found all that a total turnoff. In fact, she was probably the *reason* that sometimes he couldn't get a—

Jack gulped down the rest of his drink and summoned a vision of the flame-haired Cindy Lou Mallory standing in a dark corner of WWEZ-TV's tape vault. She'd shown up late one night after he'd broadcast one of his film reviews. He'd made *her* hot enough that time, hadn't he? Now, there was a woman who was so oversexed she'd do it upside down in a trash can.

The group at Simon Hopkins's table stood up as if preparing to depart. Jack set his empty glass on the bar and strolled purposefully in the direction of the deserted bandstand. He halted ten feet away from Daphne who, by this time, had changed into slacks and a demur white, long-sleeved cotton shirt.

Jack watched as his ex-fiancée received plaudits from family and friends.

"Bravo!"

"Hey, great job, Daphne!"

"Splendid, my dear!"

He ambled toward the group with greetings of his own.

"Hey, Daphne. Quite an act you had goin' tonight. Can't wait to give your mama my review of your… ah… *performance*."

What he sure as hell wasn't going to tell anyone was that he'd checked on a few things when he'd heard she had the hots for this guy and couldn't believe what he'd discovered about Simon Chandler Hopkins of San Francisco, California. Meanwhile, Daphne had turned her head and was staring at him with an expression that went from shock to fury.

"Why do you do this, Jack?" she demanded, surprising him with her directness, especially in front of all these people. "Why do you follow me around like some stalker, or something? And why are you still in Natchez? Don't tell me that you traded your Texas job for running your daddy's mortuary here in town?"

The bitch knew that was just the sort of thing that would rile him the most, he thought, as cold, hard anger swept over him. However, he forced himself to smile and shook his head.

"Much as it may surprise you, Daphne, I didn't come here to see *you*." He nodded at the silent group clustered around her, and said with forced geniality, "Sorry to interrupt." He put out his hand to Simon Hopkins. "I'm a former journalist and TV arts critic and a great admirer of yours, Mr. Hopkins. I just had to come over and say hello. Over the years, I've reviewed a couple of your books. I recognized you tonight from your picture on the jackets and I just wanted to have a chance to meet you in person."

The photographer looked at him skeptically, but made no challenge.

Jack glanced swiftly at the others standing nearby. "I once ran an Internet search on this man when I was doing those pieces, and I'm sure he's far too modest to tell you 'bout all the things he's accomplished." He returned his attention to Hopkins and smiled in a fashion he hoped the jerk found ingratiating. "Pretty impressive credentials. A double PhD in biology *and* ornithology from Stanford, huh? Plus a wife who's considered one of the smartest, most hardworking young attorneys in San Francisco ever to make full partner in one of the city's big law firms out there, am I right?"

"Ex-wife," Simon corrected. "I guess you need to update your Internet information."

Oh. Well, so what, sucker, Jack thought.

All the better for *his* purposes that Francesca Hayes wasn't married to the guy anymore, although it would have given him great pleasure if Daphne had picked another married man to make a fool of herself over.

So, he thought, making his farewells, he'd succeeded in nailing what he came here to find out. The toughest anti-environmental lawyer in the country was the former wife of *this* particular Simon Hopkins. What a piece of luck. He could kill two birds with one stone, so to speak. He nearly laughed aloud at his own joke.

He was startled when a short, white-haired member of Daphne's party took a step forward and rudely waved a finger at him. "Didn't I see you up in Jackson last week?" the old man demanded belligerently.

Jack was alarmed. He preferred that no one in Natchez know what was going on in the state capital. Let everyone think he was merely checking up on the latest funeral home his parents had purchased. The deal in Jackson was a stealth operation, and, for sure, Able Petroleum wanted to keep it that way.

"Hmm?" Jack temporized, reluctantly giving his attention to the pesky gadfly he'd seen at the hearing. "I don't think I've had the pleasure." He addressed Hopkins again. "Well, it was nice meetin' you in person. So long, everybody. Take care, Daphne," he said, smiling faintly in her direction.

"Now, just you wait, young man," the old goat persisted, visibly agitated. "You were with all those folks at the legislative subcommittee hearing who are trying to force those blasted toxic chemical dumps down our throats here in Mississippi."

"Bailey, I think you may be mistaken," Madeline Whitaker intervened gently. "Mr. Ebert works for Able Petroleum out of Texas."

"My point, exactly," the elderly physician exclaimed. "Able Petroleum also manufactures those pesticides and defoliants they've been spraying on cotton and everything else 'round here for forty years. It's been killing the birds, and probably the *people*. This fella and his ilk are wanting to bury that crap right next to my Caroline's bird sanctuary." He slammed his fist on the nearby cocktail table so hard that the red candle wobbled precariously.

"Of course, y'all know that there's another side to this story," Jack said smoothly, for the benefit of those standing nearby, "but you're probably too fatigued after Daphne's electrifyin' performance to listen to it, so I'll just say good night."

And as swiftly as he could, Jack Ebert headed for the exit.

Bailey Gibbs calmed down sufficiently from his discussion with Jack Ebert to gallantly offer to give Cousin Maddy a ride home so Sim and Daphne could take a walk by the river after the show.

Daphne faced the gentle, cooling breeze that swept up the bluff to where she and Sim stood looking down at the moonlit Mississippi far below. They both leaned against the encircling railing of a bandstand where summer concerts were offered for the enjoyment of Natchez's citizenry. The band gazebo was in the park adjacent to Rosalie, an impressive red brick mansion fronted by tall white columns built near the spot where once an eighteenth-century military fort had stood.

"I can't believe Jack Ebert had the nerve to show up at the club like that," Daphne fumed.

"What do you think he's actually doing up in Jackson?" Sim asked, gazing below at the path of moonlight dancing on the water.

"Spin doctoring. He's the public relations point man for Able Petroleum. He's probably orchestrating his company's entire campaign to site some of those toxic dumps in Mississippi, and that's why he's still hanging around here, more's the pity. Maybe it means that he's not deliberately bugging me," she said hopefully. "I should have known he'd be involved in something disgusting like this." She turned to study Sim's profile, and added, "Doesn't it give you the willies to know he's done a search on the Internet about you... and your wife?"

"Ex-wife," he reminded her gently.

"He even could describe her as the 'most hardworking attorney in San Francisco.' How would he find that kind of detail?"

"Newspaper clips online... that kind of stuff. Hey... it's a free country—and now it's a *wired* free country. There's very little privacy anymore." Then he smiled and glanced around at the grass carpet that blanketed the bluff. "However," he added with a wolfish grin, "it's pretty secluded right here at twelve thirty at night. I finally have a chance to tell you... privately... just what a terrific performance you gave tonight."

Daphne stared at her hands clutching the white wooden railing. "Thanks," she murmured. "It will seem really strange to go back to my normal life in New York on Monday."

Except it won't be normal because I'll have to scramble fast to find another steady orchestra job.

"So... you head for New Orleans tomorrow to get a plane back to Manhattan?"

Daphne glanced at her watch. "Yes. In less than... ten hours, in fact."

Sim pointed toward the river. "By tomorrow night, you'll be looking at the Hudson."

A moment's silence ensued.

"Hard to believe," she murmured.

"You know, Daphne, you were *more* than terrific tonight. You were sensational."

"I was *lucky*. Thank God Althea's such a pro. She saved my fanny more than once tonight. Literally. But, *really* thanks," she said with a grateful smile. "I was scared out of my wits to appear on public looking like I did... but Althea reminded me that it was time to retire my angel act."

Sim gently rested the fingers of one hand under her chin. "That was what was so fabulous about it," he insisted quietly. "You still looked like an angel... but no man in that audience tonight could possibly not want to—"

Sim didn't finish his sentence but instead leaned forward and slowly closed the short distance between them. His kiss was firm and confident, as if no heavenly intervention could save her from experiencing the softness of his lips, or the faint smell of the cognac they'd shared at the bar after everyone else had said their farewells. When the tip of his tongue gently, inquiringly brushed her mouth, it seemed the most natural thing in the world to welcome his touch. They moved toward one another as easily as if they'd decided to dance, pressing their bodies together to steady their kiss, which deepened, and was heading for the stratosphere. A warning voice in Daphne's head began its usual chatter, but all she wanted was to *feel*... feel Sim's thighs pressed against hers, feel his pelvis and the broad expanse of his chest crushed against her breasts.

Peel me a grape...

The seductive tune flitted through her consciousness with a consuming awareness that all she felt like "peeling" were the clothes off his back. When Sim's arms tightened around her shoulders, she felt an irresistible urge to pull his shirttail out of the waist of his trousers so she might touch his skin there... and in other places... intimate places. Sim's thoughts apparently mirrored her own, for he had begun to tug at the hem of the white blouse tucked neatly into her slacks.

"Telepathy..." she whispered.

"Do you have any idea what that last song of yours tonight made me want to do?"

"Me too." She reached up and framed his face with the palms of her hands, telling him wordlessly that she was perfectly aware that the attraction she felt when she was singing "Peel Me a Grape" was mutual.

You've got to wine me... and dine me...

The man had certainly done that, and now he was kissing her again in a fashion that could lead only in the direction of the huge plantation bed in Room 23 at Monmouth—and what a delicious idea *that* might be…

Sim sensuously brushed his lips against the base of her throat and then worked his way around to the sensitive spot near the nape of her neck. Not to be outdone, she bowed her head slightly and returned the favor, flicking her tongue against the hollow near his collarbone, sampling the salty taste of his skin. She felt as giddy as a teenager necking in a car. When Sim's hand cupped her breast and his thumb strafed her nipple through the fabric of her cotton blouse, she pressed her own hand on top of his, wanting more.

"This is getting… kind of silly…" he whispered into her ear between nibbling kisses. "We're both grown-ups, aren't we? Come to Monmouth with me tonight?"

"Oh… Sim…" she murmured, not wanting him to speak but merely to continue kissing her hair, her eyes, the tip of her nose.

"The song said you're hungry… remember?" He slid both his hands down to her hips and pressed their bodies together, the evidence of his stimulated state impossible to ignore. "Well, so am I."

Strangely, the exquisite feel of this man fully aroused brought her back to reality with an unwelcome thud.

Don't try to fool me… bejewel me…

Who was she kidding, demanded the sane part of her cerebral cortex. This man was just passing through town. There were no jewels in her future, no commitment of any kind. This was the classic setup for a one-night stand. The shocking thing was: part of her said "Why not?" while her core fought against any action that would leave her feeling bereft—again.

Breathless, she broke their kiss and shook her head.

"This isn't silly… this is nuts!" she said, meeting his puzzled gaze.

"What do you mean?" he asked warily.

"I come to Monmouth with you, and then what? Rush home to Bluff House, pack, and drive like a madwoman to catch my plane in New Orleans for New York? And after that, what exactly do you see happening?"

"We'll have a chance to see where all of this is leading," he proposed.

"Long distance?" she asked, attempting to make her voice sound light and pleasant. "Honestly, given the geography involved, how realistic is it that this could lead to anything other than a great, big diversion that, eventually, we'd give up?"

Sim studied her thoughtfully. "Since it's true… living on opposite coasts is definitely a challenge, why don't we just take this thing one step at a time?" He shot her a crooked grin, and said teasingly, "Step one: the Lovell Room at that temple of Southern romance, Monmouth Plantation."

Daphne stiffened and took a step back. She turned toward the river and spoke into the darkness that stretched toward the *Lady Luck* below.

"Here's the deal, Sim. There is absolutely no question that I'm highly… drawn to you," she began, searching for words that would express how she truly felt. "But at this point in my life, I'm not interested in casual—or difficult—relationships. I'm just not." She turned to gaze directly into his eyes. "So I guess I'm not the type of woman that a traveling man should ask back to his hotel room. And I totally apologize for not thinking all that through before we started… kissing," she finished lamely.

"But *you're* the one who's traveling this time," he protested.

"Right—and I'm not coming back to Natchez."

"There's always our cell and video phones, not to mention email and texting each other," he pointed out. "And of course, frequent flyer miles, of which I've banked thousands."

"I don't think so…"

"But we haven't had enough time to know where this… this obvious attraction for one another might go. Can't you take a chance that if we're together tonight, it could lead toward something very important for both of us?"

"With an emphasis on the *could*, I presume?" Daphne asked tartly. "What you've just said makes my answer easier. I can't afford to take any more emotional risks right now. Frankly, I just don't trust *my* judgment."

Sim seized her hand and pressed it against his heart. "Can't you trust *this*?" he demanded, almost angry.

"I'm sorry… but no. *Especially* not that."

They stared at each other in silence.

"Well, then…" he said with finality, "I guess that's it. I seem to remember we wandered down this road a few days ago."

"You're right. We did," she said, her voice tight. "I'm so sorry, Sim."

Ignoring her apology he replied, "Shall I take you home?"

She nodded and they walked silently back to his car. Thankfully, the drive to Bluff House took less than three minutes. Daphne smiled sadly at Sim.

"Good night," she whispered finally, turning toward the passenger door to make her exit. Then she looked back across the short distance between them, gazing at his striking profile one last time. "All the best with the Audubon project. I can't wait to buy the book."

Sim merely nodded as he stared out the windshield. Then he turned his head toward her, and said softly, "Good night, Daphne. You were great at the club tonight. Whatever you decide about your musical future, you have a fan who'll buy all your CDs."

Daphne did her best to ignore the lump in her throat as she fumbled for the handle to the car door. Once she'd made her escape, she strode quickly toward the welcoming beacon Maddy had left on to guide her to the veranda.

"Hey, Ms. Magnolia!" Sim called after her in the dark.

She turned.

"What's your email address?" he demanded, and then exclaimed, "Oh, damn! I don't have anything to write with."

"It's really easy," she announced, unable to suppress a pleased smile. "HarpHoney—all one word—at Gmail dot com."

"I can remember that," he said. Then, Sim put his well-traveled Range Rover in gear and swiftly disappeared down the drive.

CHAPTER 13

MARCH 28

THE NEXT MORNING, DAPHNE opened her eyes in her room atop Bluff House and immediately felt a blanket of depression settle over her as heavily as the handmade quilt that rested on the bottom of the mahogany bedstead.

New York...

Good God, was she ever not in the mood for rude cab drivers and crowded subways and hauling her harp down sidewalks and over curbs! Nor was she in the mood for her harp teacher's theatrics, or for facing the embarrassment of telling music colleagues around Manhattan that Rafe Oberlin had deep-sixed her from his chamber orchestra.

Myriad images drifted through her mind as she idly watched the frayed dimity curtains on the dormer window flutter on the river's breeze. She pictured herself, dressed to the nines, playing a marathon of teatime gigs at fancy hotels—just to make a buck—while she auditioned for another "big time" orchestra job which she would ultimately grow to hate.

Then, of course, there was the twice-weekly chore of carrying her groceries in heat and humidity, rain, sleet, or snow from the corner One-Stop—where the packages of Twinkies were at least three years old—up five flights of dingy stairs to her tiny apartment on Sixteenth Street. And what could be more annoying than sitting in the Washing Well for hours waiting for her clothes, sheets, and towels to dry, or running for a bus, only to discover she didn't have the exact change?

Was she ever not in the mood to go back to New York!

Was she ever not in the mood to deal with the high-pressured ego-maniacal rat race that constituted the modern world of classical music.

And was she ever *not* in the mood to leave Natchez.

A soft knock on her door interrupted her unhappy reverie. "Daphne, dear," Maddy called softly. "Much as I hate to tell you for my own sake, it's nearly seven o'clock, darlin', and I think you'd better—"

"I don't want to go," Daphne announced, sitting bolt upright in bed.

The door inched open and Maddy poked her head inside the room.

"What did you say, dear?"

"I don't want to go. I don't want to fly back to New York and start that life all over again. I just *don't*! And besides, I got fired from the chamber orchestra for coming to King's wedding instead of playing our concert debut at Lincoln Center."

Madeline advanced into the room, concern etched into her features. She gestured questioningly at the bottom of Daphne's bed where Groucho was curled up, fast asleep.

"Yes, please. Sit, Maddy," Daphne urged, her heart pounding in her chest with the same velocity it had the evening she told five hundred wedding guests in Saint Louis Cathedral that the ceremony was off. "I want to move to Natchez."

"You *do*?" Maddy exclaimed, an expression of delight erasing the furrows on her brow. "Are you *sure*, sugar? You're not just feelin' bad 'bout gettin' fired?"

"No..." Daphne said slowly. "I'd like to try it out here for a year. Explore a different sort of music... blues, jazz, Dixieland. Learn from musicians like Willis McGee and Althea."

"Did I hear my name taken in vain?" asked a husky voice from the hallway. Maddy's other houseguest appeared in the doorway clad in a threadbare bathrobe, toothbrush in hand. "Man, oh man," Althea complained, "what I let this white girl get me into." She shook her head and added good-naturedly, "I've got permanent indentations on my rib cage from that danged bustier."

"Daphne's just said she wants to move to Natchez for a year… to study jazz and such," Maddy announced, astonishment written all over her.

"She *what*?" Althea exclaimed. A broad grin spread across her face. "Well, whaddaya know? Our harp angel's heading back down to earth?" Then her eyes narrowed, and she said, "This doesn't happen to have anything to do with Bird Man, does it?"

Daphne blushed and remained silent for a moment. It was a fair question. She turned the query over in her mind and then shook her head. "No," she answered simply. Her decision had nothing to do with the whereabouts of Sim Hopkins, and that knowledge buoyed her spirits tremendously. "Bird Man will move on to the next assignment before long, and since I declined to accompany him back to his hotel suite after our gig last night, who knows if I'll ever hear from him again."

"Pity…" Maddy murmured and then appeared embarrassed for thinking out loud.

"Okay…" Althea said, ignoring her hostess's lapse. "But do you mind telling me the *other* reasons for doing this wild thing, girl?"

"Because I *want* to," Daphne replied, moving to the edge of the bed and dangling her feet over the side. Groucho jumped to the floor with an indignant yowl and headed for his food bowl in the kitchen. "I had more damn fun with you and the McGees this week than I've had the entire month rehearsing for an effing concert at Lincoln Center." She flushed slightly and turned toward her cousin. "Sorry, Maddy."

"Land, nothing you've been saying upsets me," Maddy said, waving her hand in the air. "What do y'all take me for? A fossil? I was the mother of a son, remember? I know you young people look at things differently than in my day… and in some ways, it's an improvement," she declared staunchly. "Now, back to the matter at hand. You propose to spend a year in Natchez playing and exploring jazz and popular music, am I right?"

"Exactly. I deserve to have a little enjoyment in life, for once."

Maddy patted Daphne's hand. "Well, first of all, I want you to know, darlin' girl, that you are most welcome to stay here. Have the whole top floor to y'self, if you want to. You'd be doing me a favor."

"Really?" Daphne said, her excitement mounting. "But I want to pay rent so you can get that homeowners insurance policy you've *got* to buy, Madeline Whitaker," she said sternly. "And I could help you with your harp students." She turned to look at Althea. "Don't you think I could get some weekday gigs at the restaurant in the Eola Hotel and places around here?" Althea nodded affirmatively. Then Daphne laughed, adding, "Maybe I'd even get a job playing electrified harp dressed as a dance hall girl in the bar on the *Lady Luck*?"

"If you really want to learn jazz," Althea said skeptically, "why not give yourself a year back in New Orleans?"

"With Magnolia Mama breathing down my neck? Are you crazy?" Daphne asked with mild irritation. "I'd have a *horrible* year!"

Althea grimaced. "Oh, yeah... I forgot."

"Why set myself up for trouble?" Daphne shrugged. "But on second thought, I'd certainly consider coming down to New Orleans for a job once in a while, if you asked me," she volunteered slyly. "I could hide out at Corlis and King's place in the Quarter when I'm in town. Mama doesn't dare walk in there unannounced."

"And I'd come up to Natchez for a job, if you asked me," Althea countered with a grin. "After all, now that we've launched the Aphrodite Jazz Ensemble, why don't we see if we can turn ourselves into *really* top women musicians?" Althea gaily wagged her toothbrush. "Maybe we could find some other players from around Miss-Lou?"

"What a great idea."

"You gotta make money to live on while you're here, right? Well, we won't get rich, but we might each clear two fifty, three hundred dollars apiece on the weekends headlining at a place like the *Lady Luck*... and maybe we could even get a slot at the New Orleans Jazz Fest by next year."

"You'd really commit to this thing?" Daphne asked with amazement.

"Sure!" Althea said, nodding. "I thought it was a total gas

last night, even though I 'bout split a gut trussed into those rigs we wore."

"You *did*?" Daphne said. "Loved playing last night, I mean?"

"You betcha," Althea replied.

"But, what about your job at Cafe LaCroix?"

"Don'tcha think I get tired of being bossed 'round by those brothers of mine on the bandstand, not to mention my daddy hollering at me to bring 'em all coffee? I love 'em all to death, but playing up here in Natchez is like a *vacation*. Why don't we figure out a schedule and see if we can get a steady booking for the weekends, once you get y'self back down here? My brother, Rufus, can double on keyboard in New Orleans on the nights I'm up here."

"Okay. We'll look for a steady job here," Daphne mused. "But we don't want to steal Willis's regular bread-and-butter gig at the Under-the-Hill Saloon." She gazed at her cousin questioningly. "If the *Lady Luck* turns us down, Maddy, maybe we could persuade the owners to have live music at the Pig Out Inn, on their back patio."

"You could certainly ask," Maddy replied encouragingly. "And there's also Biscuits and Blues... and maybe even the Magnolia Grill would consider hiring you to play nice and quiet a night or two during the week?"

"Boy, the Pig Out Inn and Biscuits and Blues are a long way from Lincoln Center, Ms. Duvallon," Althea said, suddenly doubtful. "You sure 'bout this?"

Daphne looked from Althea to Maddy and back to Althea. Her friend had a point. Did she really dare to do something as drastic as this? Did she honestly have the guts to kiss good-bye the opportunities she had in New York as a rising star in the world of orchestral music?

"Look," she said, as much to convince herself as Althea, "I can always go back to Manhattan if this doesn't work out."

But *could* she? Would her highly competitive friends and classical music colleagues in New York accept her again, or figure she'd been a total flop down south and give her the brush-off—while laughing behind her back?

Probably.

I'm just taking a year off, she reassured herself silently.

It would be like a sabbatical that academics are granted after a decade or so of teaching. For more than fifteen years now, she'd either been studying classical music or living the life of a professional musician. Considering her chronic stomachaches and the roller-coaster life she'd led thus far, wasn't it about time she took stock of where her life was heading?

"How long do you think it'll take you to close things down in New York and get back here?" Maddy inquired, beaming.

"If I'm lucky, I can wind things up in about a week, two at the outside. That'll give you time, Althea, to serve Cafe LaCroix notice that you'll be playing in Natchez on the weekends, right?"

"Right. While you're up north, I'll line up Kendra, for sure, and see if she knows anyone else around here of the female persuasion who can play drums."

"And what about a sax player—"

"Daphne, dear," Maddy interrupted, pointing to the bureau where a priceless cobalt blue, French enamel antique clock kept accurate time behind a cracked glass face. "If you plan to be on that plane out of New Orleans by three o'clock this afternoon—and you, Althea, intend to drive down with her—you've both got to get cracking, sugar pies!"

"Are we actually doing this?" Althea demanded in wonderment.

"We are actually *doing* this," Daphne replied emphatically.

The two women looked at each other, burst out laughing, and then clapped each other's palm in a joyous high five.

Daphne had no trouble selling her furniture and transferring the two-year lease on her apartment to a piccolo player in the chamber orchestra who had just broken up with her boyfriend and was thrilled that Daphne Duvallon was abandoning New York. However, Eleanor Beale, her harp teacher, was not at all pleased to hear Daphne's news.

"Are you out of your mind?" she cried. "You've decided to change the entire course of your life just because you sat in on some jam session and then played with a microphone stuck up inside your harp, as a... as a... *novelty* act... in some dive in a tiny town in the swamps of Louisiana?"

"Mississippi," Daphne corrected.

Ignoring her, Eleanor declared flatly, "Rafe will kill your career if you ever want to come back to New York. Granted, he thinks you're a brilliant talent, but if you bail out of the profession like this, he'll ruin you if you ever show your face here again. He'll tell colleagues that you're a flake... or hint you had a mental breakdown, or something."

"If Rafe thinks I'm such a 'brilliant talent,'" Daphne repeated quietly, "then, one year from today—should I decide to come back here—I'll be able to prove to other conductors that I'm still a good classical harpist."

"In this cutthroat old world, Daphne," Eleanor Beale replied with weary finality, "one must learn to play by the rules. And unless you do things 'the Rafe way,' even being top talent won't be good enough."

Eleanor's pronouncements gave Daphne pause. What if the old warhorse was right, after all? If Daphne insisted on pursuing this brave, perhaps foolish dream, was she royally burning all her bridges?

Shaken by the frigid smile her teacher had plastered on her heavily made-up features, Daphne had no choice but awkwardly to bid her a final farewell and not look back when the chilly stranger closed the door firmly behind her.

In the subway heading downtown, Daphne replayed the scene in Eleanor's music room, wondering briefly if she *had* completely lost her mind. Should she head for Juilliard, burst into Rafe's office, and beg the maestro to give her her job back?

By the time the train whizzed by the Forty-Second Street station, she found herself comparing the excitement and joy she'd experienced playing jazz and blues with Althea and Willis to the sheer dread that clutched at her stomach as a browbeaten member of the Oberlin Chamber Orchestra.

"No guts, no glory," she muttered ten minutes later when she opened the triple locks at her apartment. It was now empty except for the last of the cardboard boxes that Daphne's neighbor promised to give to UPS the following day. She glanced at her watch. The phone was due to be turned off at five o'clock. Her plane was at seven. She'd have a few moments before the cab arrived to take her to JFK to check her email on her laptop and write the last of her farewell notes.

Under "new mail" there were several messages from friends wishing her well, a short missive sent three days earlier from King and Corlis who had logged on at some cybercafe in Rome to tell her they were having a fabulous honeymoon, and a final entry monikered *Fogcityphotog*.

How long had it been there? she wondered, checking the date. It had arrived five days earlier. Her pulse beat a shade too fast for her to ignore. Her life had been so chaotic since she'd gotten back to New York that this had been her first chance in a week to check her email. She clicked the "read" button and quickly scanned Sim's brief note.

Greetings from the wilds of the Trace.
Hope the Big Apple still has bite.
Best, Sim.

Light and polite. Nothing more.

Well, what did she expect?

Should she answer?

What could she say—as briefly—that would match the minimal amount of effort he had expended in this cryptic communication? Her entire life had turned upside down. Try putting *that* into a two-line electronic message, Mr. Fog City Photog!

Just then, the buzzer sounded on her intercom. The cab had arrived.

"Gotta go," she said aloud. She pushed the intercom's talk button, and shouted, "Be right down!"

She swiftly clicked the "save as new" button, shut down her laptop, packed it inside its black leather case, and made one last survey of her five-flight walk-up.

She'd answer Sim's email when she arrived in Natchez.

Or not.

❧

Daphne's rented minivan was filled to overflowing with her baggage. She could barely see out the rear window as she drove north on Interstate 10 from the New Orleans airport. The April air positively had a *tang* to it, she thought happily as she sped past Oak Alley where azaleas and tulips bloomed everywhere in the surrounding gardens.

Unfortunately, she'd missed King and Corlis's return from their honeymoon by two days. However, they would likely be horribly jet-lagged, and she was anxious to get settled into her new routine. Furthermore, Daphne didn't want to risk running into her mother and father on the streets of the Big Easy. She'd tell everyone of her decision, once she knew what her daily routine would be.

A quick stop at South of the Border for a soft-shell crab sandwich, and before long, she was just minutes away from downtown Natchez. When she turned onto John Quitman Parkway, she noticed the sign pointing to the entrance to Monmouth Plantation. By her watch, it was two o'clock, with a bright sun high in the sky. A good day for shooting photographs. Simon Hopkins would be out in the woods someplace, stalking some rare bird life. Before she could stop herself, she turned into the long, curving gravel driveway and pulled into an empty space in the visitors' parking area.

"I'd like to leave a note for a guest?" she inquired politely of a pleasant-faced woman manning the reception area.

"Certainly," the desk clerk replied genially in her soft, lilting accent. "Here... let me get you some paper and somethin' to write with."

Daphne smiled gratefully and jotted down the news that she was back in Natchez and that she'd explain why when she saw Sim.

She folded the paper and handed it to the woman behind the desk with a broad smile. "Please give this to Mr. Hopkins when he returns tonight."

"Oh... but he's checked out," the desk clerk informed her. "'Bout a week ago, I think it was. I wasn't on duty that day. I can ask Mrs. Riches if he left a forwarding address... or perhaps you're friends? You can contact him at home."

"Oh…" Daphne said faintly. "Yes… I'll do that."

Well, that was short and sweet, she thought, fighting an avalanche of disappointment. Simon Hopkins… a man on the move. Was that such a surprise?

Daphne chastised herself roundly for the crushing sense of bereavement that overcame her. Bleakly, she nodded her thanks to the desk clerk and made her way back to the gravel parking lot, the scene of the dreadful confrontation with Jack Ebert.

She hadn't given Jack a single thought these last pressured days. Simon Hopkins, however, had been another matter. She had allowed mildly lascivious thoughts of him to filter through her brain while half asleep during the flight to Louisiana. And just this afternoon, as she cruised north into Mississippi, the pleasant notion that he'd be here in Natchez, waiting for an answer to his email, had made her impending new adventure even more exciting.

She climbed into her rented van and turned on the ignition. She recognized it as the moment when an entirely new life had begun. She was starting fresh. A totally clean slate. No personal complications. Hopefully, no more strange visitations from the "other" Daphne. And Simon Chandler Hopkins had done what he'd been doing for ten years: he'd moved on to the next location.

Perhaps it was better this way.

Perhaps.

CHAPTER 14

APRIL 6

I N THE COLD LIGHT of day, the Under-the-Hill Saloon looked like a... well... *saloon*, Daphne judged ruefully. Dust motes hung in a shaft of sunshine that illuminated a path from the front door into the gloomy interior. The stale cigarette smoke from years past, and the beer spilled on the bar and tables from the previous night, infused the air with an odor more reminiscent of a Tulane fraternity house than a jazz and blues club.

"Hey there, Miz Harpist," Willis McGee called, sitting at his electronic keyboard in a corner next to an upright piano. "Welcome back to Natchez!"

"Thanks. Hi, Kendra," Daphne replied, smiling at his daughter, dressed in Capri pants and a skintight, psychedelic green cotton T-shirt. "It's good to *be* back. I think," she added wryly. "It was such a whirlwind, getting myself out of New York, I'm still in kind of a daze." She reached for one of the spindly chairs tucked under a small cocktail table nearby and sat down on it, back to front. The seat felt slightly sticky, and she was glad she'd worn jeans.

"I'm sorry I was too under the weather to play our last gig," Willis apologized.

"Well, thank goodness you look a lot better than when I saw you last," she declared. "How're you feeling now?"

"Doc said I nipped the pneumonia in the bud."

Daphne was relieved to note that Willis actually looked pretty fit. His porkpie hat was cocked at a jaunty angle, and his face was clean-shaven.

"Well..." she drawled, looking from father to daughter. "Tell me the truth. Do y'all think I've lost my mind?"

Willis peered through the gloom from behind his thick, black-rimmed glasses and shook his head. "Not from the reports I keep getting about you Aphrodite gals." He pointed to his daughter. "She showed me the outfits y'all were wearing that night." He clucked his tongue a few times and a sly grin spread across his face. "I *said* 'You gotta do something these days to get folks to walk in the front door'—but man, you gals took me mighty seriously!"

"Blame Althea," Daphne said with an embarrassed laugh.

"Kendra's told me kinda what y'all are thinking of doing... but, maybe I have a suggestion that'll work out good for all of us."

Intrigued, Daphne grabbed herself a cup of coffee so potent, a spoon was likely to stand up on its own. "So... what are you thinking, maestro?"

Willis chuckled at the nickname and sounded pleased. "Well... Kendra and me have had a couple of good talks while you was up in New York. I told her that me and the boys is gettin' too old to play till two, three a.m. every night, you understand? So what I propose is this..." He pointed at some music charts piled on top of the piano. "She says you wanna spend a year learning 'bout the blues... jazz... all that stuff. So I think you've first gotta work at expanding your repertoire, you understand what I'm sayin'?"

"Definitely," Daphne agreed.

"Add more numbers for you and Althea to sing—solos and duets. That's gonna take some time. Meanwhile, you need a drummer and a sax player, and they've gotta be gals, if you're gonna keep this Aphrodite thing going, so..."

"So... Daddy thinks we should get my sister Jeanette to be part of the Aphrodites," Kendra intervened without preamble. "He just doesn't want you to think he's taking things over, or nothing." She pointed to the deserted set of drums in a darkened corner of the club. "Jeanette's real good on drums, believe me."

"That's a *great* idea!" Daphne had worried about finding such a key player. Then she added, "Let's run that by Althea."

"I already did," Kendra announced. "Jeanette drove down to New Orleans and sat in with Althea last Sunday afternoon while you was up north. She says 'fine.' And I have a friend who played very cool sax in my high school band. Sunny's her name. She'll come try out later this week, okay?"

"Terrific," Daphne replied, nodding. "But what about you, Willis? I said in the beginning of all this, we don't want to steal your gigs."

"Here's the rest of my idea," Willis proposed, warming to his subject. "Management here's glad as could be to have you singing and playing jazz harp, you know? So, let's say that when you do your thing with my trio—we'll get real fancy and call it the Willis McGee Quartet, okay? We'll just do one long set every evening with Daphne in regular clothes, and then you *gals* can come on for the late sets in your Aphrodite rigs, trying out new numbers every couple a nights, got it? A few days a week, I'll teach you more songs and help Althea with the arrangements, and, at the end of the day, we'll split the proceeds from everything both groups do, fifty-fifty. You pay yourselves and *your* extra musicians out of your pockets, I'll pay *mine*. Kinda like a music company, you see what I'm saying?"

"And once we get our whole act together," Kendra chimed in excitedly, "we can look for bookings all over the place, and Daddy'll still have his job here."

"By that time, girl, I hope y'all are making so much money I can do what your mama wants me to do and *reeee-tire*. Or, at least, just play daytime wedding receptions and stuff like that."

"That sounds really generous," Daphne said, touched by the amount of thought that the McGees had given to everybody's welfare. "I've got some savings to tide me over, but I'd better get busy hustling up a daytime job, maybe playing the tea service at the Eola Hotel, or someplace, so I don't get too far in the hole with this scheme."

"Don't forget Monmouth and the Governor Holmes House," Kendra suggested helpfully. "They do *tons* of swanky weddings and engagement parties. They'd probably love somebody playing harp

and dressed all fancy, along with Daddy's group, don'tcha think?"
she asked her father.

Willis grinned at Daphne. "You'd be a good addition and then
I can charge 'em more."

Daphne groaned. "I hate to say it, but you're probably right."

"When's Althea due to come up?" Willis inquired.

"By lunch on Friday," Daphne replied. "On the weekends
when she's in town, my cousin Madeline Whitaker's renting her a
room, too. Works out well, all around." She bit her lip in thought.
"We'd better meet with Jeanette and Sunny as soon as Althea gets
here so we can go over all the numbers we already know."

"That'll be cool," Kendra said, nodding. "Jeanette works the
lunch shift as a waitress at the Pig Out Inn and she's off by three.
Sometimes I help out, too."

Daphne merely nodded, thinking that the Pig Out Inn was
a far cry from the elegant Cafe Des Artistes where a lot of New
York musicians had been known to augment their incomes by
waiting tables.

Get used to it, Daphne. This is your new life.

"Now, no arguments, darlin'," Maddy insisted. "You'll have the
whole top floor to y'self. On the weekends, Althea can have my
old room on the second floor, and I'll be downstairs in the place
I fixed up for m'self after Marcus died... so all of us'll have some
privacy in this boarding house we've got going here."

"Thanks, Maddy," Daphne said gratefully. She handed her a
check for four hundred dollars. "And here's my first rent check."

Maddy stared at the amount. "Oh, Daphne, dear, that's way
too much."

"Four hundred dollars for a two-bedroom suite with
parking and a great view of the river?" Daphne scoffed. "In
Manhattan, I was paying twelve hundred for a one-bedroom, fifth-
floor walk-up!"

"That was New York. This is Natchez. I can't accept it.
You're family."

"How much is that insurance policy a month?" Daphne demanded.

"Three hundred and fifty dollars," Maddy admitted.

"I rest my case. The extra fifty goes toward the utilities, and I'm giving you cash for a grocery kitty. Otherwise, I can't stay," she said firmly.

Maddy remained silent and pensive. "Oh, all right! You've let that Yankee stuff rub off on you some, but I deeply appreciate your doing this, darlin' girl."

Daphne gave her cousin a hug. "And I wouldn't be able to throw myself into such a harebrained scheme, if it weren't for your hospitality," she replied seriously. "I just hope Mama doesn't put a contract out on the two of us."

Maddy grew somber. "I think it's a very healthy thing that you're starting to live your own life, Daphne Whitaker Duvallon."

Daphne gazed at her cousin for a long moment. "So do I..." she murmured. "But I have to admit it's a little scary."

"Course it is... but that's all right, darlin'. You've got Althea and me backing you up."

"It's probably a lucky break that my parents aren't speaking to me," Daphne noted wryly. "That way, my move to Natchez won't be a subject for debate."

When Maddy returned downstairs, Daphne set about getting her rooms organized into living quarters, with an office in the second bedroom. Another phone extension had been installed earlier that day, and an Internet connection and wifi modem were put in to handle her computer. Daphne glanced around her suite, surveying her handiwork, and was pleased with the results.

Maddy had donated a desk that had once been used by her husband, along with his handsome burgundy leather office chair. Daphne sat down, and tackled her to-do list, starting with a number of calls to people she wanted to invite to the opening night performance of the new-and-improved Aphrodite Jazz Ensemble. She glanced at the list and dialed the first number.

"Hello, is this Liz Keating?" she asked, "This is Daphne Duvallon... the harpist? You and Otis were kind enough to come to—"

"Why, Daphne!" Liz exclaimed. "I'd heard from Maddy when I saw her at the Piggly Wiggly yesterday that you were back in Natchez. When you get settled, I'd be pleased if you'd come out to the Trace and have supper with us."

Daphne murmured thanks and then launched into her invitation. "We're a real jazz ensemble now," she finished. "We actually have five members—all women."

"Why, Otis and I would be delighted to come," Liz replied promptly. "Does Sim Hopkins know you're back?"

"Sim? I heard he'd left Natchez," she said, trying to ignore her racing pulse. "I stopped by Monmouth to leave him a note, and the clerk there said he'd left town."

"He left Monmouth, all right." Liz chuckled. "Bailey Gibbs offered him the cottage on his place to use as a sort of base camp. Sim's been out there... oh... I'd say a week or more. Off in the woods, mostly, Bailey says. Even sleeps out there, brave man."

Maybe that's why he hasn't responded to the email I sent when I got here, Daphne thought, gratified.

"Wow... well... ah... if you see Sim or Doctor Gibbs in the next few days, please tell them I've made the big move, and that I'd love to have them join you and Otis at the Under-the-Hill Saloon Saturday night."

"Will do," Liz replied cheerfully. "Bye now."

By Thursday morning, Daphne had secured a twice-weekly job, commencing immediately, playing her harp during the tea service and into the cocktail hour at the Eola Hotel on the corner of Pearl and Main Street. Prior to her four o'clock assignment, she checked her voice mail and her email one last time.

King and Corlis had called from New Orleans and left word that they were just checking in to see how she was faring in her new life. There was also a message from Bailey Gibbs who telephoned from the state capitol in Jackson, sending regards to Maddy and welcoming Daphne to Natchez.

"Liz Keating gave me a ring," he explained in a hearty voice.

"If these danged legislative hearings 'bout the toxic dump site wind up Friday, I surely won't miss a chance to cheer you on. And, dar-lin' Maddy, save me a seat for Daphne's show Saturday night and I'll do m'best to get there. Bye, now."

But nothing from Sim.

More disappointed than she cared to admit, she quickly dressed and sped the short distance to town just as a pair of gargantuan tourist buses pulled up in front of the hotel. All afternoon, a stream of travel coaches had been disgorging eager visitors to the last four days of the Natchez Spring Pilgrimage. Some thirty-two grand mansions on this year's home tour had enjoyed a steady flow of sightseers who now sought refreshment in the cool, dark green confines of the Eola's cocktail and tea lounge.

In a stall in the ladies' room, Daphne donned her "uniform": a long-sleeved, black crepe, floor-length gown, a string of pearls, and demure black pumps. She strode past the foyer and positioned her gilded harp discreetly in one corner of the lounge. For the next three hours, she dutifully played "Greensleeves," excerpts from *Swan Lake*, and other "romantic background music favorites" from a pile of charts perched on her music stand. A few inebriated male customers attempted to engage her in conversation from time to time, but she easily deflected their advances with the skill of a sea-soned New Yorker who had no qualms about politely telling the pests to get lost.

At seven o'clock, she swiftly wheeled her harp through a door marked "Employees Only." She darted back into the ladies' lounge, and reemerged in jeans and a T-shirt with "The Boston Pops" emblazoned across her chest. Then, she packed her unwieldy instrument into its wheeled traveling case, pushed it out a side door, and hoisted the harp inside a slightly rusty, silver-colored Jeep Cherokee that she'd purchased the previous day at River City Auto for five thousand dollars.

Daphne sat quietly behind the wheel, reflecting that Cousin Maddy was having dinner tonight with a friend, and Althea wasn't due in from New Orleans until tomorrow. Somehow, she couldn't face having dinner at the hotel employees' dining room, loading her stomach with smoked ribs at the Pig Out Inn, or coping with the cluttered kitchen at Bluff House. She felt restless and out of sorts and aimlessly began driving up Main Street. Before she admitted what she was doing, she found herself on Highway 61, the road that led north to the Natchez Trace Parkway.

I'll just tack a note on his door…

Dr. Gibbs was up in Jackson. Sim was likely camping deep in the woods, and Liz Keating probably hadn't been able to inform him of Daphne's decision to spend a year in Natchez. It would be perfectly reasonable to leave Sim a note. So why was she feeling like such a jerk driving out to Gibbs Hall?

The simple fact was Sim was still in the Natchez area. Why should she act like a martyr and deprive herself of his good company? Wasn't it about time she learned to make decisions in her own interest, instead of worrying what Mama—or anybody else, for that matter—thought she should be doing?

Twenty minutes later, Daphne was still questioning the wisdom of her impulsive act when she discovered the closed gates at the end of the drive leading to Bailey Gibbs's stately residence. She left the car running and investigated.

Bolted and impassable.

"Damn!" she exclaimed into the cool April air.

Before she allowed herself to think about how ridiculous she probably looked—or the fact that she was a blatant trespasser—she turned off the ignition and grabbed a flashlight from the glove compartment. Then she locked the doors to her car and scrambled over the white wooden fence to the left of the gate. In the lengthening dusk, she walked along the gravel drive as ducks settled near the pond for the night and the wind rustled the graceful willow trees near the water's edge. Gibbs Hall loomed on her right, a solitary veranda light illuminating its columned facade.

She set off across the back lawn toward the stand of oaks and the meadow dotted with a dozen birdhouses that lay beyond. Gingerly, she kept the beam of her flashlight a yard in advance of her feet, always mindful of snakes that hopefully, at night, were asleep in their underground lairs. The breeze ruffled the branches overhead, and Daphne could hear the call of a mockingbird and the scurrying of quail not far from the footpath.

When she emerged from the trees into the wide meadow, she could just make out the six-sided cottage sitting like a miniature pasha's palace with its white wooden finial perched atop its onion dome of a roof, poking at the night sky.

Cautiously, Daphne crept onto the mini-veranda past the pair of empty rocking chairs, certain the place was deserted, yet still feeling like an interloper. She opened the screened door and knocked.

No response.

She cracked the second door a few inches and peered inside. Briefly, she wondered how a large man like Sim could feel comfortable in a place with the dimensions of a luxury dollhouse, and then nearly laughed out loud. For an adventurer who'd camped in igloos in Alaska, and huts along the Amazon River, this jewel of a structure must seem like a suite at the Ritz!

She found a matchbook next to a kerosene lantern and lit the wick. With a guilty thrill, she absorbed the sight of a neatly made daybed pushed against one wall. In a recessed area stood a Bunsen burner stovetop and a pint-size refrigerator powered by a cylinder of propane. Behind a muslin curtain she could just see a shower stall, a toilet, and an old-fashioned pedestal sink, probably salvaged from some outbuilding near the main house. A large-size khaki shirt was flung over the arm of a chair. On a side table next to the bed, Daphne was surprised to see a book about the origins of New Orleans-style jazz lying open and facedown. On a minuscule round table near the efficiency kitchen stood a portable CD player and a collection of disks of female blues vocalists and one of jazz harpist Deborah Henson-Conant.

Pleased that Sim obviously loved the same kind of music she did, Daphne dug into her purse, searching for a pen and paper. She had nearly finished her short note when she froze at the sound of footsteps on the porch.

"Daphne?"

Her breath caught and she whirled in place, but could see only a shadowy shape on the other side of the screen door.

"Wha—" she said with a startled gasp. Her heart was hammering in her chest like a timpanist on amphetamines.

"Don't be scared… it's me… Sim. What in the world are *you* doing here?" He opened the door, and suddenly the room shrank when the six-foot-two-inch figure, clad in muddy, hip-high rubber waders, took a step inside. She pointed to a puddle of water seeping onto the wooden floor. "Oh, God!" he said, retreating quickly to the porch. "I was so startled to see you, I just—"

"I'm so sorry," she interrupted in a rush, embarrassment infusing her cheeks. "I-I… was just… leaving you a note to say—oh—can I help you with those?" she interrupted herself inanely.

Sim backed out onto the veranda where an enormous backpack and bedroll had been deposited on the bottom step.

"Thanks for offering, but I don't want you to get all dirty," he said as he sat on one of the wooden chairs and began extracting his left leg from his waders. He looked up and grinned. "It's good to see you. Tell me why you're *here*," he reiterated.

Daphne leaned against the doorjamb and watched Sim kick off the second leg of the rubber waders. He was only wearing running shorts underneath, providing her a distracting view of his long, muscular legs.

"Well… I-I've decided to take a year off from New York… to learn more about blues and jazz from Willis and Althea. She's agreed to come up to Natchez every weekend so we can really see what we can do as the Aphrodite Jazz Ensemble."

Sim stood up and met her nervous glance.

"Why, that's great!" He paused and asked in a mildly reproving tone, "Didn't you get my email?"

"Yes. Did you get mine?"

"No. Well, I don't know," he amended. "As you can see, I've been nonelectronic for about a week, and I didn't have a chance to check my laptop up at the main house the morning I set out." He approached the door in his stocking feet, staring intently at her through the open screen. His face was unshaven and several days' growth of black beard stubbled his cheeks and chin. He looked hot and tired and probably was dying to shower and then dive into bed and sleep for twelve hours.

CIJI WARE

Daphne pointed to the pair of porch rocking chairs. "Do you mind if we sit on the veranda for just a minute? Then, I'll get out of here and let you get cleaned up." Sim nodded and she sat down on the chair beside him. She inhaled deeply, wondering that she should feel so ill at ease if this was just a friendly visit.

"I didn't answer your email right away because... because I would have had to explain about all the decisions I was in the process of making," she began. Sim relaxed into his chair and gazed at her steadily. "The morning after our show at the Under-the-Hill Saloon, I realized that I absolutely *dreaded* going back to my life in Manhattan."

"And why was that?" he asked quietly.

"I don't know, for sure. But I knew I needed some time off to... to think and to learn more about the kind of music that made me so... so—"

She searched for words to express the soaring feelings she had experienced singing and playing her electrified harp that night in front of the wildly appreciative audience.

"To play the kind of music that made you happy?" Sim suggested encouragingly.

She beamed. "Yes! The kind of music that made me *happy*. So I decided right then and there that I would go back to New York, sublet my apartment, postpone auditioning for orchestras and chamber groups, and see where this new road would take me." She smiled soberly. "It all happened so fast, and, frankly, I didn't even know if you'd... be interested one way or the other. Especially when I... I didn't go back with you to Monmouth that night."

"Oh, I'd have been interested."

She let Sim's remark pass. Then she blurted, "I stopped by Monmouth as I drove back into town on Monday." She suddenly felt shy making the admission. "All the lady on the desk said was that you'd checked out. I'd thought you'd gone to some other location way north of here, or maybe back to San Francisco."

"I can see how you'd think that," Sim allowed, a smile quirking the corners of his mouth.

"Liz Keating just happened to mention that you were still here and that Doctor Gibbs had offered you the cottage while you continued your Audubon project. That's when I thought I'd leave a note inviting you to come hear the new-and-improved Aphrodite Jazz Ensemble, and I…" Her words trailed off a bit breathlessly.

"That was fast work, getting the band together again, but then, I'm not surprised, considering the great response you got that first night."

"The debut show's this Saturday. I was afraid you might not run into Doctor Gibbs and you wouldn't get the message in time."

"Well, thanks for taking all the trouble to drive out here."

"You're welcome," Daphne said, gazing intently at one of the birdhouses to avoid Sim's gaze.

"Look for me in the front row."

"Really?" she said, turning. "You're willing to come hear a lot of the same songs?" She gave him a sidelong glance, "At least we have a new drummer and a saxophone player. Both women."

Sim rose from his rocking chair. "Sounds pretty wild. Hey," he said, switching subjects. "I'm starved, are you? Would you like to drive into town, or can I rustle up an omelet? That's about all I'm equipped to do out here."

"Oh, I can't stay to dinner," she replied hastily.

"Why not?"

She felt heat flood her cheeks again, and offered weakly, "Well actually, you look exhausted. You're probably dying just to grab a shower and hole up tonight and—"

"On my last mile back, I certainly felt that way," he acknowledged, "but now I'd love to have your company. Will you stay for a bit and have dinner with me?"

"Actually," Daphne said, suppressing a smile, "I could eat an alligator. I've been playing 'Claire de Lune' at the Eola Hotel for a bunch of drunks all afternoon and, believe me, that really takes it out of you."

Sim put his head back and laughed. "You've already got a day job? You're amazing!" Then he swung a khaki-cloaked arm around her shoulders and gave her a brief hug. "Playing 'Claire de Lune' is kind of like sitting for hours in waist-high water waiting for a red-eyed vireo to show up. It can get to be a real drag."

"Exactly," she said, suddenly feeling giddy. "Tell me what I can do to help get supper on the table."

"Easy. You pour the wine while I take a quick shower."

❦

Sim pulled shut the shower's muslin curtain and rid himself of his shorts and T-shirt while he stood inside the stall that Bailey had added on to the hexagonal building. His previous sensation of grinding fatigue had miraculously disappeared, and an unnerving sense of expectation had taken its place.

Man, what a surprise to see a light glowing through the trees as he dragged his body back to the cottage after days of grueling work. His backpack had felt like it was filled with lead bricks the last few miles he'd tramped along the Trace, and his only thought had been to strip off his clothes and fall into bed.

A feeling of deep contentment washed over him as he stuck his head under a cascade of hot water. He recalled his amazement at his first glimpse of a slender figure with a mass of wonderfully curly blond hair silhouetted against the screened door. The wildest thing was that he had been *thinking* of Daphne Duvallon the last few hours... disappointed that she hadn't responded to his email. He'd figured that their timing and geography had become impossible obstacles even to establishing a friendship, let alone anything more serious. He'd assumed by her silence that, after she'd thought better of going to bed with him, she'd simply blown him off. It had been a depressing thought, and it had led to *other* depressing thoughts, such as how long could he keep living like some man without a country? Without a reason to tramp through the woods and come home? Then, he'd seen that light winking through the stand of oaks, and in an instant, his entire outlook had changed.

"Hey, shutterbug... you ever coming out of that shower?" called Daphne.

Sim poked his drenched head around the curtain and grinned. "Took a while to wash off all the mud. I'll be right out."

❦

After their hastily assembled dinner of eggs, bacon, and toast consumed at the tiny table where Sim's CD player had been, Daphne could see that overwhelming fatigue had begun to reclaim her host.

"Look... you've got to get some sleep, Sim, and I'm bushed, too." She seized her flashlight and pointed to the door. "I'm going to go on home, but thanks so much for a lovely supper."

"I'll walk you to your car."

"Oh, you don't have to do that," she protested. "You look as if you're about to drop right where you're standing."

"I am, but even so, a bit of air will do me good, and, besides, I want to see you safely past those unpredictable ducks in Bailey's pond."

"They bite?" Daphne picked up her purse off the day bed while Sim threw on a pair of tennis shoes.

"No... I was making that up," he said, laughing. "It's a private joke between me and myself. I dislike ducks. They're the only one of our feathered friends I could do without."

"Ducks?" Daphne repeated, astonished. "They're such benign creatures. Why don't you like them?"

"I don't blame the ducks," Sim hastened to say as he held open the door to the veranda for her. They set off in the direction of Daphne's car. She felt the comforting, steady presence of his hand on her arm as they strolled down the footpath toward the stand of trees that separated the meadow and the lawn surrounding Gibbs Hall. The birdhouses, perched on their poles, towered in the darkness above their heads.

"Then why don't you like our daffy little friends?" she teased.

Sim's voice had lowered in the silence surrounding them. "It's one of those association things."

"What do you mean?" she asked, puzzled.

Sim was silent while they walked several more yards down the path. "I associate ducks with one of the worst periods of my life," he said finally.

"How so?" she asked, attempting to sound casual, although she instinctively knew this conversation was turning into anything but.

Sim was staring straight ahead. "I was in a duck blind when my former wife, Francesca, went into labor with our daughter. It was in a remote area outside Sacramento and I was photographing mallards and a rare pair of Peking ducks that had apparently ridden the air currents in a Pacific storm and landed on a pond. No one could reach me for two days. And so, I've always associated ducks with... with that sad time. It's stupid, really."

"No, it's not," Daphne said softly as they arrived at the edge of the rolling stretch of manicured lawn that surrounded the main house. She was both amazed and gratified that Sim had finally opened up a little about this previous taboo subject. "It's a silly analogy, but I feel exactly that way about 'Claire de Lune.'"

"Really?"

"It's not the composer's fault I hate that pretty melody," she said matter-of-factly. "It's just that my mother used to nag me to play it for friends at the most inappropriate moments... just to show off that she had spawned such a *talented* darlin' lil' girl!" Daphne's voice mocked her mother's Southern drawl. "I associate that music with the feeling that my mother only cared about how I performed... not who I was as a person. I wanted her to love me because I was her daughter, not a trained seal." She gently pulled Sim's sleeve to halt then-progress on the path. "To this day, if I hear the first four bars of 'Claire de Lune'—and especially if I play it myself, like I did today—I go into a total funk."

"Remind me never to hum Debussy."

Daphne smiled at Sim's attempt to jolly himself out of his pensive mood. "So, maybe," she suggested gently, "the mere quack of a duck automatically triggers all those sad, painful feelings about... losing the baby." She gently squeezed his hand. "I don't know how any parent survives the loss of a child, Sim. I can only imagine what sorrow comes with such tragedy."

"Francesca just couldn't get past the fact that I wasn't there when she... when she went into labor."

"Why did you accept the job, if she was so close to her due date?" Daphne asked softly.

"The baby wasn't supposed to be born for another four months."

"Oh... Sim... how awful. But when you left on the Sacramento shoot, you had no reason to believe the pregnancy was in trouble, did you?"

"No…" he said, gazing sightlessly at the starlit sky. "Francesca was still putting in brutally long hours at her law firm. Whenever she did have some free time, she wanted to go to some San Francisco society thing, or entertain colleagues. We never just took walks or lay around the apartment reading the paper." Sim paused, as if replaying the scene in his mind. "The day I left for Sacramento, everything seemed perfectly normal, except…"

"Except what?"

Sim was silent for a moment. "Even before Francesca knew she was pregnant, she'd been… out of sorts. Moody. Later, I just chalked it all up to her hating the fact that some of her fellow lawyers were teasing her about her pregnancy beginning to show." Sim smiled slightly. "Francesca had been the epitome of San Francisco chic, and she couldn't stand the way she had to dress. She refused to stop smoking and still drank wine. She avoided any discussion about how she was feeling, but I think she really hated her body at that point." Sim shrugged. "You know… the usual stuff I imagine a lot of professional women go through when their lives and their physiques are changing so drastically."

"Who finally called it quits to the marriage?" Daphne asked, unable to stem her curiosity.

"She did," he said shortly.

"Is it something you're… willing to talk about?" Daphne asked cautiously.

Sim paused a long moment and then took her arm again, guiding her across the lawn in the direction of the front gate as he spoke.

"About two months after she lost the baby, I finally felt I had to accept a photography assignment. That it was time to *try* to start getting on with our lives. When I got back from that trip to Alaska, the entire apartment on Taylor Street had been cleared out."

"Oh, my God…"

"It was empty of every single thing, except for—"

Sim broke off in the middle of his sentence. It was too dark for Daphne to read the expression on his face, but she peered at the outline of his profile. Instinctively, she reached up and grazed the back of her hand gently against his face.

"Empty, except for what?" she murmured.

"The only furniture left in that whole damn apartment was the mattress to our queen-size bed… and a baby's bassinet."

"Sweet Jesus…"

"She hadn't wanted any baby stuff in the house until the child was born, but my mother couldn't wait that long to give us that bassinet. She'd used it for both my sister Brooke and me and was very sentimental about it, so she had it delivered to our apartment as a surprise."

"That's so touching… what happened?"

"Francesca was upset. She said it was bad luck and had the delivery men shove it in the guest room closet."

"So, when you returned from Alaska, you found the bassinet… and what?" Daphne asked delicately.

"It had obviously been yanked out of the closet because it was tipped over on its side. I found a blue legal folder with divorce papers stuck to the crib mattress ticking with a couple of diaper pins."

"Jesus, Mary, and Joseph, Sim! How cruel."

"She was pretty angry."

"I can understand that she would be devastated to lose her baby," Daphne protested. "But why would she feel that your not being there when she went into early labor was *your* fault?"

"I should have arranged some way for her to track me down." He shook his head. "Cell phones weren't used as widely back then, but I could have been more aware—"

"Bad stuff happens," Daphne interrupted stoutly. "It was a horrible tragedy, but you didn't *cause* it. Even if she didn't accept that truth, why do you continue to carry this… this burden of blame?"

"Because it was more than just being in that duck blind," he insisted soberly. "She also holds me chiefly responsible for why the marriage didn't work. The traveling, the long hours. Maybe I deserved her fury. I honestly don't know anymore."

"Wait a minute," Daphne countered. "You weren't the only

one working hard. You just said that she put in long hours too, and didn't take very good care of herself, even when she was pregnant. Surely she had to travel occasionally for her job?"

"She did, but not as much—or for such long times away—as I did. She specialized in environmental issues."

"Not on the side of the tree huggers I'll bet."

Sim chuckled. "We eventually agreed not to discuss subjects like the endangered spotted owl," he noted dryly.

By this time, they had reached the wrought iron gate. Sim leaned against the fence and gazed at her contemplatively.

"Sounds to me," Daphne ventured, "like you and Francesca dealt with a lot of the usual issues that cause the marriages of two working professionals to break up. Why are you still taking so much on your own shoulders, Sim?"

"I guess it was that stripped-down apartment, and the way Francesca delivered the message that she didn't want to be married to me anymore. Those diaper pins said it all." He shook his head. "I wasn't there when our baby died, and got back too late even to see… my daughter. When I went to Alaska two months later, that did it, I guess. Apparently, Francesca couldn't forgive me for either of those things. End of story."

"Look," Daphne said shortly, "maybe you acted like a complete bastard in other ways—which I doubt—but take it from another woman. Her attempt to punish you in such a cruel way, for something that was totally out of your control, seems like major overkill. Something just doesn't add up here, Sim. Really."

Sim looked thoughtful and then shrugged. "Well… thank you for that. And you've given me a lot to chew on. And you're also right about one thing: I'm getting really tired of carrying this weight everywhere I go."

Daphne smiled reassuringly. "Well, I can't wait to see your latest photographs, considering what you must have gone through to get those shots these last few days. And, by the way… thanks for the scrambled eggs."

"I wanted to do a real omelet but—"

"You were dead tired, and that takes concentration, right?

Besides, I always give a good guy like you a second chance," she added, and swiftly vaulted over the fence before he could reply. "See you Saturday."

"Look for me front row, center!" He touched his forefinger to his lips and then anointed the tip of her nose through the wooden railing. "And thanks for being such a good listener. I haven't talked about that... subject... for a long, long time."

"Not even to your dad before he died?"

"Not the part about the overturned bassinet."

"Well, that's some very tough stuff."

"Very."

They gazed at each other steadily until, at length, Daphne murmured, "Gotta go. Thanks for letting me trespass in your cottage tonight."

"Anytime. Oh, and by the way, I like your T-shirt."

Daphne felt a rush of pleasure, since she instinctively knew that he meant exactly what he said. And she also realized that for the first time, Sim hadn't dodged the bullet when it came to the subject of Francesca Hayes.

"Thanks," she replied with a grin. "I liked your shorts."

CHAPTER 15

APRIL 10

"Holy Mother, will you look at all those tour buses in front of the *Lady Luck*?" Althea exclaimed as Daphne drove down Silver Street searching for a parking place near the Under-the-Hill Saloon. "Good thing you off-loaded your harp yesterday for rehearsal and left it here, or we'd be toast."

The last week of the monthlong Natchez Pilgrimage was always a busy time for the city. This year, a goodly number of tourists seemed as intent on gambling aboard the *Lady Luck* as visiting the three dozen mansions in the Town That Time Forgot. Cars, bumper to bumper, snaked down the one-way street amid knots of people tramping on foot toward the mock steamboat moored at the riverside.

The old-fashioned streetlights were aglow along the narrow thoroughfare and the temperature had dropped ten degrees since sunset. The lively sounds of the newly named Willis McGee Quartet blared through the saloon's open door and windows, amplified by the water as the river sluggishly headed for the Gulf of Mexico, downstream.

Daphne wasn't due to perform with Willis's group until the second half of the first set, but still, she was nervous to be inching forward so slowly in traffic like this.

"Okay if I let you park?" she asked, hopping out of the driver's seat and onto the pavement. "I can't believe all these people are here," she remarked, buoyed by the sight of customers pushing past the front door and into the bar.

Althea climbed out of the passenger seat and hurried around to the driver's door. "Maybe the ad in the *Natchez Democrat* with the picture of us in full battle gear did some good."

"Yeah… when in doubt, there's always the old adage: 'Sex sells,'" Daphne replied dryly, waving her skimpy costume on its coat hanger as she prepared to cross the street. "See you backstage."

"Good luck, Harp Honey."

Daphne rolled her eyes in mock disgust and went around to the back entrance.

The narrow vestibule near the restrooms was dark, except for the naked bulb at the end of the hallway. She swiftly shed her coat and stowed it, along with her Aphrodite costume and her handbag, in a locker in a corner of the minuscule ladies' room. Willis and his group were playing one of the last songs scheduled before she was due to make her entrance, so she gave her newest cabaret outfit the once-over, quickly refreshed her lipstick, ran a comb through her hair, and took several deep breaths to steady her nerves.

When she opened the door, her breath caught at the sight of the man lounging against the wall outside her makeshift dressing room.

"What are *you* doing here," she exclaimed in a hoarse whisper.

"I saw the ad in the newspaper," Jack Ebert drawled. "Keepin' up with everythin' that's goin' on in this state is part of my job," he added pompously. "Saw that picture of you and your soul sisters in those getups. How could I resist attendin' the grand debut of the new-and-improved Aphrodite Jazz—what do you have the nerve to call it—'Ensemble'? It's a pity I'm not reviewin' for *Arts This Week* anymore," he noted with the ghost of a sneer. "I'd have m'self a Mardi Gras ball with this one!"

Daphne felt herself starting to hyperventilate both with anger and alarm. She was nervous enough about tonight's performance without her malicious ex-fiancé sneaking into the vestibule to rattle her cage.

"Get out of here, Jack," she snapped. "You're *really* bothering me."

"And I don't really much care."

She thought briefly of King, who had never been intimidated

by Jack and had never hesitated to push back, as she found herself doing, much to her amazement.

"Why are you still slithering around Natchez like this?" she demanded. "I thought you were based in Jackson these days, looking for *bird sanctuaries* to dump your company's toxic chemicals into."

Jack's eyes narrowed indicating that she'd drawn blood.

"I've got a lot of big things goin' on up in Jackson, but how could I miss bein' front row, center for a great event like this?" he asked sarcastically.

Daphne guessed that the takeover at his father's newest funeral parlor in Natchez might mean that Jack was forced to serve as a troubleshooter in his off-hours, much to his displeasure.

"Look, Jack... get a life." She desperately needed time to collect herself before going onstage to perform. "You've done your best to disrupt my concentration and you've succeeded, so score one for you. Just *leave*, will you?"

"Sure." He shrugged, casting a critical eye at her stretchy black, long-sleeve, scoop-necked T-shirt and her long black skirt with its provocative side slit. His gaze meandered down her legs to her feet, clad in sheer black stockings and stiletto heels. Never had Daphne felt so vulnerable or exposed, and she gave silent thanks that at least she wasn't wearing her Aphrodite outfit during this unpleasant encounter. Her physical intimacy with Jack seemed as if it'd happened a million years ago on another planet to some android—not her.

Jack ambled down the hallway just as Althea walked through the back door.

"Well... look who's here?" he said in an insulting tone. "My favorite classmate, Althea LaCroix." His eyes raked her figure from high heels to curly Afro hairstyle. "You two are quite a pair. Always wondered 'bout the nature of that buddy-buddy thing you got goin'." He raised an eyebrow and pointed to the abbreviated length of Althea's miniskirt. "Doesn't take much to figure it out, does it, now? No wonder you're callin' yourself after a bunch of Greeks. Didn't Aphrodite come from the Isle of Lesbos?"

"No, Jack. You're probably thinking of the Isle of Crete, where cretins like *you* come from."

Jack slowly shook his head. "Well, well, Althea, still an uppity n—"

"Jack!" Daphne interrupted, pointing angrily toward the exit sign. "You've got exactly two seconds to get out of here, or the bouncer'll *throw* you out."

"I just came by to say 'break a leg' tonight, sugar," he said, his hand on the doorknob. "And, believe me, I mean that sincerely."

Just then, Willis's amplified voice announced, "I bet y'all've been wonderin' what this big, ol' concert harp is doin' here. Well, put y'hands together and give a big, warm welcome to Natchez's newest arrival on the jazz and blues scene... Miz Daphne Duvallon of New York and New Orleans!"

Out of the corner of her eye, Daphne saw Jack slip out the back exit as she made her way through a thicket of chairs and cocktail tables. She immediately spotted Sim seated down front among the small group of her friends and Cousin Maddy. It took every ounce of will to shut out the thought of Jack Ebert's unwelcome appearance and to shift into performance mode. Fortunately, the bright lights screened from her vision all but the first row of tables, where every seat was occupied.

Much to her amazement, considering the degree to which her run-in with Jack had upset her equilibrium, the set with Willis went off without the slightest hitch. During the break, Daphne only had time to think about jumping into her miniskirt and bustier, and she succeeded in putting the creep out of her mind.

However, five minutes into the Aphrodites' first set, the group swung into a slow, seductive rendition of "Damn Your Eyes," and Daphne suddenly noticed that Jack was standing against the brick wall, not ten feet from her harp. He crossed his arms tightly across his narrow chest and stared at her in an obvious attempt to jar her concentration. She could almost smell his malevolence.

As if she'd been struck dumb, Daphne was not only unable to remember the words to the next verse—if pressed, she would probably have had trouble recalling her own name. Her mind had become an utter blank, as free from cogency as a blackboard wiped clean by the teacher's eraser or a computer with the "delete" button depressed. As the moment to sing again approached, she turned desperately to Althea, who also had spotted Jack's reappearance and seemed, in the mysterious way of jazz musicians, to read her thoughts. The black woman nodded imperceptibly, and attacked the keyboard as if it were her turn to take the solo. Daphne turned her back on the side of the room where Jack continued to glare at the band with undisguised hostility. Silently, she ordered herself to calm down.

Listen to the beat! Concentrate on the meaning of the lyrics.

When the beginning of the verse rolled around again, Daphne had recovered her wits sufficiently to finish the song and launch smoothly into the next. By the third number, she'd blocked out Jack's presence entirely. The beat, the blossoming synchronicity of the quintet, created in Daphne the distinct sensation of a key fitting smoothly into a lock, opening up a world of full-flavored, melodious sound. Now it seemed that she, Althea, Kendra, Jeanette, and their latest addition, Sunny on sax, were suddenly performing as one instrument.

Toward the end of the last set, Daphne glanced at her childhood friend playing hard on her electronic keyboard and saw Althea shaking her head in wonder, a triumphant grin spreading across her face. Except for Daphne's brief lapse, the quintet had been able to forge wordless lines of communication between themselves—and with their audience. Several times, the crowd talked back to the musicians or burst into spontaneous applause.

As for Daphne herself, her fingertips pulled sounds from her harp she had never heard before, and her voice felt strong and capable of phrasings she'd never even contemplated prior to this magical night. In fact, she felt as if she'd entered a soothing alpha zone where there was nothing in her consciousness but the music—and her love of it. If the roar from the crowd after her solo, "Peel Me a Grape," and the spontaneous clapping in time to the group's final rendition of "I Got the Will" were any yardstick, the Aphrodite Jazz Ensemble had batted a thousand tonight.

The five women were still taking their bows when the club's owner, bearing a handful of roses, barreled his way through the packed room. He handed a single stem to each of the women and then leaned into the mike.

"Thank y'all for comin' tonight, and thanks to the Aphrodites, who'll be at the Under-the-Hill Saloon…" he looked happily at the standing-room-only crowd and declared, "indefinitely!"

Sim and Cousin Maddy continued to clap, along with everyone else. Daphne grinned at the photographer and impulsively pitched her rose directly into his lap. He seized it and promptly inserted the stem between his teeth while the applause and wolf whistles swelled to ear-splitting intensity. Althea, noting Daphne's gesture, followed suit by throwing her solitary bloom into her landlady's lap—much to Madeline's delight.

Then the members of the band turned on their high heels and scampered offstage in the wake of unabated cheering.

⇛

The front porch of Bluff House was swathed in purple shadows pierced by the glow of a single candle flickering in a clear glass votive, set on a round wicker table that had ridden out several tornado warnings in recent years.

Daphne heaved a sigh of contentment and turned to look at Sim, who sat across from her sipping the champagne he'd brought to Maddy's house after the show. Althea and their hostess had long since trundled off to bed, yawning as they disappeared into the darkened house. However, Daphne felt keyed up and not in the slightest mood for sleep.

She raised her glass in a toast to his generosity. "Thanks for this—and thanks for so loyally showing the flag tonight."

"The pleasure was definitely all mine." He was smiling but she wondered if he was tired after a week camping in the woods and was thinking about the half-hour drive to Gibbs Hall.

"You've probably had a long day tracking… whatever you were tracking today, but I'm still wired," she said apologetically. "Please feel free to take off. I like just sitting here feeling the cool air from the river." She leaned back in her wicker chair and closed her eyes happily, the sound of the music still reverberating in her head. "God, those lights on stage were *hot!*"

Sim leaned across the table, and she felt the backs of his fingers skim along her jaw line. Startled by his feathery touch, she opened her eyes and smiled, his face only inches from her own.

"I'm fine right where I am," he said quietly. "I'm enjoying the champagne, the view… and the company."

"Veuve Clicquot…" she murmured, relaxing as his fingers began to knead the muscles of her tired right forearm. "Mmmm… that feels so good. How did you ever find a bottle of that around here?"

"Oh, I have my ways."

She closed her eyes once more and allowed herself to enjoy his gentle massage as he worked his way down to the muscles and tendons in her wrist, her hand, and finally to her fingers that were always fatigued after hours of plucking harp strings. Momentarily she was self-conscious of the thick calluses on her fingertips, but soon gave in to the delicious sensation of Sim's touch.

"Oh, that is *heaven*," she whispered. "I'm such a sucker for a massage." After a few moments he switched to her other forearm and hand, repeating the vigorous motions. "You wouldn't consider standing behind me and—"

Without answering, Sim rose and positioned himself behind her chair, his long fingers firmly stroking her sore shoulder and neck muscles.

"Good?"

"Oh yes," she mumbled. "I'll be putty in your hands if you work on my neck for another two minutes."

"Good," he repeated with a chuckle.

All was quiet except for a light wind rustling the bamboo stand to the rear of the property and the hoot of a river barge's horn alerting nearby boats as it glided past on the churning Mississippi two hundred yards below Maddy's front porch.

"Daphne?" Sim said softly, continuing to knead the muscles in her right shoulder. "I don't want to worry you, but I saw—"

Her eyes flew open. "Jack? I saw him, too." She patted his

hands where they'd come to rest on her shoulders and then swiveled in her chair to look up at him. "He appeared without warning backstage, just as I was about to go on to sing with Willis."

"Jesus! That must have given you a start," Sim declared, reclaiming his chair across the table from her.

"It did."

"You don't think he's turning into a… stalker, do you?"

"No…" she considered. "He's just… doing what he does best, which is to stir up trouble and try to make people uncomfortable and upset. It's always payback time with that guy. Did you see where he stood during the show?" she asked indignantly. "Right down in front! I told him earlier to get lost, and after a while, I completely forgot about him, amazingly enough."

"Not me," Sim countered. "Once I'd spotted him, I kept my eye on him, and then, after your last song, he just sort of melted into the crowd heading for Silver Street."

"All that applause probably put him in a bad mood." Daphne swallowed the last of her champagne. "I'm praying he finds some new female to distract him, and eventually just leaves me alone. Besides, he has to return to Texas *some* time, right?"

"Let's hope so," Sim replied grimly. "Meanwhile, Ms. Harp Honey… isn't Monday your day off?"

"Yes." She sank into her chair and closed her eyes again while she inhaled air laden with the scent of dogwood and night-blooming jasmine. "We have an earlyish show tomorrow, and then a blissful Monday with no gigs and no rehearsal and no 'Claire de Lune' or *Swan Lake* at the Eola Hotel."

"Do you want to sleep all day, or would you let me pick you up tomorrow night after your gig and bring you out to Gibbs Hall? If we get a decent start on Monday, I'd love to show you some of the beauty spots I've found on the Trace," he said, enthusiasm lighting his handsome features. "I've finally honed in on an area where I spotted a few of those elusive yellow-rumped warblers and even a couple of much rarer yellow-throated wood-warblers that Audubon probably painted in the 1820s—maybe even while he was staying on Washington Street, like you said."

"You're kidding! You finally captured a yellow-rumped little guy on film?" Daphne said, laughing. "Well this *is* big news." She sat up straight. "Do you think sighting that bird is a sign from heaven that you're doing exactly what the ghost of Audubon would have wanted?"

Briefly, she wondered if the "other" Daphne Whitaker had ever met John James Audubon. And then, she immediately chided herself.

Audubon's ghost? The last thing she needed was to summon more specters and spirits. She gave silent thanks that she hadn't experienced any uninvited visions since she'd returned from New York. Perhaps starting to lead a life of her own choosing had put an end to those eerie mental wanderings of a few weeks earlier, she considered gratefully.

"Just how early do you propose to set out on this excellent warbler adventure?" she inquired dubiously.

"For you... how's nine o'clock? I'm stretching things, but you musicians need to get your shut-eye."

He'd just asked her to sleep at his place Sunday night, she realized with a sudden intake of breath, so as to "get a decent start" on the day. An unbidden image of Rafe Oberlin popped into her head. Handsome. Charming—at first. Very interested in taking her to bed—at first. She certainly couldn't deny that Sim's invitation was extremely tempting, but considering her track record, it was probably best not to allow things to get unduly complicated.

"I'd love for you to show me those little critters out on the Trace, but how about I sleep in my own bed Sunday and drive out early to your place Monday morning... by nine?"

Now, she would have a chance to see what Bird Man was *really* interested in. Without a slumber party at his place, would he still be enthusiastic about taking her into the woods?

"Sounds great," Sim replied without hesitation. "I'll have everything packed and ready by the time you get there." He tweaked her nose gently and then rose to his feet. "Just arrive by the appointed hour and bring your leather knee boots."

"Snake prevention, right?"

"Clever girl."

"Believe it or not," she replied happily. "I even know what carton I packed them in."

"The snakes?" he laughed.

"No, my boots, Bird Man!"

✎

Daphne woke up Monday morning rested and excited about her coming foray to the Natchez Trace with Sim as her guide. She waved good-bye to Maddy and hugged Althea, who was heading back to New Orleans for the week.

For once, the drive through town was pure pleasure. The Pilgrimage had ended on Sunday and the crowds and tour buses had diminished significantly. Daphne delighted in her unobstructed view of brilliant banks of red and white tulips, flowering azalea and camellia bushes, and a riot of other spring flowers in glorious shades of peach, pink, coral, purple, and yellow that filled local gardens on both sides of the streets. The magnolias weren't yet in bloom, but the air was filled with the scent of Confederate jasmine and honeysuckle. Along the Natchez Trace Parkway, the bare branches of English dogwood trees had sprouted white lace, and the green shoulders of grass beside the highway were dotted with volunteer iris, daffodil, and jonquil.

No doubt about it, Daphne thought happily, spring had sprung in Mississippi.

Bailey Gibbs's wrought iron gate was standing wide open when Daphne wheeled her Jeep down the dirt drive to Gibbs Hall. The doctor's housekeeper hailed her from the back porch while Daphne was locking her car, explaining that her employer was still up in Jackson.

"I've made y'all some fried chicken and a thermos of my blueberry lemonade," Leila said with a knowing smile. "Mr. Sim said you heading onto the Trace this morning and I told him I didn't want you starving out there. Do you mind taking this basket down to the cottage?"

"Not at all." Daphne lifted the tea towel covering the food

and sniffed appreciatively. "Ummmm! Yum-ola!" she chortled. "Thanks so much, Leila. I can't wait for lunch."

"Y'all have a lovely day, y'hear," she replied in her soft, lilting accent.

Daphne found Sim stuffing the last of his equipment into a backpack that he'd propped on one of the rocking chairs on the cottage veranda. He glanced up as she strode across the meadow, nodding approvingly at the sight of her jeans, sleeveless shirt, light-weight jacket, and knee-high leather boots.

"The temperature's almost eighty, and due to go even higher today," he predicted. He opened the end of his pack. "I saved just enough room for our lunch and one of those blue ice packs." Just as Daphne had, he inhaled the aroma of Leila's picnic fare tightly wrapped in aluminum foil. "Maybe we should eat first," he proposed jokingly.

"You don't have one of those big things for *me* to carry, do you, Bird Man?" she asked with a doubtful glance in the direction of Sim's enormous pack. "What you need to know about me is that I spent most of my life indoors under my mother's watchful eye, practicing a harp. I've never been much of an outdoorsy type."

"I've taken that into consideration," he said, smiling, "My backpack is big because I've got camera gear in there, just in case we see something."

"Well, what's *that*?" she asked, pointing to a camera with "Canon EOS" stamped on its face. The piece of equipment sported a lens that looked to be at least two feet long and was mounted on a single metal tube painted in camouflage.

"This is my favorite camera. Eight hundred millimeter lens for distance shots. Mono-pod so I can carry everything, ready to go, over my shoulder."

"You have to lug that thing around *and* the backpack, too?" she sympathized.

"I'm used to it," he replied, with a shrug. "Well, are you ready to put the moves on a yellow-throated wood-warbler?"

"What about the *yellow-bellied* guy?"

"Him, too. We'll take what we can get."

They set off down the path through the open meadow and into the woods bordering Whitaker Creek, walking in companionable silence. Farther along the way, Sim pointed out flora and fauna, providing more identifying information when Daphne asked questions. He spoke quietly of integrated ecosystems and the need for sustainable development within urban areas and rural zones, and for protection of declared wilderness regions like the Trace.

"It's important that ordinary citizens begin to connect the dots between an endangered spotted owl or an extinct ivory-billed woodpecker and the eventual fate of *all* creatures inhabiting this planet, including us," he said quietly. "If we *don't* pay attention to the loss of these guys and their habitats, eventually you and I won't have enough food to eat or clean air to breathe or safe water to drink."

"Not to mention that our great-great-grandchildren may all die from toxic poisoning a century from now."

Sim paused and brought his forefinger to his lips. "Shhh," he warned softly. He cocked his head, and whispered, "Hear that?"

Daphne froze in place and listened to a soft, soothing birdcall and the sound of rustling leaves in a nearby tree. Without further warning, a pair of grayish-blue birds dove with lightning speed. They alighted on the roots of the tree and pecked a beakful of small insects before darting into the branches overhead once again.

"Warblers," Sim whispered.

"They flew so fast, I didn't see which part was yellow... their bellies, or their throats," she whispered back.

"Their throats."

The birds apparently had noted their presence, for they remained overhead, out of sight.

"What you've just witnessed is a rare appearance of the yellow-throated wood-warbler," Sim explained in his normal voice. "Audubon described them in his journals as birds 'that threw themselves by the thousands into all the cypress woods and canebrakes.' In his day, these warblers were common as crows."

"And now, I suppose, they're a real find," Daphne commented sadly.

"I'm afraid you're right. Thanks to us humans crowding the land and using all our toxic chemicals on the soil, the groundwater is being poisoned and pollutants are thinning the eggshells of the birds that *have* survived. I got some great shots in this area a few days ago when I camped here overnight."

Daphne stood very still, remembering the swiftness and beauty of the warblers as they dived to scoop up insects. "If there aren't any insect-eating warblers anymore, then there will be too many of certain insects, right?"

"With tainted groundwater or other pollution, you're left with a lot of dead birds and certain insects that survive, or that mutate into something you don't want to take home to mother."

"That's what you mean by 'connecting the dots'?"

"Yep," he nodded. "We nature photographers crawl through mud or climb to the tops of granite crags or spindly trees in hopes that the images we capture in the wild will help people understand what our planet's in danger of losing."

Sim gestured that she should follow him, and they set off on a path that meandered along the creek. Occasionally he held up his hand like a crossing guard. He swiftly put the Canon to his eye and squeezed off a rapid succession of shots of some bird that Daphne couldn't even see.

At one point Sim pointed through a clearing within a stand of trees, and whispered, "Well... well... look who's here."

"Where?" she demanded under her breath.

"Up there... straight ahead of us. Top of the third tallest tree."

Daphne peered through the branches at a cloudless sky. A large, compact, chocolate-brown bird, with a wingspan that appeared to be nearly a yard wide, took flight and made lazy, downward spiraling circles.

"A hawk?" she queried softly.

Sim flashed her an approving smile. "In search of his lunch. Very rare sight here. Until recently, on the endangered list, in fact," he said, his voice filled with awe. "*Falco peregrinus*... a peregrine falcon, also known as the great-footed hawk in Audubon's day," he disclosed in hushed tones. "Mr. A. painted a pair devouring prey when he was in Mississippi and wrote in his journal that he and his companions killed upwards of fifty of them in one day."

"Audubon, the naturalist?" Daphne whispered, aghast.

"Audubon, the painter," he reproved gently. "He killed them so he could study them. His friends killed them for sport."

"And they're on the endangered list."

"In some regions. Westward expansion nearly did them in." Sim raised his camera and squinted through the eyepiece, following the hawk's lazy movements in the sky. "In the mid-seventies, there were less than four dozen in the whole damn country." Soon, thanks to the camera's automatic focus capability, a hail of staccato clicks filled the air like shots from an automatic pistol equipped with a silencer. When, finally, Sim lowered his camera, an expression of pure bliss had settled on his features.

"You've brought me luck, Harp Honey. Maybe getting you outdoors a little is a good idea all around."

She glanced overhead at the empty expanse of sky. "It's a truly magnificent bird," she said quietly. "What a privilege to have seen one."

"Hungry?" Sim asked. "We've earned our lunch."

"Has a bird got tail feathers?" she retorted good-naturedly. "I'm starved!"

Within minutes, they were back at Whitaker Creek.

"Oh, look! There's a pretty spot." Daphne moved toward a tree-shaded area beside a quiet pool created by fallen rocks and broken tree branches.

Sim unpacked a silver thermal blanket and stretched it out on the bank of the stream. Daphne pulled off her leather riding boots, checked for snakes, and thrust her feet into the creek up to her calves.

"Ohoooo," she moaned with rapture. "The cool water feels so good!"

"Soup's on," Sim announced, and without further conversation, they fell to eating Leila's delicious picnic fare.

"Ow!" Daphne exclaimed, slapping her upper arm. "Damn! *Why* do mosquitoes love me so much?"

"Women's body temperatures are higher and—*hell*!" Sim slapped his cheek. "So much for that theory. Now they're after me too." He glanced at the creek and the still waters nearby. Water had also gathered in puddles on the lower side of the stream. "I think we've managed to pick a mosquito *breeding* ground for our picnic spot."

"That's what you get for letting an amateur decide where we should eat lunch," she said, chagrined.

"That's what I get for letting a pretty woman distract me from putting repellent on both of us." Sim glanced through the branches overhead. "It's gotten hot and it rained last night so it's Happy Birthday time for a new generation of mosquitoes. Ouch!" He began pawing through his backpack. "I've got some Cabela Canadian Formula stuff in here somewhere…"

"Sorry, but I've got to get out of here," Daphne declared, scrambling to pull on her socks and boots while Sim swiftly repacked the chicken in its foil wrap. "Yikes!" she cried, slapping her upper arm twice in quick succession. She donned her long-sleeved cotton jacket, but not before she suffered several more bites, as did Sim.

"Here," he said, handing her a small plastic bottle. "It's probably too little, too late, but at least put some of this on your face and hands." They slathered themselves with insect repellent and headed back through the steaming woods. A half hour and a dozen yelps later, they caught sight of the cottage.

"You go first and hop in the shower," Sim directed, shedding his pack and depositing it onto the veranda floor. He helped her out of her jacket, then sat her down in one of the rocking chairs and pulled off her leather boots.

She padded across the porch and was halfway to the front door before she turned, and said apologetically, "Do you need help with anything?"

"No… thanks. Go on inside. I left the air-conditioning on, so it should be nice and cool. Clean towels are on the stool next to the shower."

Daphne scratched her neck and arm where welts the size of

dimes had risen. "Gad, these things always do this to me! Do you have anything to stop the itch?"

"Do you know the old Aussie trick? Dab a bit of toothpaste on those bites. It works wonders."

Daphne stared at him. "You're kidding, right? I'll look ridiculous, considering where some of these damn things bit me."

"No, I'm serious," he said laughing. "Toothpaste works in a pinch. But I have some industrial strength stuff I'll give you later. First, though, you'd better shed all your clothes out here. We don't want any of those critters invading the cottage. I'll shake out your stuff while you're showering."

"Oh. Right. I get it. Take off *all* my clothes. Ah…"

Sim considerately turned his back, continuing to unpack his gear while Daphne divested herself of jeans, blouse, socks, and underwear. "Hurry up, or you'll have to fight me for that nice cool water waiting in there," he chided.

"Hmmmm," was all Daphne said. The thought of Sim whipping her bra and panties in the air like signal flags to launch any leftover mosquitoes into the Great Beyond made her blush with embarrassment. With as much dignity as she could muster, she made a beeline for the blessedly cool sanctuary inside.

CHAPTER 16

S IM STOOD NUDE IN the middle of Bailey Gibbs's guest quarters with Daphne Duvallon—similarly unclad—not five feet away behind a shower curtain. He quickly donned his cotton bathrobe and ordered himself not to stare at her slender silhouette moving behind the drape as the sound of cascading water ceased and a slender arm appeared reaching for a towel folded on a nearby stool.

"Here's some Bactine," he announced. "Shall I hand it to you? It should stop the itching."

"That'd be great. Thanks. I wish I'd brought a change of clothes," she fretted. "Even if you shook mine outdoors to a fare-thee-well, I hate the thought of—"

"Want to borrow a shirt and some drawstring pants?" Sim intervened. "They'll be pretty big, but you could roll up the legs."

There was a long pause, and then he heard a brief "Good idea. Thanks."

Sim rummaged through a duffel bag stowed beside his bed and found a pair of cotton sailing pants and a lightweight button-down dress shirt he hadn't worn since he'd arrived in Mississippi. "Stick out your arm again."

A moist hand, wrist, and forearm poked through the shower curtain and retrieved the donated articles. He noted the blunt nails and callused fingertips, slightly incongruous on such slender hands. Daphne Duvallon might be the daughter of a Southern belle, he thought, and schooled in the manners of a debutante, but she was no magnolia. She'd been a trooper despite the swarm of hungry mosquitoes.

"I'll be right out," she said. "Just give me a sec to—"

"Take your time," he interrupted. Then he heard Daphne giggling. "Way too big?" he asked.

"Way, *way* too big, but nice and clean," she said, still laughing. "No one but you will see me between here and Bluff House, anyway, so what the hey?"

The heightened intimacy developing between them was becoming highly erotic. Here he was, stark naked under his robe while Daphne, only a few feet from where he stood, was struggling to make herself presentable in his outsize clothing.

"Don't laugh, okay?" she called.

"Promise."

When she pulled back the curtain, his breath caught in his throat.

Her golden curls were piled on top of her head with a tortoise shell clip she must have retrieved from her purse. A few tendrils lay against a cheek flushed pink from the heat of the shower. She'd rolled up both the shirtsleeves and the pants legs, transforming the makeshift clothes into a set of stylish loungewear. Her long legs—and breasts, obviously minus her bra—prompted all sorts of uncensored yearnings.

Fresh-faced and smiling, she looked about eighteen years old.

"Actually…" he observed slowly, "you look great."

"Mmmm," she said, smelling her arm as she padded into the room in bare feet. "I loved that soap. What is it? Lemon something?"

"Verbena. Found it in France and always carry a bar wherever I go. Makes me feel civilized when my surroundings aren't." He noticed her take in the sight of his robe and bare feet and then lower her eyes self-consciously.

"Your turn," she mumbled. "I'll drown myself in some more of this anti-itch stuff while you take your shower."

In the small, hexagonal room, Sim had no choice but to walk within inches of his visitor on his way to the minuscule bathroom. As he drew near, he inhaled her scent, an intoxicating blend of the lemony soap mixed with an indefinable aroma as seductive and womanly as any he'd ever come across. Unable to stop himself, he reached out and tucked a wayward curl behind her ear.

"I like your hair pulled up that way," he murmured, locking

glances as he read her expression of wariness mixed with—what? he wondered. He rearranged the unbuttoned collar on her shirt, teasing, "Now I can see your swan-like neck."

She was actually *blushing*, he marveled.

"You Bird Men say that to all the girls," she retorted in a self-mocking approximation of her mother's Southern drawl.

"No, I don't."

And with that, he stepped inside the recessed shower, pulled the curtain closed, divested himself of his robe, and turned on the water full blast. He stood under its soothing cascade for several minutes while trying to restrain his rampaging imagination.

Daphne had declined his invitation to spend Sunday evening here, he reminded himself sternly. *So just cool your jets, Hopkins.*

Ah, but she had come here *today*. And what a glorious day it had been! Despite her having been raised as a hothouse flower by a domineering mother, she'd tramped the woods without complaint, laughed at his jokes, and appeared genuinely interested in learning about his work. A bout with a few mosquitoes didn't send her into a sharp decline as it would most women of his acquaintance. She was courageous in more important ways, too. It took real moxie to abruptly pull up stakes in New York to spend a year exploring the world of blues and jazz. He wondered when he'd tell her that it was his favorite music and always had been.

As the cool water washed over his body, Sim luxuriated in his recollection of the day, last week, when Daphne suddenly materialized at the cottage to inform him that she'd returned to Natchez. The vision of her mass of curly blond hair, backlit by the kerosene lamp near the bed and visible through the screen door as he approached from the meadow at dusk, was etched in his memory like a favorite photograph.

He absorbed the sight of his semi-aroused condition. You could fool the mind, but you couldn't fool the body, he mused. And hers was so lovely... honey-colored, like her hair. He found himself speculating on what the rest of her was like beneath clothing that had also touched *his* skin...

He abruptly turned the cold tap on full blast, letting it engulf his head and run down his back. Then he swiftly soaped, rinsed, and toweled himself dry, directing his thoughts to photographic subjects like aperture settings and shutter speeds.

The lady's still licking her wounds from her last encounter with a man.

But that was two years ago. As for himself, he'd put a decade between his own personal disaster with Francesca and this lovely April day. Surely, by now, he was fit company for a woman who'd intrigued him from that first arresting moment he'd glimpsed her playing a harp and singing in that husky voice of hers inside the cool, elegant parlor of a Mississippi plantation house.

Sim donned his bathrobe once again, assailed by sudden doubts. Was he honestly ready for a serious relationship with Ms. Daphne Duvallon—and all the complications that would entail? He knew that if he advanced beyond simple friendship today, this could be no casual affair. For reasons he couldn't even explain to himself, he knew intuitively and positively that Daphne was not merely a ship he'd pass in the night.

Cinching his bathrobe tightly around his waist, Sim yanked back the curtain, the swiftness of his motion startling Daphne, who was sitting on the daybed dabbing antiseptic on her ankle.

"Squeaky clean?" she asked finally as he stood rooted to the spot.

"Yep." He took a step toward the bed. "Show me your mosquito bites," he commanded.

Slowly she raised her eyes to meet his gaze, and bit her lip. In that instant, he knew instinctively that she was feeling every bit as sexually charged as he was. Her dark eyes widened and her lips parted slightly, just as they had when he held her in his arms on the dance floor the first night he'd taken her to Biscuits and Blues.

"They got me everywhere," she revealed, her glance never wavering from his.

"Here. Let me help."

He held out his hand and she placed the plastic bottle of antiseptic into his palm without looking away. "See?" he said, pointing to a spot under his ear. "Everywhere, too." He sat down beside her on the bed and searched for some cotton swabs in a first-aid kit he'd stowed in the bottom of the duffel. "Show me the ones you couldn't reach," he demanded gently.

"On my… back. They bit me right through my shirt!"

"Me too. Show me."

He had absolutely no idea whether she'd comply with his directive, and when she turned her back to him and unbuttoned the front of the oversize shirt, he felt his heart hammering in his chest. She discreetly lowered the shirt from her shoulders and employed it as a shawl, revealing her upper back only. "See them? About halfway down to the right of my spine?"

And what a lovely spine it was, he thought. Her fragrant skin was still warm from her shower. She had a tiny mole in the middle of her back adjacent to several small red marks where he began to dab antiseptic. Slowly, and with a sense that every move should be savored like a sip of fine wine or a taste of caviar, he patted the saturated cotton ball against the small swellings and then leaned forward to blow each spot dry.

"How's that feel?" he asked, leaning close to her left ear, riveted by the golden skin on her shoulder now dimpled with goose bumps.

"Mmmmm," she said, and Sim knew she had her eyes closed. "Not as itchy."

"How about this one at the base of your neck?"

"Uh huh. And there's one at the bottom of my spine." She lifted the hem of the shirt while pushing down the edge of the drawstring pants.

He patted both spots with icy antiseptic and then blew them dry.

"Oh, God! Here's another one," she offered, raising her forearm and pushing the cotton sleeve up to her elbow.

He repeated his ministrations. Again, gooseflesh.

"Let's see that ankle."

"I already did it."

"I'll give it a second dose."

She modestly returned his dress shirt to her shoulders, holding it closed over her bosom, and shifted on the bed in order to face him.

"That's the worst spot," she groused good-naturedly. "I must have gotten ten bites down there when I stuck my feet into the creek. Duh-umb."

Sim slid his hand over the arch of her foot. Her skin felt warm there too, and wonderful to the touch. "Ah... I see," he murmured. "There's one... and there... and..."

His fingers now encircled her slender ankle while his other hand attended to the mosquito bites. She was watching his every move. Slowly her glance shifted and he found himself staring into dark eyes as brown as espresso. The look flickering behind her lashes contained the kind of wariness and desire he'd seen in female birds at the beginning of the age-old dance that always ended as instinct had forever dictated.

"Sim?" He didn't answer, but merely continued to gaze into her lovely, questioning face. "What about you?" she whispered.

"Are you inquiring about my mosquito bites?" he asked softly, "or the rest of me?"

She paused, carefully considered his question, and replied, "Of course I mean your mosquito bites."

Feint... counterfeint.

In nature, the female of the species affected disinterest until the male proved his intentions. Even so, he briefly wondered if he hadn't mistaken mere friendliness for desire... No, he assured himself. She would have allowed him and his mosquito bites to fend for themselves. She'd just offered to—what?

Let's just see what the lady intends...

He shrugged his bathrobe from his shoulders and allowed it to pool at his waist. He pointed to his exposed back. "I'll match you, bite for bite."

"Well, we'll just see about that, won't we?" she declared softly.

Daphne changed places on the bed and rather primly, Sim thought, set to work soaking a new piece of cotton in the antiseptic and dabbing it on the itchy bites on his back. He felt himself relax while she administered first aid to far fewer mosquito bites than she had certainly suffered.

"Anything else?" she asked.

"Oh, yes," he replied, laughing softly. He turned to face her, drawing one leg beneath him on the bed as she had. "I have a confession to make."

"What is it?" she asked warily.

He gently took her chin between his fingers. "For a while now I've been imagining you in my bed... and now... here you are."

She took a deep breath and nodded. "Here I am."

"And I've imagined... I've *been* imagining," he amended, "making love to you in all sorts of beds, beginning with that gigantic four-poster at Monmouth Plantation—"

"I remember," she said solemnly.

"And here in this cottage, on this skinny little mattress," he continued, patting the white cotton bedspread. "And if those damn mosquitoes hadn't interfered, even in the woods near the creek." He paused, allowing time for his next words to sink in. "But, I know from experience that it takes quite a while to recover from certain kinds of wounds and so I—"

"May I say something?" Daphne intervened.

Sim merely nodded, feeling as if he were watching a skittish warbler through his camera lens. If nothing else, he was a patient man. He'd learned that skill while waiting on mountain ledges and in leafy jungles and knee-deep in swamps until the object of his interest was ready to show itself.

Daphne smiled faintly and then, to his surprise, trailed a piece of cotton from a spot beneath his ear to the base of his neck where she had apparently discovered another mosquito bite "I blush to admit it," she said, her repressed Southern drawl creeping into her speech, "but a few of those very same notions have crossed my mind."

"I thought... I *hoped* they might have. At least you're willing to admit it."

"Sim, do you remember our first dance at Biscuits and Blues?"

"Do I ever."

"You'll never know how tempted I was that night to... well, *you* know," she murmured with a self-deprecating laugh. "I *am* a recovering magnolia, after all, but I do try these days to... to be a straight shooter."

"And so?"

"So part of me says 'What in the world are you doing, Daphne, sitting on this guy's bed? He always moves on, and you'll get your heart broken... maybe for real, this time.'"

"For real," Sim murmured. "What a sweet thing to say." Actually, he was tremendously touched. "And what's the other part of that conversation going on in your head?" he asked, lightly combing the fingers of one hand through her caramel-colored hair.

"Another part of me says... 'in for a penny... in for a pound,'" she replied. "You said that night, before I left to go back to New York, that you wanted me to come to your room at Monmouth Plantation... to see where this... this... *electric* thing we've got going between us might lead."

Sim allowed both hands to fall gently into his lap. "That may have been a bit premature on my part," he allowed, "but I couldn't help it. I meant exactly that. Later, I realized that it was asking too much of you to fly on faith like that, given... well, given the short time we'd known each other, and considering what had happened to you before."

"That's right," she said, nodding. "As of today, we've only known each other a little under a *month*?

Sim heaved a faint shrug. "You know something, though? The oddest thing of all was that after you'd gone—and then didn't answer my email right away—I-I felt a terrible sense of bereavement... as if a friend of long-standing had simply flown out of my life."

Daphne appeared startled by this confession. "I felt a bit like that myself, but did my best to ignore it. I didn't want my decision about coming back to Natchez to have anything to do with you or any other man—or my mother. I wanted it to be purely about doing something that was good for *me*, Daphne. I hated the fact I was dragging myself to rehearsals in New York and dreading each day in a profession I'd worked so hard to be part of."

"And *I* hated the fact you'd left Natchez," he replied, gently clasping one of her hands between his two. "I checked out of the hotel the next day and asked Bailey if I could camp in his woods."

He glanced around their cozy nest. "He immediately insisted, of course, that I make Caroline's cottage my headquarters. I think he made the offer as much for having company to drink mint juleps as for anything else."

"And you're going to stay here for... how long?" she asked quietly.

Sim knew that everything hinged on the answer to this very legitimate question.

"At least a couple more months. Then I'm scheduled to go back to San Francisco to prepare the photographs and write and edit the text of the Audubon book." He released her hand and reached up to smooth a strand of hair from her forehead. "There's no denying it, Daphne. As I said that night, we are definitely geographically challenged here, but other people have coped with this stuff while they figured things out."

Daphne stared at him wordlessly for a long moment. Then she said, "I'm beginning to believe that there are no guarantees in this world. Just stupid—or intelligent—risk-taking."

"That's... exactly what I've been thinking too," he marveled. He sought her gaze once again and said, "I haven't had a serious relationship with a woman in a decade. A few flings, I admit, but nothing even remotely like this. So what's happening here is all pretty new territory for me too, you know."

"All I can do is go by my instincts, Sim, just as I did about my decision to come back to Natchez." Surprising the hell out of him, she reached up and gently cupped his face in her hands. "It's kind of a moment-by-moment deal, you know?" she murmured, leaning closer. "And most of it scares me to death."

If Sim were honest with himself, he would have to acknowledge that he was suddenly feeling pretty apprehensive about this obvious next step as well. This had the makings of a serious liaison. If it didn't happen to work out, one, or both of them was going to get hurt. Daphne, too, had to be absolutely sure she was willing to take the risk.

"Even waking up each morning has its dangers," he said. "It's a risk we *both* have to be willing to assume. So, what's it to be? Do we make this leap of faith tonight... or not?"

Silence fell between them until she said, finally, "I'm feeling that… I have this strange connection with you too… and that I… I want what is happening… to *really* happen." She grinned at him crookedly, and added. "Now, if that's not a remark by a nearly recovered magnolia, I don't know what *is*!"

"You're not your mother," Sim reminded her firmly, "In fact, I don't think you have any idea how totally unique you are in this world, *mah de-ah*," he added with deliberate irony.

"A woman of the New South, right?"

"A magnolia with moxie…" He chuckled. "It's an irresistible combination." He leaned forward and kissed her lightly on the mouth and then he moved his head to brush his lips beneath her earlobe in an all-out frontal assault. The time for talking was at an end—if that was how she wished it.

"I'm trusting you, Mr. Outdoorsman, not to be one of those trophy-collecting hunters," she said softly, leaning into his kisses, "or I'll have your license revoked."

"Oh, I'm not that," he said, surprised by the husky tone of his voice. "Maybe I'm other things, but I'm also a throwback to that strangest of all male breeds… a one-woman man. Like swans. I always thought I'd mate for life. And even when it didn't turn out that way, it would take a lot to beat that notion out of me."

"All I'm asking," she said, tilting her head to gaze at him soberly, "is that you be a one-woman-at-a-time man until we know… we know how all this might play out."

Sim put his hand over his heart, and swore solemnly, "Till we know what we've truly got going here, I pledge to be monogamous to the core."

"Thank you," she said simply. "Thank you for having the guts to use the *m* word."

"You're welcome. It's not as hard for me as you think."

She smiled again. "The gentlemen of my experience didn't even have the word in their vocabulary." She leaned closer, her scent only slightly less alluring than the promise in her gaze. "Here's how I figure it, shutterbug," she murmured, casting him a sidelong glance that was as come-hither as any mating dance he'd ever chronicled on film. "How can I know if I really love jazz and blues if I don't play them, right?"

"A wise woman," he commended.

She drew even closer and brushed her lips lightly against his.

"And how can I know what I feel for *you*, Simon Hopkins, if I don't discover it, firsthand?" Then, to his utter amazement, she whispered, "Shhh... quiet, Daphne! Stop talking and just ask this man to kiss you senseless."

We are creatures first, and rational beings second, he thought as he seized the initiative and did as he'd been requested, reveling in the warmth of her lips, the tip of her tongue tentatively exploring his own, and the faint taste of blueberry lemonade, tart, and astringent.

When she wrapped her arms around his shoulders, the shirt she'd been wearing gaped open and he felt her naked breasts against his chest. With a little sigh, she invited him to deepen their kiss, and suddenly he found that they were stretched the length of the narrow daybed in a tangle of bathrobes and shirts and entwined legs—one pair naked, the other cloaked in drawstring sailing pants.

Laughing, she sat up and held his gaze while she shrugged out of his shirt.

"Ever play strip poker without the cards?" she asked.

Then she waited with a mischievous smile while he stood, peeled off his bathrobe, and threw it on the floor like a matador divesting himself of his cape. He remained standing by the daybed and allowed his gaze to float lazily from her face to her slender throat to her beautiful bare breasts, lovely in their fullness and form. He sensed that his sudden nudity had unnerved her to some degree, so he remained stock still so as not to frighten or alarm her with any sudden moves. His mouth felt parched now, but he held off swallowing, even. He would wait as long as it took. He would allow her to grow accustomed to his presence. He would let her send him a signal... a sign. Meanwhile he drank in the sight of her naked torso, slender waist, and long legs still clad in outsize sailing pants.

When, finally, she licked her lips nervously and looked up at him through her lashes, he pointed to her drawstring trousers.

"May I do the honors?" he inquired.

She merely nodded and, smiling faintly, lay back against the pillows, allowing him to fumble with the strings and then indulge in the exquisite pleasure of skimming the cotton cloth from her waistline, down the length of her shapely legs. He paused before he tossed her clothing onto the floor in the pile that included his robe.

"I knew you'd be beautiful, but…"

"Me, too, you," she whispered.

He shook his head, unable to speak. Then he sat on the side of the bed and drew her onto his lap, absorbing the sensation of her smooth, golden flesh against his, caressing a breast with one hand while kissing her wherever his lips happened to fall. And then, somehow, they were lying on the narrow mattress once more, and she was beneath him. He gloried in nuzzling each breast while she arched her back in an unmistakable gesture of acquiescence. He sampled first one, then the other, like a ravenous hummingbird that would not leave the flowerbed alone until he'd drunk his fill.

He lowered his head, tasting her freshly scrubbed skin where her breasts creased her rib cage, licking, grazing his lips against her navel, and then glancing up to assess her reaction. Her eyes were closed and a ghost of a contented smile played about her open lips. He lowered his head once again and experienced his own slight intake of breath at the sight of a golden triangle of curls he'd only imagined. The reality of those erotic musings was now within view and he grew hard and short of breath. Her lovely scent assailed him again, a powerful agent that set his course like unseen radar, toward the target of his desire.

Penetrating this all-consuming haze of rampant craving was the sensation of her fingertips grazing his head. "Sim… Sim…?"

He raised his eyes to meet her questioning gaze. Her expression was a potent blend of shyness, alarm, and unquenched arousal.

"Oh… yes, darling Daphne," he assured her gently. "I'll wear a condom… but not yet. All in good time." And then he continued his quest for the exquisite sweetness only inches away.

As for Daphne, Sim's promise erased the last barrier, the last bastion that a thirty-one-year-old woman, burning up with desire for this man, would think to put in their path.

It had been the verbena soap that ultimately did her in, she reflected in the part of her brain that was still making sense. That, and the knowledge that here was a man who would look after her mosquito bites and wasn't afraid to say the word "monogamous."

Earlier, when she'd donned Sim's shirt and sailing pants and found herself sitting on his bed, she was fairly sure, then, there was no turning back. That, despite all the warnings ringing in her head, she wanted nothing so much as for him to kiss her blind and to feel the length of his long, muscular body pressing against her own.

Peel me a grape.

The beguiling lyrics of the sexiest song in her repertoire mercifully replaced the alarms as Sim continued his rapt exploration of her navel and the creases between torso and legs. Wherever he touched her, he laid claim to another inch of her skin that would never be the same after this day, never *not* know what it was like to be driven mad with pleasure.

Peel me a grape? she thought, near to laughter that bordered on hysteria.

She was the one being peeled down to the deepest layer of desire, stripped bare to the core of her voluptuousness, calling forth a sensuality she'd never fathomed she possessed. She could only pray that he continue his selfless ministrations, for she yearned for his lips to brush her there... and there... and, oh my God... *yes*! There!

It had been so long since she'd been touched. So *long*... and never like *this* with such skill and attention to detail. Wild, fluttering sensations began to radiate a universe of incandescent warmth and tenderness. The cottage walls and the rest of her surroundings faded from her consciousness as she allowed herself to be claimed by a liquid tide of passion, while, somewhere, a vivid recollection of the peregrine falcon, soaring and darting in the heavens above the Natchez Trace, drifted through her thoughts.

Daphne heard an attenuated cry, a shattering of the silence that had enveloped the wooded landscape outside, an atmosphere utterly still, except for the whir of wind that could sometimes be heard under a falcon's wings. She realized with a start that it had been her own voice resounding in her ears. A surge of sensation unlike any she had ever known lifted her higher still, and then burst, spilling snowy white down that floated to earth, feathers shed by a bird taken in midflight.

Another rush of emotion overwhelmed her and she fell back against the bed, her lips parted, exhausted from the journey, wanting only to be held, and soothed, and embraced in the safety of sheltering wings.

Sim's head was next to hers now, and he was cradling her against his chest. He kissed her eyebrows, her cheeks, the shell of the ear nearest him. With one arm, he reached down and retrieved his bathrobe from the cottage floor and draped it over their nakedness.

Outside the window, the only sound now was a faint chattering of birds on a tree branch near where Daphne lay somnolent and sated. Far, far in the distance, she thought she heard a falcon's cry.

After a few minutes, she raised her head, her eyes growing moist.

"Hey there," she whispered.

"Hello, angel…" he said, watching her intently.

Somehow, the endearment no longer set her teeth on edge. With Sim to show her the way, she'd soared and floated and somehow landed safely.

"I have never… in my life… experienced anything like… like what just happened." She kissed him on the forehead in an act of benediction. "You are a good and generous man."

He smiled faintly and responded in kind, kissing her on each eyelid.

"Believe me," he murmured, "the pleasure was at least half mine."

Daphne propped an elbow on the mattress and cupped her chin in one hand.

"Is that so?" she challenged with a wicked gleam in her eye. She boldly smoothed the palm of her hand along his chest to below his waist and continued downward. "Well, here's the other half," she announced.

She began with a feathery touch, gentle and sensuous at once, calling on the gods of music to help her express to Sim the same unstinting passion that had left her breathless and content. Slowly, and with the attention she would bestow upon a glorious adagio or arching glissando, she stroked and caressed him, wooing him as lovers woo, as artists paint, as musicians play.

And then, before her song could come to its forgone conclusion, Sim seized her hand, raised it to his lips and murmured, "Another time, angel woman. Another time."

And in an instant, he was hovering above her like a protective eagle, his arms on either side of the pillow, his hips pressed against hers, his long legs smothering her thighs. And then he kissed her and she knew how much she wanted him.

"Yes?" he asked, as if her thoughts were transparent.

"Oh, yes, please," she sighed. Sim swiftly donned the protection he had promised, and when he'd taken her in his arms again, she drew him into her, welcoming him to a soft, sacred place where she would take off her feathered mask and give herself up once more to the beating of wings and the soaring joy of a peregrine's flight.

And then they slept.

Daphne awoke first and tucked her head under Sim's chin, pressing her cheek as close to his chest as she possibly could. She was in the falcon's lair, she thought sleepily, protected from stalkers and predators of all descriptions.

Her eyelids still felt heavy, as did her whole body, and a sprightly tune drifted through her thoughts. It was an old melody, a lively gavotte popular at eighteenth-century balls, that Cousin Maddy had taught her when she was a child just learning to play the harp with both hands. The sprightly tune always made her think of parties and laughter and whispered assignations arranged behind fluttering fans.

The tune was so familiar... so full of promise for dancers in satin ball gowns and knee breeches who glided across the floor while candlelight danced on the walls. She could hear the tinkle of crystal glasses and bursts of merriment and the crunch of wheels on a gravel drive. Behind her eyelids, she saw horse-drawn carriages pulling up before a magnificent house. A flood of newly arrived guests was ushered past stately columns and across a wide veranda toward an open front door. Inside, a liveried butler greeted the newcomers, taking their cloaks and pointing the way inside.

Through the open windows, the music swelled, and somehow Daphne knew that the night was ripe for romance.

CHAPTER 17

FEBRUARY, 1798

Don't y'all hear that music downstairs?" Mammy
demanded. The black woman stood with hands on hips,
gazing down at her several charges in various stages of undress in
an upstairs bedroom at Concord, the governor's mansion a mile
or so down the road from Bluff House. "Time to get up, y'hear
me? Kendra's here to help y'all lacin' up your corsets," Mammy
announced, drawing the curtains back so that shafts of late afternoon sunshine filled the room, "and I'll do what I can 'bout your
hair. Wake up, sleepyheads! Naptime's over."

Daphne Whitaker and her two sisters, along with the other young
ladies from the most prominent families in the Natchez Territories,
lifted their heads from linen-covered pillows and blinked drowsily.
The group of young women had been fatigued after standing on
the edge of the parade grounds at the dilapidated Fort Rosalie all
morning to greet the late Queen Marie Antoinette's cousin, Louis-
Philippe—the duc d'Orléans—on his arrival by river barge. The
youthful nobleman and his ragtag entourage had made a show of
marching up the road from the docks, royal flags flying, past the
houses of ill repute in Natchez-Under-the-Hill. The visitors, clad in
their blue, threadbare French army uniforms, and the local residents,
dressed in their finest attire, had reveled in the clear, unseasonably
warm February weather and the commanding view of the river.

Governor Manuel Gayoso de Lemos had stood at attention,
relieved, for the moment at least, of the improbable duty of ruling

over Natchez's cauldron of disparate factions: English, French, American, and his own restless Spanish countrymen. After the formal review of the troops, he extended a courtly invitation to all the young ladies present to repair to Concord to enjoy a rest and refreshments. Later that evening, a grand ball in the young duke's honor would be followed by a sumptuous repast.

"Y'all are bein' mighty pokey," Mammy complained. "Gonna miss supper, if you don' get up, right now!"

Daphne pulled a feather pillow over her head, wishing she could sleep forever. Beside her in the large, four-poster bed, her sister Maddy, and their baby sister Suki, now fifteen, struggled to sit up. Daphne, however, kept her eyes shut tight, ignoring Mammy's demands that they get dressed. Instead, she strained to listen to the twittering birds in the larch tree outside the mullioned windows and to the lilting music of the small orchestra wafting up the grand staircase.

I don't want to go to the ball! I don't! I don't! I don't!

Daphne's silent protest would be to no avail of course, for the mourning period for her father was long since past, and Charles Whitaker's friends and neighbors, believing he had slipped on an icy rock four years earlier, had other thoughts and concerns. Who had time to console a young girl who remembered her father's reassuring presence in the days before he took to drink to assuage his sorrows? As far as anyone knew, the tragedy Daphne had endured had merely been one among many that struck, without warning, in a frontier society like Natchez.

Napoleon striding through Europe—now *that* was a tragedy for planters like the Hopkins and Gibbs families who had abandoned tobacco and were finally producing plentiful crops of cotton. Simon Hopkins, the Elder, had loyally assumed wardship of the Whitaker children and taken on the responsibility of his late neighbor's plantation. Thanks to his foresight and Eli Whitney's new cotton gin, Devon Oaks was finally producing to its capacity. Nonetheless, planters in Mississippi and Louisiana regularly risked their lives and livelihoods getting their goods past blockades imposed by all parties to the conflicts still raging in Europe.

No, Daphne thought, peeping out from under her pillow to stare through the bedroom window at a stray warbler sitting on a bare branch in the cooling afternoon sun, there would be no thought for her father's demise during tonight's festivities. Nor would there be special consideration granted Charles Whitaker's eldest daughter, who was now old enough to realize that she was often laid low by the same dark moods she so abhorred in her mother. Life went on... and nobody knew how miserable it was to keep the secret that Daphne felt like shouting to the heavens.

My father drowned himself! He left us! He didn't care enough...

Nobody knew the truth except both Simon Hopkinses, father and son, and during the intervening years they had made an art of rarely alluding to Charles Whitaker. She was alone in a prison of silence. No lively gavotte or pretty ball gown or sweetmeat or fine wine was likely to distract her from the dark tunnel her life had become.

"Oh, Daphne," Maddy whispered loudly, poking her older sister's arm. "Look at Rachel's gown. 'Tis beautiful watered silk in the most heavenly shade of blue. Just look! Simon will be smitten for sure, don't you think?"

Grudgingly, Daphne shifted her gaze, but merely stuffed the pillow behind her head and refused to sit up. She didn't give a fig if Simon Hopkins, budding young botanist and sketch enthusiast, proposed tonight on bended knee to that priggish Rachel Gibbs. For all she cared, he could make an ass of himself in front of the gaggle of mincing French courtiers and the entire town of Natchez! Love was not for the likes of her... no, *no!* Daphne thought mutinously. The violent scene she had witnessed as a child between her parents in their upstairs bedroom had been enough to put her off courtship and marriage for all time. If a man took a drink... well, a woman took her life into her hands, she thought glumly.

She regarded Rachel Gibbs with a jaundiced eye as the dark-haired beauty stood patiently, both hands on the bedpost, while Kendra tugged on the laces of Rachel's corset to create the eighteen-inch waist every self-respecting young woman desired.

Everyone except *her*, of course, Daphne thought with peevish satisfaction. Often, these last four years, she'd refused even to dress and would remain alone in her bedchamber on the second floor of Devon Oaks. Even when the family was in town at Bluff House, she flaunted convention and wore her bed gown downstairs to play her harp.

Daphne's gaze wandered to the lime-colored silk ball gown draped over a nearby chair that she would be forced to wear that evening. No one had listened to her complaints that the sickly greenish shade gave her complexion a sallow appearance that even a set of diamond ear-bobs and a necklace—given her by Grandmother Drake—could not ameliorate. Her mother still wore widow's weeds and seemed to take pleasure in her permanent state of grief, Daphne thought resentfully.

Oh, what's the use? she cried out silently as the dull throbbing in her head began, as it always did, whenever she thought about her father. There had been safety in his arms before Charles Whitaker began to drink heavily. When she was small, he had petted her and told her she was pretty and that she played her harp like an angel. Her father had *loved* his eldest daughter… surely he had? But he had drowned himself and left his family to fend for themselves. She hated him for that. And she *hated* her dead-eyed, sniveling mother! She hated them all, and she most heartily hated the thought of attending tonight's ball.

Candles illuminated every window of Concord, and cast a mellow glow over the mansion's ballroom with its satin-clad musicians at one end, and whirling dancers gliding across the polished floor as if on golden ice.

I will not cry!

Daphne plastered herself against the wall opposite the small orchestra playing a lively reel and blinked her eyes hard.

No one had asked her to dance. Adding to her misery, she was hot in her finery and could barely breathe, thanks to the fierceness and determination with which Mammy had laced her into her stays. Her blond hair lay in fat sausage curls plastered against her neck. She felt faint with the heat. The room was filled to over-flowing with guests who probably hadn't risked bathing in many months, and the stench of perfume was nearly as awful as the odors it was meant to mask.

"Miss Daphne?"

A kind voice startled her. She turned as Governor Gayoso gently took her hand with a courtly bow.

"Your Excellency…" she murmured, gazing into the dark eyes of the smooth-shaven gentleman, resplendent in a lacy cravat and ivory waistcoat under a coat of midnight blue velvet adorned with magnificent silver buttons down the front and encircling the deep cuffs.

"I am delighted that you grace us with your presence tonight, my dear *señorita*," he said compassionately. "May I say… it pleases me to see you looking so well."

The man was a blatant flatterer, considering the color of her dress, but he obviously meant to be kind. Daphne inclined her head, and murmured, "Thank you."

"I can only imagine how difficult it has been for you and your poor mother since the loss of our dear *amigo*, your father… a man who contributed much to our society here in the Territories."

"'Tis good of you to speak of him thus, Your Excellency," she said a bit stiffly. She was uncomfortably aware that many eyes in the room were observing this exchange.

"Your grandmother, *Señora* Drake, made mention of her recent gift to you on the occasion of your birthday," he offered genially, referring to Daphne's magnificent diamond necklace and matching earrings. "These are exquisite and suit you wonderfully well. Wear them in good health."

"You are very kind, indeed…" she murmured, blushing with embarrassment that so distinguished a personage should have taken such public notice of her.

The governor leaned forward and smiled encouragingly. "Would you do our guests the honor of joining the musicians on Concord's harp for the next reel?" he asked, his black brows knitted in inquiry above dark eyes. He lifted a velvet-clad arm and gestured toward the orchestra with lace-frilled wrist and manicured hand. "Your father often spoke of your exceptional talent. Would you be so good as to indulge us?"

The governor had indeed been a close friend of Charles Whitaker, and the reminder of this fact touched Daphne deeply. Gayoso was singling her out in memory of her father, and thereby encouraging the young swains in the room to pay her court. She smiled at him with genuine pleasure and nodded her assent before the fright of being thrust unexpectedly into the limelight took hold. She allowed the genial governor to lead her to a padded stool positioned beside a small golden harp and nervously took a seat. Her hands suddenly grew clammy and perspiration trickled beneath the back of her gown. Her stomach lurched alarmingly when the musicians played the first, familiar strains of the lively tune.

Dancers leapt to their feet and skittered about the ballroom. Remarkably, Daphne acquitted herself reasonably well. When she had finished, she was greeted with more than polite applause. The governor stepped forward, still clapping, with a handsome young member of the royal entourage in tow.

"May I present one of the duke's gentlemen, Monsieur Jacques René Hébèrt?" Governor Gayoso said with a wink. "I should have asked your mother's permission first, but after listening to you play, Monsieur Hébèrt pleaded with me so eloquently to be introduced immediately that I did not have the heart to refuse him."

Dumbfounded, Daphne turned to regard the stranger clad in a worn—but once fashionable—burgundy frock coat, buff knee breeches, and discreetly darned ivory silk hose. Despite the loss of their country and their fortunes, the visiting dignitaries had done their best to keep up their spirits and appearances, and Monsieur Hébèrt was no exception. This band of refugees from the French Revolution had straggled down the Mississippi River on a barge from St. Louis en route to what they hoped would be a warm welcome among Francophiles in New Orleans.

"My friend, the Marquis de Vaille, and I were entranced by your command of your instrument," Hébèrt declared charmingly, "and I wagered him the price of a supper in *La Nouvelle Orléans* that I would be introduced first." Daphne glanced across the dance floor and saw a squat young man in a plum satin suit place a hand over his heart and make a slight bow in salute to his friend's apparent success.

The sandy-haired Jacques Hébèrt was without powdered wig, but his hair was pulled back and tied with a black ribbon, periwig-style, at the nape of his neck. Slender, of moderate height, he respectfully bowed over Daphne's hand, and murmured, "You were enchanting on the harp, *mademoiselle*. Beauty *and* such talent… all in one lovely lady." He was rather attractive in an intense, ascetic fashion, putting her in mind of an underfed, pedigreed greyhound.

Blushing for a second time that evening, Daphne met his glance as Monsieur Hébèrt raised his eyes and resumed an erect posture. No one had complimented her like this except her father… long, long ago, before the greedy bankers, the succession of dead babies, and his melancholy wife had driven him to suicide and changed his daughter's life forever.

"If you will excuse me, the young duke beckons," the governor declared jovially.

"Would you care to dance, *mademoiselle?*" Jacques inquired politely. "*C'est une gavotte.* I'm sure you will put these rusty feet of mine to shame."

Daphne gazed in horror at the lines of dancers preparing to launch into a series of figures that originated as a gamboling French peasant dance.

"Oh… I've rarely—"

"Come, *mademoiselle*," her escort commanded. "I will show you how 'tis done in Paris! Just observe the lifting of my feet, and we shall outshine them all."

The next hour was a fantasy of fun the likes of which Daphne had not sampled in her entire life. Jacques was a superb dancer, schooled in the French court, and passionately devoted to the terpsichorean arts.

And his manners! Daphne mused, filled with gratitude for the young aristocrat's effusive attention and the string of compliments he showered on her throughout the evening. He showed her every respect, fetching her refreshments,' delicately clasping her hand each time they returned to the dance floor, and bowing often to demonstrate to everyone present his sincere regard.

Jacques Hébèrt was not at all like the younger Simon Hopkins, who had made no secret of wanting to kiss her and had clutched her hand until she had been forced to push him away one moonlit night the previous summer. If Simon would not speak of what he had witnessed that cold, January day when her father had killed himself, Daphne refused to entertain any thought of an alliance, despite the proximity and business ties of Hopkins House to Devon Oaks and her youthful fondness for her neighbor. Her erstwhile suitor had finally given up, and Daphne was relieved that such ardent wooing had now unleashed itself upon Rachel Gibbs, leaving Daphne free to enjoy the attentions of the visiting Frenchman.

At length, when the orchestra paused, Jacques declared, "'Tis insufferably hot in here, *non?*"

Daphne nodded, speculating worriedly that the perspiration she felt soaking her bodice might have made itself known to sensitive French nostrils.

Before she could reply, however, Jacques gestured toward open doors. "Would you join me on the... how you do call it? The veranda?"

Daphne closely regarded the duke's fellow traveler whose arm she clutched as he swept her past her somber, vacant-eyed mother, who looked for all the world like a skinny black crow sitting next to Simon and Rachel Gibbs. The trio stared curiously as Daphne and Jacques escaped the stuffy ballroom for the balmy night air outside. Simon rose abruptly from his chair, but mercifully did not follow them.

"When we are cool again, I shall fetch you some refreshment and you shall tell this wanderer all about life in this exotic land," Jacques proposed.

The poor man is lonely, reflected Daphne sympathetically. She knew too well the dark despair that loneliness could engender. She smiled faintly and nodded. "Perhaps you will do us the honor of visiting Devon Oaks while you're here? The countryside is lovely, full of woods and birds and streams. It might make you feel less homesick to see land that would make you welcome."

"You are too kind." He sighed heavily. "You are… *sympathique* with my sad fate?"

"*Sympathique*," she said softly. "Yes… I believe I am."

They walked down the porch steps and along a garden path until they reached a shadowed arbor, bereft of leaves on this mild February evening.

"When the orchestra has recovered its strength, perhaps you will play an encore on your harp?" Jacques inquired gallantly.

"I fear I will not be a-asked," she stammered. "I struck a few false notes earlier."

"'Twas the orchestra that faltered," he assured her blithely. He paused and indicated a bench where she might sit down. His pale brown eyes looked into hers intently.

"'Twas I who made the mistakes," she demurred.

"Surely not!" Jacques insisted. "I have witnessed many an entertainment at court and know whereof I speak. You played brilliantly!"

"Are you a royal cousin to His Grace?" Daphne asked shyly, wishing she had her fan to cool her perspiring forehead. She was greatly relieved to be inhaling the sweet-smelling night air and prayed that her overheated face would quickly lose its flush.

Jacques tilted his head and laughed mirthlessly. "Ah… *non, mademoiselle*, I have noble, but no royal blood. I am a *journaliste*. I was known everywhere in Paris as *Le Terroriste*… for in my newspaper I gave opinions on political affairs, you understand?"

"You were not a royalist?" she asked, startled. "But then, why are you with—"

"I am a Frenchman, and loyal to *La France*," he declared in rather a sharper tone of voice than he had used earlier. "The newest duc d'Orléans wants the best for our poor country now—as do I. So we have found common ground. *La Revolution* has made for strange bedfellows. I quite think my skills with the pen make me valuable to him… do you take my meaning?" he added, with a mysterious smile. "He, the Marquis de Vaille, and I shall do well together when we arrive at *La Nouvelle Orléans*."

Daphne didn't understand the import of the stranger's words, but she enjoyed the warmth of his glance and the praise he heaped on her about her performance. After all, surely he had heard the finest music in the world at the French court. Hadn't her father once told her that the queen herself had been noted for the beauty of her harp playing?

The French visitor's command of the English language was remarkably good. Jacques explained that in 1793, when blood had flowed in the streets of Paris, the elder Philippe—"Philippe Egalite," as the father of tonight's guest of honor had come to be known—paid dearly for his daring and had himself become a victim of *Madame Guillotine*. His surviving son fled to North America with the hope that he might one day be summoned back to France to assume the vacant throne. Meanwhile, the penniless young royal depended on the kindness of strangers in a land where France no longer held sway.

"Come, *ma petite*," Jacques coaxed. He took Daphne's arm and gently guided her farther down the moonlit path that curved to the right of the governor's mansion, its windows aglow with candlelight. "You must tell me more about this great Mississippi River of yours. How far is it beyond *La Nouvelle Orléans* until one arrives at the Caribbean Sea? We hear that the plantations are *magnifique* in that part of the world and that a thousand slaves do one's bidding night and day."

Jacques fervently hoped that the Marquis de Vaille was spying on them through the ballroom window, as his companion would be forced to admit that their wager had nearly been decided. Seducing this pathetic bit of Natchez fluff in a single evening would be child's play, with the added bonus that he would relieve her of her diamond jewelry, and the marquis would have to stand him to a good cognac—that is, if they could secure one in this godforsaken outpost!

The necklace and earrings belonging to this gullible *jeune fille* would come in extremely handy. He would certainly need to have new clothes and a decent mount in order to impress the widows and orphans who clung to their plantations in Santo Domingo—or whatever the island was called where they had been assured their fortunes were to be found.

Jacques summoned a practiced melancholy smile to his lips and gazed at the moon as he recounted the horror that had befallen his family in France.

"Forgive me, *mademoiselle*, for burdening you with the sad tale of my parents' fate."

"Oh, 'tis no burden," she assured him in hushed tones. "'Tis indeed tragic that your mother and father met such a terrible end. I am touched that you should honor me with your trust, for I know, myself, how heartbreaking such violent losses can be."

He could see that Daphne Whitaker had been deeply moved by his solemn recitation of the mournful last mile to *Madame Guillotine's* embrace—a tale he had invented out of whole cloth to deify a drunken sot of a father and a whore of a mother who dwelled in the stews of Paris to this very day. How fortunate for him that the governor had unwittingly disclosed details about the plantation heiress's unfortunate situation—the tragic death of Daphne Whitaker's sire and the instability of a *maman* whose perpetual melancholy rendered her a poor guardian of her daughter's virtue.

However, he would have to proceed swiftly and cleverly, for he'd spied the girl's black house servant watching him closely when he guided his intended prey out onto the veranda. He would woo the moony *mademoiselle*, pierce her maidenhead, and depart by dawn's light with her jewels. He'd collect de Vaille's wager once their barge arrived in *La Nouvelle Orleans*.

He slowly extended his hand and fondled an earring, saying softly, "*Sacre coeur*, but you are as lovely as the greatest beauties I ever saw at Versailles. I never thought to find such a flower in this wilderness."

Daphne Whitaker raised her chin and said with more spirit than she'd shown all evening, "Natchez, sir, is considered among the finest cities on this continent. New plantation houses are being built each year, and the town itself has many fine mansions to its credit. If you gaze around the ballroom, you will find many women pleasant to behold."

"But no jewel as dazzling as you," he whispered softly. "I must see you again. I must—"

Daphne had the expression of a startled deer, and took a step backward just as a voice bellowed from the shadows.

"I fear I must interrupt this unseemly exchange."

Daphne whirled in her satin slippers and went slack-jawed. Stalking down the path were two gentlemen of similar aspect, but far different age.

"How dare you, sirs?" Jacques said icily.

"You are taking savage advantage of our hospitality, my man, to entice my ward into such a compromising situation. I am Simon Hopkins, and this is my son, whom I am pleased to say noticed your actions and hastened to inform me that you—"

"You have been *spying* on me!" Daphne looked scathingly at the younger Hopkins, and Jacques instantly sensed that she held no fondness for the young man who had summoned his *père*. Her eyes flashed and her hands formed fists beside the folds of her ghastly green gown. "How dare you presume to treat me as a child. I'm practically as old as *you* are!"

"That is of no import whatsoever," the elder gentleman replied heatedly. "You are my ward and my responsibility, Daphne, and if you have no better sense than to slip into the shadows with a knave like this, then I must, perforce, save you from your own folly." He seized Daphne's hand and addressed his namesake. "Son, should you be thinking of anything so foolhardy as to challenge this villain to a duel, I command you as my only heir to *desist*." Then he turned to address Monsieur Hébèrt directly. "By dawn tomorrow," he declared in tones dripping with disdain, "you, sir, and the other dishonorable wastrels who call themselves *noblemen* will be miles downstream, and we *Americans* shall have no need to dirty our hands with you."

Jacques took a step forward and glared at the intruders. "I, sir, demand satisfaction from you and this ill-mannered pup."

"Father?" Sim said, his fists clenched in fury. "How can we stand by and—"

The elder Hopkins ignored his son. "Monsieur, you'll not say another word to my son or to my ward. Simply make your fare-wells to your host, Governor Gayoso, as if nothing is amiss. Then you will immediately retire to your quarters on the barge. If not, I shall personally escort you to my plantation, and there shoot you myself. Do you understand what I've just said, or shall I translate it into French?"

At this, Daphne covered her face with her hands and began to cry tears of fury and mortification.

"Stop that at once!" her guardian demanded gruffly. "You'll cease sniveling like your mother, dry your eyes, and dance one last quadrille with my son, as if nothing has occurred. Then you will withdraw politely from the festivities and be taken home by your mammy and we will not speak of this again." He addressed Jacques. "And you, sir… I have had about as much of you Frenchies and your damnable insolence as a body can endure."

And with that, Simon the Elder bid his son take Daphne's other arm. The trio advanced rapidly toward the columned entrance to Concord—abandoning Jacques René Hébèrt to the shadows and his own smoldering humiliation.

The night is still young, ma petite pigeon… *'tis still young…*

CHAPTER 18

DAPHNE DUVALLON RECKONED THAT she had slept curled up next to Sim in the one-room cottage for an hour or more. At least, that was what she desperately *hoped* she had been doing, for she had awakened just now with a clear recollection of having witnessed her namesake naively falling for the oldest line in the world.

You are so beautiful… you are so talented… come, let me seduce you, my pretty little nincompoop!

She lay quietly beside Sim, who slept peacefully on the day-bed, and felt her heart thumping heavily in her chest. What a strange vision—or hallucination or *nightmare* perhaps. She replayed the scenes, blushing at the thought that she had been nearly as naive with Jack Ebert—not to mention Rafe Oberlin when he came on strong with flattery and Veuve Clicquot champagne during her first year at Juilliard. Worst of all, it was positively unnerving to have encountered an eighteenth-century version of her former fiancé Jack Ebert, whose name popped up as Jacques René Hébèrt. Even the French rake's profession as propagandist to a kingly wannabe eerily echoed Jack's work as a PR flak for Able Petroleum.

What was it that the French always say, she mused? *Plus ça change, plus c'est la même chose.* The more things change, the more they are the same, indeed.

It was insane, she thought worriedly. She had felt certain that these ghostly visitations would cease to plague her now that she had made her momentous decision to escape New York and the intense stress of her life there. But here she was, having just made love… delicious, staggeringly wonderful love, in fact… and then, bingo, she dreamed about *another* Simon Hopkins in *another* century that *another* Daphne had apparently grown to detest because she preferred being wooed by an obvious cad.

It was just a dream…

But was it? She wondered what had triggered the little virtual reality show *this* time. Was this latest foray backward in time some sort of warning? Was the Simon Hopkins sleeping next to her everything he seemed to be? Had she made another stupid choice?

The last thing she'd remembered was basking contentedly in Sim's arms and listening to the birds twittering. An old dancing tune she'd known since childhood had drifted through her thoughts, and then—abracadabra! There she was, watching Daphne Whitaker wake from a nap in an eighteenth-century four-poster in a Natchez house called Concord.

Once again, it had been the surrounding *sounds* of chattering birds and the memory of music that had apparently provoked the extraordinary parallel journey into the lives of people who seemed to have been her ancestors. According to her family tree, Daphne Whitaker was a real person. Her birth and death dates were no doubt a matter of public record. However, these flip-backs couldn't be chalked up to past life memories—reincarnation—because she didn't experience these events *as* her namesake. She *witnessed* the other Daphne's emotions and psychological turmoil rather than experience them herself.

She bit her lip, lost in thought while idly gazing at Simon's sleeping form. If these events had truly taken place once-upon-a-time, it would seem that their repercussions were somehow still rippling down through the centuries and affecting her life today. Had the other Daphne's terrible taste in men become part of her *own* DNA?

What a thought!

Daphne was struck, suddenly, by another electrifying notion: what if a person's major psychological and emotional traits were also handed down from one ancestor to another, just as were brown eyes or curly hair or diabetes? Could it be that some unhappy ancestral memories continue to impact events these many generations later?

There were so many parallels. Both she and her namesake played the harp and had thorny relationships with their mothers, along with serious, unresolved issues of abandonment with their fathers.

And, like Cousin Maddy's distant forebear, Susannah Whitaker, Maddy had admitted to battles with the "Whitaker blues," as she'd describe the debilitating despondency she'd endured following the traumatic deaths of her husband Marcus and her son Clay. Was her reaction to those tragedies normal, or was something else at work here?

These thoughts were sobering, and Daphne was determined not to dwell upon them for very long. Her only wish now was for these phantoms from the past to stop appearing in dreams—or in any other fashion.

"You look as if your thoughts are a million miles from here," Sim said quietly.

Startled, Daphne turned to gaze at her new lover, and couldn't help smiling. Sim's bathrobe, which they'd been using as a blanket, had slipped down, and she allowed herself the pleasure of gazing at his bare, muscled chest. A faint stubble shadowed his jaw and highlighted the sharp angle of his cheekbones.

Erotic memories skittered across her mind. She reached over and trailed the backs of her fingers along his cheek.

"No... actually, I was wondering if, somehow—way, way back—you aren't, in fact, related to the Hopkinses whose plantation was destroyed in that horrible tornado Bailey told us about. It feels so natural to me that you're here. Or rather, that *I'm* here."

Sim rose up on one elbow. "What a nice thing to say," he said softly, capturing her wandering hand. "Wouldn't it be something if we turned out to be kissing cousins?" He leaned toward Daphne and bussed her on the cheek before flopping on his back once again. They lay quietly beside one another for a long while.

Her instincts told her Sim was a good man. But then, her instincts had been wrong before. She marveled at the roller-coaster afternoon they'd had, and without thinking, she began to laugh.

"What?" Sim demanded, lifting his head off the pillow.

"It just occurred to me," she said, chuckling. "Mosquitoes can be good things, can't they? Look what they accomplished."

Then, for a split second, she thought of the deadly yellow fevers that had felled so many of her Southern ancestors in centuries past. She was grateful she lived in an age when that sort of plague had been banished by modern science, and even a bottle of Bactine could prevent a Mississippi mosquito from doing further harm.

"Absolutely mosquitoes can be good things," Sim said, nuzzling the base of her throat as if he were a friendly vampire. "Eef it veren't for zose pesky eensects," he agreed, doing a fair imitation of Count Dracula, "who knows, my dear, how long eet might have bee-an before I finally lured you eento my caa-stle bed?"

"You *tink* so, do you?" she said, doing her level best to sound like Zsa Zsa Gabor. "Veil, Countess Daphne has some veee-ry een-teresting ideas about vat to do vit zis laf-ly, laf-ly part of you!"

And then she ceased her teasing, and vowed to stop obsessing about a dream. Instead, she set about to show Sim that, once again, the pleasure would be all theirs.

Daphne sat in a chair beside the small, round table in the middle of the cottage. Clad again in Sim's outsized shirt, she watched with unabashed pleasure while he donned his bathrobe. For at least an hour, as they lay in bed, their conversation had been intimate, comfortable, and full of laughter.

"Here," Sim invited, handing her a glass, "have the last of the lemonade."

"Thanks," she said, draining the glass while handing him half a cookie, the remnants of a bag that Sim had produced from the backpack he'd left on the veranda. She gazed at the late afternoon sunshine slanting through the windows and wondered briefly if the little house were truly as isolated as it appeared.

"When does Doctor Gibbs get back?" she wondered aloud.

"Tomorrow," Sim replied, resuming his seat across from her.

"I FedEx-ed him a bunch of bird and landscape color photos to use in his testimony today before the legislative committee up in Jackson. He thought they might help him and his fellow bird lovers show the powers-that-be how irreplaceable these habitats are in and around the Trace."

"You two have become really good friends in a very short space of time, haven't you?"

Sim gazed at her thoughtfully. "It's strange, actually. I've been such a loner for ten years, and yet I arrive in Natchez less than a month ago—and you two suddenly appear in my life." He tweaked her nose lightly. "You, my lovely Daphne, who can play and sing all my favorite tunes... and Bailey, who shares my passion for animals and the environment, not to mention the pleasures of wine, women, and song."

"Doctor Gibbs?" Daphne asked skeptically.

"He may be in his seventies, but that man likes his mint juleps, right enough, and as for women... sometimes, he cheered louder than I did when you Aphrodites strutted your stuff."

"You're kidding!" Daphne laughed at the notion of Bailey Gibbs getting hot and bothered by stiletto heels.

"You better believe it. And he never stops talking about his late wife." Sim shook his head. "I thought my parents, after nearly forty years of marriage, were pretty cute, but Bailey and Caroline Gibbs must have been something to see."

Except for her brief stays in Natchez with Maddy and Marcus when she was younger, Daphne realized now that she'd never witnessed a husband and wife enjoying their life partnership. The family atmosphere in the Duvallon household had either been nuclear war or an uneasy truce.

Her head full of disturbing childhood memories, she reached across the table and allowed her thumb to graze the top of Sim's hand. "Do you still think about your father a lot?"

"I suppose I've been thinking about him more than usual now that I'm around Bailey so much," Sim acknowledged somberly. "Bailey says he's got his prostate cancer under control at the moment, but I went through all that with my dad. I just hope to hell he gets his wish about protecting this bird sanctuary. A loss in Jackson is bound to demolish his morale, and…"

Sim rose from his chair and gazed out the window at the meadow.

"Do you think he'll win over the key legislators?" Daphne asked.

Sim heaved a resigned sigh. "I don't know. I've watched these battles go both ways." He turned to face her. "I'm not some obsessed crusader, you know? I don't take pictures anymore just to advance some cause."

"Why *do* you take them, then?" Daphne said, startled. She'd assumed he was an ardent conservationist. "Why go through so much mud and misery if you're not passionate about saving the environment?"

"Oh, I know full well what's at stake and I want it saved. And I'm not opposed to my photographs of animals in the wild and what's left of our wilderness being used to inspire folks to do what they can to protect the planet, but I…" Sim appeared to be searching for the words. "You can burn out really fast, if what you're trying to do is save the world. And it gets very discouraging to play David against Goliath all the time. I do what I do now to make sense out of my *own* life. I came to the conclusion, after my marriage broke up, that I had to find a way to live so that I wasn't doing more harm than good. Nature photography and traveling to remote places seem to… *seemed* to," he corrected himself, "accomplish that goal."

"Who did you think you were in danger of harming?" Daphne inquired quietly.

"I… I wasn't harming *anyone* if I stayed out there on my own," he replied, neatly avoiding her question.

"Wasn't that choice a little bit tough on your family?"

"I didn't think about it. Then."

"And Francesca? After the divorce, was she glad you'd banished yourself to the wilds?"

"Probably. Or, more than likely, she didn't give a damn *what* I was doing as long as I wasn't in her line of sight." He shook his head. "It's been a long time, Daphne. I don't even remember, anymore, all the factors that launched me down this road. I guess living *on* the road so much has become more habit than anything else. A way to put some distance between me and my troubles."

"A way of avoiding your troubles, perhaps?" Daphne asked lightly.

Sim shot her a look that seemed to say *touché*.

"As I think back on it, it *was* kind of the chicken's way out, you know? I didn't have to deal with Francesca's rejection anymore, or the strains within my family after the baby died and our divorce... or any of it."

"And now?" she asked, wondering how any sane woman would reject a man like Simon Hopkins if he really was the man he seemed to be.

"My father's terminal illness forced me to go home for a while and work out whatever stuff he and I had avoided."

"And that was..."

"My not telling him what had really gone on between Francesca and me... and my hitting the road afterward and not staying in touch with him and my mother."

"And he forgave you?"

Sim paused, and then nodded. "He forgave me—and himself—for being such a hard-ass." He turned and cast a thousand-yard stare out the window once again.

"And now?"

Sim looked over his shoulder. "Well... at the moment, I'd have to say that the wild blue yonder doesn't hold quite as much appeal." He crossed to the table and sat down. "These days, I've a hankering to stick around to see what's going to happen in *this* neck of the woods." He cuffed her gently on the chin. "With us, certainly, and with Bailey's crusade. I'm aware that pictures like mine can help—some—to make the issues at stake more understandable to the average Joe."

Stick around? She wondered for how long.

She pointed to a large photograph of a nesting mockingbird that Sim had leaned against the wall. "You know, Mr. Hopkins," she said quietly, "these amazing images have the power to make people *care* whether peregrine falcons are on the endangered species list or not. I think it's wonderful that you've given Bailey some support in this fight. Maybe you're still more of a crusader than you think."

"Well, as sort of a tribute to my dad, I've decided that I'm going to do whatever I can to help the guy," he said with a self-deprecating shrug. "But these fights always take a *community* rallying around the cause to shake some sense into the politicians. I hope people around here will wake up and smell the coffee before it's too late—but they very well might not—and I can't allow myself to get crazy over that."

"Hmmm," Daphne said, digesting Sim's remarks while considering the picture of the mockingbird nest. "Most of the folks with big houses around here don't have unlimited funds anymore to donate to their favorite charities. Hiring lawyers and going up to Jackson can get expensive."

Sim cocked his head and gazed at her shrewdly. "What about a local fundraiser to mount a legal challenge against Able Petroleum? Do you think that's an option?"

"Uh... oh... I don't know," Daphne mumbled, immediately thinking of her own crowded calendar.

"Well," Sim said, resuming a seat at the table, "if I decide to volunteer my services to raise some cash to help the cause, what about you? Don't you think it's the least we can do to repay the good doctor for his hospitality?" he finished with a rakish grin.

"What kind of a fundraiser are you thinking of?" Daphne asked suspiciously.

"Oh... I don't know," Sim said, with an innocent expression. "You know this area a lot better than I do. What do you think would work around here?"

"Sim Hopkins, if my gut instincts didn't tell me otherwise, I might think that you'd deliberately lured me into your bed today in order to get me to co-chair the Bailey Gibbs Bird Preservation Extravaganza."

Sim's grin was unabashed now. "Maybe this is a classic case of killing two birds with one stone."

"You are *so* bad," she scolded.

"And you are *so* good... in bed."

"Wicked man!"

Sim pulled her to her feet and wrapped his arms around her shoulders. "What a great idea to have you as my co-chair! Thanks for suggesting it."

"I did no such thing!"

He kissed her on the nose. "Will you? Help me, I mean? For starters, I'm willing to donate a signed set of large-format bird prints I've done in the area to auction off to the highest bidder."

"That's a terrific idea," Daphne said thoughtfully. "That kind of thing isn't too hard to pull off. I could organize a silent auction or something. People in Natchez have a ton of antiques up in their attics they'd probably love to donate to a good cause."

"Ah... you don't get off that easily, Harp Honey. Ever since I heard you were going to live here for a year, I've been thinking about how great it would be to stage a benefit concert. You know... all the kinds of music you hear around Natchez... classical... blues... Jazz... rock 'n' roll?"

"Oh, I don't know..." Daphne countered reluctantly. "I've got an awfully full plate as it is... and if it's going to be a music-based fundraiser, a ton of responsibility would naturally fall on my shoulders."

"Wouldn't your cousin Maddy help?" Sim asked hopefully. "And Althea and the McGee family? I bet if you combined all your talents and your contacts here and in New Orleans, you could put together a program that would attract more people than the Natchez Pilgrimage."

"Oh, Sim... get real."

Ignoring her comment, he pressed, "And, you're right, we could track down other things to auction off besides my pictures. Antiques are a good idea, and what about a night's stay at Monmouth Plantation? What about a dinner party donated by some of the other plantation owners? And—"

"Whoa, there now... it sounds to me like you've done this kind of thing before."

"My mother and... well, Francesca... used to be big in the charity circuit in San Francisco. I've been to more than my share of fancy black-tie events."

"Well… at least it sounds as if you know what you're talking about," she allowed.

"It'd be something *for* the locals *by* the locals," Sim said, his excitement evident. "Something to save the birds that live in their own backyards… something—"

"I've *got* it," Daphne exclaimed, pointing out the window at one of Bailey's bird feeders that was casting a long shadow across the meadow in the fading afternoon sunlight. "A concert 'For the Birds'! A benefit concert *in aid of* the Mississippi Flyway, and with the express purpose of blocking a toxic dump adjacent to private land where birds have been protected for years."

"That's *brilliant*," Sim said softly. "I can already see the posters and ads."

"Every single piece we play at the concert could have some connection *to* birds!" she said with a rush of enthusiasm.

"*Swan Lake*," Sim volunteered.

"Ugh! But okay." Then her eyes widened excitedly. "*The Firebird Suite.*"

"Where you going to get an orchestra?" he asked doubtfully.

"Natchez has an opera season, Bird Man," she proclaimed. "Maybe the orchestra conductor would be willing to put together a small chamber orchestra for one night."

"*Double* brilliant. Let's see…" he said, rubbing his chin. "Bird songs… bird songs…"

"Easy! They're only about a million of 'em," Daphne said, waving her hand dismissively. She immediately began to warble the tunes. "*Bye, bye, blackbird… When the red, red, robin goes bob, bob, bobbin' along… Skylark…*"

"Okay, okay! I *believe* you," Sim protested, laughing as he cupped his hands over his ears. He drew her into the circle of his arms once more. "You are something else, Ms. Magnolia," he whispered into her ear. "You understood this bird stuff so fast, it took my breath away today."

"I learned about fighting to save the environment at my brother's knee," she murmured, snuggling beneath Sim's chin while they remained with their arms clasped around each other.

"You mean King's saving all those buildings?"

"In his own way, he's battled for years to preserve what he calls 'the historic environment.' I bet if I call him, he and Corlis will do what they can to help." Then she bit her lip.

"What are you thinking?" Sim demanded. "You looked as if a black cloud just appeared over your head."

"Jack," she pronounced. "My getting involved in this project means I'm going to mix it up with Jack and Able Petroleum and I worry that—"

Sim put a hand on each of her shoulders. "Jack cannot hurt you, Daphne. Just keep telling him to get the flock outta here, if you'll pardon the expression," he said jocularly. "And tell him you've got some big bruiser in your life now—a wild man from the tundra—who's totally got your back."

By this time, the sun had slipped behind the stand of trees encircling the cottage, and shadows turned the room into a dusky den. Sim crossed the room and lit the kerosene lamp on the table beside the daybed.

Then he turned, and declared suddenly, "We've *got* to help Bailey, Daphne. This is a doctor who fought to save the lives of people like Marcus Whitaker and Caroline Gibbs. People... like my father. And he's fighting, still, to save the birds. He's a valiant old man who's much more exhausted from these battles than he lets on. But I can see it. He's got cancer and—"

Sim's voice broke, and Daphne walked the short distance across the room, raised her hand, and gently tweaked his nose in a tender mockery of all the times he had made the same gesture.

"Hey... what are you worried about?" she asked softly. She thrust out her hand in a gesture of solidarity. "Harp Honey to the rescue. Gimme a high five!"

Sim's eyes were so full of gratitude that Daphne forced herself to push away any doubt that she could help produce a money-raising show *and* keep her own financial ship afloat. She smiled while Sim ceremoniously shook her hand and then, suddenly, leaned down and scooped her up in his arms.

"Since I owe you my eternal gratitude," he said with an evil chuckle, "*I* just had a brilliant idea for a change." He strode over to the unmade bed and carefully laid her upon the rumpled sheets.

"Gee… let me think," she said, rolling her eyes heavenward. "What could that be?"

Sim flung off his bathrobe. "Guess."

"Why, Mr. Hopkins," she drawled, "I do declare… you are naked as a jaybird."

᷈᷈

A routine, of sorts, began to take shape for Daphne and Sim during the subsequent weeks. Tuesday mornings, Sim headed deep into the Trace, stalking a list of birds painted by Audubon so many years before. Often, he camped in the woods, returning by Friday to sit front row, center at every weekend performance of the Aphrodite Jazz Ensemble.

For her part, Daphne spent her days running between rehearsals, teatime gigs at the Eola Hotel, teaching harp students with Cousin Maddy in the parlor at Bluff House, and contacting various community leaders about raising money to protect Bailey's bird sanctuary. Twice a week, she and Willis McGee met in the studio he'd built in the garage behind his house. During those sessions, Willis unveiled his amazing storehouse of knowledge about jazz riffs and "finding the groove" in the scores of tunes they rehearsed together.

When Sim and she could find the time, Daphne delighted in showing him her favorite Natchez hangouts. They often had chopped pork sandwiches, homemade baked beans, and miniature pecan and sweet potato pies, served in grand style by drummer Jeanette McGee at the Pig Out Inn.

"I especially like the decor," Sim mumbled with his mouth full. He nodded in the direction of an inflatable pig hanging above the window and a bright pink porker with angel wings floating on a string from the overhead fan.

Occasionally, they drove a few miles out of town to eat at Mammy's Cupboard, a hallowed icon where the primary part of the restaurant was housed in the red brick skirt of the gargantuan mammy figure.

"The place is not exactly politically correct, but everybody loves Mammy's," Daphne admitted, relishing a bite of Mammy's Mile-High Lemon Meringue Pie.

"I can see why." Sim groaned, patting his bloated stomach with a pained expression. "I don't think too many eateries in America can claim to serve sour cream corn muffins *and* broccoli corn bread, *and* Mexican corn fritters all on the same menu."

Sim even made it to Natchez the day the historic *Delta Queen* docked next to the *Lady Luck*. That morning, Daphne conferred with the activities director to offer her paid services the next time one of the three paddle-wheelers paid another visit to Natchez-Under-the-Hill. After the successful conclusion of the negotiation, she and Sim ate corn dogs on the deck and listened to the old-fashioned calliope whine out nineteenth-century favorites like "In the Good Old Summertime!"

Their idyll came to an abrupt halt one hot Monday afternoon in early June when Daphne wheeled through the gates of Gibbs Hall and continued on foot to the cottage. Sim was not his usual, cheerful self. He handed her a glass of iced tea and pointed to one of the two chairs that flanked his minuscule dining table.

"Got something to tell you," he said without preamble.

"What?" Daphne asked, conscious of the hum of the air-conditioner in the window nearest the daybed.

"My mother called from San Francisco today."

"Is she ill?" Daphne asked with alarm.

"Oh, no… nothing like that," Sim assured her. "She just called to warn me."

"About what?"

"That I should expect to hear from Francesca sometime soon."

"Really?" Daphne said carefully. "And why is that?"

"She's coming to Mississippi on a case. She wanted my mother to give her a number where she could leave a message when she arrived."

"Did your mother give it to her?" she asked stiffly.

Why am I giving this poor man the third degree?

"Francesca can be very persistent. She said she knew what

project I was working on back here and wore poor Mom down with a battery of questions. My mother said that afterward, she felt like she'd just given a deposition. She felt terrible that she'd told Francesca where I was staying and called me today to apologize."

"How in the world did Francesca even know you were in Mississippi?"

Sim paused and arched an eyebrow. Daphne knew instinctively that bad news was on its way.

"She's been hired to act as legal consultant for Able Petroleum in the environmental battle shaping up in Jackson."

Daphne sat up straight in her chair. "Oh, my God…" she said, stunned. "It's Jack, isn't it? Jack, the *agent provocateur*. Jack the Internet wizard. Remember what he said that night at the bar when he admitted he'd done a Web search on you and your wife?" She stalked to the door and held it open. "Do you mind if we sit out on the veranda? I need some air."

"Sure," Sim said, and followed her outside. "It's starting to cool off."

"That son of a bitch!" Daphne began to pace the porch. "He finds it *amusing* to stir things up like this. He does it just for the perverse entertainment value."

"Well, obviously he also wants to win this battle very, very much if he's willing to pay Francesca's enormous consulting fee. Her firm is one of the top corporate litigation outfits in the country."

"Able Petroleum is footing the bill, so what does Jack care? He's hell bent on sweet revenge, and figures, somehow, that Francesca's just the person to help him get it."

"It's a legislative battle, Daphne. It'll be decided in a bunch of hearings, not here in the Natchez Trace. It's not personal."

"Oh… it's *personal*, Sim. Trust me," Daphne said bitterly. "I *knew* Jack wouldn't just leave me be. I knew he wouldn't let go until he felt he'd humiliated me as much as I humiliated him. He won't be satisfied until he's stripped me of every happiness he can."

"Look, Daphne," Sim said. "Aren't you being a little—"

Daphne turned on him and felt her heart begin to pound.

"If you say 'dramatic,' I'm going to walk right out of this place, because you *have* to believe me when I say that there is something very, very scary about this guy."

"I think he's really just a pest," Sim said gently.

She turned and stared at the bird feeder replicating Monmouth Plantation. Then she faced Sim again.

"You said the day that I agreed to help you with the benefit that you'd stand by me if Jack threatened any trouble. But if you won't…" she said, her hands on her hips, "if you're not up for dealing with this kind of a mess—an ex-fiancé and an ex-wife, both up to no good—then let's just put that on the table right *now*, before I get my heart handed to me."

"Daphne, why are you making such a—"

"Sim… *stay with me*, here! You said a long time ago, 'We're all grown-ups' and I believe I am… or at least I'm getting there. So, I'm asking you, Simon Hopkins, to *trust* me when I tell you Jack's latest move to involve your ex-wife in this is *serious* and can cause us nothing but trouble unless we stay vigilant. You have to take my word on this. And if you take the attitude of 'there, there, little lady, don't exaggerate,' I will pack my toothbrush right now and clear out. I mean it!"

Sim stood silently behind one of the rocking chairs, his long fingers tapping the white wicker in concentration.

"This is really visceral with you, isn't it?" he asked. "Gut instincts?"

"Higher up," she declared, planting an imaginary dagger into her chest. "A stake in the heart."

"Okay…" he said slowly. "I get it. Jack's unpredictable." He stepped toward her, but before he could enfold her in his arms, Daphne put the palm of her hand on his chest to ward him off.

"Sim, you and I have to be absolutely clear about everything," she said in a voice that vibrated with intensity. "Jack is far more than 'unpredictable.' I'd go so far as to say he's got a screw loose," she said, thinking back to the day Jack locked King inside a big family crypt on the grounds of a New Orleans cemetery in the heat of the day to prevent her brother from testifying at a building demolition hearing. "*Believe* me, if Francesca is working as a legal consultant for Jack Ebert, he's just upped the ante about fifty levels regarding the toxic dump controversy. As far as I'm concerned, they're both the enemy now. I learned that from my brother King. And if you don't see it that way, that's your right, but then *I'm* not signing on to help you or Bailey Gibbs with the fundraiser to challenge Able Petroleum—and putting myself in harm's way." She removed her hand from his chest and turned to face the veranda railing, staring into the stand of trees that encircled the cottage. "So, just tell me," she said softly, her back to him. "Are you up to being a *totally* united front about this—or not? If not, fine. I won't feel rejected. I'll just know that you're being straight with me."

The air crackled with an emotional charge. Daphne could sense Sim gazing at her ramrod-straight back as they stood silently on the veranda. At length, he answered her question by closing the gap between them, pressing her against his chest, and gently wrapping his right arm around her upper torso, pulling her close.

"I take that as a yes?" she murmured, tears suddenly filling her eyes. She felt the knot in her stomach miraculously untie and she could breathe again. She turned in place and allowed Sim to take her properly into his arms. "Now, what do we do?" she whispered into his collarbone.

"Nothing," he said. "We'll be patient. We'll stay alert… 'vigilant' as you put it. And we'll go on with the business at hand."

Daphne leaned back and gazed at Sim with a watery smile. "You learned a lot, didn't you, during those ten years in the wilderness? The wait-and-watch stuff."

"I learned a lot about myself."

"So have I," she murmured.

And then he led her by the hand inside the cottage, cooled by the humming air-conditioner, and made love to her, telling her without words, she supposed, that he had signed on as one half of a united front.

CHAPTER 19

DAPHNE RECEIVED ANOTHER UNPLEASANT and unanticipated jolt within an hour of leaving Sim's place and returning to Bluff House. At the end of Maddy's driveway, a burgundy late-model Cadillac with Louisiana plates was parked haphazardly on the grass, as if its driver couldn't care less about the unsightly grooves his Michelins made on the lawn. The owner was easy to identify.

Steeling herself, she mounted the back stairs of the old house and prayed for courage to break in on the diatribe bouncing off the walls of her cousin's kitchen. She stood on the back porch for a while and peered through the screen door.

"It's plain mortifyin' for everybody concerned, and you, of all people, know perfectly well it is, Madeline Whitaker!"

"I don't see it like that at all, Antoinette—"

"Well then, you're as certifiable as *she* is," Antoinette exclaimed, "Isn't she, Waylon?"

Daphne's father sat at the kitchen table with an untouched glass of lemonade in front of him. Waylon Duvallon appeared as uncomfortable in his brown suit and buttoned-down shirt as when his short, stout frame had been squeezed into white tie and tails the fateful evening he'd walked his only child down the center aisle in Saint Louis Cathedral.

"She looks like a damn tramp in that picture," he growled. "First King pisses off every friggin' developer and politician in New Orleans, and now my daughter joins a rock 'n' roll band with a bunch of nig—"

"*Hello*, Dad," Daphne said, pushing open the back door with a bang. "Mother."

"Where the hell have you been?" her father demanded. "Your mother and I have been sittin' 'round here for more than an hour, waitin' for you and—"

Maddy jumped up from the kitchen table, wringing her hands nervously. "They left a phone message that they were in town, dear, and planned on comin' by for a visit, but I was teachin', and you were…"

"Showin' your tail in a bar somewhere, probably," Waylon declared, banging his fist on the kitchen table.

Meanwhile Antoinette, too, had risen from her chair. She was impeccably groomed, her periwinkle-blue silk jacket setting off her flawless complexion and jet black hair, pulled back, as always, in a smooth chignon at the nape of her neck. Her white linen skirt just skimmed her knees and showed off her shapely legs to good effect.

Standard issue for a Magnolia Suprema, Daphne thought, attempting to keep her sense of humor and self-confidence intact.

"Quiet, Waylon," her mother snapped. "Let's let Daphne explain to us why she has abandoned her thrivin' career as principal harpist in the Oberlin Chamber Orchestra in New York and returned to this backwater to sing with a bunch of blacks in costumes even hootchie-kootchie dancers would be ashamed to be seen in." She narrowed her hostile glare and pointed a perfectly manicured vermilion fingernail at Daphne. "Just tell us, daughter. I'm curious to hear exactly what led to your latest *brilliant* decision regardin' this travesty you call your *life*!"

Before Daphne could even attempt a reply, her father waved two newspaper clippings in her face. "You've outraged the family one time too many, young lady." Squinting, he read aloud, "'The Aphrodite Jazz Ensemble's scanty attire is an insult to the Natchez community where music and art have long enjoyed an honorable tradition.'"

Daphne stared at cousin Maddy and then at her father. "Where did that come from?"

"The *Times-Picayune* in New Orleans," her mother shot back. "And surely you've seen the photo of yourself in the *Natchez*

Democrat? You don't think you can keep such scandalous behavior a secret, do you?"

Daphne stalked to the kitchen table and snatched the *Picayune* article from her father's fingers. Eyeing the byline, she announced with disgust, "Bitsy Worthington's so-called society column! You *know* she was Jack's old boss at *Arts This Week* and got fired at the same time he did when Lafayette Marchand took over. This is a planted item, Daddy, designed to disparage me." She turned to address her mother. "Jack's up to his usual dirty tricks, and, as usual, you get mad at *me*?"

"Oh... I'm not just angry about the public humiliation you're causin' *us*, young lady. You are a Juilliard-trained classical harpist," she declared icily. "We made tremendous sacrifices to send you there. You are also the daughter of a family whose Louisiana roots go back nearly two hundred years. Your mother was a Mardi Gras queen, for pity's sake, with all the privileges and responsibilities that entails. And here you go, takin' a cheap job in a cheap bar that's got all of New Orleans and Natchez talkin'—not to mention the damage you continue to do to Flowers by Duvallon—"

"Stop this right now, Mother!" Daphne shouted, interrupting Antoinette's harangue. Two years of silence had unleashed a tidal wave of pent-up resentments on both sides. "What you so conveniently forget is that *I* earned the music scholarship to Tulane. *I* played about a million jobs to pay for most of Juilliard, and I'm *still* in debt because I paid you back every cent you were out from the wedding!"

By this time, Daphne was feeling as if she were the victim of an emotional hijacking. Trembling, she shredded Bitsy Worthington's article and threw it on the floor.

"And if I want to play jazz in a *brothel*, I will! I'm thirty-one years old, Mama. What part of my decision to live my own life don't you understand?"

"Why, you little—"

"Antoinette, forgive me," Madeline Whitaker broke in sharply, barely in time to prevent Daphne's mother from slapping her daughter across the face. "But I'm afraid I'll have to ask you to leave if you continue to assault poor Daphne like this under my roof."

Antoinette Kingsbury Duvallon drew herself up and shifted her ire to her first cousin by marriage. "You're throwin' *me* out of this dump? Now, that's a laugh, isn't it, Waylon?" She glanced around the cluttered kitchen and laughed mirthlessly. "Madeline Whitaker's gonna show me the door? No wonder you two have cooked up such a ridiculous scheme here. I hear you're even rentin' a room to some jungle bunny piano player."

"*Althea*, Mother," Daphne said, heartsick that her mother would deliberately speak of her friend in such a bigoted manner.

"Althea LaCroix, Madeline Whitaker, and Daphne Duvallon!" Antoinette spat. "What *is* this place? The House of the Risin' Sun?" She turned on Maddy, and said, "It's one slattern offerin' shelter to another, isn't it, Maddy? Only the problem is, cousin mine—my own daughter has practically ruined our flower business—"

"Oh... so *that's* why you can only afford to drive that new Cadillac, is it?" Maddy retorted sweetly.

Antoinette continued, oblivious to Madeline's interruption. "Everyone in town has said for years that you and Marcus and Clay were practically poor white trash, livin' in this dump, and now it's in the *newspapers* that that's what you're tryin' to turn my daughter into."

Antoinette's expression was that of a triumphant debate captain who had finally won the battle of words. Waylon, too, exuded a satisfied air. As for Daphne, she felt sick to her stomach. She took a step backward and leaned against the kitchen sink for support. She was startled when she heard Maddy speak up.

"You have to leave now, Antoinette," the older woman declared softly, her voice more arresting than all of her visitor's histrionic fulminations. "You, too, Waylon." She pointed to the back door with its top hinge falling off. "I see perfectly well how you've regarded Marcus and Clayton and me all these years, and I do not have to tolerate your contempt in my own house—ever again."

"For God's sake, Maddy, Antoinette is just tryin' to make the point—" Waylon began.

"Leave at *once!*" the owner of Bluff House insisted, slamming her fist down on the kitchen table in a rare show of wrath.

Seething, Antoinette snatched her blue clutch bag off the table and glared at her husband, as if expecting him to defend her honor. Meanwhile, Maddy, her gentle face etched with sorrow, walked slowly to the back door and held it open.

"I learned some awfully hard lessons when Marcus and Clay were sick... and then died," she said, her tone conversational now. "Here's the main thing I've discovered: we only have *today.*" She glanced at Daphne with a reassuring smile. To the Duvallons she said, "You have a lovely, talented, hardworking daughter whom I love like I loved my husband and son. I hope for your sakes that someday you two will come to appreciate Daphne for precisely the darlin', precious woman she is." She shrugged her shoulders as if there were nothing more to say on the subject. "Y'all have a safe journey home."

And without further exchange, Antoinette and Waylon Duvallon marched out of the kitchen and down the rear stairs, and swiftly backed their late model Cadillac out of the drive before Daphne leaned over the sink and was desperately sick to her stomach.

When, finally, Madeline led her to a chair and applied a damp dishcloth to the back of her neck, Daphne began to cry deep, cleansing sobs that came from a place too primal for words or explanations. The older woman pulled up another chair and eased her cousin against her narrow chest, rocking Daphne as if she were an injured child.

"I know it's crushingly sad, darlin'!" she crooned, swaying rhythmically. "Crushingly sad."

As if to underscore her cousin's heartfelt sympathy, Daphne burst into another round of tears.

"Maybe th-they're r-right!" she sobbed. "M-maybe I'm crazy t-to be doing a-all this..."

"Oh, Daphne, please..." Maddy said, holding her close. "Don't turn this on yourself, darlin' girl! You've got to *accept* things as they are, don't you see? And if you can, try to *give up* any notion you might nurture in that lovin' heart of yours that your parents will ever behave any differently toward you than they did today. From what we've observed all these years, chances are good they won't. 'Course, there could be a miracle," she said, dabbing Daphne's eyes with the dishcloth, "'cause we never rule those out, do we?"

Maddy handed Daphne a second cloth to mop the tears streaming unchecked down her cheeks.

"Th-they did the same th-thing to King." Daphne hiccuped, pressing the cloth to her eyes. "When he f-fought all those people trying to demolish h-historic buildings in New Orleans, I mean. They disparaged every thing he did, saying he was hurting their business just for spite, when all he was doing was trying to keep New Orleans beautiful!" She dropped the cloth into her lap and stared at Maddy with tortured eyes. "But *why*? W-why wouldn't they be *proud* that he'd help save all those wonderful places from the wrecking ball?"

"'Cause it's more important to them what the powerful people in New Orleans want—the ones who buy their fancy flower arrangements and make money buildin' big hotels—than what you *or* King thinks is the right thing to do," she pointed out matter-of-factly.

"I know..." Daphne said, shudders wracking her shoulders. "That's w-what just *gets* me. I wanted... I w-wanted..." She couldn't finish her sentence.

"You wanted them to love you, no matter *what*, didn't you? And they should... but they don't love *themselves*, darlin'—not one little bit—so how in the world can they love anybody else? What they did to you this afternoon is what you're likely always to get—no matter if you're playin' harp in a sailor's bar or at Carnegie Hall."

"I know..." Daphne moaned as another wave of emotion overwhelmed her. "I know that... what you say... is true." She shook her head slowly and took deep, steadying breaths, calmer now. "It's just that I feel as if... someone has *died*."

"Well... in a way, someone has. Maybe you're grieving for the parents you wish they were. But if you can just start accepting the way they truly *are*—over time—their bad behavior won't hurt so much, 'cause you won't be surprised by it anymore."

"I guess you're right…" Daphne replied, feeling spent. "There are some things you just can't fix."

They remained quiet for a long moment. Finally Maddy said softly, "I think you're very wise to see it in that light. If you understand… deeply… *truly* understand that you have no power to change your parents' behavior… you can get rid of the poison, as you just have, and not take any more into your darlin' soul. The way I see it," Maddy said, giving Daphne's hand a soft squeeze, "whatever choices Antoinette and Waylon make—or don't make—have very little to do with you, actually, so you needn't feel responsible for any of it." She gently patted the younger woman's forearm. "I know that probably leaves you feelin' pretty cut off from the people who brought you into this world, but none of us is ever truly an orphan, Daphne, if we take the trouble to surround ourselves with kindred spirits."

Daphne gazed at her cousin, deep in thought. "You… King and Corlis… Althea… Willis McGee… all of you have been so good to me," she whispered, her eyes filling with tears once again. A memory of Sim solicitously dabbing her mosquito bites with antiseptic nearly prompted another flood of tears.

"That's because we all love you, darlin'," Maddy said brightly, giving Daphne a big hug. "Just the way you are—you kindred spirit, you!"

"Thanks," Daphne murmured gratefully, dabbing her eyes one last time.

Bone weary from her emotional outbursts, she stumbled up to bed, turned off the ringer on her phone extension, and fell into a sound, dreamless sleep. At ten o'clock the next morning, she awoke to Maddy gently shaking her shoulder.

"It's Sim on the phone, sweetheart," she said apologetically. "I thought you'd want to talk to him. He says it's important."

Daphne sat up, looked around her cozy room under the eaves, and blinked. Thirteen hours of sleep, along with a glimmer of a new understanding concerning her parents, had made a world of difference. She grinned crookedly at her cousin and declared, "I actually feel pretty good, considering."

"Well, that's truly a blessin', dear," Maddy responded, smiling broadly. "I'll make you some coffee."

Daphne padded in her bare feet into the room she was using as her office and picked up the receiver.

"Hello, sleepyhead," a deep voice said. "I've shot about a thousand images already when I'd much rather be between the covers with you, darling."

"Sim!" Daphne protested, laughing in spite of herself.

"Listen... a slight change of plans. Just got a call from an editor from one of the magazines I shoot for occasionally and he's sending me to the Amazon on a story about contraband parrots. I can't do lunch at South of the Border this week, but I'll be back in Natchez by your next day off, on Monday."

The man was winging to the Amazon and he considered that a *slight* change of plans?

"Wow... South America and back in a week?" Daphne murmured, her emotional elevator plunging to the basement. She despised herself for feeling this way. This was his *job*. This was the globe-trotting world Simon Hopkins had inhabited for more than a decade. It was childish of her to be waylaid by an unwarranted sense of abandonment. Yet, these were the very issues Sim said had arisen between his wife and him. How could two people conduct a sustainable relationship when one was sent to remote jungles at a moment's notice?

"Daphne? Are you okay with this?"

"I hate it," she declared.

"Well, there's an honest answer."

"But it's what you do, Sim. It's your job," she said hurriedly. "I understand that... but I... well, I just had a huge fight with my parents who were lying in wait for me when I got back to Bluff House last night. So, I think, right now, I feel a bit like a kid someone forgot to pick up at school." She laughed with embarrassment. "I'll get over it."

"Your folks don't like your new career, right?" Sim asked quietly.

"Among about a million other things they don't like. Jack got another creep journalist to write in her New Orleans newspaper column that I was a disgrace to all music lovers."

"That bastard—"

"But actually, I'm glad everything's on the table now," she

interrupted. "Same with you, shutterbug. I hate that you're going away right at this particular moment, and I'll miss you madly, but I'm trying to stay focused on how happy I'll be when you get back. Don't do anything dangerous, promise?"

"Oh, I promise," Sim assured her, his deep voice soothing to her ruffled heart. "I'm going to take very, very good care of myself, because I want you to figure out a way for me to feed you those fried green tomatoes with crawfish rémoulade in bed the night I get back. Deal?"

"Deal. See you… when?" she asked.

"Let's make it Sunday night. After your show. I'll come to town to pick you up en route from the Jackson airport."

"Oh Sim, it's out of your way to come into town."

"After the miles I'll have traveled by Sunday… not a problem."

And, suddenly, Daphne felt like a grown-up again.

～

Willis McGee's family lived just off Martin Luther King, Jr. Street, not far from a tire plant. The McGee residence, a batten-board farmer's cottage that had been added on to over the years, was a neat and tidy house in the predominantly black section of the city. Daphne's aging silver Jeep barely fit into the driveway next to a battered van marked "The Willis McGee Band—Parties, Weddings—You Pay… We Play!" The telephone number to call for bookings was printed in bold red letters.

The hot June sun beat down on Daphne's back as she eased the mammoth harp case out of her car. The front door opened and Mrs. McGee welcomed her cordially, as always, and pointed to a side entrance to the garage.

"I'm just feedin' Willis his lunch. I left the door open, dear," she said cheerfully. "You jus' go on out there and make yer'self at home. He'll be out shortly, and Kendra and Jeanette are due back from the Pig Out any time now. It'll give you time to set up. Can I bring you a soda or somethin'?"

"No, but thanks," Daphne replied. "It'll take me a while to tune the harp."

"Well, let me know if you change y'mind."

Daphne nodded her thanks and continued down the path toward the garage. The interior of the converted space was completely covered—floor, walls, and ceiling—in squares of vibrantly colored carpet samples. Willis had glued them on every available surface to create a soundproof space in which to practice and record. A small, electronic mixing board with numerous knobs and dials stood behind a glass wall. Music stands piled high with charts dotted the room, as did a variety of musical instruments, including Jeanette McGee's drum set.

Daphne unpacked her harp, pulled up a metal folding chair, and began to tune the strings. After ten minutes or so, her glance fell upon a piece of sheet music propped on a music stand nearby. She leaned forward and stared at it intently. The notes were hand drawn—by Willis, she assumed. The notations were extremely complex. Black notes flew like tiny crows across the page.

She reached out and fingered the paper on which the music was written, making a soft tap-tapping sound as she plucked the corner of the page with her thumb. Oddly, it was a familiar sound, a sound that resonated somewhere in a place long forgotten... a place where musicians had left their hand-drawn music charts and abandoned their violins and gambolas on velvet-covered chairs in an ornate ballroom. A place where dancers, too, had departed for a late supper, and only a short, squat young man in plum velvet carelessly seized a piece of music off a mahogany music stand, fingering it for a few moments.

Tap... tap... tap...

The man's thumb continued to pluck at the piece of paper as if in time to unheard music. Without warning he ripped the parchment's corner. Swiftly, he thrust the torn piece into the hands of his companion—a slender young man with sand-colored hair and dark, furtive eyes.

"No!" Daphne whispered aloud as the gayly carpeted walls of Willis's studio began to fade to gray. "Not now! Not again..."

CHAPTER 20

FEBRUARY, 1798

*A*TTENDEZ, *JACQUES!* HERE'S SOMETHING to write upon," the Marquis de Vaille declared, indicating the corner of parchment he'd just torn from the conductor's score. "See if you can find a quill in the study and scribble a note on the back of this. Beg to see the girl one last time. Deuced, if I won't find a way to thrust it into her hand!" His round face had assumed a leer that journalist Jacques René Hébèrt had often observed when the *aristo* was seriously in his cups. "Quickly, though," the marquis urged. "I heard her guardian call for their coach."

As far as Jacques could fathom, the marquis's principal achievement in life was to have spent many long hours at the gaming tables in Paris with the notorious Italian libertine Casanova. The tipsy nobleman slapped Jacques on the back, irritating him even further. "Be assured, *cher ami*," chortled the sot, "you haven't yet won those thousand francs from me, but I yearn to stand witness to your success... that is, if you can somehow devise a way to pierce her maidenhead!"

Jacques slipped into the study unobserved and dashed off the requisite *billet-doux*. Then, the marquis managed a semiprivate farewell with the young *demoiselle* in question at the moment her guardian turned his back to allow a servant to assist him with his cloak.

"*Adieu, ma petite*," the rotund marquis murmured as he kissed the chit's hand. His words could barely be heard above the sounds of musicians tuning their instruments inside the ballroom. "Enchanting to make your acquaintance. Your handsome cavalier bids me give you this…"

The Marquis de Vaille slipped a folded missive into Daphne Whitaker's gloved hand and melted into the crowd streaming back into Concord House for another round of dancing. Jacques doubted much would come of it, but for a thousand francs and a handful of diamonds, he was willing to hazard one last try. Discovering the location of Bluff House was an easy task.

As for Daphne Whitaker, the silent journey home seemed to go on forever in a coach crammed with the reproachful Hopkins men—father and son—three unhappy Whitaker sisters, and their melancholy mother.

Several hours later at Bluff House, Daphne sat dressed in her ballroom finery on her narrow bed. In her trembling hand she clutched two objects. She leaned toward the candle's light and unfolded the piece of music with its message written on the back.

Mon Ange… meet me in your beautiful dress at the edge of the cliff two hours before dawn…

A white silk rosette with dark brown droplets staining its folds lay in her satin lap. Jacques had included the cockade along with the note that the Marquis de Vaille had stealthily slipped into her hand. Daphne's wide-eyed gaze moved from the *bijou tendre*, as Jacques had called his love token, to his hurriedly penned note, which she read, once again, from its beginning.

This cockade is stained with the blood of my late, sainted mother. I consign it to your care to prove my honorable intentions, merely to hold you in my arms once more. I pray one day that I can make you my noble bride in this vast, new land.

Ma très chère chérie, never did I dream to meet someone so sympathetique to the wretchedness that has been my lot these last years, someone whom I instantly knew to be the other half of my heart that I thought shattered forever.

Prove to me I am not alone in believing that our meeting is a blessing from God, that we should find each other and give comfort and care in the years to come. I wish only to tell you of my pledge to return, Mon Ange…

Votre Jacques

Tears spilled down Daphne's cheeks. Jacques's loving words tapped a wellspring of emotion and need that she been denying to herself since her father's cruel death. Someone cared for her. Someone else in this lonely world had suffered, as she had, and wished to offer comfort. Jacques would shelter her from the melancholic humors of her mother's world that had tortured the woman for as long as Daphne could remember.

She carefully slipped the precious note beneath her pillow, doused the candle, and crept downstairs. Bluff House was shadowed and silent, as were the outbuildings that housed the kitchen, the smithy's shop, and the slave quarters.

She peered through the gloom, searching for a figure to beckon to her. Slowly, she descended the back steps and scanned the lawn that surrounded a large oak tree dripping with clouds of Spanish moss.

"Mon Ange…" a voice whispered hoarsely. Daphne raised one hand to her breast and could feel her heart leap. *"C'est moi!"*

"Jacques!"

Daphne didn't remember running toward him, or hurling herself into his arms. All she knew was that this French tornado had blown into her life less than six hours earlier and—for the first time in four years—she was able to feel as keenly for the terrible pain and loss *he* had suffered, as for her own piercing bereavement. For once, she could forget the vision of her father floating in Whitaker Creek, and, instead, behold the visage of Jacques Hébèrt between her hands, a man upon whom she could shower her love, care, and concern.

"Ah… *ma petite*," he said, crushing her to his chest. "You came!"

"Of course I came!" she whispered fiercely. "I, too, felt you were the other half of *my* shattered heart."

"Ah… *chère, chère* Daphne," he murmured, his lips beginning to roam from her cheek to her mouth, to a spot beneath her ear. "Come, my darling... we have so little time..."

He led her behind the oak and settled her back against its broad bark. Without further conversation, his hot, seeking lips nibbled her skin, searing the flesh on her neck.

"Jacques... I—wait! What are you doing?" she cried as he roughly began to nuzzle her earlobes, skillfully removing first one diamond earring, and then the other.

"I am making love, *ma petite*," he muttered. And, as if to underscore his claim, his lips moved lower to the base of her neck, licking and nibbling her tender flesh while he unlatched the catch on her diamond necklace. Swiftly, he stowed it in the pocket of his velvet frock coat, along with the ear-bobs. "I must see you naked as God intended you to be."

Shocked beyond words, Daphne began to struggle, pushing the palms of her hands against his linen-clad chest.

"No!" she cried. "Stop this! I don't want you to—"

Young, inexperienced, craving affection rather than adult passion, Daphne was stunned when Jacques began to insinuate his hands roughly inside her satin bodice.

"*Reste tranquille...* relax... relax..." he mumbled, and when she turned her face away from his voracious kisses, he grasped her shoulders and gave them a sharp shake. Then he seized the front of her gown with both hands and yanked the fabric, splitting the garment's seams and her underclothing to her waistline. Horrified, Daphne's hands instinctively flew to cover her breasts. Her attacker grabbed her wrists, clasped both hands behind her back with one hand, and used his other to push her to the ground and hike up her skirts.

Daphne began to scream as a kaleidoscope of terrifying images shot through her brain. Her father lying listless on the bank of Whitaker Creek. Her father, naked, hovering over her terrified mother like a great bird of prey. Her father... her father... how could anyone be so cruel?

She felt Jacques's weight pressing down upon the length of her body. Within seconds, however, he went utterly limp, his form becoming heavier still. The next thing she knew, Jacques René

Hébèrt rolled off her and lay face up upon the grass, staring at the night sky with glassy eyes. The canopy of leaves and moss overhead became a grotesque umbrella.

"Miz Daphne? Miz Daphne? You all right? Mistah Hopkins, he don' tol' me to keep a sharp lookout tonight, and I did. I surely did!"

It was Willis, Mammy's husband, his large, brown, bare feet planted in the grass beside her head. Dazed and sore, she pulled herself up to a sitting position, her satin skirts askew, her bodice in tatters.

"Mistah Hopkins say they might be two of 'em, and he was surely right! I done run off dat other fat man with *dis*!" he declared triumphantly.

Willis clutched a length of rope in one hand and a piece of wooden board in the other. Swiftly, the avenging giant trussed up Daphne's attacker—who was just regaining consciousness—and threw him facedown on the turf while Daphne gaped in stunned silence. By this time, several pinpoints of light had begun to converge on the trio under the massive oak tree. Mammy, Daphne's mother, and a wide-eyed Maddy ran toward them while Daphne buried her face in her hands and began to sob.

"Miz Daphne…" Willis asked hesitantly. "Did he… did he…"

"No," she said barely above a whisper. "No, no, nooooo…"

Her answer ended in a shriek. When her cry died out, she pressed her hands and arms across her violated breast and stared into Willis's dark eyes. His brows were furrowed with concern. The slave pulled off his homespun shirt and draped it around her trembling shoulders, tying the sleeves to cover her. In full view of her family and servants, Daphne pointed to the front of Jacques's woolen breeches, the buttons down the front still intact.

"No…" she said brokenly, "My jewelry is in his pocket, but he didn't… hurt me. Not like what Daddy did to Mama…"

❧

The meeting in the late Charles Whitaker's study at Devon Oaks Plantation was brief and to the point.

Simon Hopkins, the Elder, along with the widow Whitaker and Judge Ebner Stimpson sat facing one another over Charles's large, leather-topped desk.

"As Daphne's guardian, I have done my best to make this offer as generous as I can, Judge," Simon declared to the fifty-seven-year-old widowed jurist whose passel of children by his only slave, Leila, was the talk of Adams County.

"So you mean, sir, that I'm not to wed Madeline, but rather her little strumpet of a sister who made cow eyes at the Frenchies at Concord House two nights ago?" Judge Stimpson inquired peevishly. "That's not what I understood last week from her mother," he added with a disgruntled look in Susannah Whitaker's direction.

"Daphne's mother and I are now in full accord," Hopkins said sternly. "Either the eldest sister becomes your bride, or take your search elsewhere, Judge. You have debts and you have no white heir. So how say you? Daphne Whitaker is your only option, for I gave you no firm indication that Madeline was to be the answer to your pecuniary and dynastic troubles, sir."

Ebner Stimpson stroked his chin in an attempt to mask his astonishment at this bizarre turn of events. "Hmmm. 'Tis most unorthodox, you must admit. I dance the gavotte with one sister and marry the other? I shall mull over this proposal, sir, and give you answer in—"

"You will give us your answer now, or our offer will be withdrawn—for both sisters," Hopkins snapped.

Astonished, the judge's gaze drifted from Hopkins to Susannah Whitaker to Hopkins once again. He cocked his head, a slight smile pulling at the corners of his mouth. "And I will be master of Bluff House?" he inquired politely. "That is, sir, in addition to holding shares in the profits of Devon Oaks Plantation?"

"That is what this document says in very specific terms," Simon Hopkins replied impatiently, indicating the sheaf of papers lying on the desk. "It also says you will conduct your husbandly duties in such a fashion as to bring honor and *propriety* to this household, so watch your consumption of brandy, and sell that slave girl of yours, is that also understood? We will have no further hint of scandal at Bluff House or any other Whitaker property, do you hear?"

Judge Ebner Stimpson settled back in his leather chair, his flushed face growing even rosier after Hopkins's ringing admonition. Then he smiled faintly as he considered Hopkins's confirmation that he would have complete management and control of his wife's portion of the Whitaker estate—which included his favorite abode in all of Natchez: Bluff House.

He turned slowly toward Mrs. Whitaker, whose eyes were lowered to her hands that she held clasped in her black silk lap.

"My dear Ma-ma…" he murmured, doing his utmost to still his racing pulse, "I accept your terms with pleasure."

❧

"You can't mean it!" Maddy cried, her horrified gaze moving swiftly from her mother to her sister to her guardian's face.

"You were not promised to Ebner Stimpson," Simon Hopkins said gruffly, "and there are many other finer fish in the river, my girl."

Maddy pointed a trembling finger at Daphne. "But Ebner will be miserable with her. He never gave her a glance! He *liked me*!"

Daphne recoiled as if she'd been struck. "I have no wish to marry anybody! Especially that drunken sot who chases his servant around the woodshed!"

"Daphne, silence!" her guardian bellowed.

"You're just saying that because Ebner chose me first. *You're* the harlot," Maddy spat. "You disgraced yourself with that horrible Frenchman and ruined everything for Ebner and me!"

"Quiet, both of you!" Simon Hopkins shouted. In a softer tone that revealed a Herculean attempt to keep his sorely tried temper in check, he said to Maddy, "I fear the judge appreciated the Whitaker dowry more than he did either of you. And due to that ignoble fact, my dear Madeline, he is perfectly agreeable to make your sister's reputation whole again." He patted Maddy's hand in an awkward gesture of compassion. "I suggest, my dear, that you try to find solace in this. There's no doubt a young man in your future who will be more suitable in age and with whom you are much more likely to get on happily."

"And what earthly good is *that*?" Maddy screamed. "If I like such a person, and you find him a better match for my sister Suki, you'll take *him* from me." In a voice risen to a pitch that could shatter glass, the teenager sobbed, "I hate you! I hate all of you, and most of all, I hate Daphne and Ebner Stimpson." She whirled on her sister Daphne. "I hope you both rot in hell for what you've done to me!"

And with that, the young girl stormed out of the study, slamming the door in her wake.

"Come back here, Madeline," Hopkins called after her sharply. He glanced at Susannah Whitaker, whose face was a blank mask. "Can you not teach your daughters to behave properly?"

"Judge Stimpson," Susannah said, in a tone as flat as if she were discussing the weather, "at first paid court to *me*. But the man smells of spirits and I always find that quite distasteful."

She rose from her chair, nodded politely in the direction of the man in charge of her financial and familial affairs, and drifted out of the room, vanishing upstairs.

Simon gazed at the last member of the Whitaker family remaining in the study and sighed heavily. "I am only trying to see to your father's wishes that you be settled sufficiently to end the incessant drama that holds sway in this household," he said. "Can you not comprehend my good intent?"

Daphne glared unforgivingly at her guardian. She jumped up from her chair beside her father's desk and strode out of the chamber without even bidding him farewell. She continued through the front door and down the steps, walking without the benefit of a cloak toward the woods that led to Whitaker Creek. The truth was, she thought disconsolately, she didn't much care what happened anymore.

Fortunately, the sun was at its zenith, providing the February day with its warmest hour. She followed the old horse path toward the river, forcing herself to focus on the trees and the cloudless blue sky beyond… anything other than to dwell on the last few days. If she were forced to marry the toad, she would live at Bluff House, she assured herself. It was a place she loved. She would not have to see her mother's long face and sad, sad eyes as often. She would ask for Mammy to come, as she was an old lady, now, and would prefer to supervise a fine town house rather than a vast plantation.

And Daphne would insist that the drunken old judge make his quarters on the second floor so that she might command the top of the house with its spectacular view of the river. She would bring her harp upstairs and create a private sanctuary for music and...

Her mind a million miles away, she approached the narrow path that meandered close to the bank of the swimming hole before she realized where her feet had taken her. As she drew nearer Whitaker Creek, she could hear the sound of the babbling water rushing over rocks. She never came here, she realized with a sudden jolt of fear and apprehension. She hated this spot!

And then she saw it—a figure floating in the water, skirts ballooning below the still surface like a giant lily pad. Beside the stream lay a small pile of stones the size of apples. It was her sister. And she had deliberately drowned.

Daphne Whitaker's keening cries could be heard as far away as the open study window at Devon Oaks.

"Maaad-dy... how did you know about Papa? No, no, NO! Maddy, how *could* you?"

⤴︎

The raucous sound of the McGee sisters' laughter roused Daphne Duvallon from a stupor that had left her near to tears. The tragic suicide scene she had mysteriously witnessed beside a bend in Whitaker Creek was so at odds with the merriment just outside the music studio at Willis McGee's that she wondered if she were awake or asleep. A door banged open and two young black women burst inside.

"Hey there, girl... whatcha know?" Kendra McGee declared, untying her waitress apron and tossing it on a chair. "Did you know, I've got this goofball for a sister? She was willin' to work another shift just so she could have a piece of pecan pie comin' out of chef's oven."

"Oh, go on," Jeanette said, laughing. "I was just kiddin', and look! The guy gave it to me, didn't he? Hey, Daph, want a bite? It's the best thing you ever ate in your whole white life," she announced, waving a small paper bag containing her trophy. She flounced into a shabby love seat and divested herself of her pair of thick, rubber-soled waitress shoes.

"N-no thanks," Daphne stammered, pinching the bridge of her nose and trying to clear her head of the disturbing images she'd just seen. She glanced around the McGee's makeshift studio. The rainbow of carpet squares blanketing the floors, walls, and ceiling seemed surreal after the strange events she had—what? Witnessed? Dreamed? Daphne Whitaker's younger sister had drowned herself in the creek in the same manner and place as her father and one of their slaves. Was it possibly *true*? she wondered. Was there any way she could prove whether this terrible series of tragedies in the Whitaker family had actually taken place? Or was she just getting loonier by the day?

This last question was upsetting to contemplate so she forced herself to pay attention to her companions.

"We grabbed some stuff at the Pig Out 'cause we knew we were late gettin' here. Sorry. Have you been waitin' long?" Kendra asked.

"N-no... I don't think it's been... very long," Daphne replied staring at a piece of sheet music she held in her hand. She was in an old garage, she reminded herself sternly, renovated into a music studio. Why in the world would such surroundings whisk her back two hundred years to the governor's mansion and calamities that happened a half century before the Civil War? She set the music on the stand and held out her hand. "On second thought," she declared, "I'd love a bite of that pie. I need a sugar rush. For some reason, I feel kind of light-headed. I think I forgot to eat breakfast."

"The girl *must* be in l-o-v-e *love* with that bird man," Jeanette warbled as she dug into the paper bag and pulled out a clear container with pie and a plastic fork nestled inside. "When I fall for a guy, I go straight to the refrigerator."

Just then Willis McGee appeared at the door.

"Hey, girls... sorry I'm late. Just got a great gig for Daphne, Kendra, and me, though," he said, dropping his date book on top of Kendra's apron.

"What about Althea and me, Daddy?" Jeanette protested.

"Sorry, no sax, sugar, and we don't need keyboard. It's a nice lil' ol' afternoon engagement party at the Governor Holmes House in early July." He addressed Daphne, adding, "No rock 'n' roll, they said, but cool jazz is okay, and you 'sposed to play regular harp in the parlor during the pourin' of the tea. It's a real good gig, 'cause not much happens 'round here in the hot summer months, y'know?"

"Willis?" Daphne asked softly. "Have you any idea where that old mansion, Concord, used to be around here?"

Willis gave her a puzzled look at the abrupt change of subject and then grinned. "Hasn't Miz Whitaker tol' you nothin' 'bout your Natchez history, girl?" he demanded. "You're *sittin'* in it!"

Dumbfounded, Daphne said, "You're joking."

"Well, you're practically sittin' in it. This housing tract was part of the original lands belonging to the Spanish governor's place way back when."

"Gayoso? Manuel Gayoso de Lemos?"

"Yeah... I think that's the guy. He got tossed out by the Americans. Then the old mansion burnt down in the early nineteen hundreds, my mama tol' me, but the double staircase survived a lot longer, till it became a hazard, and then they pulled it down too."

Double staircase? Daphne's strange sojourn to the past had featured no double staircase and she took that as a welcome sign that, perhaps, it had all been some crazy daydream.

Willis looked at Daphne quizzically. "Now, why you interested in a thing like that? Nobody talks 'bout Concord no more... 'cept my ninety-two-year-old mama, and she's dead five years now."

"Oh, I don't know," Daphne replied vaguely. "I just heard about it somewhere and wondered where it had been, exactly."

"Mama used to tell all kinda stories 'bout *her* great-grandmama takin' care of white girls goin' to all the fancy balls, y'know?" Willis shook his head. "Mama thought it was kinda funny that so many of

the black folks in Natchez live practically on the spot where that ol'
mansion used to stand." He shifted his attention to his daughters.
"Well, y'all ready to get down to some work?"

Willis spent the rest of the afternoon coaching the three women
through several new numbers. Daphne was grateful she could put
aside thoughts of her latest historical flashback and concentrate on
matters at hand. Before they broke up in time for Daphne's steady
teatime obligation at the Eola Hotel, she laid out her idea for a
benefit to aid Bailey Gibbs's bird preserve and his efforts to keep a
toxic waste dump out of the Natchez area.

"A 'Concert for the Birds'... what a great idea," Kendra said
enthusiastically. "We got these cute lil' sparrows or somethin' that
hang out in the pecan trees all 'round here, but there've been less
and less of 'em since we were kids. Somebody says it's the smoke
from the ol' tire plant's killin' 'em off, but I dunno if that's true."

Jeanette and Willis nodded agreeing with Kendra's assessment.
Then Jeanette said excitedly, "Maybe you could even get our sister
Mary Jo's kindergarten class to sing the 'I tawt I taw a puddy tat'
song. Remember? From the old cartoon? I saw 'em do it at the
Spring Sing this year. Some kids play the kitty cats, and the others
play the birds. They're cute as can be."

"That's brilliant!" Daphne said, relieved to have gotten all three
musicians to sign on to the idea. "We want to involve the entire
community. I'll let you know when we have a date nailed at the
auditorium... probably in late September or early October, when
folks are back into their normal routines."

The rest of Daphne's week was filled with performance dates,
as well as a series of phone calls to line up the auditorium, along
with booking Althea and the LaCroix brothers from the family jazz
band in New Orleans and a few other possible participants in the
benefit concert. Several times a day she wondered how Sim was
doing tracking down the story of illegal shipments of exotic parrots
from South America and prayed he was keeping to his promise to
stay out of danger.

On Thursday, Maddy called her attention to an article in
the *Natchez Democrat* detailing the passionate testimony given by

Dr. Bailey Gibbs in front of a low-level environmental committee hearing in Jackson. The story referred to the meetings held to discuss "possible Southern sites for disposal depots that would allow for the safe disposition of chemicals no longer allowed in the environment." The article mentioned that Able Petroleum had attended the confab with several of its "scientific staff members" in tow, as well as "a veteran from industry-environmental skirmishes in California, corporate attorney Francesca Hayes, who has been hired by the company as a legislative consultant."

"Sim's former wife," Daphne announced to Maddy, pointing to a picture showing an army of witnesses sitting at a table dotted with microphones. "Jack tracked her down in San Francisco through the Internet and hired her to work for AP. She's a celebrated corporate pit bull, specializing in getting big, polluting companies off the hook."

"Oh my land!" Maddy peered more closely at the photo. "Hmmm…" she said, and Daphne knew her cousin thought Sim's former spouse looked very attractive, even in the grainy newspaper picture. It showed a slender woman with high cheekbones and dark, shoulder-length straight hair conferring with her colleagues. Attorney Hayes wore a classic dress-for-success suit that Daphne would bet her next paycheck had an Armani label inside.

She turned the article facedown on the kitchen table and began to outline the entire situation concerning Bailey Gibbs and the controversy simmering in the state capital. Earlier, Maddy had readily agreed to help with any enterprise aimed at raising money to protect her old friend's bird sanctuary.

"Jack sure likes to stir the pot, doesn't he?" Maddy murmured, retrieving the newspaper article and scrutinizing the picture carefully.

"That's exactly what I tried to tell Sim," Daphne exclaimed.

Maddy pointed to the picture showing Jack and Francesca bent close in consultation. "To think that he deliberately brought this *particular* lady all the way back here to help him persuade the bigwigs in Jackson to put toxic dumps in Mississippi."

Suddenly, a thought struck Daphne like a lightning bolt in her solar plexus. What if Sim had *not* actually gone to South America?

What a perfect way to tell everyone he was totally out of touch and couldn't be reached, and, instead, had slipped up to Jackson for a reunion with—

Daphne, get a grip! she castigated herself. She was shocked at how quickly her thoughts went to The Dark Place when it came to a man in her life. *Sim probably left the state before Francesca could even call him here...*

The following day, Maddy and Daphne set off on a recruiting mission for the benefit concert. They headed for the downtown office of Amadora Bendhar, the East Indian-American orchestra conductor and executive director of the Natchez Light Opera, an organization that had developed as an offshoot of the world-famous Natchez Opera Festival.

"There are those who love *Carmen* and those who love *Cabaret*. Amadora's outfit does the lighter stuff," Maddy explained on the short drive from Bluff House. "Her father was from India and came to Boston to study and met her mother there, whose people were Italian."

"And was she welcomed in Natchez?" Daphne asked carefully, knowing that the conductor's race would be a factor in a state like Mississippi.

"She was one of the first women of color ever to get a job conducting an orchestra in the Deep South," Maddy replied. "I was on the search committee eight years ago and cast the decidin' vote," she added proudly.

Dr. Bendhar's office was on Pearl Street, not far from First Presbyterian Church where King and Corlis had been married. The June morning promised to be the first really hot day of the summer. The building's air-conditioners were humming full tilt as they entered from the steaming pavement and made their way to the second floor.

"Doctor Bendhar is expecting you," said a young woman who Daphne guessed doubled as a local music student.

"Why, Maddy Whitaker, how wonderful to see you," Amadora exclaimed, rising from a desk littered with file folders, a large portfolio that Daphne suspected contained a conductor's score, and a small glass fishbowl full of coffee candies. On shelves above her desk sat a variety of unusual stringed instruments one of which Daphne knew to be a sitar, an eastern cousin to the western guitar.

The artistic director of the Natchez Light Opera was a tall, stately fortyish woman with a prominent nose and cheekbones that looked round and pliant as persimmons. Her wide mouth was defined with a slash of bright red lipstick that contrasted well with her honey-hued skin. Her eyes were nearly as coal black as her hair, which was severely drawn away from her dramatic features and fastened in a coiled bun at the nape of her neck. Amadora's lush figure, clad in a navy blue sari, was bedecked with gold jewelry that dangled from her ears, throat, and wrists. When she stepped from behind her desk to shake hands, Daphne noticed that on her feet were gold lamé sandals, and her toenails were painted the same five-alarm red as her lips.

She was stunning. A star. And she filled even her small office with an unmistakably grand presence. Daphne could only imagine the audience's reaction when the glamorous woman mounted the podium and raised her baton.

The conductor's arrival eight years earlier had been a watershed of sorts in the cultural history of the town, Maddy had said. Dr. Bendhar's charm, training, talent, and arresting looks had won over not only everyone on the search committee—but the season ticket holders as well. Slowly, she'd built her part of the music festival into a nationally recognized event.

Daphne and Amadora exchanged smiles, and the conductor invited her and Maddy to sit.

"We're here to ask a huge favor, Amadora," Maddy declared bluntly.

Dr. Bendhar laughed. "Well, I have one to ask as well," she replied genially. "May I go first?"

"Of course," Maddy said.

"Considering your stellar training, Daphne," the conductor began. "I hope that I can interest you in serving as principal harpist in my orchestra next spring. Our season only runs the month of March, so it wouldn't cut into your jazz performing too terribly much."

"You've heard about my straying from the fold," Daphne said dryly.

"Oh, yes indeed. I was present at your official debut at the Under-the-Hill Saloon," Amadora said with a twinkle. "How could I not have been, given the article about your Juilliard background and that intriguing picture of you in the paper?"

"I didn't see you there," Maddy exclaimed.

"I was way in the back and slipped out at the end. Didn't want to cause talk with my benefactors, you know," she said, winking. To Daphne she added, "But I loved the Aphrodites, and I especially loved your musicianship, my dear. I know you've headed off in another direction, musically, but perhaps you'd still like to keep one oar dipped in familiar waters?"

Astonished by the conductor's positive reaction, Daphne gratefully smiled her thanks. "By next spring, I might well be dying to play a little Bernstein or Andrew Lloyd Webber. I'm honored to be asked."

"Excellent." The conductor nodded, appearing pleased to have accomplished her mission so easily. "Now, tell me why you're here."

"We want your help with something that's very, very important to this community… important to its survival!" Maddy announced dramatically. Then Madeline and Daphne launched into their explanation and a request for musical assistance from the celebrated artistic director.

"We need you to organize and conduct a Natchez-based chamber orchestra to be the centerpiece of the concert," Daphne explained. "We want every single part of the benefit to show the scope of music to be found in Mississippi and appeal to all musical tastes in the community—black and white. That means we could use your advice and counsel on every aspect of the concert. Most of all," she said earnestly, "the evening should be *fun*." She took a deep breath, and said, "For once, race should be set aside in this city. A toxic dump in this region could affect the health and well-being of everyone."

Silence filled the room. Amadora smiled sadly, and then said,

"Believe me, as a woman of color, I straddle those two worlds, as you know, so of course I endorse your aims. And the beautiful birds…" She heaved a small sigh. "Remember, Maddy, when Doctor Gibbs and his wife hosted a wonderful party for the Friends of All Opera out at Gibbs Hall our first year?" Maddy nodded. "That sweet Caroline Gibbs gave me a personal tour of her birdhouses modeled after the historic homes of Natchez. What a dear woman she was…"

"And she died of a rare brain tumor that's been *linked* with the type of chemical waste these petroleum people want dumped next door," Daphne said urgently. "Doctor Bendhar, we need your help so much to make this benefit a success."

"Call me Amadora, please," the conductor urged. "And of course I'll help."

"You will?" Daphne asked, realizing, suddenly, what a pleasure it was to deal with a musical director so unlike the self-absorbed Rafe Oberlin. "That's absolutely wonderful!"

"Some of your contributors may have conflictin' opinions about this," Maddy warned. "They might grow cotton and need to fumigate and defoliate, and others may get their money from investments in the oil business in these parts."

Amadora shrugged. "I'm sure I'll hear from people whose ox is gored in this controversy, but I'm used to dealing with that sort of problem."

"Do you think we could actually field at least twenty-five decent local musicians for a chamber orchestra?" Daphne asked with a worried frown.

"As you probably know, we import a lot of our solo musicians for the festival, so it might take scouring the colleges throughout Mississippi and across the river in Louisiana, but yes," Amadora said, banging her bangled wrist on her desk. "If I can tell them Daphne Duvallon's agreed to be principal harpist, I'm sure others will help us as well."

"Sign me up," Daphne replied. She pointed to the shelves above their heads. "What about playing something on those exotic instruments of yours as part of the program?"

Amadora glanced overhead and laughed. "I think they're a bit *too* exotic for Natchez, my dear." She paused, and then revealed, "I use them as a form of therapy, actually. The vibrations when I play the sitar, for example, soothe me and literally transport me to my father's family home in the mountains north of Delhi. I can practically hear the temple bells ringing and the laughter of little children outside on the street." She laughed. "It's a good antidote for homesickness."

Startled by this revelation, Daphne said, "Really? How's that so?"

Amadora's eyes took on a dreamy cast. "The intensity of the sound almost has the effect of putting me in a trance. I allow my mind free rein to wander where it will and magically it takes me wherever I want to go." She laughed and added, "On a *good* day, that is."

The vibrations transport me... I can practically hear bells ringing...

Amadora rose from her chair, and said apologetically, "I'm afraid I must excuse myself. I'm due at a board meeting in five minutes and need a moment to look at my agenda." She glanced at Daphne, who had swiftly stood up, preparing to leave. "Call my secretary, Daphne, and come for supper one night next week. I'd love to have a little shot of New York."

"That'd be great. I'd love to," she said, wondering silently if she had the nerve to ask the renowned conductor what, exactly, she had meant when she'd described the power of certain sound vibrations to serve as a musical magic carpet?

On Saturday afternoon, Daphne made her way to the back entrance to the Eola Hotel, wheeling her bulky harp case through the kitchen and past the stainless steel warming tables. A waiter kindly held open the double doors that led into the adjacent lounge where afternoon tea was served prior to the cocktail hour. Mostly black cooks and busboys bustled about, banging pots and pans and shouting to each other. The pace of their labors picked up with the approach of the dinner hour. Eric, the maitre d' of the tea service, waved as he directed his minions to pile teacups and saucers on trays in the pantry nearby.

Daphne positioned her harp unobtrusively in the corner of the lounge. She had learned long ago that for "I play, you pay" jobs like these, she was just part of the furniture, and in a sense, she preferred it that way. Fortunately, the harp had remained decently in tune, and within ten minutes, she entered the ladies' room. There, she donned her long-sleeved black performance gown and reapplied her lipstick, then headed back to the pantry to have her own quick cup of tea before her mini concert began at four o'clock.

"Got milk?" Eric joked, ordering a busboy to take down more cups for a private party that was being served in a tucked-away corner of the restaurant.

"Yes, thanks," Daphne replied, peeking through the small window of the kitchen's double doors to see how many people had made reservations for tea.

She had raised her teacup to her lips for a final sip when her hand froze midway to her mouth. There, at a table for two, not ten feet from her harp, sat Jack Ebert and a woman Daphne recognized instantly from her newspaper photo—Francesca Hayes. She was certain that their presence there was no coincidence. Eola Hotel's weekly ad in the *Natchez Democrat* for "Afternoon Tea" featured a picture of the harpist posed beside her instrument. Jack knew exactly where he could harass her in a public place.

The question was, what was behind his latest attempt to "stir the pot"—as Cousin Maddy had so eloquently put it? Had he told his new consultant that her ex-husband and the teatime harpist were an item these days—as Jack had no doubt concluded by now—citing chapter and verse to Ms. Hayes of the times he'd seen them together?

Daphne leaned against the kitchen wall amid the shouts of the cooks and the clanking of cutlery and tinkling of glassware. Her heart had begun to pound and a feeling of vertigo suddenly came over her. She was vaguely aware of a busboy racing past her into the pantry to seize a tray full of teacups off a nearby shelf. Clattering crockery and the steady murmur of a roomful of voices pulled her into a spiral of confusion as she watched guests swarm the buffet. Their chattering seemed to grow louder as they grazed among a cornucopia of delicacies: thin, crustless watercress and egg salad sandwiches, marzipan tarts, hot buttered Scottish scones, and berries piled high in crystal bowls.

How strange, Daphne thought bemusedly, that the guests were wearing such heavy clothing when it was so hot... when the atmosphere outside was sticky and oppressive and foretold of rain.

And then she realized that the guests in long skirts and starched collars were not clanking teacups at the Eola Hotel, but rather were partaking of a feast set out on a long sideboard in the dining room of a large house not far from Whitaker Creek.

JUNE 16, 1806

Porcelain teacups clinked genteelly as young Simon Hopkins tugged at his ivory brocade waistcoat. He inserted a finger between his neck and the stiff collar of his starched shirt and wished he were swimming in Whitaker Creek. He wondered how in tarnation the poor women attending his homecoming gathering could bear to be corseted and swathed in such heavy fabrics while sipping hot tea served them from his family's ornate silver samovar.

His gaze drifted from the dining room to the parlor where Daphne Whitaker—now the widow Stimpson—dutifully played the small golden harp that his mother had often strummed before her death when he was a mere boy. His sister Emma had no interest in music whatsoever, so the instrument had stood silent, until now. It pleased him greatly to see Daphne seated demurely in a corner of the chamber, her honey-colored hair glistening in the afternoon sun that streamed through the parlor windows. Her glorious mane nearly matched the gilded harp, and her black bombazine widow's weeds only heightened her fragile beauty. According to strict etiquette, a bereaved spouse should wait an entire year before performing music in a public setting. However, today's gathering was merely for family and close friends, and he doubted few would criticize her too severely. In the insufferable heat, he'd wager that Daphne must be the most miserably uncomfortable person in the room.

Simon had heard already from several sources the sad tale of Daphne's recent loss, even though he'd only just returned from Edinburgh, Scotland, where he'd toiled at his botany studies in hopes of improving the cotton yields at the Hopkins and Whitaker plantations.

Gossips loved to relate that Judge Ebner Stimpson "jilted one sister and married the other." Maddy Whitaker, it was whispered, had drowned herself in Whitaker Creek over the snub. "Like that slave had," they murmured. Like her own *father*, as Simon well knew. The elder Simon's hair was now snow white. The young girl's tragic suicide had aged his father prematurely.

As for young Simon himself, he had willingly sailed for Great Britain as soon as he heard of Daphne's forced engagement and Maddy's subsequent demise. That Judge Stimpson died of heart failure within six short months of his marriage seemed just desserts for such an overly ambitious man, or so the town's tattlers had pronounced. Piling tragedy upon tragedy, Charles Whitaker's anemic son, Eustice, perished from an infection this spring and died like his twin, Phaedra, had back in 1793.

Now, Daphne made her home at Devon Oaks and Bluff House with her mother, Susannah, her unmarried sister, Suki, and her sole surviving brother, Keating, who at twelve was a handful if ever there was one.

"Simon, you surely seem to be woolgathering at your own party."

Dark-haired Rachel Gibbs, teacup in hand, approached, flanked by two handsome young men who towered above her petite frame. One lad was her brother, John Gibbs, equally dark-haired and two years older than Rachel. Her other companion was a newcomer to Natchez, a Harvard classmate of John's, late of Boston.

Aaron Clayton was half a head taller than John, with a muscular frame and neatly coiffed ginger hair. The two newly minted attorneys were rumored to be forming a law firm in town, and John, obviously, was seizing the opportunity of Simon's welcome home soiree to introduce his new partner to the cream of Natchez society.

Earlier that afternoon, Simon had overheard a conversation in which Aaron Clayton had been asking about the disposition of Judge Stimpson's will, and the likelihood that the sickly young Keating would survive many more fever seasons. John Gibbs had happily informed his friend about the advantages of becoming acquainted with such a socially prominent plantation family as the Whitakers.

"The young widow may be shopworn goods, old chap," John declared slyly, "but that doesn't alter the attractiveness of her purse, eh what? The good judge hadn't much to leave her, but she's heir to a goodly portion in her own right."

"Ah…" Aaron Clayton had replied with a faint smile. "I've always meant to marry a little lady with a little money." The two young men had exchanged knowing looks.

Now, as they nodded politely in Simon's direction, the younger Hopkins cast a jaundiced eye at the outsider while Rachel made the introductions. After a decent interval, Simon withdrew with the excuse that he must attend to his ailing father, who was resting in a wheelchair in the library.

When he returned to the parlor, he was alarmed to see that Aaron Clayton was seated next to Daphne while the two chatted pleasantly over their teacups. In Sim's prejudiced view, Clayton looked foolish, indeed. The hulking man's big hand, covered with a sprinkling of sandy-red hair, dwarfed the delicate porcelain cup he was holding. His massive legs and knees jutted out from the spindly chair, and his boots were as long as a pair of river barges. Yet Daphne appeared aglow in the light of the interloper's complete attention.

"Aren't you just dyin' for a breath of fresh air?" Rachel asked brightly when she spotted Simon's return from seeing to the welfare of his father. She nodded in the direction of an open door that led to the front gallery. "It's so close in here, and I'll bet there's a bit of a breeze to be found on the veranda."

She'd all but asked him to escort her outside, and for a moment, he nearly acquiesced. Rachel was a lovely girl… kind, interested in plants and animals and in art, just as was he. She was comfortable to be with, like his sister Emma, and therein lay the rub. During his time away from Natchez, it had been Daphne that had filled his mind's eye those long, wintry nights in Edinburgh. It was Daphne who made his heart ache with longing to touch her golden hair and to hear her play her harp. He'd hardly given Rachel Gibbs a passing thought while abroad.

"Simon," Rachel said tartly. "Are you listening?"

Simon liked the sprightly Rachel and had no wish to hurt her feelings. He glanced down and took her gently by the hand.

"It's good to see you, Rachel," he said quietly. "I've brought home from Britain all sorts of interesting specimens I'd like to show you, but I'm afraid I must now see to my guests. Father isn't up to making an appearance, so I must play the attentive host. Forgive me, will you?"

"I very much want to see your specimens, Simon Hopkins," Rachel replied, removing her hand from his. "But more than that, I want to see *you*. I know that Daphne… pulls you like a magnet to the north, but… I urge you to discover for yourself what she's like these days, won't you?"

"She has endured much tragedy," he murmured.

"She and that blighted family of hers have brought much down on their own heads," Rachel declared matter-of-factly, "but I do believe men are far more likely to forgive women with golden curls—and that's my final word on this subject." She curtsied and said with touching dignity, "I will leave you to your guests."

Simon nodded, both guilty and relieved that he was free to turn his attention elsewhere. He paused briefly at the buffet table and then approached Clayton and Daphne with a plate in hand.

"Have you tried the Scottish scones?" he said with a smile only for the pale, angelic-looking woman seated to Clayton's right.

"Ah, yes. Excellent," Aaron Clayton declared heartily. "Did you enjoy them?" he asked his female companion.

"Oh yes… lovely," Daphne murmured.

Simon was vaguely aware that a house servant had wheeled his father's chair into the sitting room and that several of his old cronies had gathered around.

"Daphne," Simon began, as if Aaron Clayton weren't even in the room. He had only a few seconds to make his request. "As you can see, my father's health has declined drastically during my absence. There are several questions we must discuss regarding his continuing guardianship, especially of young Keating." He nodded faintly in the direction of a thin, sickly-looking child who nevertheless had the stamina to play tenpins on the lawn outside with several black children while everyone else drank tea in the parlor.

"Keating?" Daphne said vaguely.

"Yes. May I call on you on Sunday? Perhaps you, your mother, and I can have supper together and discuss some important issues?"

Daphne laughed shortly. "I doubt you will find Mother very good company."

"Well, then, may I call on *you*?" He sensed keenly that his pressing the issue irritated Aaron Clayton.

"If you wish," Daphne said, sounding faintly vexed.

"I shall ride over in the late afternoon, if that would suit," Simon insisted, wondering at his forwardness in the face of such obvious disinterest. Daphne glanced through her lashes in Aaron's direction and then at Simon.

"We will be so pleased to have you as our guest," she said softly, and he wondered, suddenly, if there was a faint note of sarcasm to her tone.

From the far side of the parlor his father beckoned.

"Simon!"

Startled by the commanding ring of his father's voice, he rose from his seat. "Till tomorrow, then," he said, bowing slightly. He threaded his way through the crowded sitting room, greeting well-wishers on either side, until he arrived beside his father's wheel-chair. "Yes, Father," he said. "May I have someone bring you some refreshments?"

"Take me back to the library, please," the senior Hopkins demanded abruptly.

"But, you've just come from there," he protested mildly. "Don't you wish to speak to—"

"I tire of all this, and besides, I wish to speak with you. *Now.*"

Simon could see that his father would brook no argument. He dutifully wheeled the chair down the hallway and back into the book-lined chamber.

"Close the door," his father ordered. The older man settled his elbows on the arms of his chair and drew his fingers into a pyramid upon which he rested his bearded chin. "I saw you speaking with Daphne just now."

"Yes..." Simon said slowly. "It was our first chance to greet each other since my return. I wished to compliment her on her playing."

"And how did you find her spirits?" his father asked, his gaze intent.

"I found her... a bit frail... but pleasant."

"And that creature, Aaron Clayton?" the elder Simon asked brusquely.

"He bears watching."

"Yes," his father agreed, "but not in the way I assume you mean."

Simon tried to interpret his father's expression. "I don't like him," he volunteered, "and I think he has pecuniary designs on Daphne."

"His attentions might result in one fewer problem for us to be saddled with."

"Father!" Simon said, shocked. "You are Daphne's guardian. It is your solemn duty to have a care for her welfare and—"

"Don't you presume to lecture me on duty, young man." His father pounded his fist on the arm of his chair. "I've taken on the burden of Charles Whitaker's will for about as long as any human could endure, given the chronic melancholy and unhealthy impulses that run rampant in that line. Tainted blood, I say," he declared. "I'm too old and feeble to run two plantations for much longer."

"Now that I've returned from abroad, I hope you realize how willing I am for you to turn over some of that burden to me, Father," Simon ventured carefully.

His father's eyes narrowed and gazed at him speculatively. "And would 'turning over some of that burden' include getting into the pantalettes of a certain blond member of that damnable family?"

"Father!" Simon exclaimed. "I have nothing but honorable intentions toward Daphne Whitaker." He felt suddenly shy. "I hope someday to make her my bride."

"Would that you only wished to *seduce* the jade and be done with it," his father shot back. "She's got tainted blood, I say," he repeated. "Perhaps 'tis not the poor girl's fault, but there are nothing but crackbrains in that clan. For the good of *our* family line, I implore you—before things get out of hand—to banish all notion of a marital alliance with Daphne Drake Whitaker Stimpson, my boy."

"'Tis not just of you to tar Daphne with the brush of madness that touched poor Charles," Simon said stoutly.

"*And* her sister, Madeline, though God knows how hard I've tried to keep that bit of news from the town criers around here."

"But Fa—"

"And let us not forget the mother," the elder Hopkins declared hotly. "Susannah's moods are most unpredictable, and her servants say she rarely rises from bed, most days. Daphne, too, I'm told, will go weeks without dressing properly."

"So you've set the Whitaker servants to spying," Simon said contemptuously.

"Absolutely," his father growled. "For I wish my son to know the sink pool he proposes bathing in."

"Daphne has suffered loss after tragic loss. Compassion and the passage of time will surely aid in a complete recovery of her spirits. See how she so eagerly plays her harp."

"So she will not have to converse. No, my son, I say this for your good and the good of our own family. You know botany. You know horse breeding. Time generally proves that within close-knit societies such as ours, the effects of tainted blood are only likely to worsen with each generation intermarrying. You must trust me when I warn you that beauty like Daphne's tarnishes with age and familiarity. I must ask you to cease all thoughts of paying court to our neighbor's daughter." He lowered his chin and gazed at his only son from beneath his grizzled eyebrows. "Do I have your word?"

The air was rife with tension, and neither man spoke for several moments.

"I cannot give you my word, but... I will give what you have just said my deepest consideration."

Simon's father looked as if he would say more on the unhappy subject, but did not. Instead, he sighed heavily, nodded, and patted his son's hand. "Good boy. At least, you make a show of listening to your weary old father. I am grateful you came home immediately when I wrote you in Scotland. I don't think I'll live past spring planting."

"Father, you mustn't say that! We cannot predict these things, nor should we."

"I'll predict something else then," Simon said gruffly. "You are correct in thinking that the Harvard man is after Daphne's purse, and I'll wager he will succeed. Furthermore, I say good luck to him! Now, would you be so good as to pour me a brandy. To the brim of the glass, please. My joints ache and I wish to sleep."

Simon turned toward a wheeled trolley where his father kept spirits in a variety of crystal decanters. He lifted one filled with amber liquor and reached for a snifter. His mind far from his task, he recalled the sight of Aaron Clayton murmuring into Daphne's shell-like ear and felt an uncontrollable jolt of anger. Without warning, the crystal snifter slipped from his hand.

"Jesu!" he cursed as the glass shattered on the silver tray with a crash. "The damnable thing has broken to smithereens!"

And with it, perhaps, had Simon Hopkins's heart.

CHAPTER 21

A BUSBOY, HIS FEATURES contorted with alarm and dismay, stood beside the remains of an entire tray of teacups that he had unwittingly dropped on the Eola Hotel kitchen floor.

"Oh, Christ, Henry," Eric, the maitre d', exclaimed. "You're supposed to look through this window before barrelin' out of here," he admonished, pointing at the double doors that the waiters used to enter and exit the hotel kitchen. With exasperation, Eric stared at the rubble and then at Daphne, who appeared equally dismayed. "You okay?" he asked hurriedly. "No cuts from flying crockery?"

"I-I don't think so," she stammered. "No," she added more confidently. "I'm fine. I'm sorry if I got in the way."

"No... no, Henry here just got an attack of butterfingers, and I was probably movin' too fast through those doors, myself." He turned to the busboy. "Just clean all this up," he directed. "And look next time, okay? I will, too."

Shaken, both by the loud crash and this latest glimpse of long deceased ancestors, Daphne peered once again through the windows of the kitchen's double doors into the lounge. With dread, she scanned the cluster of small tables, each covered in a starched linen cloth and decorated with a bud vase containing a single rose.

"Oh, my God," she exclaimed aloud.

I wasn't hallucinating, she thought. *At least, not about this. Jack and Francesca Hayes are still sitting right there!*

"What?" Eric demanded.

Daphne bit her lip and shook her head. "Oh, nothing. It's just not my day either." Eric gave her a quizzical look, shrugged, and returned to his post at the restaurant reservations desk.

As for Daphne, she resolutely inhaled five even breaths to steady her nerves, lifted her chin, and crossed the carpeted lounge where afternoon tea was well under way. How long had she been "gone," she wondered, glancing at her watch. It was just a few minutes after four. The chill she felt had little to do with the sight of her ex-fiancé and Sim's ex-wife sitting together at a cozy table ten feet from her harp.

Why were these distressing vignettes happening with increasing frequency? she wondered worriedly. She thought of the ominous predictions the senior Simon Hopkins had made about "tainted blood." Had the modern Whitaker line—and thus, the Duvallons, too—been saddled with some questionable DNA?

Disturbed, she swept past Jack and Francesca without a glance, reminding herself that the inbreeding endemic among old Southern families like hers might have been mitigated by the injection of new Yankee blood. That is, if the opportunistic Aaron Clayton turned out to be Maddy's direct ancestor—and in a roundabout way, Daphne Whitaker Duvallon's as well!

Saved? Or a case of double jeopardy? she wondered grimly.

Well, as they say in N'awlins, 'round here, everybody's related to everybody, sugar! And in my case, that's probably twice as true.

Daphne focused her attention on the first musical selection. Despite her best efforts, however, she was acutely aware of the oddly matched pair sitting to her right, and she willed them to finish their pot of Darjeeling and be on their way.

No such luck. Forty minutes later, Jack and Francesca ordered a second pot and another round of tea sandwiches and appeared to be settling in for the new millennium. Just about the time Daphne was scheduled to take her break, Francesca leaned down and drew out some legal-looking briefs from a heavy, black leather briefcase. Daphne seized this chance and made a dash for the ladies' room. Within minutes, she realized she'd miscalculated.

She was standing at the sink washing her hands when Francesca Hayes walked in.

"You play wonderfully," Sim's former wife volunteered with a warm smile. Her voice had a rich timbre that probably carried well in a courtroom.

"Thanks," Daphne said stiffly, reaching for a paper towel.

Francesca was even more attractive in person than her picture in the newspaper. She was a tall woman, slender, and elegantly attired in camel slacks and a tailored silk shirt the color of cappuccino. Her straight, shiny brunette hair was tucked behind ears adorned with gold jewelry that Daphne knew must be eighteen karat. The woman had the unmistakable look of a thoroughbred.

"You don't know me," the attorney said, waiting for Daphne to toss her towel into the wastebasket so she could shake her proffered hand.

Oh, yes I do!

"I'm Francesca Hayes. I'm working with your... with Jack," she said, as if no further explanations were required.

"Yes," Daphne replied, barely masking her annoyance. "I read the paper."

"He told me I'd love your playing, and he was right. I'm a member of the San Francisco Symphony Guild and—can you believe it—I always put my chair backstage during Saturday morning rehearsals in a spot where I have a clear view of the harpist." She chuckled as if the joke were on her. "It's always been a secret desire of mine to learn to play but, of course, I've never found the time."

"Really?" Daphne replied coolly.

"And it's also pretty strange, isn't it," Francesca said with a laugh, "that Jack met my ex-husband in Natchez and then, through him, discovered that my legal specialties dovetail perfectly with the mission of Able Petroleum—and *voilà*—here I am!"

"So all these happy coincidences are due to Jack's skill as an Internet sleuth?" Daphne remarked tersely.

"Look," Francesca said, shrugging, "there's no need for us to create *The Clash of the Titans* here. Jack has already told me that you and Sim are... friends."

"Oh, I'm sure he has."

"Sim and I have been divorced for nearly ten years," she said. "As far as I'm concerned, we're friends now, and I wish him all the best." She smiled at Daphne. "You, too," she added encouragingly.

"I adore classical music, and I really loved your playing just now. I hope that while I'm working in Mississippi, we might get to know each other better. Jack says—"

"Speaking of Jack," Daphne interrupted, "you and he are working together to finesse a toxic dump next to an established bird sanctuary. I'm totally *opposed* to that," she added flatly, "so even if you took Simon Hopkins out of the equation, I don't think we have much common ground for friendship, Ms. Hayes."

Ten years as a single woman in a big city was a long time, Daphne reflected, sizing up the woman's chic persona. Maybe Sim's perceived sins didn't seem so bad, now that his former wife had had a decade to think about them. Why would a hotshot trial lawyer from the West Coast accept a run-of-the-mill consulting assignment in a small potatoes place like Mississippi? Had the worldly Ms. Hayes ambushed her presumed rival in a hotel ladies' room to scope out the competition and rattle her a bit? Hadn't legal pit bulls like her been known to employ such tactics before?

The woman appeared startled by Daphne's overt lack of Southern graciousness. "I'm sorry to hear that you don't think we can even just be pals," Francesca replied pleasantly. "I try to keep my professional and personal lives separate. I've merely been hired to do a job here. The basis of our democracy is that everyone is entitled to representation, even corporations, wouldn't you agree?"

"The standard lawyer's defense when defending the indefensible," Daphne replied.

Wow, did that sound acid, she thought ruefully. She hated that Jack's sneaky maneuvers ruffled her feathers so much that she suspected the worst of anyone associated with him—but there it was. If Francesca Hayes was willing to work for Jack, she could be no friend of hers. Worse still, the woman had come to Mississippi to help defeat Bailey Gibbs's effort to save the nature preserve on his land, and that fried her oysters big time.

"I didn't chase any ambulances," Francesca noted mildly. "I was called in on this case. And when the public has a chance to see the specifics of what Able Petroleum proposes to do when it comes to responsibly disposing of toxic waste, I'm certain fair-minded people will frame these issues differently."

"Do you include Sim in that 'fair-minded' category?" she asked, despite her best intentions to keep her mouth shut.

"Sim's always been a fair man."

Now that she'd brought it up, Daphne wanted to get off the subject of Simon Hopkins—pronto. "So, according to you, it's responsible policy to site a toxic dump next to a bird sanctuary?"

"The specific placement is all part of the ongoing debate," Francesca responded smoothly. "I'm just in Mississippi to help find a compromise that everyone can live with."

Daphne's rat detector had started to twang from the moment she'd spotted Jack and Francesca through the small windows in the kitchen's double door. She was faintly chagrined for acting so churlish, but there was something about Francesca that instinctively made her want to scratch the woman's eyes out. For a take-no-prisoners lawyer with a national reputation as Queen of the Mean, she was being too nice and too tolerant of overt rudeness, Daphne judged. Francesca Hayes and Jack Ebert had stayed overlong at tea, and the consulting attorney for Able Petroleum was trying much too hard to become her new best friend. Something definitely was up.

"You know, Daphne," Francesca said as if they knew each other well, "Jack would have turned up my name pretty fast as a potential consulting counsel even if he hadn't run into Sim." She paused, and added pleasantly, "And I really *do* love harp music. It was foolishly impulsive of me to run in here and tell you how good I think you are."

Impulsive? This was a woman who probably didn't make a move without five good reasons.

Then Daphne admonished herself for her visceral reaction. Maybe her instinctive antipathy toward Sim's ex-wife was motivated by simple jealousy? Meeting her like this was just plain weird, not to mention ridiculous on about ten different levels. She could easily be reading things into the situation that weren't really there. Daphne composed her features into what she hoped was a neutral expression.

"I appreciate your kind words about my playing," she said evenly, "but, honestly, Ms. Hayes, I doubt you and I could be much in the way of kindred spirits."

"We could try," Francesca ventured with a friendly grimace. "It looks like I'll be around for a couple more months."

Daphne glanced at their reflections in the mirror above the sinks and found to her surprise that she had begun to feel a little sorry for Francesca Hayes. Who knew better than a musician how lonely it could get plying one's craft away from home? She hoped her next words sounded conciliatory and made up for her testiness earlier.

"Maybe under other circumstances we could be… friends. Given the reality, though, I think I'd better just skadaddle back to work."

Daphne had reached the door by the time Francesca spoke again.

"I'm sure you're probably wondering why it didn't work out for me with a dishy guy like Sim."

Daphne halted her forward motion, one hand on the door-knob. She turned her head toward her right shoulder, listening. The awful truth was, she was dying to know.

Francesca saw her hesitation and continued. "You seem like a really nice person, so I'm going to tell you."

Unable to help herself, Daphne turned around. "Look, I—"

"Here's the deal in a nutshell," Francesca interrupted. "Ten years ago, Sim Hopkins valued his Canon camera a lot more than the woman in his life. I have no idea if things have changed. In fact, I'm rather curious to find out."

Daphne wondered if Francesca expected her to provide an update—Or was the woman's game plan to explore her past relationship with Sim while she was in the area? For a long moment, Daphne stared at Sim's former wife, suddenly imagining her pregnant, frightened about possibly losing her baby, and then miscarrying in a San Francisco hospital while her husband was off in some wilderness, unavailable and out of touch. Daphne sensed that there could easily be a lot of unresolved emotions on Francesca's side, as well as Sim's.

What have I gotten myself in the middle of here? she wondered bleakly.

She advanced a step back into the restroom, grateful no one else had barged through the door. "I know it can be hard balancing two major careers with home and family," Daphne replied softly. "I'm sure you both tried your best."

Francesca appeared startled by the clear show of empathy in Daphne's tone. Then her lovely features hardened. "Is that what Sim told you? That we *both* tried?"

"No," Daphne said slowly, reaching for the doorknob that offered her only escape. "I just surmised that part on my own— knowing Sim—and meeting you like this. My guess is that there were probably no major villains at work in this case. Just sadness and disappointment on both sides that it didn't work out."

After all, each of them had suffered the loss of a child…

"It was a bit more complicated than that," Francesca replied sharply.

"Isn't it always?" Daphne said, wondering, now, exactly what details Sim might have left out—and Jack might have included—in the stories of how these two wildly different, but equally unhappy relationships ended?

"I really am interested to hear the version Sim gave you," Francesca said in a tone one degree shy of nasty. "Tell me… did he describe how 'desperately sorry' he was that I lost the baby?"

For Francesca, too, the wound was still raw.

"He did, actually," Daphne replied, gazing at the thin, com- pressed slash of coral lipstick that Francesca's mouth had become. "And I believed him."

"Oh," Francesca said shortly.

"Listen," Daphne intervened. "This is not a conversation that two complete strangers in a ladies' room should be having."

"Why not?" Francesca demanded, shifting gears suddenly and sounding like the hardball attorney she was trained to be. "Wasn't Sim supposed to be back from South America by now? Aren't you interested in getting an expert's opinion about the man I married and that you're probably sleeping with?"

"From you?" Daphne interrupted, abruptly pushing the door open. "In a word, *no*. Gotta go."

She bolted from the restroom and virtually ran through the rear of the restaurant toward the lounge, seeking the safety and anonymity of plucking out "Claire de Lune" on her gilded harp. Jack Ebert had apparently paid his bill and cleared out. Mission accomplished.

The question was: what were they after? Information? Revenge? Or had Francesca Hayes her own agenda that had nothing to do with Jack Ebert? Had she eagerly accepted an assignment that would bring her in contact with the husband she both loved and hated, and may have, at times, regretted she'd walked out on ten years ago? She'd already managed to find out—probably from Bailey—that Sim had gone to South America. What better tactic than to suggest to his current ladylove that he was nothing but trouble?

And then again, what if Simon Hopkins *was* nothing but trouble? A man who didn't show up when the chips were down?

Stir the pot, she thought grimly of Jack, who'd started it all. *Stir the pot, indeed.*

Cousin Maddy greeted Daphne with news that made her wonder if she shouldn't have pumped Francesca Hayes for a hell of a lot more information.

"You just missed Sim's call," Maddy reported sympathetically. "The bush plane had engine trouble wherever he is in South America, which means he can't get to Rio to catch a jet back to Miami. He's not even sure when he'll get out of there. Probably not till the end of next week."

"Next *week*?" Daphne wailed. She suddenly had a clearer notion of what it must have been like for Francesca Hayes to play lady-in-waiting to Sim's errant knight.

"He sounded so sorry on the phone," Maddy assured her quickly.

"Yeah… sure."

Maddy gazed at her cousin with look of concern. "Daphne, dear," she said gently, "It's not Sim's fault if an airplane has engine trouble. I know how anxious you are to have him safely back. Frankly, I thought it was a miracle that he got a message through from wherever he was in the jungle. He had to ring off because his cell phone battery was about to go dead. What's upsetting you so, darlin'?"

Daphne heaved a sigh. "I just met Sim's ex-wife. She and Jack chose this afternoon to come all the way down from Jackson to have a cozy cup of tea at the Eola."

"Goodness me!" Maddy said, patting the back of one of the kitchen chairs. "You poor thing. Sit down, sugar. I'll pour you a cup of coffee and you can tell me all about it."

"Thanks, but no thanks," Daphne said, shaking her head. "I've got to dash upstairs and get ready for tonight. I'm due at the Under-the-Hill by eight thirty and I need to wash my hair. I wish I could take a nap. I feel totally beat."

"Did Sim's wife tell you what a bad person he was, or somethin'?" Maddy coaxed.

"She told me he cared more about his work than his wife. That he apparently didn't try very hard to strike a balance between his career and his home life."

And she also admitted to me that she was curious to find out if he'd changed his wandering ways...

"Well, if I heard him right, he sounded pretty concerned about not gettin' back to Natchez and to *you* when he said he would," Maddy declared flatly. "If it were me, I wouldn't put too much stock in what an ex-wife says. Can you imagine the version of events Jack Ebert gives out 'bout you leaving him at the altar?"

Fair enough, Daphne allowed silently, *but neither Jack Ebert nor I have any second thoughts about wanting to get back together...*

Daphne shook her head. "I'm sure I *wouldn't* enjoy hearing Jack's version, believe me." She gave Maddy a brief hug. "I'll just be glad when Sim's back."

"So will I," Maddy said with a satisfied smile. "I miss that boy. He reminds me a bit of Clay."

"Oh, Maddy..."

"No, it's a nice thing! He's thoughtful in the same way Clay always was. Clay called his mama when he was gonna be late... brought little gifts when he came back home... things like that."

Daphne was brought up short by Maddy's description of Sim's consideration and good manners. Francesca had said she was interested to find out if Sim Hopkins had changed much in ten years. What if he had? What if a leopard *could* change his spots? Which leopardess would he then invite to permanently share his lair?

Dusk had fallen on the river by the time Daphne reappeared downstairs to eat a bowl of red beans and rice before heading off for the Under-the-Hill Saloon. Maddy swiftly placed supper on the kitchen table and sat down across from her.

"Daphne, dear, I think I should tell you that I saw the young doctor who took over Bailey Gibbs's practice today."

Alarmed, Daphne paused with her spoon halfway to her mouth.

"Why? What's wrong? Haven't you been feeling well?"

"I feel fine," she assured her. "It's just that I felt a funny lil' thing on my shoulder, near the base of my neck, and I thought I should have someone look at it."

"What kind of thing?" she asked carefully.

"It's tiny, tiny," Maddy said. "And not exactly a lump. It's raised a bit, and rough when you run your finger over it."

"A mole?"

"Not really that, either." She waved her napkin in the air. "I 'spect it's nothin', but they did a biopsy, just to be safe. I've done a lot of gardenin' in my day. The doctor said it might be sun-related."

Or related to God-knows-what around here, Daphne fretted silently, thinking of Clay's, Marcus's, and Bailey's bouts with cancer. Was it happening all over again, and to Maddy this time? A primal jolt of fear took hold.

"How long have you noticed that the… whatever it is… was there?" Daphne asked, her heart sinking.

"I don't rightly know. Maybe a couple of months. Not more. I was just so preoccupied with the bluff crumbling, and all, that I kinda put it out of my mind." She glanced up at the kitchen clock. "Oh, land! Look at the time. You'd better run along, darlin'. And don't worry 'bout this. It's probably plain ol' sun damage and not anything really bad. All those years I paid my dues to the Natchez Garden Club, you know," she said with a brave smile.

"Probably that's what it is," Daphne echoed faintly.

But she knew they both were worried.

❧

During the next few days, Daphne found herself increasingly edgy and apprehensive—both about the outcome of Maddy's biopsy and Sim's whereabouts. Adding to her anxiety were the strange forays into the past that had kicked in again with a vengeance since her return to Natchez.

On Monday, she rang the office of Amadora Bendhar and, to her surprise, spoke directly with the conductor.

"Why, I'd love to have dinner," Amadora said delightedly over the phone, "but you must come to my house and let me cook you a curry."

"Oh... you work hard all day like I do," Daphne said quickly. "I don't want you to go to all that trouble."

"It's no trouble," Amadora assured her. "For me, it's a form of relaxation. I figure that a former New Yorker won't find my food too exotic for her tastes."

Daphne sensed that the conductor was actually eager to cook at home. "If you're sure you won't rue your words after a long day tomorrow..."

"Not at all. If I do, we'll just go out. And besides," she said cheerfully, "you're probably one of the few people in Natchez who would actually mean it when you say you like my food."

"I adore curry," Daphne replied enthusiastically, "and I'd love to talk to you a bit more about the benefit concert... and also about your theory that music can... well... transport you mentally to faraway places. I've—I've had a version of that experience myself," she finished lamely.

"Oh, it's more than just theory," Amadora declared. "There's some interesting, albeit controversial, scientific inquiry into the subject, and—" she laughed apologetically. "I can already see that we'll have plenty to talk about tomorrow night. Is seven thirty all right?"

"Sounds like a plan," Daphne said, her spirits lifting. "See you tomorrow night."

~

Sim knew that *if* he put the call through, he'd be waking Daphne and Maddy at some ungodly hour, but his cell phone was useless in this remount place and the airport pay phone was his only hope. Despite this, he slowly enunciated the familiar Natchez number to the international operator and waited impatiently. The roar from the single-engine plane fifty feet away on the tarmac nearly drowned out the sound of a blessedly clear ring. He was grateful that days of cooling his heels in this South American backwater were finally at an end.

"Hello?" a voice laced with sleep croaked.

"Hello, angel," he shouted into the receiver. "Why is it I've always been awake for hours and you're just coming to?" he said jokingly. In truth, he'd be glad to hear the sound of Daphne's voice at any hour.

"What? Hello? I can't hear you! Who is this?" Daphne demanded, sounding highly incensed at having been awakened from a deep sleep. The line crackled on the other end and he cursed the government not only for its corruption, but also for its godawful phone service. Just then the revving engine throttled back and he could hear himself speak.

"Hey, baby… it's me, Simon of the Jungle!"

"Sim? Oh Sim! It's great to hear from you. Where are you?" she cried, and he could tell she hoped it wasn't still South America.

"You don't want to know," he shouted into the receiver. "But I'm heading home. At least, I think I am. They had to fly in a major engine part and then fly in a mechanic who could install the damn thing. If we can just make it to Rio in time, I'll get on a real plane and be in Natchez in a day or so." He briefly described his ordeal of the last few days, realizing, suddenly, how much he yearned to be back in the peaceful little house on Bailey Gibbs's back forty. "On top of everything, some damn parrot bit my arm and I had to take a course of an antibiotic no U.S. doctor has ever heard of."

"God, Sim… are you okay now? It sounds awful."

Listening to Daphne's voice again convinced him, as if he needed it, how much he'd missed her. "I'm getting too old for this shit," he declared ruefully.

"Good. Glad to hear it. When do you think you'll get here?"

"First, say your prayers that I make it to Rio… then to Miami and through customs. If I get lucky, I should arrive in Jackson—via Atlanta—Wednesday or Thursday. I'll be majorly jet-lagged and probably look like an ape-man, but can I see you?"

"Oh shoot," Daphne lamented. "I've got rehearsals both nights this week and there are too many other people involved to change them at this late date."

"Well, I'll call you when I get in and we'll figure something out," he replied, disappointed. "Maybe a nice sleazy motel in town?" he suggested hopefully, shouting above the static on the line.

"Before we settle on a motel, Bird Man, just show up this time. You've been getting some very bad press from your—"

Just then, the phone went dead.

"Señor! Señor!" a member of the ground crew shouted, beckoning him to the plane.

Slowly, Sim replaced the phone receiver as Daphne's last statement echoed unpleasantly in his head. Her supposedly teasing words "Just show up this time…" had a definite edge to them, he thought, as he made a dash for the two-seater parked outside the Quonset hut. He yanked open the plane's door and jumped into the copilot's seat. The pilot revved the engine and began to taxi toward the end of the runway. He stared with unseeing eyes out the dusty windshield, remembering that same sort of faintly critical tone that women in his life—and especially Francesca—assumed when his traveling schedule was not to their liking.

Yeah, he was returning to Mississippi more than a week later than he'd predicted, he thought, starting to fume. Wasn't a faulty landing gear a good enough excuse for the lady? He'd just called her, for God's sake, to let her know he was on his way back. And when he'd first had engine trouble, he'd rung then and left a message with Madeline Whitaker—just as his cell phone was dying, no less—instead of calling his editor, who'd been trying to get ahold of him for two weeks.

Sim grabbed his seat belt and fastened it with a vengeance. Daphne's last remark rankled like a burr under a saddle. *You bet* he'd learned a few lessons about "showing up" from his failed marriage, for all the good it'd done him with Daphne just now. She couldn't even change her rehearsal schedule for two nights running! Why should he be confined to the doghouse because of a bush plane that had very nearly done a fatal belly flop?

I'm exhausted and my arm hurts like hell, he cautioned himself. It wasn't the best time to draw conclusions about anything. Especially since it was six a.m. and he hadn't been to sleep yet.

The little plane sped down the runway and managed to get airborne just before the tarmac ran out. Sim watched the world beneath the wings grow smaller and smaller. In the pit of his stomach he recognized a feeling that was very old and very familiar—and he didn't like it. He didn't like it one bit. He had not signed up for this kind of misery again.

A thousand feet below, the dense foliage was thinning and turning into terrain dotted with small, primitive houses. Their miniature size reminded him of the cottage at Gibbs Hall. For a moment, he pictured Daphne sitting on the daybed, dabbing her mosquito bites with a wad of cotton and gazing across the little bungalow at him with a come-hither expression he would remember to his dying day.

Where was the truth? Was it in that exquisite moment, or in the painful, distant past of his relationship with Francesca? he wondered. And why did these thorny questions always arise with the women in his life whenever he began to look toward the future?

I am really, really *too old for this shit.*

CHAPTER 22

DAPHNE STARED AT THE telephone, wishing she could bite off her tongue for implying that Sim didn't keep his promises.

Now, why in the world did I say that? she wondered, listening to the dial tone after the line went dead.

In fact, she knew exactly why, under the guise of humor, she'd fired off the crack about his showing up "this time." Her run-in with Francesca at the Eola Hotel had been far more troubling than she'd admitted even to herself and had infected her with nagging suspicions about Sim's alleged penchant for disappearing at crucial moments.

But let's be fair here, she admonished herself silently.

After all, Sim's ex-wife was a lawyer, and lawyers were trained to put a certain spin on the facts. Who knew exactly what circumstances surrounded the events leading up to Francesca's miscarriage? In Natchez, Simon Hopkins had been nothing but courteous, thoughtful, and kind. He should be judged innocent until proven guilty, right?

Daphne returned the phone to its cradle and wished mightily that she could ring Sim back and apologize for her flippant remark. As for Francesca's hidden motives and Sim's likely reaction if, indeed, his former spouse had come to Natchez to make a grandstand play—well, why look for trouble… and what could she do about it, anyway?

Just tell Sim you're sorry for whining on the phone and be done with it.

❧

Tuesday night, Daphne stopped briefly at the Eola Hotel and

persuaded the bartender to sell her a good bottle of California Chardonnay. She arrived at Amadora Bendhar's precisely at seven thirty and parked at the curb in front of a cunningly restored Victorian cottage on Washington Street, a few blocks west of the home where Audubon had once resided. She rang the doorbell while inhaling a wonderful aroma of herbs and spices emanating from within.

"Come in! Come in!" her hostess greeted her, opening the door. A tangy blend of cardamom, cumin, ginger, and cinnamon infused the air as Amadora made way for her guest to enter the house. The music director was swathed in a sari of rust-colored silk. She was devoid of jewelry and makeup and appeared five years younger—and extremely relaxed.

"Mmmm…" Daphne breathed. "It smells just marvelous."

She glanced around at the walls, painted linen white, and admired the elaborate millwork of the cornices, baseboards, and door frames. The furniture consisted simply of carved wooden tables inlaid with mother-of-pearl, and plump pillows covered in colorful paisleys and ample enough for a large man to sit on comfortably. Scattered over the hardwood floors were silk rugs in jewel tones of garnet, emerald, and sapphire. An arresting statue of a reclining gilded goddess adorned a low table against a wall to the right of a brick and wood fireplace, also painted white. Placed before the figure was a small, clear glass vase holding a single yellow flower.

Daphne gazed around the restful living room, absorbing its rich simplicity and calm. Low, rhythmic music wafted from stereo speakers tucked into a wall of bookcases lined with leather-bound volumes. A slender stick of incense burned in a brass holder on a middle bookshelf, imbuing the venerable Victorian house with a feeling of Far East exotica.

"What a wonderful retreat," Daphne exclaimed, sinking gratefully onto a pile of plush pillows. "This place definitely exudes a 'Peel Me a Grape' ambiance."

Amadora tilted back her dark head and laughed appreciatively. "It's certainly different for Natchez, wouldn't you say?" She handed Daphne a glass of the white wine her guest had brought. "No hors d'oeuvres," she announced. "I don't want a thing to distract us from this curry I've slaved over."

Amadora laid out the meal on a sideboard, buffet style. Beside the main dish was a large bowl of rice. Several smaller bowls were filled with condiments, including sliced bananas, pine nuts, minced scallions, chopped peanuts, currants, and a pungent mango chutney.

"I've mixed elements of Indian, Indonesian, and Thai cuisines," she explained.

"Kind of a Far Eastern gumbo," Daphne teased. "Mmmmm… it looks fabulous!"

An hour of dining and drinking later, Daphne felt relaxed enough to ask casually, "Amadora… tell me more about those theories you mentioned the other day. You said that there was actually some science behind the notion that music might be able to whisk you back to the land of golden goddesses?" She nodded toward the gilded statue nearby.

"She's Thai, by the way," Amadora commented. "Are you talking about my statement that the sound of the sitar has the ability to transport me—mentally—back to my father's homeland?"

Daphne nodded again.

"Why do you ask?" Amadora inquired, gazing at her guest intently. Though her dark, expressive eyes invited confidence, Daphne hesitated.

"When I play the harp," she replied finally with an affected shrug, stalling for time, "sometimes the sound of the vibrating strings has… well, you know… created another world for me, too."

"For the listener, as well as the musician," Amadora agreed.

"And sometimes, when I'm singing and playing, it's almost as if my body is also an instrument—kind of a vibrating tuning fork— and I'm feeling *my* reactions to the music as well as something of what the audience must be experiencing hearing the same notes. It's as if we're all *connected* through hearing the same sounds."

"There are those in Eastern cultures who take this sense of connectedness one step beyond," Amadora said slowly. "They believe the vibrations produced in one era—through music, speaking, crying, screaming, laughing, and so forth, don't ever end, but continue to vibrate forever, connecting people throughout time. After all, the human body is ninety percent water, and water is one of the best conductors of sound."

"And everybody knows that music, especially, evokes nostalgia," Daphne added, thinking of the moment when the strains of "Frère Jacques" had sent her thoughts careening back to her childhood when Cousin Maddy sang to her and played the harp.

"One theory is that sound is a kind of audio album of our shared human experience," Amadora proposed, "a species of memory that's beyond the merely rational."

A species of memory? Daphne was suddenly dumbstruck by the notion that musical phrases might encode a record of past events. An audio album, indeed.

Amadora stood and scanned the bookshelf behind them. Selecting a volume, she resumed her seat on a crimson pillow and asked, "Have you ever read *Molecules of Emotion* by Doctor Candace Pert?"

Daphne glanced at a cover that looked rather like a medical school text. "No," she replied.

"Well, for me, Pert's research is the underpinning for a theory to explain the phenomenon of the sitar creating in my mind a sense of the sights and sounds of India when I play. You'd have to read it yourself to learn about neuropeptides—in other words, chemicals produced in the body—and the way they attach themselves to cells in the cerebrum and our other organs," she advised, pointing a vermilion fingernail to her skull. "Scientists now understand that memories can remain *lodged* in the nervous system inside the cells' 'receptors.'"

"Sort of like in a cellular filing cabinet?"

"More like sticky cellular lily pads," Amadora replied, laughing. "In brain studies, Pert also found that strong emotions—along with reaction to trauma—can activate a particular circuit in the brain's cortex that retrieves a certain kind of memory."

"You mean like those post-traumatic stress reactions

experienced by Iraq and Afghanistan vets, even after they left the war zone?"

"Right," Amadora said approvingly. "What if those kinds of traumas and strong feelings and memories were not only stored in the brain, but encoded in *cells*—and thereby inherited by the next generation in their DNA?"

"Wow... What a concept. Your grandmother is rescued from a fire and you are born with a deathly fear of bonfires?"

"Something like that," Amadora replied, smiling. "And since the flute, the drum, and the harp are the oldest instruments known to humankind, the memory of *their* sounds may actually be indelibly imprinted in almost everyone's deep memory."

"Oh, my God," Daphne murmured.

"And perhaps," Amadora continued, her own excitement evident, "these sounds—or the *memory* of these sounds, encoded in the cell receptors of early humans—have been handed down over the ages, along with physical traits like blue eyes or big feet."

"I've wondered about that, too. So when a harp vibrates—what?" she queried, her confusion returning.

"Perhaps those vibrations tap into memories not only that have accumulated over your lifetime, but also the memories of those who went before you."

"Unbelievable! But you're the first person I ever heard describe an experience at all similar to... to mine. Why doesn't everybody experience this?" Daphne asked, suddenly dubious.

"Perhaps non-musicians and non-music lovers don't have the same opportunities to encounter this phenomenon of being 'transported,' so to speak, as do people like you and me who are in the music world," Amadora suggested, refilling Daphne's wineglass. "We're exposed to music every day. Our flesh and bones—being the excellent conductors of sound that they are—may allow us to pick up on the 'vibes,' as it were, and thereby access sights and sounds and emotions, stored on a cellular level, that are similar to what our ancestors experienced."

"This is all so... amazing," Daphne said quietly. "The chemistry of memory..." Slowly, shyly, she began to relate the unworldly events that had happened to Sim Hopkins and her, and spoke, too, of their burgeoning relationship.

"So, are you saying," Amadora asked somberly, "that the first time you heard that harp playing by itself, your friend Sim did too… and at the same hour of the night?"

"It was a different harp in a different parlor across town from Bluff House… at Monmouth Plantation… and both of us heard it after midnight some time, but yes, we *both* heard 'Frère Jacques' being played on the same night by a harpist who wasn't there. And besides the same family names popping up, there are some other bizarre parallels." She then gave Amadora a brief recitation of the mother-daughter conflicts that existed between Antoinette and her today, and Daphne Whitaker and her mother, Susannah, generations before.

"As for Daphne, the harp-playing ghost," she said grimly, "from what I've seen so far, this lady's life was pure hell."

"It sounds as if the woman you were named after used music as an escape."

"Exactly. And from that first night when I believe I heard her playing, onward, various sounds—music, birdsong, clattering dishes, sounds in *my* world that also existed in my ancestors' day— seem to act like some magic carpet sweeping me back in time. It's as if I'm viewing a video of the *other* Daphne's life, recorded in sound and picture nearly two hundred years ago."

"And has Simon Hopkins continued to experience this as well?" Amadora asked.

"I don't know," Daphne said slowly. "He hasn't said he's heard anything after that first night. And anyway, he's from an old-line family in San Francisco. So as far as I know, none of these folks I've encountered are relatives of his, even though there was a family named Hopkins around here way back when."

"You two are lovers and you haven't discussed these encounters?" Amadora asked, incredulous.

"Not since we first met." Daphne blushed.

"Well, *I* suggest you do."

Daphne shook her head. "He'll think I'm loonier than he probably already does."

"Not if he's experienced it too," Amadora insisted. "Was he forthcoming about the experience at Monmouth?"

"Yes," Daphne admitted thoughtfully. "He raised the issue before I did."

Amadora gave a satisfied smile. "I like the sound of this man."

Daphne lowered her eyes and stared at her wineglass. Suddenly, the strangest thought entered her head.

I don't like getting left!

She thought about her last, uncomfortable conversation with Sim. On some deep level, she'd felt that he'd left and wasn't coming back. That was her problem in a nutshell, and always had been, she thought with a growing sense of wonder. The other Daphne "got left" in the most traumatic way possible: her father committed suicide and her mother suffered depression from all those pregnancies spaced too close together and the trauma of her other children dying in infancy.

For reasons Daphne understood much more clearly now, her own mother and father had also "left" her in a sense. Daphne and her namesake might as well have grown up as orphans for all the parental nurturing they received as children.

"What a legacy," Daphne murmured. "Generation after generation of Whitakers, Claytons, and Duvallons abandoning their nearest and dearest either physically or emotionally."

"Ah… but that's just it, don't you see? By this strange gift of yours, perhaps you will learn that there are other choices we humans can make as we go along in life. We need not be condemned to cause or endure the same pain."

Daphne sat quietly for a long moment, her eyes slowly filling with tears.

"What is it, Daphne?" Amadora reached out and touched her arm.

Briefly, the younger woman sketched for Amadora the sorry tale of her relationships with Rafe Oberlin and Jack Ebert.

"Well, it certainly sounds as if you've chosen more wisely this time with your Mr. Hopkins," Amadora said kindly, handing Daphne a tissue.

"I wonder," she said with a sigh, thinking of Francesca's acid comments and Sim's on-the-road lifestyle. Daphne took a sip from her wineglass. "I can't believe we've just met and we're just sitting here like normal people calmly discussing this crazy stuff."

"It's not crazy," Amadora said sharply. "Use what you've learned here, tonight, and be grateful for it. It's happening to you for a reason." She gathered several books into a stack and handed them to her visitor.

"Is that what Eastern religions believe?" Daphne asked, pointing to the golden statue. "The 'there are no accidents' philosophy?"

Amadora smiled indulgently. "Yes… that's part of it. But the psychologist Carl Jung also wrote on similar themes. I urge you to make his work your next reading assignment after you finish these books," she said, laughing at the stack Daphne held in her arms. She patted the younger woman's shoulder. "Many of us with this special awareness are on parallel but distinct paths. Yours is just more interesting than most."

"Hmmm…" Daphne replied noncommittally.

"And also," Amadora encouraged, "you could do some checking of your own with local historical records to see if any of the details of your experiences can be verified."

"And if they can be? That might scare me even more!"

"My guess is that, once you satisfy yourself that these people actually lived and had lives similar to those you've viewed through this amazing lens of yours, you won't call these experiences 'crazy' anymore, and your anxiety will subside. Like many seers of other dimensions," she said with a mischievous smile, "you'll merely come to accept this gift and eventually to be thankful for it."

"Maybe…"

Amadora clapped her hands briskly, as if she were asking for the attention of a roomful of musicians.

"Let us now have some *chai* and discuss the order of music to be played 'For the Birds.'"

❧

In the days following her extraordinary dinner with the singular Amadora Bendhar, Daphne was relieved to discover that she felt much less anxious about her relationship with Sim. And though she continued to fret about the awaited report concerning Maddy's biopsy, she even began to feel more relaxed about the unwelcome "visitations."

Unfortunately, this feeling of budding personal serenity lasted exactly three days. On Saturday morning her cousin picked up the downstairs extension and called up the stairwell excitedly, "Sim's on the phone! He's back at Gibbs Hall."

Why wasn't he standing on Maddy's veranda, knocking on her door—as promised? Daphne wondered with a mild jolt of annoyance. She walked to her desk and lifted the receiver.

"Well, welcome back," she said when Maddy hung up downstairs. "When did you get in?"

"Late last night, in the middle of all that rain," Sim answered.

Daphne sensed immediately the slight chill on both sides of the conversation. An awkward pause followed, and then he continued to speak while she stared out the upstairs office window at a cluster of dark, roiling clouds gathering on the Louisiana side of the river. The weather was sultry. The rain had been soaking the countryside on and off for a day and a half.

"I could only drive about ten miles an hour down the highway from the Jackson airport. By eleven o'clock last night it was a monsoon."

"Poor you! Was the flight horrible, too?" she asked sympathetically.

"Pretty bumpy." Another pause. Then Sim said finally, "Look, Daphne, I'm afraid I can't get into town for a while. My book editor arrived from New York this morning."

"Were you expecting him?" she asked, surprised.

"I'd known that he wanted to get together sometime this month," Sim replied, "but we got our signals crossed because I accepted that last-minute magazine assignment and flew off without telling him. Our deadline to get the coastal bird book to the printers is next week. My cell phone died in the jungle and he couldn't reach me to tell me he was coming in today."

That's right, Daphne remembered, attempting to stem a wave of disappointment. Sim had used his mobile phone to leave a message with Maddy that his bush plane had engine trouble. A rush of remorse for her selfish reaction prompted her to blurt, "Sim... look... I-I wanted to say that I realize what a tough trip you had and I'm really sorry I—"

Sim cut her off before she could finish her sentence.

"The message that Greg was heading here from New York was waiting for me when I got in at midnight. I slept about three hours, then got up, and went back to the Jackson airport this morning to pick him up. Bailey has been good enough to give him a guest room in the main house while we work on the captions."

He clearly was not in the mood to discuss anything personal.

"You sound absolutely beat. Can you get some rest, at least, before you have to tackle all this?" she asked, trying to sound like a good sport.

"Not likely, given the deadline."

Daphne recognized that cool, preoccupied tone of voice. She'd heard it from Rafe Oberlin often enough.

"Oh. Sure. Well... of course. What can you do?" she said, attempting a dignified retreat. "I'm pretty busy too right now. I'm playing for an engagement party at the Governor Holmes House on Sunday afternoon, plus three shows this weekend." Impulsively she added, "If you get your work done, maybe you and your editor could catch our last set at the Under-the-Hill Saloon tomorrow night? I'd love to meet this slave driver."

"From the red pencil marks on the pages he's brought with him, I doubt we'll finish in time. I have to take him back to Jackson to catch a plane early Monday and then I'm going to head pretty far north up the Trace for a couple of days. Bailey spotted some great crested flycatchers, and I want to track them while we know they're around."

Another awkward pause. Daphne felt as if she were in the sixth grade forcing a male classmate to keep talking to her on the phone.

"Sim," she said in a low voice. "What's wrong? It feels as if you're still way off in the jungle."

"I can't go into it right now," he replied tersely.

"No?" she shot back, angry now. "Well, what a shame. First

things first, right?" She knew she was being childish and unreasonable, but she couldn't hold back her disappointment at his air of chilly detachment.

"Greg McKinney has flown in from New York, Daphne. Leila's feeding him breakfast right now, and then we have to start revising the manuscript. I still have a long list of Audubon birds to capture on film before autumn, and then *write* the other damn project. What do you expect me to do, here?" he declared, making no attempt to cloak his exasperation.

He was exhausted.

He was also frazzled, jet-lagged, and feeling behind the eight ball.

I'm making excuses for him, Daphne thought.

There was no ignoring the fact that Sim Hopkins was distant—bordering on rude—for the first time since they'd met. It would appear that the honeymoon was over.

Wow… that didn't take long…

Daphne blinked away tears that fogged her view of yet another impending storm that had blown up from the Gulf of Mexico.

"Here's what I expect," she said in a choked voice. "I expect you to tell me straight out what's going on with you, and I expect you to act like a *friend*."

She heard Sim heave a sigh as she continued to gaze out the windows while rain began falling in a steady stream. She waited a few more seconds for him to speak, and when he remained silent, she murmured, "Well… good luck with your projects. And y'all take good care, y'hear?"

During the split second she waited to hear if Sim would offer something conciliatory, she realized that she hadn't told him about Maddy's cancer scare. Then she gently hung up the phone, knowing *exactly*, now, how it must have felt to be the former Mrs. Simon Hopkins.

Stormy weather hung over Natchez all weekend, the air as dark and gloomy as the black mood that held Daphne in its grip. The bad weather drastically reduced the size of the audience Saturday night at the Under-the-Hill Saloon. At one a.m., when the lights were turned off and the last stragglers drifted onto Silver Street, she half expected Sim to emerge from the shadows and take her for a ride along the river as a peace offering. He didn't appear, however, and Daphne drove with Althea to Bluff House in a deepening funk.

Sunday, she arrived at the Governor Holmes House on Wall Street a half hour before the time the engagement party was slated to begin. She parked her Jeep in front of the old brick residence that had been transformed into an elegant bed-and-breakfast. The innkeeper was a man who had returned to the South after thirty years serving as manager of the celebrated Algonquin Hotel in New York. He was famous among locals and visitors to Natchez alike for his warm hospitality, scrumptious breakfast fare, and his distinctive attire, which consisted of black silk knee socks and impeccable Bermuda shorts secured by a revolving wardrobe of fancy suspenders.

"The weather's too chancy for us to hold the party in the court-yard," Bob Pully explained in the soft Virginia drawl of his child-hood, "so I've set up cocktails in the parlor in front of the fireplace instead. Will you be all right stuck in that corner over there?" he asked apologetically.

Before Daphne could nod agreement, a gust of wind ripped a branch off the mammoth oak rooted in the side yard and hurled the amputated limb against the house with a crash. Startled, Daphne and Bob dashed to the window on the left of the carved, white wooden fireplace and peered out. The exterior atmosphere had taken on a peculiar greenish tinge, as if they were looking out on Emerald City in *The Wizard of Oz*.

"Tornado weather," Bob murmured grimly.

"In June?" Daphne protested. "This kind of stuff is supposed to happen in springtime, isn't it? Shouldn't it be over by now?"

"Anytime you have moist, hot air colliding with a mass of cool air from the West, you'd better start watching for funnels, honey chile," he advised with a worried smile. He glanced at his watch. "You need any help settin' up?"

"No, thanks," Daphne said. "I'll just start tuning the harp, but where do you want Willis and the group to play, since we won't be outside? They're due here in forty-five minutes."

Bob pointed through a door that opened to a center hallway leading toward the middle of the house. "The foyer?" he suggested.

"That should work just fine," Daphne assured him. "Everything looks gorgeous, as if you'd planned to have the party inside from the beginning."

"Bless you," said Bob, heading back to the kitchen to check on last-minute arrangements with his small staff. He called over his shoulder, "The engaged couple knows to come downstairs right at noon. When the first guests come wanderin' in, just start playin' your little heart out."

It was an engagement party that neither the happy couple, nor their family and friends, nor Daphne, Bob Pully, and his staff of Thelma and Lucille would ever forget. By twelve thirty, the wind had grown so fierce that the boisterous toasts could not be heard over its roar. Just as the groom-to-be raised a glass of champagne in honor of his betrothed, a piercing blast from the tornado warning system, less than a block down the street, sliced through the sound of the storm raging outside. For a full minute, the horn's ear-splitting decibels left Daphne feeling as if she were plucking imaginary harp strings. From the wide door at the entrance to the parlor, Bob Pully loudly clapped his hands to gain everyone's attention.

"I hate to interrupt, but y'all've *got* to get to a safe place! Here's what I want you to do," he shouted over the wail of the siren as the group of twenty guests turned around, mouths agape. Swiftly and calmly, Bob assigned groups of four to make a dash for interior bathrooms scattered throughout the old house. "Pull a mattress off one of the beds, get into the tub, and put the mattress on top of you—and *stay put* till you can hear y'self think again!" He looked at Daphne, and said, "Do you mind goin' into the powder room under the stairs? It's only got room for one person." He pulled a beige silk brocade cushion off the sofa. "Here," he shouted over another crack of thunder. "Crouch down under the sink and put this over your head and shoulders."

Just then, a crackling round of lightning, followed immediately by rolling thunder, rent the air. The startled mother of the bride-to-be screamed as the rain, furiously lashing the windowpanes, shattered one square of glass nearest the fireplace. Daphne ran to the window on the opposite side of the room and thought she saw a funnel cloud faintly visible in the direction of the river. She suddenly thought of Willis and the band driving into downtown Natchez in the battered McGee van, and of Cousin Maddy, alone at Bluff House—and felt her heart lurch.

And what about Sim and Bailey at Gibbs Hall? she wondered in a rush. The wind could do terrible damage to old plantation houses and flatten all the beautiful trees on the Trace. *And what about the poor birds?*

As if to reinforce her fears, the tree that had earlier lost a branch gave a groan, followed by an ominous sound of bark splitting, as its roots were yanked skyward by the falling trunk. She was relieved to realize that the mammoth pine had fallen away from the two-hundred-year-old brick house. By the time Daphne squeezed herself into the diminutive bathroom and wedged the couch's seat pillow between the bottom of the sink and her back, the screech of splintering trees and howling winds had become deafening.

She winced when another tree cracked and crashed to its death somewhere nearby. And then, strangely and suddenly, the wind's roar began to fade, and all Daphne could hear was the rain... a steady downpour that seemed destined never to stop.

CHAPTER 23

JUNE 25, 1806

SIMON HOPKINS THE YOUNGER peered through the downpour and grabbed his heavy cloak from the peg near the back door. He slipped out of Hopkins House and swiftly made his way to the stable and saddled his horse.

The rain hadn't cooled things down at all, he thought with annoyance, urging his horse down the path through the woods. Even when it let up a bit, hot, damp mist hung in the air and rose from the saturated leaves underfoot. Dark clouds overhead threatened another downpour and served to trap sultry air like a lid on a pot of steaming rice. Simon had already sweated through his frock coat and shirt, and his cravat had become a wilted tangle of linen. Though his cloak made him still more uncomfortable, without it he would have been a thoroughly sodden mess by the time he arrived for dinner with the widow, Daphne Whitaker Stimpson, of Devon Oaks Plantation. Despite the rain and his discomfort, young Simon would willingly ride through the eye of the storm to pay this call.

A jagged bolt of lightning lit the night sky, closely followed by a long clap of thunder. As he had feared, the heavens opened up once more and for a second time, driving rain lashed his face.

"Whoa... steady there, boy," he crooned. "I can see a light from the house," he announced, far more for his own benefit than for that of his horse. "Steady there, now."

A youthful slave, barefooted and soaked to the skin, scampered around the plantation house and met him at the foot of the broad stairs that led to the front veranda. The lad reached up and relieved the visitor of his reins while he dismounted and dutifully led the horse to the stables as Simon ascended the steps to the front door.

"Good evenin', sir," the butler mumbled. "Miz Daphne and Miz Suki are in the parlor."

Simon divested himself of his drenched cape and strode through the darkened foyer where few candles were lit in welcome. Behind the wide-planked door of the front room, voices could be heard, shrill and complaining.

"Mama said she won't come down to dinner, and that's the end of it, Daphne! You'll just have to cope on your own."

"You go right back upstairs and tell her she'll go without supper then. And, for pity's sake, Suki, wash your hands and face and tidy your hair. You aren't fit to dine with pigs."

Startled by this acrimonious exchange, Simon hesitated to knock.

"You can't order me 'round like some slave, Miss High-and-Mighty," Suki declared petulantly. "You go up and tell Mama yourself, and stop calling me names, or I'll tell Simon what everyone in Natchez is calling *you* ever since that Yankee friend of Johnny Gibbs arrived and—"

"How *dare* you—"

Simon rapped sharply on the parlor door and silence descended immediately. He slowly turned the knob, suspecting that his entry had prevented the two sisters from coming to physical blows.

The young women flanked a gilded harp that stood to the left of a cherry wood pianoforte. Suki's disheveled appearance matched Daphne's description. The twenty-three-year-old spinster's hair was in disarray and she looked as if she'd slept in her indigo gown. Daphne, on the other hand, was neatly attired in gray silk, signaling that she had declared herself to be in the final stages of mourning. Simon's heart swelled at the sight of her delicate beauty, her mass of golden hair held atop her head by a cunning collection of tiny tortoiseshell combs. Could he dare to think she was happy that he had come to press his cause?

"Good evening," he said, looking warily from Suki to her older sister. He stepped into the sitting room and bowed slightly. "'Tis a great pleasure to see you both and good to come out of such inclement weather. 'Tis a monsoon out there."

It was insufferably hot in the room, the windows being kept shut against the rain. Both young women looked flushed and out of sorts in their high-necked, long-sleeved gowns and tight corsets. Suki glared at Daphne and then made a perfunctory curtsy in Simon's direction. She whirled to face her sister again.

"I will tell Mama that you request her presence at dinner," she said icily. "As for myself, I'm feeling poorly this evening and have told Mammy to bring a tray to my room." She nodded at Simon. "Please excuse me," she murmured, and flounced out, closing the door none too quietly.

Daphne pursed her lips, but said nothing about Suki's rude departure. Her shoulders heaved a little shrug before she declared with forced politeness, "May I pour you some spirits? You could die of thirst before anyone 'round here will see to your pleasure."

"No, thank you, but you're kind to offer," Simon replied with a warmth he hoped would put Daphne at ease. Her hands fidgeted in her lap and she had a distracted air. "I'd be mighty pleased, though, to accept a glass of wine with dinner, if you'd join me." He was happy to find himself alone with her and hoped to use this rare opportunity to advance his suit. His father was an old and weary man, and Simon was convinced that the elder Hopkins would eventually come to accept his son's choice.

Unfortunately, the ensuing conversation never proceeded beyond small talk. His hostess steered Simon's every effort at intimacy back to the topic of the dreadfully oppressive weather, and then launched into a lengthy description of the various ailments such inclemency had occasioned in the slave population at Devon Oaks.

A few minutes later, the butler reappeared and announced that dinner was served. Daphne led the way to the foyer, casting an annoyed grimace in the direction of the curved staircase. From over their heads, Simon thought he heard a woman moan, followed by a series of loud, steady thumps.

"I fear you will have poor company tonight," Daphne said, ignoring the alarming sounds as they marched across the threshold and into the dining room. She swiftly took a seat at the far end of an elegant mahogany table. "Apparently, my mother *and* my sister are indisposed—as usual."

Simon indicated to a servant standing silently against the wall that he would prefer to be seated to Daphne's right hand, rather than at the opposite end of the long table where his place had been set. The crystal, silver, and chinaware were moved. Taking her seat, Daphne immediately shifted her chair a few inches to the left, as if she desired to put as much distance between them as the end of the dining table allowed.

Thus far, Simon judged, the evening was not going well. He concentrated his attention on the sight of her caramel-colored curls, burnished by candlelight glowing from a set of sconces on the wall.

"And young Keating?" Simon asked of the purported raison d'être for his visit to Devon Oaks. Obviously, relations among the women in the household had seriously deteriorated during Simon's long sojourn in Edinburgh. The atmosphere inside the grand house seemed every bit as gloomy and dank as the wretched weather outside.

"Well, you know twelve-year-old boys," Daphne said sourly. "They're young savages. I told Mammy to give him his supper at six with the servants."

Simon felt a momentary flash of irritation that the natural bois-terousness of the poor lad had caused his banishment in this house where women dictated daily decorum.

Their conversation throughout the soup course remained stilted and filled with awkward pauses, rescued from utter silence at times only by the movement of servants in and out of the shad-owed chamber. Throughout dinner Simon did his utmost to gently draw out his hostess on the subject of her recent bereavement, wondering if this latest tragedy had indeed dealt a fatal blow to her beleaguered spirits, as his father had asserted during Simon's homecoming soiree.

"Another purpose for my calling, Daphne—besides speaking of young Keating's future—is to express my sorrow for the sad fate that befell Judge Stimpson," he said quietly. "It must have been a bitter blow for so recent a bride."

Daphne's expression, across the candlelit table, was unfathomable. "I would have to say, Simon," she declared at length, "that the marriage itself was more bitter than was the judge's taking leave of it."

Simon was frankly flabbergasted by the tartness of her reply. "Why, Daphne," he said, "pray, what do you mean?"

"What I mean," she said with an astringent smile, "would certainly not be polite to voice to mixed company."

There was something strange and remote about her behavior, something far different from the young, vulnerable girl he had held in his arms when she caught sight of her father floating in Whitaker Creek. She had become guarded and unapproachable. He wondered what other terrible blows had befallen her since that fateful night at the Concord ball to render her so unlike the angelic girl he remembered.

She glanced at the servant awaiting her directions. "We shall have coffee in the parlor." She returned her attention to her guest, and asked brightly, "Shall I play for you? And then you must tell me your father's plans for reining in young Keating. Boarding school, I should hope."

Somehow, the evening had not followed the track Simon had hoped. Gloom engulfed him as he followed his hostess once again into the front sitting room. Daphne immediately took her seat at the harp and played a standard, rather mundane rendition of "Greensleeves" without the slightest nuance of feeling. Then she rose from her music stool and swiftly poured them each a cup of coffee from the porcelain pot the servant had left on a silver tray—as if the sooner they got this polite ritual over with, the better. Simon caught her glancing at the brass-faced clock on the mantel. Surely, he wasn't such a great, yawning bore that she wished only for him to leave? He fingered the velvet box containing a marquis-cut diamond ring that he had purchased in London en route home to

Natchez. His father would bellow with outrage if he knew what his son had been planning this evening, but he didn't care.

Thanks to the wine they had consumed at dinner and the continuing heat, Daphne's cheeks were more flushed than usual, and she appeared nervous for reasons he could only surmise. She had been married and widowed, and thus Simon assumed that she would not feel awkward to be dining with an unmarried man. Why would an old family friend put her so out of sorts? he wondered.

Suddenly, she commenced chattering intensely about Aaron Clayton, the newcomer in their midst, and heaped praise on what she characterized as the forward-thinking law firm of Clayton and Gibbs.

"The partners appear to be doing very well, even though they've just opened their practice, and Aaron says by next spring, they might be quite the most sought after attorneys in all of Natchez. Personally, I think you would do well to consider Clayton and Gibbs as your legal representatives before they have more clients than they can handle."

"You call him Aaron?" Simon said, arching an eyebrow. "I had no idea you had become such... intimate acquaintances... in so short a time, especially in view of the tragic and recent loss of your late husband."

He knew he sounded priggish, but there was something about the mere mention of Aaron Clayton that made his hackles rise. For her part, Daphne actually had the grace to blush to the roots of her blond ringlets. Her flushed face turned positively scarlet.

"Oh, don't be a scold, Simon," she said peevishly. "I am, of course, still in mourning, but I think it only proper to extend the traditional hospitality of Devon Oaks."

"Aaron Clayton has called here this week?" he demanded. "A perfect stranger visiting a household of women?"

Daphne raised her chin a notch, and replied stiffly, "And, pray, why not? Suki and I entertained both gentlemen yesterday afternoon. I would have thought your travels abroad would have made you less parochial, Simon. Aaron Clayton is a fine, upstanding, Harvard-trained attorney who—"

"Who would like nothing better than to become the master of Devon Oaks, I wager." Simon wondered, suddenly, if the insinuating Mr. Clayton was due to pay a late call on the grieving Mrs. Stimpson after her supper guest departed for home this rainy evening.

Simon set his coffee cup on the table with more force than he had intended. He had difficulty stomaching Daphne's dewy-eyed enthusiasm for a man he would not honor with the title gentleman. Simon considered Aaron Clayton a damnable poacher of the first order.

"You are behaving like a very silly woman," Simon admonished crossly.

"And will you join your father in opposing yet another of my suitors?" Daphne jumped to her feet.

"I will oppose anything that my father and I deem would not be in your best interest," he said, his temples throbbing with frustration.

Daphne began to pace in front of her harp, her distress and agitation obvious. She halted abruptly and whirled to face him.

"I will not abide your interference, do you hear me, Simon Hopkins?"

"Our *interference*, as you so unwisely term it," Simon replied, "will only become necessary if you do something so foolish as to continue to accept the attentions of a man of Clayton's stripe. Your previous suitor—since you have raised the unfortunate subject yourself—nearly… nearly ruined you, Daphne, not to mention the physical peril he put you in the night of the ball at Concord. You showed then, as I fear you are doing now, that you are not fit to guide your own destiny. My father and I have done everything humanly possible to—"

"Leave here at once!"

Simon stared, dumbfounded, at the woman who had inhabited his daydreams and unguarded fantasies since he was fifteen years old. There she stood, hands clenched by her sides, glaring at him with loathing.

"You cannot mean that," he protested. "I have nothing but your well-being at heart, dearest Daphne! I am not my father, though heaven knows he's given the greatest attention to the welfare of the Whitaker household ever since—"

"Do not *dare* to speak of that!" Daphne shouted. Simon was shocked into silence while she continued her tirade. "You and your father have cruelly forbidden the words 'Charles Whitaker' to be uttered in my presence all these years past, so you will *not* bring his name to your lips in this household, do you hear me?"

"Please, Daphne. You are displaying precisely the sort of behavior that warrants my father's intervention as your guardian and requires him to—"

Before he could finish his sentence, his hostess snatched the blue-and-white porcelain coffeepot off the tray and hurled it straight at him. With quick reflexes, Simon stepped to one side as the chinaware crashed into the baseboard at the far side of the room. Daphne's breathing had grown ragged, and her lovely features were inflamed with rage.

"Just leave this house! I didn't want you to come here. No one at Devon Oaks wanted you to come. You merely invited yourself, as you well know."

"Daphne… please," Simon pleaded, his voice low with intensity. "You're upset. You've had so much to contend with. You're—"

"I have endured you Hopkinses and your dictatorial, self-righteous *charity* about as long as I can stand," Daphne cried contemptuously. "If I am not allowed by you and your father to run my own affairs, then I shall find a male quite willing to grant me the privilege."

"Aaron Clayton?" Simon murmured as if to himself.

"I am a twenty-five-year-old widow with an unbalanced mother who has an unbreakable habit of striking her head against her bedroom wall for hours at a time. I have an incorrigible little brother, and a sister I detest as much as she detests me. My father *and* my other sister took their own damnable lives and left me with this unholy mess to contend with. No one will fault me if I turn to a man who has promised to help me steer my own ship."

"But you've only just met this man," Simon replied quietly, hoping an unemotional tone would serve to calm the roiling waters. "He's an interloper. He's a *Yankee*, for God's sake! An opportunist! Are you sure you know him well enough to trust him with such a precious charge?" He studied her agitated features, taking in the sight of Daphne's glittering gaze and the frantic, unnatural way she paced the room as if she were strung as tightly as one of the strings on her harp. "What if the jackal only pretends, now, to give you your head as means of gaining entry to your heart—and to your purse?"

Daphne stared wide-eyed at Simon, as silence filled the air. Then, suddenly, her face crumpled and she sank her head into her hands and began to sob. "You don't understand..." she moaned, shaking her head from side to side. "You've never understood what it was like to live in this house... what it was like to have a mother who's as mad as a hatter, and to have my own father—"

Daphne's desperate cries and her face, so contorted with pain, were alarmingly like the portrait she had just sketched of her mother's melancholy madness. Simon took a step forward and attempted to enfold her in his arms, but she flailed against his chest with her fists and sank in a huddle beside a chair. In the blink of an eye, the strident, willful rebel had metamorphosed into an inconsolable child, tears cascading down her cheeks, her keening cries rending the air and drowning out the steady downpour that continued to soak the countryside bordering both sides of Whitaker Creek.

"Daphne, please," Simon implored softly, kneeling beside her as gingerly as he would a traumatized faun. "If I can't be more to you than just a friend, at least let me be *that*." He reached out with the intention of embracing her as he had the day Charles Whitaker had taken his life.

"No... *no!*" she screeched, as if she'd been seared by fire. And without warning, she jumped to her feet and fled the room.

Simon sat back on his heels for a long moment. Then he slowly pulled himself up and sank into a silk-clad chair. He stared at the silver tray, minus its coffeepot, and reflected upon the malaise that had come to infect all who lived at Devon Oaks Plantation. A few minutes later, the butler who had first welcomed him appeared at the door, his eyes wide in his brown face.

Simon drew himself up, and announced, "Miss Daphne was feeling poorly and has retired for the night."

"Yessir," the butler replied, nodding wisely.

Simon's heart brimmed with a melancholy nearly as piercing as that which he now recognized held the entire Whitaker household in its grip. Slowly, he shifted his weight in the chair and pointed to the smashed crockery heaped on the floor. A dark brown stain discolored the wall just above the wooden baseboard.

"There's been an accident," he said. He rose unsteadily to his feet. "Would you be so good as to fetch my cloak?" Then he added more forcefully, "I shall be returning to Hopkins House before the next cloudburst engulfs us."

CHAPTER 24

DAPHNE DUVALLON PEERED THROUGH the gloom from her cramped position under the bathroom sink in the powder room at the Governor Holmes House. The heavy pillow from the sitting room couch that she'd wedged between her body and the porcelain sink weighed heavily against her back. The muscles of her thighs and calves ached from kneeling within her bathroom refuge, riding out the storm.

The storm!

Which storm? she wondered, her heart thudding heavily in her chest. One minute she'd been running for cover during an engagement party, and the next, she was witnessing another storm, in another era, at another grand old house—Devon Oaks Plantation.

She recalled the harrowing scene of Daphne Whitaker hurling a china pot against the parlor wall. Her namesake's behavior was that of a woman in the midst of a full-blown nervous breakdown. And probably the most peculiar aspect of the entire event was that she'd experienced this latest foray into her ancestors' pasts from the viewpoint of a *man* this time—the poor, beleaguered young Simon Hopkins.

"Oh, God," she gasped. "Sim!" Where had the Simon Hopkins *she* knew been during this storm? Was Maddy all right? What about Willis and the band?

The air inside the small bathroom was stifling and Daphne couldn't stand her close quarters for another second. She disentangled herself from the couch pillow and the sink and slowly, painfully, rose to her full height. Then she cocked her head and listened intently. No more thunder and lightning, no more howling winds, she thought thankfully. The only sound she could hear was a steady downpour—not the cacophony visited upon the brick house just before she had slipped into this latest crazy time warp.

"Daphne? Daphne!"

She yanked open the powder room door and beheld hotelier Bob Pully standing in the foyer amid the distraught members of the aborted engagement party. His worry and concern evaporated at the sight of her, and he rushed forward to enfold her in a hug. Then he looked over his shoulder, and proclaimed, "Well, thank heavens! Everyone present and accounted for."

A feeble cheer went up from the assembled storm survivors and the remaining bedraggled guests descended the stairs from the second floor.

"Is your house okay?" Daphne asked worriedly.

"Fine, 'cept we lost that big ol' tree in the side yard, the electricity's off, and the phone is dead," Bob replied. "Guess we should count ourselves lucky."

"I've got to get back to Bluff House and check on Cousin Maddy," Daphne exclaimed. "May I leave the harp in your sitting room, Bob?"

"Of course. Let me get your raincoat, and you be careful now."

Within minutes, Daphne was in her Jeep, headed down Washington Street at a snail's pace thanks to the continuing monsoon-like downpour. She could hardly see the road as she made a right turn onto Canal Street and picked up speed, heading in the direction of Cousin Maddy's. She dodged the uprooted trees and debris that littered the street.

"Bless you, four-wheel drive," she muttered.

Behind her, two bright headlights flashed in her rearview mirror and the driver of the car began to honk incessantly. Annoyed, Daphne speeded up as much as she dared. So did the mystery car behind her, tooting its horn even more furiously.

Despite the pouring rain and the empty thoroughfare, she dutifully made a stop at the intersection with Jefferson Street, and winced when the car behind her slammed on its brakes, screeching to a halt on the slick pavement only inches from her rear bumper.

Daphne glanced angrily into her mirror and was frightened witless by the sight of a man bursting out of the driver's-side door and sprinting toward her side of the car.

"Sweet Jesus," he cried. "I've been chasing you for two blocks! Didn't you see me?" he shouted through the car window that was nearly opaque with rain. "Thank God you're okay."

Wordlessly, Daphne unfastened her seat belt and opened the car door. A man in bright yellow foul weather gear with water cascading off his billed hat stood beside her car in the pouring rain. Scooting out of the driver's seat, Daphne absorbed the close-up sight of a dented Range Rover with a distinctive black rack on the roof. She returned her gaze to the face of her pursuer.

"Sim! Oh, my God!" she shouted through the rain. "It was pouring so hard, I couldn't see a thing! I had no idea it was you!"

"What did you think? That I was a carjacker?"

"I was just trying to get home to see if Maddy's all right. How did you know where to find me? From Maddy? Oh, my God... is she okay? Is Bluff House all right?"

The rain continued in a steady downpour, although the wind suddenly lessened enough for them not to have to shout.

"I haven't been there. I just remembered you said you were playing at the Governor Holmes House today. As soon as the worst of the storm blew past, I raced down here. If I hadn't had the Range Rover I'd never have made it. Trees and power lines are down all over."

"Is Bailey all right?"

"I left him having a bourbon, straight up," Sim said.

"I saw a funnel cloud." She glanced overhead at the ink-black sky, struck by the terrible danger they had miraculously avoided. She lowered her eyes to meet Sim's worried gaze, and began to tremble. "I was wedged under a sink in a tiny bathroom... by myself. Oh, Sim... I saw... I... it was so..."

Her words trailed off as Sim threw his arms around her, pulling her close. Daphne wrapped her arms around his waist, her cheek against his slicker, and held on tight, reveling in the refuge and strength of his embrace. Sim peered down at her through the drizzle that had finally begun to taper off.

"I'm sorry I was so disgusting and stupid on the phone when I got back to Natchez," he apologized.

"Ditto, me too, you, in Brazil or wherever you were. I was just worried and missing you," she said, sniffling.

"I think I had some sort of weird flashback to the way it used to be with Francesca and me whenever I couldn't make it back on the dot. You're not her. I'm sorry."

"Apology accepted, especially since I've met the lady."

Sim looked at Daphne in amazement, "You did? How'd that happen?"

"Tell you later, but first..." She held up her right hand as if she were swearing on a Bible. "A double ditto apology for getting testy whenever I think somebody's not playing it totally straight with me. I automatically imagine the worst. It's a nasty habit that I *really* want to break, trust me, Bird Man."

Sim glanced at the fallen branches and broken electrical wires strewn across the street. "All I could think of when trees started crashing down around Bailey's place was, what if you were driving alone, or you were somewhere where you couldn't take cover. Suddenly, all that stuff on the phone just seemed stupid. Nothing else mattered except to get to you," he said, enfolding her in his arms again.

After a moment, Daphne leaned back to touch Sim's face. "I had the same pictures in my mind of you in trouble out on the Trace. What if something had happened to you after our horrible conversation?" Her voice choked and she couldn't speak.

He pulled her roughly against his chest again and they hugged each other tightly. Then he kissed her so soundly, no other words of apology or explanation were necessary.

At length, Daphne broke their embrace.

"Maddy!" they pronounced simultaneously.

"But wait!" she said. "Before we get to Bluff House, there's something you should know. Maddy's waiting for the results of a biopsy that her doctor has sent down to New Orleans for a second opinion from the pathologist down there."

"Oh, God, no! What do they think it is?"

"Some kind of skin lesion. I'll tell you everything I know about it later. Let's go."

They made a dash for their respective cars. Sim drove his Range Rover around Daphne's Jeep and led the way.

⤝⤜

Bluff House, as it happened, sustained only moderate damage to a section of its roof. Despite branches and debris scattered about the yard, the rest of the house came through the storm unscathed. Sim and Daphne found Cousin Maddy on the first floor, shaken but unharmed.

"I was mighty glad I took cover in the downstairs bathroom," the older woman exclaimed. "I saw the funnel cloud on the other side of the river, comin' straight across the water, and I just high-tailed it in there! By the time I had the gumption to look out the window again, that mean ol' cloud'd disappeared."

Maddy made a pot of tea on the gas stove, which fortunately was working, and they sat around the kitchen table telling their war stories about the storm. When they all felt calmer, Sim set off to check on the Richeses' welfare at Monmouth Plantation and confirmed that the McGees came through the storm in one piece. Then he called Daphne's cell phone from his own wireless, which miraculously worked, to say he was heading back to Bailey's to help remove the fallen branches and repair the birdhouses knocked over by the high winds.

The next day, the *Natchez Democrat*, ever mindful of the tourist trade, declined to categorize the storm as a tornado, describing the funnel cloud as "straight-line winds." The front-page article quoted Maddy as one of several citizens caught without sufficient insurance coverage.

"I had the check all made out, mind you," Madeline Clayton Whitaker had disclosed to the reporter who stopped by the house, having spotted the damaged roof, "but with one thing and another, I'd forgotten to mail it and found it on the floor of my kitchen, can you imagine? The envelope was soaked through because a window had blown open in the storm." In the next paragraph, Mrs.

Whitaker noted that she would mail the letter to her insurance company the very next day.

"While you argue with the insurance guy, I'm paying for the repairs so we can get the roof fixed right away," Daphne announced firmly to her cousin. "You can just consider it raising my rent."

Maddy shook her head vehemently. "If you pay for the roof then you're *not* payin' rent! But, you are a lifesaver, my dear. I get so overwhelmed by payin' bills and takin' care of all the things that Marcus used to do, that I'm terribly forgetful sometimes. But this was such a *stupid* mistake."

"Look, Maddy," Daphne reassured her gently. "Remember, you've had some pretty weighty matters on your mind. We all do stuff like forgetting to mail things. I'm so grateful you weren't hurt that I'd gladly pay for the whole damn roof to be replaced, if we needed it."

Just then the phone rang.

"Praise be, the lines must be working again," Maddy declared jubilantly. She picked up the receiver and immediately her expression grew grave.

"Maddy, what is it?" Daphne whispered.

Her cousin mouthed the word, "Doctor." Then she murmured, "I see. Yes, of course. Let's schedule it right away Thursday would be fine. Will I have to stay overnight at the hospital? Oh, good. Right. I'll call your nurse later today 'bout everything. Thank you, Doctor Gilman."

Daphne felt her heart contract as Maddy sank onto a nearby kitchen chair.

"What?" she demanded, trying to read the expression on her face.

"The biopsy came back. Doctor Gilman calls it an 'evolving melanoma.' He plans to remove it surgically as an outpatient procedure this week."

"Is it sun-related do you think? People get those all the time."

"He said the cells were a bit unusual, but it could be caused by sun. He said we'll know more once they cut it out and get a full report from the pathologist."

"True." Daphne leaned down and gave Maddy's shoulders a

squeeze. "We'll take this a step at a time," she proposed, privately thinking that even the doctors probably dreaded accepting the possibility of a cancer spike going on in the South. She brushed a stray strand of gray hair off Maddy's forehead. "Look... we'll deal with this. We'll get through this together."

"I know we will," Madeline replied staunchly, her eyes filled with tears. "I'm just so grateful to have you in my life, you know? If this had happened to me a year ago, I'm not so sure I'd even fight this thing."

"Oh, we'll fight it, all right," Daphne vowed. "Why don't you call Bailey right now, tell him what Gilman said, and get his opinion about all this?"

She seized the phone and dialed the number, handing the receiver to Maddy before she could decline. Then she ran and picked up another extension.

"'Evolving melanoma' sounds like 'sorta pregnant,'" Bailey scoffed. "It's kinda a CYA diagnosis... 'cover-your-ass.' Basal cell carcinomas won't kill you. Squamous cell carcinomas can be tricky but are usually not life-threatening. And melanomas you don't wish on your worst enemy. Get Gilman to send me the New Orleans pathology report, and I'll see y'all Thursday in Gilman's office, Maddy darlin'."

"Well, that's mighty kind of you, Bailey, to be there for the surgery."

"My hands shake a bit, these days, but thank God, my brain still works. I'm keeping an eagle eye on Gilman every second, sweetheart. Don't you worry one bit 'bout this. I honestly think it's gonna be fine. Doctors these days get mighty nervous not preparing you for the worst so you won't sue 'em later for not warning you life can lead to death!"

❧

Daphne and Sim sat in the waiting room while Maddy had the growth removed from the top of her shoulder as scheduled. Within twenty minutes, Bailey Gibbs appeared in green operating room scrubs.

"The growth *was* slightly atypical, as these things go, but nothing definitive. I made sure we had a pathologist standing by during surgery to confirm that Gilman took enough tissue on all sides out to where the margins were cancer-free. I'm bettin' he got it all, but she's committed to regular checkups every three months and you can be sure that I'll stay on the lady's case."

Relieved to hear this news, Daphne threw her arms around Bailey, and Sim pumped his free hand. Choking back tears of relief, Daphne said, "Well, now we've *really* got to sell every single ticket for the 'Birds' benefit, don't we? We need money for more than just hiring a few lawyers. People've got to know they're *all* at risk."

"Getting that kind of a story into the public's consciousness takes some mighty deep pockets, believe me," Sim warned.

"True," Daphne replied tersely, "but I've learned from my brother King that people can do the most amazing things if each volunteer *delivers* on what he or she has promised to do. That's the way to pull off a miracle."

∼❧∼

From the day of the storm onwards, Daphne and Sim never again spoke of their first spat. For the rest of the summer they enjoyed each other's company whenever their complicated schedules allowed for a rendezvous. During the ensuing weeks, Sim was photographing in the field nearly five days out of seven. He spent his time systematically tracking down the remaining birds that Audubon had painted in the 1820s.

For her part, Daphne was busy dawn to dusk. Maddy's cancer scare had galvanized the younger woman's commitment to the benefit concert like nothing else could have. She spent every free minute coordinating the myriad production details. Three days a week, she took on the instruction of several of Maddy's most advanced harp students. Tuesdays through Saturdays, she played during tea service at the Eola Hotel, and she appeared at the Under-the-Hill Saloon on weekends. Twice a week she had her tutorial sessions with Willis. Late Sunday night and Mondays were sacrosanct, however. Maddy didn't even ask anymore if Daphne would be home for dinner.

"Mmmmm…" Sim whispered sleepily one evening, taking Daphne in his arms as she slipped into his bed in the cottage at Gibbs Hall. It was just after midnight following her Sunday session at the Under-the Hill Saloon. "I think I'll have *you* for a late supper…" he murmured, nibbling her ear.

A few days after Maddy's surgery, Daphne had related to Sim the details of her unwelcome exchange with Francesca Hayes in the hotel ladies' room, though she omitted her theory that Sim's ex-wife had come to Mississippi with an additional goal besides pounding Bailey Gibbs into submission. In August, she had finally given in to her curiosity.

"Has Francesca ever called you since she's been here?" Daphne had asked, doing her darnedest to keep her tone casual.

"She left a message on my cell phone," Sim replied. "She said she has some 'creative solutions' to suggest regarding the toxic dumps."

"And?" Daphne demanded. "I suppose she wanted to get together to talk?"

"I left a voice mail telling her to call Bailey directly when she puts something in writing."

Daphne had been satisfied to hear this answer and let the subject drop. Since then, she'd made a good-faith effort to banish Francesca Hayes and Jack Ebert from her thoughts. Even so, after each week's absence from Sim, she had to bite her tongue not to ask if the persistent attorney hadn't tried to contact her former spouse a second time.

The weeks telescoped, one into the other, as the hot, sultry summer months flew by. Amadora Bendhar rehearsed weekly with the ad hoc "Birds" chamber orchestra, which had been miraculously recruited from musicians on both sides of the Mississippi. Daphne accepted the role of harpist in this group. Meanwhile she, Althea, the McGee sisters, and Sunny, their sax player—with the help of Willis McGee's new arrangements—began rehearsing jazz and blues numbers with the word "bird" in the title, which they unearthed from lists of songs they downloaded from the Internet.

By early September, Daphne had enlisted a quintet of Maddy's youngest harp students to form the Angel Choir. Next, she signed up a barbershop quartet from the paddle steamer *Delta Queen*, along with twenty-two members of Mary Jo McGee's kindergarten class to sing "The Tweety Bird Song," which Daphne knew had all the makings of a show stopper.

All Natchez was abuzz about the coming benefit concert. Sim assembled a collection of his most representative works and sent them to New York to have prints made at his own expense. They would be sold at the charity auction to be held in the foyer of the Margaret Martin Auditorium before the show, along with some prized antiques that Maddy and her committee had recruited from the attics of friends all over Natchez. Bailey and his "Birders" visited the social and fraternal organizations throughout the region selling theater tickets and chances on prizes that ranged from a complimentary weekend at Monmouth Plantation to a free lunch at Mammy's.

When, at last, the entire coterie of performers assembled for their final rehearsal on Saturday, the afternoon of the evening's benefit, an exhausted Daphne sat in the middle of the leased hall with Bailey Gibbs and cousin Maddy, watching their handiwork take form and substance on stage. Due to the whirlwind of preparations for the one-and-only performance of "For the Birds," scheduled to begin at eight o'clock, she hadn't seen Sim all week. Finally she had a moment to wonder where he was.

When the afternoon run-through came to a close, Bailey rose from his seat, and said, "You are somethin' else, Daphne Duvallon. It's gonna be terrific!"

The temperature outside was still warm, but the "crushin' heat," as Maddy described the dog days of summer, was nearing its end. The nights had been cool enough this third week in September to require a jacket or sweater when the sun went down over the Mississippi, offering a welcome early taste of fall.

"Thanks, Bailey," Daphne replied to the physician's compliment with a tired grimace. "Your kind praise is a balm to my tattered soul. The Angel Choir is cute, but the kids need to work on getting on and offstage." She glanced up the auditorium's empty center aisle. "Where's Sim? I thought he was coming back to Gibbs Hall last night. Didn't he drive in with you? He was supposed to be here hours ago to mount his photographs for the lobby display."

"Oh, I meant to tell you earlier, but there was so much goin' on when I got here," Bailey apologized. "Sim said he'll be front row, center by curtain time. He called me from Jackson. He's sending the last of his photos down with somebody else today and hopes one of your volunteers can set them up in the lobby."

Daphne's jaw dropped slightly. Sim had been in *Jackson* during this last week of rehearsals? When they'd spoken on his cell phone a few days earlier, Daphne had assumed he'd been deep in the woods, somewhere northwest of Natchez—not in the state capital. Suddenly she wanted to ask Bailey a dozen questions.

"Did you actually see him up there?"

And where—exactly—was his ex-wife all that time?

"Just on Wednesday," the doctor replied. "I asked him to help me button-hole as many senators and representatives as possible, now that the legislature's headin' back in session. I want to persuade those folks to vote no if the toxic dump proposal comes out of committee—which it's expected to real soon."

"Was the opposition also prowling the corridors of power?" Daphne inquired, unable to keep a touch of sarcasm out of her voice.

"You betcha," Bailey said with disgust. "The Able Petroleum people and our group were practically playin' tag team goin' in and out of the legislators' offices."

On stage, Maddy had called her students together to run through their number another time. The covey of Angels still bumped into their harps and each other like a bunch of pint-sized Keystone Cops. Rehearsal was nearly at an end and time was short, but all Daphne could think about was that Sim was a no-show, and worse—he hadn't disclosed he'd been in Jackson all week. The co-chair of the benefit wasn't even going to be here to set up his own photographic exhibit, she fumed.

Just then, two figures appeared at the back of the hall and proceeded to make their way toward the foot of the stage where

Maddy and Daphne had gathered to confer about altering stage directions for the young harpists.

"Hello, y'all," Jack Ebert said in a loud voice from halfway up the aisle. "You remember Francesca Hayes?"

Daphne glanced briefly at Maddy, whose startled expression registered the same surprise that she was feeling. "Yes, of course," she said, nodding curtly in the direction of Sim's former wife. Francesca looked excessively chic in an ecru linen pantsuit and pale pink, scoop-necked tee. Daphne shifted her gaze to Jack, who was by now only a few feet away. "What are you doing here?"

"Looking for Sim," Jack said brusquely, as if she were an unhelpful secretary. "Did he beat us down here from Jackson?"

"Nope. Not yet," Daphne replied, masking her surprise at his question.

"You're 'sposed to meet him again tonight, right?" he asked his companion.

Daphne stared at the unwelcome intruders, dumbfounded by this exchange.

"That was the plan," Francesca agreed, adding, "Who should I give Sim's photographs to?" Her gaze drifted from Jack to Bailey to Maddy and finally settled on Daphne.

Daphne stretched out her hand to receive the large manila envelope. She didn't know who she was furious with most—Sim or his ex-wife.

Francesca smiled faintly, and asked, "How's the benefit going to be tonight?" as if their conversation was the most normal thing in the world.

Daphne flashed on an image of the socially connected Ms. Hayes slumming in the wings of the San Francisco Symphony during rehearsals. "I expect this will seem pretty down-home if you're not from Natchez."

Bailey Gibbs spoke up harshly, "We have a sellout house, so we'll have money to hire our *own* fancy lawyers to support our cause."

A cause that Jack Ebert and Francesca Hayes were working night and day to thwart, Daphne thought, her hackles rising. What were these two *doing* here? she thought angrily. Why was Sim planning a rendezvous with his ex-wife *tonight*, of all times? And what did Jack mean that Sim was supposed to meet Francesca "again"?

Daphne pushed away ugly thoughts about "consorting with the enemy" and abruptly excused herself while Maddy bustled about, herding her students off to the wings to prepare for one last run-through.

"See you tonight and good luck," Francesca called after her. The barbershop quartet began warbling in the back of the hall.

Amazed by the woman's gall, Daphne slowly turned around at the bottom of the steps that led backstage and stared at Jack and his hired gun.

"There aren't any more tickets," she repeated in as neutral a tone as she could muster. "Like Doctor Bailey says, we're completely sold out."

"Oh, we've got tickets," Francesca informed her cheerfully, patting her Chanel handbag with interlocking brass *C*'s on its leather flap. "Sim gave them to us. We wouldn't miss it, would we, Jack?"

Jack flashed Daphne a grin, and said, "Not in a New York minute."

Backstage, Althea whispered to Daphne and Maddy. "Man oh man, we're likely to *die* of adorableness here tonight."

Daphne forced a smile, mentally willing the band of harpists making up the Angel Choir to conclude "When the Swallows Come Back to Capistrano"—all at the same time, all on the same note. The bevy of six-to-twelve-year-olds were attired in identical flowing, white dimity dresses with wide, pink satin bows at their waists. Maddy had also fastened pink ribbons in their identical Alice-in-Wonderland hairdos, producing, in fact, a miniature angelic host the likes of which even Natchez had never seen.

The Angels had already marched on stage when Daphne gazed through a spy hole in the curtain in time to see Sim Hopkins slip into his seat next to Bailey in the fourth row. Even her *mother* had shown up in time for King's wedding, she thought, hurt and bewildered by the events of the last few hours. She pushed such unhappy comparisons out of her mind and did her best to focus on the business at hand.

Staring past the curtains that masked the wings, Daphne's ire went up another notch at the sight of Maddy's surgical scar, just visible an inch below the nape of her neck. Hadn't Sim drawn them all into this enterprise as partners in the effort to make people aware that the health of the Baileys and Madelines of this world was at risk just as much as that of the birds? Why, then, had he taken a powder all week?

"Can you *believe* Sim?" Daphne demanded in a hoarse whisper. "Disappears for three days, lets his ex-wife deliver the photographs being auctioned off to fight *our* side of this battle, and then arrives just as the curtain is going up?"

Maddy and Althea exchanged glances, their gazes troubled. "Bailey was upset, too," Maddy murmured comfortingly. "Sim must have an explanation."

"For going AWOL? Whatever excuse he comes up with, I'll bet it's going to sound *really* old," she retorted.

Just then, Kendra and Jeanette McGee sauntered into the wings, decked out in their black leather miniskirts and chain metal bustiers.

"Do you think the Aphrodites will offer the audience a big enough change of pace?" Kendra joked under her breath, pointing at the angelic-looking children on stage. The jazz musicians snorted with suppressed laughter, while Maddy shot them all a warning look to be quiet.

The Angel Choir, seated in a crescent arrangement of harps, next swung into a well-loved excerpt from *Swan Lake*. The pint-size musicians concluded their part of the program to wildly enthusiastic applause that nearly matched the audience's response to the next act, the For the Birds Chamber Orchestra, led brilliantly by Amadora Bendhar.

For the benefit concert, the flamboyant conductor had donned an electric blue sari with gold embroidery that winked and glinted under the lights. Following a rousing rendition of a movement from *The Firebird Suite*, the twenty-five musicians, including

Daphne, segued into a sprightly medley of crowd-pleasing pop tunes that included "Yellow Bird," "Zippity Do Da," and "When the Red, Red Robin Comes Bob, Bob, Bobbin' Along."

Next, Miss Mary Jo McGee's kindergarten brought down the house as expected with a boisterous version of "The Tweety Bird Song."

"I tawt I taw a puddy tat! I did, I taw a puddy tat!" they sang.

At intermission, some audience members drifted outside the auditorium for a breath of air. Others stood in line to bid on auction items or to purchase souvenir T-shirts that sported a picture Sim had shot of chickadees perched on the miniature veranda of a birdhouse replica of Monmouth Plantation House.

During the interval, Daphne had changed from her flowing black tea gown into her seductive Aphrodite uniform. She adjusted her skintight bustier for the tenth time, critically eyed her black leather miniskirt and sheer silk hose, and peered through the discreet slit in the red velvet curtain at the half-empty hall. She could just make out the fourth row where Bailey Gibbs, Liz and Otis Keating, and Sim lounged, chatting among themselves. Bailey smiled broadly at friends and well-wishers who were making their way outside for a smoke. Sim, on the other hand, looked subdued.

Now, as Daphne gazed at the auditorium from her hiding place, she was taken aback to see Francesca saunter down the aisle, lean over several seats, and whisper something in Sim's ear, to which he nodded agreement. As Daphne watched Sim listen intently to his former spouse, she was assaulted by the shocking notion that the most important man in her life might well be more involved with his ex-wife than he'd let on.

Bewildered, she watched Sim smile faintly at Francesca and then shrug. To Daphne, their exchange appeared so easygoing… so familiar… so *intimate*.

"Stop peeking at that man of yours and collect your wits, girl," Althea admonished, "'cause the audience is comin' back to their seats."

The acts following intermission succeeded each other in a blur.

Daphne was startled when Althea turned to her other fellow musicians and croaked "Standby, y'all! Are y'ready to rock 'n' *roll?*"

No! Daphne wanted to scream. Added to her preperformance jitters was a surge of anger over the scene she had just witnessed between Francesca and Sim.

What the hell is going on here? her mind shrieked as she strode on stage. Her gaze swept from a side view of Maddy in the wings to Bailey sitting in the audience—two living examples of why she'd given her all to tonight's effort. If she could have flung her stiletto-heeled shoe squarely between Sim's eyes, she would have. Instead, she took her place, along with the other Aphrodites, behind an opaque curtain that would become transparent as the footlights and floodlights gradually kicked up to full strength. She lightly fingered a single harp string to double-check that the microphone inside her instrument's hollow soundboard was turned on. Summoning every ounce of will, she forced herself to plaster a smile on her face and concentrate on the performance at hand. In an act of mental jujitsu, she pushed aside all other thoughts except for the opening bars of their first number. Later she would deal with the import of Sim and Francesca's little tête-à-tête. Right now, it was show time. And as she'd been taught since childhood, she inhaled a deep, cleansing breath, and waited for Althea's count.

When the lights came up on the Aphrodites wailing a double-time version of "Bye, Bye Blackbird," members of the audience began to clap in time, and some spontaneously jumped up from their seats and swayed to the music. The moment the scrim curtain was fully raised, the eye-popping quintet prompted an avalanche of hoots and hollers from all corners of the hall. The crowd's first glimpse of the scantily clad all-female band brought many patrons to their feet, and soon a few enthusiasts began dancing in the aisles. Even the most sedate among the audience were either tapping their toes or clapping their hands over their heads in time to the rollicking tune.

Another cheer went up when the group launched into "Rockin' Robin," their enthusiasm topped only by the Aphrodites' rendition of "Lullaby of Birdland." By the end of the set, Daphne had succeeded in blocking all thoughts of Jack Ebert, Francesca Hayes—and even Sim. However when the spotlight fell on her during a droll jazz rendition of "Tit Willow" from the operetta *The Mikado*, her gaze was inexorably drawn to Jack and Francesca, heads close together, conferring. Fortunately, Daphne quickly regained her concentration as she and the band began to play the first sweet, swelling strains of "The Wind Beneath My Wings." Soon, the audience, as one, rose to its feet. Tears welled in her eyes when everyone began to sway in time to the music. Some even sang along with the band, their voices raised in an anthem to courage and love.

When Daphne glanced down at the fourth row, Dr. Bailey Gibbs was holding tightly onto Liz Keating's right arm, beaming, as moisture bathed his cheeks. Out of the corner of her eye she saw Maddy smiling in the wings through joyful tears. When the last notes died, the Aphrodites left the stage waving and clapping back at the audience. It took nearly four minutes before the wolf whistles subsided. Meanwhile, two seats in the middle orchestra section that had belonged to Jack Ebert and Francesca Hayes were conspicuously empty.

Backstage, an army of well-wishers engulfed the Aphrodites, along with the rest of the performers. By the time Daphne reached her dressing room, her arms were laden with bouquets of flowers. Banks of blooms—including one from Sim—magically had appeared on the table littered with makeup and boxes of facial tissues.

Bailey and Maddy were among the first to burst into the room, giving Daphne bear hugs in quick succession. It was more than a half hour before she was able to shut the door and trade her mini-skirt and bustier for a pair of sweatpants and a terry cloth shirt. She cleaned her face of the heavy stage makeup, pulled her blond hair into a ponytail, and returned to the deserted stage to pack up her harp. Sim may have remembered to send her flowers, she thought, angrily flipping open the catches on her hard-shell case, but he sure as hell forgot to come backstage to congratulate her! Her dark musings were interrupted by Althea heading out the stage door.

"I'll see you back at the house, okay?" Althea called, hoisting a duffel bag onto her shoulder. Maddy had agreed to host a modest cast party for performers and the stage crew at her place, and everyone appeared headed in that direction.

Just then, Kendra, Jeanette, and Sunny appeared in the wings. "Us, too," Kendra declared. "But remember, you and Sim gotta behave yourselves tonight," she teased. "Don't y'all forget, we've gotta be at the Under-the-Hill Saloon tomorrow night by eight p.m., sharp. The *Delta Queen* docks in the afternoon and they expect a big crowd."

Afraid to speak, Daphne merely nodded farewell, feeling more morose by the minute. Silently, she continued with her customary routine of safely stowing her instrument into its traveling case.

"Need any help?" Amadora called from the wings.

"No... thanks," she replied, gazing around the empty auditorium. She tried to smile at the woman who had become like a sister during the summer of rehearsals and endless strategy meetings. "Want to have lunch tomorrow and do a postmortem after Bailey and I put the profits in the bank?" She desperately needed a friend to talk to.

"No can do," Amadora said smugly. "I have a hot date flying in from California for the week. I have to get my beauty sleep. How about Tuesday, next?"

Daphne nodded, pleased for her friend, though by this time, her spirits were lower than an alligator's belly.

Goddamn it! she thought, her temper advancing beyond its slow boil. What kind of co-chair of a charity event turns up missing in action?

Easy, she silently answered her own question. *An absolute* rat, *that's who.*

CHAPTER 25

DAPHNE HAD JUST EASED the harp case into the back of the Jeep when she spotted Sim in the parking lot. He was standing next to a nondescript late-model car, conversing once again with none other than his former wife.

Daphne slammed the tailgate with a vengeance and marched toward the driver's side of her car with murder in mind. Meanwhile, out of the corner of her eye, she watched Francesca pat Sim familiarly on his shoulder in a farewell gesture. The lawyer from San Francisco climbed into her rented car and drove off.

Daphne jumped into the Jeep's driver's seat and angrily turned on the ignition. She had thrust the gear into reverse when Sim rapped smartly on the window.

"Hey, angel girl, where're you going in such a hurry?"

Angel girl? Who did he think he was kidding?

Daphne stared straight ahead through the windshield for a moment, composed herself, then turned to look at Sim. Slowly, she lowered the window.

"Bluff House," she said without elaboration.

"You were great and the show was fabulous," he said. However, Daphne sensed a strange remoteness in his manner that was a toned-down version of what she currently felt toward *him*.

"Thanks," she said brusquely. "Look, I've got to get back to help Maddy with the cast party. Where were you all day, Mr. Co-chairman? Or should I say all *week*?"

Sim glanced across the emptying parking lot. "I'll follow you in my car. We can talk when we get there, though I can't stay long." Daphne arched an eyebrow and waited without making a reply.

Sim hesitated a moment longer, and then volunteered, "I apologize for not getting here in time to put up my photographs in the lobby tonight."

"We could have used your help," Daphne said, barely civil.

"And the reason I can't stay at Maddy's party is that I have to get up at the crack of dawn to meet a birder friend of Bailey's. He's going to take me to a spot on the Trace where he claims he sighted a bunch of ivory-billed woodpeckers. The bird is presumed extinct, so it's worth checking out. Plus my editor's been bugging me to submit all the photographs for the Audubon project by the end of the month, so I'm feeling behind the eight ball."

Daphne thought Sim's explanation was too long and too detailed and completely unresponsive to her original question. Her rat detector kicked into high gear, yet she merely shrugged. If she uttered a single word, she'd say something she'd regret.

He leaned through the open car window and bussed her on the cheek. Daphne tried to smile, hoping that he would seize this moment alone to explain further, but Sim only gazed at her for a long moment before he asked, "Are you okay?"

She debated her answer, then shook her head.

"Absolutely not."

"And that's because..."

A bleakness swept over her that was dangerously reminiscent of the week following Sim's return from the Amazon. "Call me crazy or simply a jealous fool, Sim, but inquiring minds want to know. Were you ever planning to tell me why you dropped off the radar screen this week—of all weeks—and why you showed up two minutes after the curtain rose tonight? Were you going to at least give me a *hint* why your ex-wife and my ex-fiancé were given house seats—which we could have *sold*, for God's sake—and why you and Francesca had your heads together just now?"

"You *do* sound jealous," Sim said, a small smile pulling at the corner of his mouth.

"I think I am," she admitted soberly.

"Well, believe me, don't give *that* issue another thought."

"So, what's with the big powwow?"

"Can't tell you... yet."

"Or *won't* tell me," she retorted before she had time to censor herself.

Just when you thought it was safe to go back into the water, she reflected grimly.

Sim looked at her a long time before speaking. "Believe me, Francesca Hayes only has business on the brain."

She remembered the way Jack Ebert had flatly denied her accusation about his affair with Cindy Lou Mallory in precisely such carefully parsed phrases of half-truths and omissions that added up to the Big Lie. When she'd confronted Rafe about his peccadilloes, he'd merely scoffed and advised her to consult a psychiatrist for her paranoia.

"Then why not just tell me what's going on?" she asked shortly. "We hit this bump once before, remember? Just level with me, Sim. Why this sudden friendliness with the enemy camp?"

"I can't discuss it," he replied tersely, "and frankly, it's not helpful to see the other side as the 'enemy.'" Daphne could tell that Sim, too, was running short on patience. "And by the way, this conversation is starting to feel like the third degree."

"One last question, then," Daphne retorted, "and then, believe *me*, I'm on my way. How come this is happening? I just put my all into a cause—mostly because *you* asked me to—and because of Bailey and Maddy, and then you, the co-chair of this event—the guy who said he'd have my back—go AWOL." Sim flinched, almost as if she'd slapped him across the face. Profoundly disturbed by the direction of this exchange, she pleaded, "Look, why can't we just be straight with each other? Tell me what's going on, or tell me to get lost. I don't do well with guessing games."

"I'm in the middle of something," he revealed reluctantly.

"In the middle of *what*?" she asked, exasperated. "What are you *talking* about? At least tell me if it's personal or professional?"

"Oh, it's *very* personal," he declared without hesitation.

"Oh," she said, feeling utterly deflated and shut out by his cryptic response. "I see. Well... that's a real conversation stopper."

Sim gazed at her with a troubled expression. "For the moment, I have to leave it at that, Daphne. I'm sorry."

They locked glances, neither of them speaking for several moments. Finally Daphne broke the silence. "You 'have to leave it at that,'" she quoted him, "and I have to leave, period. In case you've forgotten, Maddy has a house full of people who all worked hard to make 'For the Birds' a success and she could use a hand."

She realized she sounded peevish and manipulative, but she didn't care anymore. Sim had let her down in the crunch. He had let *them* down.

Sim reached out and touched her forearm that rested on the ledge of the driver's window. "There are two important things going on right now. I have to see them through."

"Is that code for 'I need some space'?" she snapped.

"No. It means I need some time."

Daphne affected a shrug. "Whatever," she replied coolly. She felt, suddenly, as if she'd donned a coat of steel armor. She reached up and adjusted her rearview mirror. There was no need for Sim to explain that he was heading out of town—whether to track the ivory-billed woodpecker, like he'd said, or for a rendezvous with Francesca. Either way, he was abandoning the "Birds" benefit… and her. She struggled for composure. "Gotta go," she said finally. "You take care in the woods, y'hear? There are some dangerous snakes out there."

Not waiting for a reply, Daphne swiftly backed out of her parking space and headed for home as the lyrics of "The Wind Beneath My Wings" echoed hollowly in her heart.

Every window at Bluff House was aglow and Maddy's downstairs rooms were filled with celebrating cast members and benefit volunteers. Althea met Daphne at the front door with a grin that turned to concern when she saw her friend was unaccompanied.

"Where's Sim?"

"Has an early day tomorrow."

"But he's the co-chair of this thing," Althea protested.

"You're telling *me*!"

Althea shook her head. "I dunno, girl… you sure can pick 'em."

"Don't say that," Daphne retorted, suddenly near tears. She felt like beating someone to a bloody pulp. Either that, or she'd run upstairs and cry for a week.

"Hey, baby," Althea crooned, pulling her friend into the powder room off the foyer and shutting the door. "I'm sorry I said that, honey, but, boy, I am *pissed* at Sim!"

"So am I. There's something going on that I don't understand," Daphne added bleakly, "and I don't know if it makes Sim a rat or a hero."

Althea's generous lips compressed into a straight line. "Well, we'll just have to see, won't we? But, if he's a rat, he's gonna hear 'bout it from me, big time!" she threatened, giving her friend a hug.

"We'll sic your brothers on him," Daphne said through a watery smile.

"You betcha!" Althea's expression suddenly brightened. "Oh! Guess who came up from New Orleans to catch our act tonight?"

"Haven't a clue," Daphne said, reaching for a tissue to dab her eyes. She pulled a brush from her purse and whipped it through her curly hair. In the bathroom mirror, her eyes looked dead and her complexion sallow.

"Chappy Barrone!"

"Who?"

"Only the main bookin' agent for the New Orleans Jazz Fest, that's who!"

Daphne turned away from the mirror to gaze at Althea with amazement.

"You're kidding? He drove all the way up here to see the show?"

"To see the *Aphrodite Jazz Ensemble*," she corrected emphatically.

"Holy cow! What did he think?"

"He thought we were pretty sensational. Wants us to come down to New Orleans to talk to 'his people,' he told me just before you got here!" Althea declared triumphantly.

Daphne gave her friend a high-five. "Way to *go*, girl!"

"Now, doesn't that cheer you up?"

"It does," Daphne lied. "It really does."

Of course it didn't, and she knew she'd cry later.

The next morning, Maddy tiptoed into the room at the top of the house. Daphne lay awake, glumly staring at the ceiling while she replayed last night's unhappy scene in the auditorium's parking lot.

"Daphne, dear… am I disturbin' you?"

With difficulty, Daphne summoned a smile, and said, "No. I've sort of got my eyes open. 'Morning, Maddy. Was that the phone?"

"Yes. It's a Libby Girard from the Farrell Funeral Home."

Alarmed by the thought that someone from a funeral home was calling early Sunday morning, Daphne grabbed her dressing gown and dashed into her office in the next room.

"Yes?" she said into the receiver, feeling her pulse quicken.

"Miz Duvallon? I'm Libby Girard, from Farrell's. I apologize for callin' you so early on a Sunday, but I was afraid that the Ebert-Petrella people would get to you first and sign you up exclusively."

"I doubt that," Daphne said dryly.

"Well, they might try," Libby said in a rush. "You see, I used to work there."

"Look, Miss Girard," Daphne said firmly, "I really don't—"

"And I *hated* it," she interrupted. "Uncle René got me to move all the way up here from New Orleans, but I should've known I couldn't work for that creep."

"Could you possibly be referring to Jack?" Daphne asked, faintly amused.

"Yes," Libby exclaimed. "I was at your weddin' and I shoulda *known* better than to think I could manage a funeral home if *he* was goin' t'be involved. Well, anyhow, I read in the *Natchez Democrat* a while back that your poor cousin, Miz Whitaker, got her roof damaged in that *non*tornado, as the Chamber of Commerce likes to call the storm that blew through here. And then a friend at the Anruss Salon told me you were so darlin' to pay to repair it y'self. So, now that I'm over at Farrell's, I'd been thinkin' to give you

a call and see if I could hire you to play at funerals here, figurin'
you'd had that big repair expense, and all."

By this time, Daphne was smiling to herself about the woman's
amazing facility for breathing in the middle of her run-on sentences, when she was brought up short by Libby's unexpected
job offer.

"Well, really, that's very sweet of you to think of me—"

"Wanted to do you a good turn, after all the rotten things Jack
did to you—*and* me, by the way," she declared hotly. "Can you
believe that he refused to pay me my bonus, even though I whipped
that ol' Livingston place they bought here last year into good shape
in less than six months? But would Jack Ebert give me the credit
back in New Orleans?" she demanded rhetorically. "Noooo! He
pounded that new Ebert-Petrella Funeral Home sign into the
ground, took all the credit for the changeover himself, and poisoned the well for me with Uncle René to boot, that old drunk! So
I quit before they could fire me, and now I'm stuck in Natchez."

Daphne was about to make a comment when Libby barreled on.

"Do y'think you could play for Abigail Langhorn's funeral on
Monday? That's tomorrow, would you believe? You'd be doin'
me a real favor, and I guess I'd be doin' the same for you—with
those roof bills, and all. By the way, I thought you and those other
gals in the sexy getups last night at the 'For the Birds' benefit were
jus' great! Seein' ya'll reminded me to call you anyway, and then
Miz Abigail up and died early this mornin'. Now I'm stuck with
gettin' her buried real quick 'cause her son can only stay one day
in Natchez, isn't that a pity? He doesn't even want to bother with
a church ceremony—which I find in very poor taste, but then
nobody asked *me* for an opinion, did they? So, anyway…"

Libby Girard continued with her stream-of-consciousness chatter while Daphne did her best to suppress a laugh. Finally, Daphne
cut in.

"I'd be happy to play for the service tomorrow, Libby," she
declared. And besides, she *could* use the extra money. "I charge a
hundred dollars an hour."

"Woo-eee! That's twice as expensive as one of Miz Whitaker's students, but don't get me wrong, you're good. You're *great*, in fact, and Miz Langhorn's family's still rich enough—though they always act as if their cotton's got a boll weevil blight eatin' away at it. Just like those tightwads, the Eberts," she exclaimed with renewed energy. "The Petrella family's a lot nicer, but René Ebert's a real creep, don'tcha think? He never did stop those awful cousins who used to drag poor Jack into the embalmin' room when he couldna been more than *five years old*. No wonder Jack's so weird."

Daphne sat bolt upright in her desk chair, her attention suddenly riveted on the bizarre turn in Libby's prattle. A hazy, long-buried memory from childhood sprang to mind. Maybe she *hadn't* imagined it—that time so long ago—when Jack tried to drag an eleven-year-old Daphne into the back room at the Ebert-Petrella Funeral Home off St. Charles Avenue. "As they've done unto you…"

Her mind spinning, she barely registered Libby's next words.

"Just promise me, you won't play anything remotely like rock 'n' roll tomorrow, will you? Play some nice, soothin' songs, y'know what I'm sayin'? Miz Langhorn's daughter couldn't stop cryin' this mornin', poor thing."

"Absolutely," Daphne assured her. "What time tomorrow?"

"Eleven o'clock," she answered promptly. "The service starts at eleven thirty. And don't forget, wear *black*, now, y'hear? And make sure it covers… everything!"

Monday, as previously planned, Daphne and Madeline Whitaker met Bailey Gibbs at the B&K Bank at ten a.m. and deposited close to twenty-five thousand dollars in a special account, with all three as cosigners.

"Well, this should hire us a fancy lawyer or two." Bailey kissed Daphne's cousin on the cheek for good measure and gave her shoulders a squeeze. "Couldna done it without you, too, Maddy girl."

"Land, go on, now," Maddy replied, blushing. "Everybody pitched in, 'specially Daphne, here."

"Thanks," Daphne replied. "Now if we could just say the same for Sim."

Bailey and Maddy exchanged looks that did little to allay Daphne's mounting sense that her relationship with Sim might surely have ended, all but for the official burial ceremony.

Bailey put a comforting hand on Daphne's shoulder. "I know Sim's not being down here this week upset you, darlin', but let's not haul him up the yardarm just yet. I've got a feeling that everything might still turn out just fine."

It won't be so fine for me if Sim Hopkins has gone back to his ex-wife…

Daphne glanced at her watch. The last thing she felt like doing was playing her harp at a funeral. Nevertheless, she waved the couple off to a celebratory lunch at Pearl Street Pasta and drove directly to the Farrell Funeral Home on the edge of town.

"Oh… I so appreciate your bein' punctual," Libby chirped, leading the way down a hushed, carpeted corridor.

Ten rows of white wooden folding chairs were set up in front of the open casket in readiness for the roomful of mourners yet to arrive.

"Is over here all right?" Daphne asked, averting her eyes as she gingerly wheeled the harp case to the corner farthest from the guest of honor. "It's not a performance, really," she hastened to add, "so I think it's good if I'm just part of the furniture, okay?"

"That's fine." Libby made her way toward a tall, white wicker basket containing sprays of yellow gladioli to straighten one stem that had tilted precariously. She turned toward Daphne, and said brightly, "All set?"

Daphne nodded and commenced unpacking her instrument. "Where should I store the case?"

"Just wheel it into the casket room, last door on the left. Nobody'll bother it in there," Libby instructed on her way out of the viewing room.

"I suspect not," Daphne commented dryly to herself.

By eleven thirty, the friends and family of Abigail Langhorn occupied two-thirds of the folding chairs. At the conclusion of the simple ceremony, the deceased's son, grandsons, and nephews shouldered her coffin and bore it to a waiting limousine for the journey to the Natchez City Cemetery, north of town.

One woman remained seated and motionless until the last mourner had followed the coffin down the corridor. Then her shoulders began to shake, and she began to cry in deep, wrenching sobs. Uncertain what to do, Daphne played the last bars of "How Great Thou Art" while the woman continued to weep. Her fingers ended in a sedate glissando, its jeweled notes shimmering in the air even after she allowed her hands to rest in her lap.

And still the woman sobbed, bereft and inconsolable. Daphne waited quietly in the corner for the woman to regain her composure. The mourner's long, rending cries tore at the heart and spoke of utter desolation and a world without hope... a world in which a pitiless God decided who lived and who died and which babies would be called back to heaven before they'd inhaled even a single breath of earth's sweet air, or heard a note of music, or saw a bird on the wing...

And Daphne knew suddenly that those heart-wrenching wails were mere echoes of generations of women who cried their sorrows into the night.

CHAPTER 26

SEPTEMBER 13, 1818

DAPHNE WHITAKER CLAYTON'S EIGHT-YEAR-OLD daughter, the image of her mother, peered inside the upstairs bed-chamber at Bluff House. The little girl with the golden curls had been told that her mama had planned to give birth in the big plantation bed at Devon Oaks. But something mysterious and alarming had happened earlier that morning and there was no time even to summon the doctor. Nobody had explained to the child exactly what had transpired in her mother's darkened boudoir, and now young Madeline was determined to find out for herself.

Maddy watched Mammy, bent over with rheumatism these days, lay a little bundle inside a wooden box that her husband Willis had hastily brought through the rear of the house and up the back stairs from the pantry.

"What you doin' here, Maddy?" Mammy demanded, catching sight of the wide-eyed youngster sucking her forefinger and gazing dolefully at the scene. Mammy's blue skirt and bodice were streaked with dark stains, as was a bundle of linens piled on the floor. "You 'sposed be downstairs, not up here botherin' your poor Mama. Your daddy and Mistah Hopkins get back from ridin'?"

"Just before sunset," Maddy informed her. "Daddy's been checking on his horse because Ovid's leg came up lame." She pointed at the box. "Is it a boy or a girl?"

"A girl," Mammy replied sorrowfully.

Maddy gazed solemnly into the servant's dark eyes, and murmured, "Baby Phaedra, Mama said… if it was a girl."

Maddy wondered why Mama always named the babies after
people who'd died young. She'd seen the headstone under the pecan
tree at Devon Oaks where Mama's sister, Madeline Whitaker, had
been buried before she'd even gotten herself a husband! Maddy
didn't like seeing her own name on a headstone like that.

There were other headstones for Grandfather Charles
Whitaker and his son Charles, too, and for the other Phaedra
and Eustice, Mama's brother and sister, who each passed away
from something horrible long before Maddy was born. And
there were tiny headstones for all of Grandmother Susannah's and
Mama's babies who'd died so young, nobody'd even bothered to
name them.

Maddy wished she'd been given a different name like Alice or
Charlotte, or even Arabella. At least Uncle Keating didn't have a
stone marking *his* grave. He was nice.

There was silence in the bedchamber, except for the sound of
her mother's quiet weeping. Maddy wondered when her uncle
would be coming back from Scotland.

"Baby Phaedra's dead, isn't she?" she declared suddenly, pointing to the miniature wooden box under the window that looked
out on the river.

At this, her mother's weeping grew louder, confirming the little
girl's blunt assertion. But before Mammy could answer or scold her
again, heavy footsteps could be heard mounting the stairs. Mammy
cast a worried glance at her patient, curled into a ball under the
quilted coverlet that Great-grandmother Drake had made, once
upon a time. The tall, imposing figure of Aaron Clayton loomed
in the doorway beside his only living child.

"What was it?" he asked Mammy harshly. Maddy's mother
suddenly ceased crying, almost as if she'd been strangled where
she lay.

"A girl chile, Mistah Aaron."

Mammy sounded scared. Mammy *never* sounded scared, Madeline
thought with alarm. But then, this long-time family retainer was

getting old and frail like Grandmother Susannah, who lived locked up in a room under the eaves at the top of Devon House.

"So we have a Phaedra Whitaker Clayton to add to our rotting family tree, do we?" Her father pronounced the names in a clipped accent, bitterly emphasizing each word.

Maddy darted a glance at her father's stern face at the same instant Mammy said softly, "The baby lived only a few minutes, Mistah Aaron. The cord was wrapped 'round her po' lil' neck and she was real blue-colored. She give only one tiny lil' cry 'fore she died. My Willis made this coffin, real quick." Mammy glanced at Maddy as if she wished she weren't in the room.

Aaron Clayton's expression hardened and he slammed his curled fist against the doorjamb, startling Maddy so that she jumped and made the mistake of clinging to her father's waist. He shoved her aside without a glance.

"Damnation! *Damnation!* That's the end of it… the absolute *end* of it!" He turned on his heel and stormed downstairs in a lather of temper. "Simon," Maddy heard him call out. "Don't leave! Stay right where you are, my man!" he shouted, apparently halting the outbound progress of the neighbor who had come to inquire after her mother's health. "Daphne's had another girl! Another *dead* girl."

Aaron Clayton spat the words as if girls were the nastiest things in the world. Despite Maddy's fear of her father's angry moods, she tiptoed down the hallway, wondering what would happen next.

"Oh, my dear Aaron," Simon Hopkins said, his voice filled with sympathy. "I am so sorry."

Ignoring their family friend's heartfelt sorrow, her father shouted, "I'm finished with doing all the work for this feckless family when it's her brother who'll inherit it all—that is, if those cursed bankers don't get Devon Oaks first!"

"Aaron… calm yourself. You're upset, as surely I would be, but—"

"I shall go to Edinburgh, myself, and bring Keating back to Natchez," her father fumed, ignoring Simon. "Let *him* deal with the accounts and the boll weevils and the blasted money changers who demand their pound of flesh. Let *him* try to cope with a mad mother-in-law living in splendor at the top of Devon Oaks. And I've certainly no use for a wife who's nearly as unhinged as her mother—and won't give me a *son*!"

"Surely, Aaron, you can't blame poor Daphne for—"

"The woman's a hopeless breeder, Simon. I shall never get a male heir to inherit what I've slaved for these last eight years!"

"Keating has always been the designated heir," Simon declared in astonishment. "Why should you have assumed that—even if you and Daphne had sons—they would inherit the Whitaker estate?"

"Who would've wagered that Keating would last a year when I first met Daphne?" Aaron snapped. "He was sickly and—"

"Jesu, man!" Simon exploded. "Has your lawyer's heart calculated all the odds down to the last nail?"

"And why not?" Aaron retorted. "I was willing to work like a damnable slave to put the estate on sounder footing, and I succeeded—until this damnable depression sacked our efforts—without a tittle of help from Keating Whitaker!"

"My father and I helped you, you might remember," Simon interjected. "Keating was but a boy. And we'll ride out this hardship, same as always."

However, Aaron Clayton wasn't listening.

"Wars and credit crises—and *madwomen*. Nothing went my way. Nothing!" Maddy heard the sound of glasses clinking and liquid being poured. "You should thank your lucky stars you picked Rachel Gibbs as your bride, sir. I am trapped with a *lunatic*!"

"Aaron, *you* are the person sounding like the lunatic," Simon Hopkins responded sharply. "Your wife is weeping because she has just suffered another unbearable loss. Her brother Keating is barely twenty-four years old. Get ahold of yourself, my man! Have you no compassion at all?"

"When I was Keating's age, I'd earned a law degree and was already making a decent living. And how does the boy spend most of *his* time? Carving up dead bodies!" he bellowed in disgust.

"Keating's finally found his calling and is studying to be a doctor, for God's sake, Aaron. You said you were pleased when I secured him a place to train in Edinburgh. The institute there offers the best medical education in the world."

"Well, let him come home then, and see if that training can cure his sister and mother," Aaron challenged truculently. "There are plenty of dead bodies produced around here for him to use his scalpel on."

"Stop it," the usually mild-mannered Simon Hopkins growled. "Don't you *dare* speak like that of the women in this household!"

The next thing Maddy heard from her listening post on the upstairs landing was the sound of a heavy object smashing against a wall.

"I'm *done* with all this," Aaron Clayton roared. "I hereby declare that you and your father are back in charge of this ship of fools, and welcome to it! You've always mooned over my wife, Simon, haven't you?" he asked, his voice full of loathing. "You're certainly welcome to see if *you* can get her with a son that will live and persuade those damnable bankers not to foreclose! I'm going to Europe to inform Keating, *in person*, that this nightmare is now all his—and I'm not coming back!"

Daphne Clayton lay in bed barely conscious of the sound of her husband's shouts. Her only thoughts were for the infant already in its small coffin.

Mammy lied to Aaron. The baby hadn't even drawn a breath. Not one.

Dry-eyed now, Daphne turned her head on the pillow and stared out the window. She thought about her own mother, the mad, bad Susannah who now howled and bit infrequent visitors to her prison under the eaves of Devon House. Was she becoming like her? Or maybe she was more like her dead sister, Madeline? Like the long-deceased Maddy, she'd often thought of putting rocks in her pockets and throwing herself into Whitaker Creek, just to end the humiliation and misery of being judged worthless because of her failure to bear a son. She regretted having named her daughter Madeline. Her well-intentioned act of contrition had probably doomed the child to suffer the family's accursed melancholia.

Dark, morbid thoughts washed over Daphne like a river churning up mud. She was like her mother, all right... and the man she had wed was frighteningly like her father, although Charles Whitaker at least had been kind in his sober moments. But he was dead, too.

Daphne rolled over and burrowed into her feather pillow. It was all so hopeless. So many deaths. So many angry words and slammed doors. She barely took notice that her eight-year-old had begun to play an etude on the harp downstairs. What did it matter? Aaron gave his sole surviving daughter nary a glance. Daphne had ceased to care even about *that* anymore. She couldn't summon the energy to fret about the little girl struggling to play an instrument that they had both once thought so beautiful.

The butler at Devon Oaks admitted Simon and Rachel into the house and stood at the bottom of the stairs as the callers mounted the treads to the second floor. Simon knocked softly on the door just off the landing and waited for a response. Nothing. He knocked harder.

"Daphne? 'Tis me. Simon. Rachel is with me. May we come in?"

Again, no response.

Rachel whispered, "Let me try."

Simon's wife of eleven years and the mother of his three fine sons gently rapped on the door's wide, cypress planking.

"Daphne darling, Simon and I have wonderful news." She cracked the door an inch. "We think you'll be so pleased..."

It had always been thus, Simon reflected, watching the greatest life partner a man could have push the door open another inch. Rachel Gibbs was a bastion of kindness and endless good sense. She was witty and intelligent, and eagerly embraced interests that also fascinated him—the natural world and all its wonders. Together they had observed and catalogued the plants and animals in the surrounding areas, and read books on botany, and painted what they'd collected during the times they weren't supervising two plantations and three boisterous little boys.

Indeed, Rachel had turned out to be the most perfect of help-mates, and the woman Simon loved with all his heart and soul. For this, he silently acknowledged that he owed eternal gratitude to his gruff but kindly father, whose judgment saw far beyond Daphne's golden curls and modest musical talent.

Whenever he thought of his father's recent passing, Simon's throat tightened and his eyes misted over. Yes, he owed his father much, and he missed his wise counsel and hardy companionship. Especially now, when so many decisions had to be made.

Rachel stood on tiptoe and whispered into Simon's ear. "I think we can go in. Look... Daphne's awake and appears quite tranquil."

Simon and Rachel advanced a step into Daphne's boudoir. It was always a shock for them to see her like this. She was attired only in a dressing gown, her golden curls an unkempt tangle about her once lovely shoulders. Although still in her thirties, the titular mistress of Devon Oaks plantation looked aged and haggard, sitting in her chair for days on end, staring blankly out the window at the wooded countryside that bordered Whitaker Creek.

Rachel knelt beside Daphne's chair, and said softly, "Your brother Keating's coming home. We've had word that he may arrive as soon as this week. He'll be so glad to see you, dear."

Simon studied the poor woman for some sort of reaction, but there was none.

"He's a physician now," Simon said, kneeling on the other side of Daphne's chair and lightly patting her hand. He always had the sense that she might bolt like a mistreated filly. "He was at the top of his class in Edinburgh, and will be able to help you regain your... spirits," he finished carefully.

Both Simon and Rachel were startled when Daphne's eyes suddenly lost their vacant stare, and she asked quietly, "And Aaron? Will my husband return to Devon Oaks?"

Simon and Rachel exchanged glances.

"Aaron's decided to remain abroad for a while longer," Simon revealed reluctantly, fearing some sort of hysterical reaction on Daphne's part. "He seeks fairer, better brokers in London for our cotton crops."

"Aaron, no doubt, has found a mistress in that city, and enjoys the percentage he makes from your labors here," Daphne said, in even tones, of the husband who had abandoned her. "I am relieved he stays away."

Rachel gazed at her husband and lifted an eyebrow. Perhaps Daphne was finally able to accept the unhappy situation and proceed with her own life. It was a hopeful sign, Simon thought with an enormous sense of relief. It was, indeed, a hopeful sign.

In truth, Daphne's outlook improved vastly upon Keating's return to Natchez in the summer of 1820. The young man had blossomed under the mentorship of the Scottish physicians with whom he'd trained. He had acquired notions about health and the treatment of disease that Simon thought were rather unorthodox, but whatever his methods, Daphne began to dress each and every day, and descended from her bedchamber more and more often.

Simon and Rachel were greatly excited by the appearance in Natchez of a wonderful painter of birds, an émigré Frenchman who had Anglicized his name to John James Audubon.

"Keating, my man, the chap's work is absolutely astonishing," Simon declared over brandy in the dining room at Hopkins Hall. "We're hosting a small party next week to display his work and perhaps gain him a commission or two." Simon refilled Keating's snifter and resumed his seat. "He intends to paint every single feathered creature in North America. Meanwhile, he'll do a fine portrait of you, should you wish to help advance his project. What do you say? Will you join us?"

"Are ladies welcome?" Keating asked.

"Have you found a new friend since returning to Natchez?" Simon teased his young neighbor with a sly smile. He felt comfortable in his new role as Dutch uncle to his late father's former ward.

"I wouldn't find it amiss if you should invite Abigail Langhorn."

"Rachel's cousin?" Simon exclaimed. "Why, that's capital! Of course she'll be invited. Nothing would please my matchmaking wife more." He sipped his brandy, and asked, "And Daphne? Do you think she's up to attending a soiree?"

Keating nodded enthusiastically. "I think 'twould be just the thing. She's playing her harp again."

Simon shook his head in wonder. "Really, Keating, you've worked miracles in the time you've been home. What's your secret? Rachel and I did our best while you and that blighter Clayton were away, but we could affect nothing…"

"She needed time to heal from all those tragic confinements," Keating said with a hard edge, "and she needed to be treated kindly within the bosom of her own family."

"Amen," Simon said, relieved that Aaron Clayton, as he'd threatened, apparently had taken permanent leave of Adams County.

Keating broke into a mischievous grin. "Perhaps my prescription of soothing, warm baths, and encouraging Daphne to help little Maddy with her harp lessons are tonics for her wounded heart," the fledgling physician declared with a note of pride. "I had cook prepare lots of vegetables and fewer heavy foods, and urged Daphne to take regular exercise and to consume a single, small glass of claret each day. This regimen has worked its magic."

Simon raised his glass in a toast. "Well, here's to fresh vegetables and to the brilliant Dr. Keating Whitaker. Long may he practice his newfangled treatments in the great state of Mississippi," he added, referring to the new status of statehood that the United States Congress had recently conferred upon the former territory.

Daphne's progress, however, was halted in a fashion that neither the young doctor, nor Simon and Rachel Hopkins could ever have foretold. Not long afterward, the families along Whitaker Creek were astonished by the sudden, unannounced reappearance of Daphne's errant husband after nearly five years abroad. Simon, especially, had his suspicions regarding the reason Aaron Clayton had returned to Natchez.

"She's *my* wife and I will do what *I* think best," Aaron declared with enough pomposity to make Simon want nothing more than to call the wretch out. However, Hopkins knew all too well the wily ways of Aaron Clayton, counselor-at-law. As they began to debate Daphne's future, he could see that Aaron had researched the matter thoroughly and had conceived a plan. If the greedy scoundrel wished to commit his wife to a mental hospital in Philadelphia, Pennsylvania, far away from family and friends—as her husband, with all rights over her person—he had a perfect legal right to do it.

"But Daphne's made remarkable progress in the last few years," Simon protested. "Surely, if you don't take Rachel's and my word for it, you will have a care for the opinion of her own brother Keating, a trained physician."

"A quack, you mean," Aaron said belligerently. "He claimed his treatments had effected a cure, yet I wasn't home a week when she nearly scratched my eyes out!" Indeed, a parallel line of narrow welts still ran along his cheek.

Simon could hardly bear to look at the man, for he could easily guess what had prompted such an extreme reaction by poor Daphne.

"Another baby might kill your wife, Aaron," Simon said in a low voice. "Can't you slake your needs in the whorehouses in Under-the-Hill? You don't love Daphne, but at least show her some respect. You abandoned her when you left for Europe. Surely you didn't expect her to fall into your arms upon your return?"

"I ought to call you out for that, Hopkins. I am her husband. Her distaste for the normal activities of married life is unnatural, and one more proof that she's unhinged, just like her mother."

Simon gazed narrowly at his uninvited visitor. "Why have you bothered to call at Hopkins House, when you know my wife and I completely oppose your idea of whisking poor Daphne to a mental institution when she's made a remarkable recovery in your absence and has family and friends willing to look after her?"

"Willing to feed off her inheritance, rather," Aaron retorted, "just as your father did all those years."

Simon rose abruptly from the chair behind his desk in his father's old study and pointed to the door. "I must ask you to leave, sir, for no one provided more care and counsel to the beleaguered Whitakers after the death of Charles, nor gave more selflessly to that poor benighted family, than did my father."

"Oh, come now," Aaron scoffed. "Your father made a tidy

enough profit merging the two cotton enterprises, just as you and Keating are doing to this day. Do you think I haven't had a look at the ledgers since I've been back? When Daphne is committed and living in the hospital where she belongs, I shall take full charge of her share, and there'll be some changes made in the business's accounting methods. You can rely on it!"

"Ah... so *that's* what all this is about," Simon said angrily. "You've squandered your supply of cash on your travels abroad, have you? Now you propose to commit your wife to a lunatic asylum and gain management and control of her share of Devon Oaks, is that it? Well, there is no need to punish Daphne in such cruel fashion. Keating and I are prepared to form a triumvirate to govern these two plantations, if you insist... but I warn you, you will be outvoted if you propose actions that are not in our mutual interests, including Daphne's."

"You are to play no role in these affairs. Keating may be the sole legal heir to Devon Oaks, but as Daphne's husband, and as one who looked after the property in his long absence in Edinburgh, I plan to sue in her interest to separate the affairs of Devon Oaks from the Hopkins plantation to keep you two from conspiring against the profits of a poor, witless—"

"And what judge in these parts would be persuaded by the transparent efforts of an interloper like you to rob your wife and her family of their birthright?"

"The courts and the wheels of justice are supposed to be impartial," Aaron replied calmly. "And merely answering my legal demands for proof regarding the way you've conducted the business of the two plantations during my absence abroad will keep you too busy and too penniless even to plant cotton seed!" He laughed mirthlessly. "I also happen to know that both of you currently owe the Natchez bankers some rather large sums since the Depression of 1819. What a problem you will have if I allege mismanagement of the land the banks hold as collateral. Your friendly bankers will panic and call your loans like *that*!" he said, snapping his fingers.

"I understand this game of greed you're playing, Aaron,"

Simon growled, "but tell me this. Why do you want to imprison your wife in the bargain, when clearly, she has recovered her spirits and begun to thrive? God knows, I could charge you with genuine neglect when it comes to the way you abandoned your wife and Devon Oaks these last years, but our two plantations are bound to recover from this temporary financial setback more quickly if we keep our assets combined."

But Simon already knew the answer. Aaron had to neutralize his wife to get what he so desired—forcing Simon and Keating to grant him a half stake, with or without a male Clayton heir. In Mississippi, the only way a Massachusetts-born husband could strip his wife of her rights in a family-owned enterprise was to have her declared insane. If Aaron's demands weren't met, a protracted legal battle would bankrupt them all. But if he later had his wife pronounced a lunatic at a hospital in Pennsylvania, he would effectively be their partner forever, even if he had no son to inherit down the line.

"What does Keating say to all this?" Simon demanded.

"He's up to his cravat in debts to his bank, just as you are," Aaron replied evenly. "He said I should take up the matter with you." Daphne's husband pursed his lips in a sour smile. "I think he is quite shaken by her taking such an abrupt turn for the worse."

Simon slammed down his fist on his desk. "Did you tell Keating how you violated your wife the instant you reclaimed her bed?" he demanded. "Did you tell him how much his sister fears you... and probably loathes you... and how this accounts for her taking 'a turn for the worse' as you so delicately phrase your effort to drive her mad?"

"No, I did not discuss my private life with Keating," Aaron said, his tone steely, "and such subjects are none of your damned business, either! Instead I warned Keating—as I warn you now—a protracted legal battle could deal the fatal blow to both your houses."

Simon glared at Aaron with loathing and contempt. Everyone in Natchez had suffered from the boom-and-bust economy since the War of 1812, but only the vilest sort of profiteer used it as a means to vault himself into affairs where he didn't belong.

"You are absolute scum, Clayton," Simon declared quietly.

"So, what's it to be, Hopkins?" Aaron demanded, brushing aside the insult. "Endless legal wrangles, or will you cut me in as a full partner with the two of you at *both* Devon Oaks and Hopkins House? You have my word that I'll be a good lad and use my legal prowess—not to sue to separate the two plantations—but to help us three make more money than you ever dreamed of from the current bumper cotton crop."

"Your word is the pledge of the devil."

"I will never expect you to like me," Aaron replied coldly, "but I do expect that you will come to respect my legal and business acumen."

A Harvard-educated man, formally trained in the law and in commerce, Aaron Clayton held all the cards and both men in the room knew it. And Simon also knew he would probably never again see Daphne Whitaker Clayton in Natchez, or—if by some miracle Aaron ever allowed her to return—he doubted she would ever again be in her right mind. The poor woman's grasp on sanity, which was held by a thread, was about to be severed forever.

How can I stand by and allow this to happen? he thought morosely. He had inherited his father's stewardship of the Whitakers, but who could have predicted Aaron's role in this mess?

Just then, there was a knock on the door, and his young son, Trey, ran into the study.

"Daddy, Daddy," Simon Hopkins III chirped excitedly. "Mama says for you and Mr. Clayton to come quickly. Mr. Audubon has arrived with a beautiful great-footed hawk he shot today on the Trace! *Falco peregrinus*," he said proudly, reciting the Latin name Audubon had taught him. "He intends to paint a picture of it for his bird book. Mama let him put it on the table on the veranda. Come and see, please, sir!"

"In a minute, son." Simon allowed Trey to climb onto his lap. Absently, he tousled the boy's auburn hair. Aaron shifted in his chair, discomforted by the show of affection between father and child. Simon put a protective arm around his eldest son and heir. He tightened his grip and thought with fierce determination that he simply could not allow Aaron Clayton to rob this boy of his birthright. Surely his late father would agree that a Hopkins's first duty was to his own?

Simon slowly allowed his gaze to meet Aaron's keen, assessing one. It was up to Keating to insure that his sister was not condemned to an institution. Perhaps, Simon thought, poor Daphne was actually safer from harm far away in Philadelphia, now that Aaron had returned from abroad. Living with such a man would drive even a strong woman insane. Simon could see that the unintended consequences of his father's kindly act toward the bereft Whitaker clan had trapped his son into an unwilling partnership with Aaron Clayton whether he liked it or not.

Well, he thought, gazing at Trey's rumpled locks, it would take slow, measured steps over time to disentangle himself from the Devon Oaks operation. With renewed determination, the owner of Hopkins House gently set his young son on his feet and addressed his hated visitor.

"You, Keating, and I will have to try to make the best of our unhappy business arrangement," he proposed, "but I will ask you not ever to set foot on this property unless invited to do so for purposes of conducting our affairs."

"What an honorable man you are," Aaron mocked.

"I'm a man who looks after his own," Simon replied, "which is a far-sight more than I can say for you."

Dr. Keating Whitaker waited in the vestibule outside the office of the chief of Philadelphia Hospital. On his previous visit, when his older sister had first been admitted, Whitaker had been surprised and even impressed by the premises, built in elegant Federalist style, with flanking wide corridors and large rooms where the wealthier patients resided. After Aaron left that terrible day, Dr. Whitaker had seen to it that Daphne was given an airy chamber where shafts of sunlight poured through broad casement windows overhead. Well-mannered attendants took patients outside to exercise along a kind of dry moat that surrounded the building, and he had thought, then, that the institution was far in advance of others observed during his medical studies abroad.

However, upon his arrival today, he had been alarmed to read a history of the doctors' orders concerning his sister's course of treatment. As a physician, Dr. Whitaker had been allowed that privilege. Perusing Daphne's chart, he'd been disturbed by the raft of purges and bleedings and doses of laudanum Daphne had endured since her incarceration. Miraculously, such treatments had not aborted the child she had unknowingly been carrying when Aaron Clayton committed his wife here against her family's wishes. When the hospital informed her husband by post that Daphne was six months pregnant, Aaron immediately cleared out his bank account in Natchez and decamped for Europe once again.

"I'm done with watching the woman produce dead babies," he'd shouted at his brother-in-law while he tossed clothes into a leather traveling trunk. "Here's the address in London to which you are to send a bank draft of my share of the yearly profits."

Keating stared out the hospital's barred windows and tried to calm his pounding temples. What a callous bastard his despised brother-in-law was!

"She was probably diddled by an attendant at that place," Aaron had pronounced upon hearing the news his wife was with child. "I should sue. At any rate, even if the thing is mine, I won't play sire to a child—male or female—tainted by Whitaker blood!"

"Do the arithmetic, Aaron," Keating had said harshly. "According to the doctors, she conceived the babe prior to being brought there for treatment."

"That's their defense," Aaron had scoffed.

Keating Whitaker had long ago recognized that Daphne's condition had only been partially responsible for her husband's abrupt departure abroad. The truth was, Aaron had soon tired of the back-breaking work of cotton production. Keating knew that Daphne's latest pregnancy had merely tipped the scales, prompting Aaron to escape his domestic troubles with a fat purse and no more hard labor. Before the lawyer left Natchez, he conferred on Keating a written legal authority—and also personal responsibility—for his wife's mental condition. Keating's duties included custody of young Maddy, the couple's only surviving offspring.

Suddenly, the door to the vestibule opened, and a white-coated physician appeared.

"Your sister's resting comfortably," the doctor announced.

"And the child?"

"Surprisingly fit. It's a boy," the doctor said with pride. "I delivered him myself."

Keating's brow furrowed. Would the arrival of a male child summon Aaron back from Europe to involve himself again in the day-to-day running of the two plantations, despite the legal documents he'd signed? There was no end to the man's machinations.

"I will spare you the trouble of informing Mr. Clayton," Keating said, "and write to him myself next post." He smiled, knowing he would do no such thing. "May I see my sister now?" he asked.

"Certainly," the doctor said. "You may see them both. Follow me."

The footsteps of the two men echoed hollowly as they strode down the ward's long, empty corridor. Strange, bleating sounds emanated from behind one door on Keating's left, while quiet sobbing could be heard behind another. At the end of the hall, they paused in front of a room where they listened to the lusty cries of a newborn child.

"Come meet Master Drake Whitaker Clayton," the doctor said jovially.

"She was... fit enough to think of a name?" Keating asked, amazed.

"She had a remarkably easy birth. Her spirits lifted immediately when I told her you were coming to take her back to Natchez. It was at that point she announced to matron and me that she'd chosen a name for the baby."

"Our grandmother was a Drake," Keating murmured. Then he frowned. "Does she also know that her husband... that Mr. Clayton has decided to make his home in Europe permanently?" he inquired carefully.

The chief of Philadelphia Hospital exchanged knowing looks with his fellow physician. "Yes... I explained that to her after I received your letter," he disclosed somberly. "I expected the worst, of course."

"And?" Keating asked, holding his breath.

"Mrs. Clayton's only reaction was a rather expansive smile."

Both men chuckled and entered the room to pay their respects to the new mother and her bouncing baby boy, whose deafening howls for his supper could be heard echoing throughout the immaculately maintained facility.

Drake Whitaker Clayton was, indeed, making his presence known.

CHAPTER 27

T HE SOUNDS OF CRYING slowly faded, and silence enveloped the viewing room of Farrell's Funeral Home.

Daphne Duvallon gazed with confusion at her surroundings. The casket containing the body of octogenarian Abigail Langhorn had been removed and the weeping mourner had also disappeared. Slowly, the scenes at the Philadelphia Hospital faded from her consciousness, replaced by one thought.

It's happened again!

It was beginning to feel like a PBS historical series where the audience was allowed to view an exciting, action-packed story one chapter at a time. Her namesake, Daphne Whitaker Clayton, had finally produced a son—but at what cost to her physical and mental well-being?

Well, the *modern* Daphne was exhausted by all this drama, she reflected grimly. She rested her forehead against the harp's sounding board, considering all she had just learned. It was of some comfort to discover that her namesake's emotional difficulties were probably not organic, but were personal problems caused by the upheavals and vicissitudes of her tumultuous life. Who *wouldn't* be on a hormonal roller coaster after multiple pregnancies and spousal rape and abuse, Daphne thought sympathetically.

Libby Girard bustled into the empty room. The manager of the funeral home began picking up programs abandoned on the folding chairs.

"You played wonderfully, just now," she said, "but then I knew you would. Look how Mrs. Langhorn's daughter just cried and cried. I've noticed that music does that to some people, haven't you?" Libby prattled on. "It kinda pulls feelings outta a person, doesn't it? I didn't even *know* Abigail Langhorn, but when you played 'How Great Thou Art,' I got all choked up, too."

Daphne politely waited out Libby's monologue and then retrieved her harp case from the casket room to begin the process of securing her instrument and packing up her music. The place gave her the willies. Next time Libby offered her a job, she'd politely say she was booked or had upped her fee or something.

"Would you like to go out the back door so you won't have to navigate those two steps out front?" the manager suggested.

"Good idea," Daphne agreed. Then she realized that Libby was leading her toward a set of double doors. She halted abruptly at the entrance and stared into a room filled with ominous-looking stainless steel equipment.

"Oh, Lord!" Libby laughed. "You should see the look on your face! Don't worry, we don't have anybody scheduled in here today, though the head nurse up at the hospital was nice enough to suggest Farrell's to the family of one of her terminal patients and I expect a call any minute now and I—"

"Ah… sorry to interrupt, but I'm late," Daphne cut in. "What's the shortest way out of here?"

Despite the bulkiness of the harp case, Daphne made fast progress through the sterile embalming room, out the back door, and across the parking lot to her car. She'd seen enough death this day to last a lifetime.

For the rest of the week, she waited in vain to hear from Sim. By Thursday afternoon, she had invented a number of possible scenarios.

He'd left for San Francisco without saying good-bye.

He'd been bitten by a snake on the Trace and couldn't get help.

He had, indeed, fallen into the arms of Francesca and was shacked up in a motel outside Jackson.

He was busy tracking and photographing the last birds on his Audubon list and had forgotten what day it was.

She suddenly remembered little Trey—Simon Hopkins III— racing into Hopkins House with exciting news that the great naturalist had just arrived with a prize peregrine falcon. The parallels in her life were positively eerie! There were so many questions left unanswered despite the clues that these journeys back in time provided. Questions whose answers very likely would impact her life *today*. Amadora Bendhar had recommended that she attempt to find out if the truth of these sorties to antebellum Natchez could be proven in *fact*.

Daphne glanced at her watch. She had a couple of hours before her Eola Hotel teatime gig. Maybe it was time she found out if she were going bonkers, or if the world she had been visiting these last few months had ever actually *existed*. At least, she could make a start.

Five minutes later, she parked in front of the Armstrong Library and made her way to the second floor. A plump, friendly woman in her thirties looked up from her desk in the reference department, and asked, "May I help you with something?"

"I'm interested in finding out about a mansion that no longer exists, called Concord, the governor's house, and another plantation that—"

"Oh, that's an easy one," the librarian said before Daphne could ask about Hopkins House and the family burial ground at Devon Oaks. "Concord used to be out where the tire plant is now," she said, confirming what Willis McGee had told Daphne. The librarian reached behind her desk and pulled out a copy of a large-format book entitled *Lost Mansions of Mississippi*. Flipping to page four, she pointed to a grainy photograph of a building that Daphne recognized instantly, except for one feature.

"I didn't remember hearing Concord had an exterior twin stairway on the front like that," she said carefully, pointing to two sets of stairs that curved from a grand entrance between stately columns.

"They're not original to the house," the librarian explained. "That exterior double marble staircase was probably added in the 1830s when everybody 'round here went mad over Greek Revival architecture."

So the Concord that Daphne remembered must have been the original mansion that had been completed in about 1795, according to the paragraph adjacent to the photo. This meant it would have existed when the duc d'Orléans came to Natchez with the motley entourage that could have included Jacques René Hébèrt. All the dates meshed!

"Concord burned down in 1901," the librarian elaborated, "except for those gorgeous sweeping stairs and metal balustrades that stood in a field for the longest time, choked in weeds. Finally, someone just pulled it all down because of the liability."

"Have you any information on an old plantation known as Hopkins House?" Daphne asked, feeling her heart start to pound. "Doctor Bailey Gibbs of Gibbs Hall told me it blew down in the Tornado of 1840."

"Oh... if that's what happened, we might have quite a lot of information 'bout it," the librarian volunteered, turning to a bank of metal filing cabinets against the wall behind her desk. "There were many eyewitnesses who wrote their accounts at the time, and the newspapers of the day went into scads of detail. Hmmm," she said, her fingers flipping through a series of manila file folders. "Let's see... Hawthorne... um... Holly Hedges... Hope Farm... ah, yes... *Hopkins House.* Here's a sketch, and here's a newspaper clipping with a series of letters to the editor bemoaning its loss."

"Great going," Daphne exclaimed, squinting at the yellowed newsprint and the date that ran above the banner headline HORRIBLE STORM!! NATCHEZ IN RUINS!!!

She scrutinized the sketch of the house and the newspaper account of the Natchez Tornado of May 7, 1840. Hopkins House, too, looked very familiar to Daphne, although there was no way she'd disclose that to the helpful librarian who offered to photocopy the file.

"Why are you so interested in Hopkins House, if I may ask?" her helper asked cheerily as the copier hummed. "Are you related to the family that owned the place?"

"No... ah... but a friend of mine might be," Daphne replied. "I have collateral cousins who once owned Devon Oaks, though, the next plantation over." On the spot, Daphne made a vow to return when she had more time to peruse the file on the home that formerly belonged to Maddy's and Marcus's forbears.

"Oh, Devon Oaks," the librarian exclaimed excitedly. "Then you and I would have been cousins way back when."

"You can't be serious?" Daphne replied, amazed.

"Absolutely." The librarian thrust out her hand, and announced, "I'm a Keating, Rosalie Keating, a direct descendent of Daphne Keating Drake, the mother of 'Crazy Susannah' Keating Whitaker, as she was known," she joked. "Daphne Keating had a brother. John Keating, who founded my line of Keatings and she was also the grandmother of Daphne Whitaker who married that awful Yankee!"

"Your name is *Keating*? Then you have to be related to Otis and Liz."

"Otis Keating is my first cousin."

"Naturally," Daphne deadpanned. "Do you know where any of the eighteenth- and nineteenth-century family members are buried?" she asked, thinking to herself that *seeing* was the only way she'd ever believe that all the people in the flashbacks had actually lived.

"Well." Rosalie Keating said thoughtfully, "'Crazy Suz' used to be buried right on the property at Devon Oaks until the family graves were eventually all moved to the Natchez City Cemetery after 1822. I 'spect you'll find the rest of 'em there, too."

Daphne slowly absorbed the fact that she and the librarian could both trace their families back to Daphne Whitaker Clayton's *grandmother*, who was the first in the line to be named "Daphne."

"*My* name is Daphne," she announced quietly.

"You're kiddin'?" the librarian marveled.

"Small town... small world, isn't it?" Daphne said with a smile. *And*, she mused, it was proof positive that she hadn't been losing her mind, even if a few Whitakers had!

"What's your surname?"

"Duvallon, through the Kingsburys, who married into the Natchez Whitakers, and yada, yada, yada."

"Oh, wait!" Rosalie Keating wagged a forefinger at her. "I know who *you* are. The wonderful harpist. You're the one who sings with that great group down at the Under-the-Hill Saloon, right?" Daphne nodded. "And you organized the 'For the Birds' benefit, which, by the way, was 'bout the hottest thing to hit Natchez, ever." The librarian cocked her head and gave Daphne's conservative outfit the once-over. "You look a lot different than you did the other night," she said, and they both laughed. "You do know, don't you, that your namesake, Daphne Whitaker, was also a harpist and supposedly mooned over some Frenchman who came through here with the duc d'Orléans way back when, and after her death—so the legend goes—plays on her ghostly harp all over town?"

"Yeah... so I've heard."

"It's just local lore, of course. Something to amuse the tourists, but it *is* pretty interesting that you're Daphne *Whitaker* Duvallon and you play the harp so well."

"Pretty weird." Daphne agreed. She opened her wallet and paid for the photocopies. "Well... thanks for all your help," she said, gathering up the copies and her purse. "Once I digest all this, I might be back."

"Anytime," the librarian said. "I specialize in genealogical research. Always glad to help out a long lost relative."

"Thanks," she murmured. "Thanks a lot."

Daphne sat in the Jeep parked in front of Armstrong Library and swiftly thumbed through the photocopies. What could possibly be the link between the Hopkins family of Hopkins House, Mississippi, and Simon's San Francisco branch of the Hopkins clan? Was *this* the reason she'd felt so drawn to the photographer from the minute they met? Had some mysterious connection between their ancestors served to catapult them both back in time—for Sim had acknowledged that he, too, had slipped the time warp the night he'd heard a harp playing at three a.m. at Monmouth Plantation.

She scanned the copy of the hundred-and-sixty-year-old letter to the editor that described in horrific detail the tornado's terrible destruction to the Hopkins plantation.

"Only chimneys remain, and little of them," lamented one eyewitness. *"Debris was found scattered far a quarter mile, as far as to the banks of Whitaker Creek. It tears the heart to think that a proud family whose members were wiped off God's earth in the blink of an eyelash should suffer such dreadful losses..."*

To Daphne's surprise and dismay, her throat tightened, and a powerful wave of sadness welled in her chest. If all the Hopkinses who had peopled her visions died in the storm, then Sim *couldn't* be a descendant. She studied the letter a second time. The missive didn't say for certain that every single member of the Hopkins family perished in the tornado, though the letter might easily be interpreted that way.

Reading the contemporary account made the tragedy seem as fresh and raw as it must have been in 1840 to the letter's author. In her mind's eye, she could imagine the devastation wrought on this house, these people, these lives.

Tears filled her eyes. The modern-day Sim Hopkins was *alive*! She could almost feel his arms around her that day last June after the tornado scare, when he'd jumped from the Range Rover in the pouring rain and held her close while they stood in the middle of Canal Street, thankful they'd both come through the frightening storm. All she wanted at this moment was to see him, talk to him, be held and comforted. To say she was sorry for acting like a jealous fool over Francesca.

And as for Sim, she sensed that something important had been bothering him. Something that surely needed clearing up between them. Though she had no idea what that might be, she made a decision right then that she wasn't going to play little-girl games anymore and wait for him to call. If he wasn't at the cottage at the back of Gibbs Hall, she could leave him a note to get in touch right away. They had to talk face-to-face—*now*.

She glanced at her watch and was dismayed to see it was five minutes to four. She was going to be one late harpist to the Eola Hotel!

❧

Later, if Daphne had been asked what tunes she played during that teatime service, she'd have been hard-pressed to recite any of their names. By six fifteen, she'd donned her jeans in the ladies' room and run for her car, then sped toward the Trace.

Night had begun to fall much earlier these September days. By the time she'd turned into the dirt drive at Gibbs Hall, the road was plunged into deep shadow. Sim's car was nowhere to be seen. She decided she'd just wait for him at the cottage until he returned, no matter how late it got to be. She parked her car next to Bailey's battered Ford Fairlane and sprinted across the lawn that fronted the grand old mansion. On the way, she began to compose what she would say when she saw Sim in person. She would level with him and tell him exactly how much he meant to her, how sorry she was for any doubts and misgivings she'd brought to their relationship as a result of her own troubled past. She even imagined telling Sim about the strange experiences she'd been having all summer, trusting gut instinct that he wouldn't think she was crazy.

"Hello there!" a familiar voice shouted from the front veranda of the big house perched on the rise. "I can guess where you're headed, but Sim's not there." Bailey Gibbs had an arm around one of the pillars on his porch and beckoned to her with the other. "I expect him back pretty soon though, so why don't you just come on in here and have some of Leila's blueberry lemonade—or somethin' stronger, if you like."

Delighted to have such good company while she waited for Sim's return, Daphne waved gaily and marched toward Bailey's front door.

"Sim called a couple of hours ago," Bailey disclosed, inviting her to sit in an upholstered chair in his cluttered front parlor. Newspaper headlines blaring the latest details about the controversial toxic dump proposal were scattered over the sofa, on the floor, and across the coffee table.

"Here, Leila," Daphne said, hurriedly making room on the coffee table for the tray laden with a pitcher of lemonade and some glasses. "Let me clear a space for you."

"Thank you, Miz Daphne," Leila replied. "It's nice to see you this evenin'. Doctor Gibbs told me how your concert raised a ton of money to fight that ol' dump," she added with the easy familiarity of a trusted member of the household. "You should be mighty proud of y'self. I thought those Aphrodites of yours were somethin' else!"

"Thanks," Daphne said with a pleased smile. "And thanks for buying a ticket."

"I've already found use for some of the money," Bailey announced as Leila handed him a glass of lemonade to which he neatly added a shot of vodka with a wink in Daphne's direction.

"Really? What?"

"I hired a private investigator to find out if that danged neighbor of mine—the one who's willing to sell his land to the Able Petroleum people for the toxic dump—is related on his mama's side to one of the state commissioners helping to decide things up in Jackson."

"You did a background check on your neighbor already?" Daphne marveled. The tangled web of associations and influences in Mississippi were all too similar to the same conflicts of interests her brother, King, used to battle in his crusade to save historic buildings in New Orleans. "Did you find out anything important?"

"Nothin' too excitin'," Bailey admitted.

"Now, Doctor G.," Leila said tartly, "you've no cause to 'spect ol' Cyrus Drake of doin' somethin' underhanded with a relative like that. You two just been feudin' for years 'cause you both courted Miz Caroline."

Daphne looked from Bailey's housekeeper to her host and back again.

"The Drake family lives next door to you?" she asked, astonished. The librarian had confirmed that Daphne Whitaker Clayton's *grandmother* had been a Drake! The original Daphne Keating had married Otis Drake, producing a daughter, Susannah—Crazy Susannah—who married Charles Whitaker and gave birth to the woman whose life had become such a part of Daphne's own. The circle went round and round. "You probably know, Bailey, that Cousin Maddy's father's name was Drake Clayton IV. That must mean she's related to your neighbor Cyrus Drake, right?" How much more convoluted could this story get? she wondered silently.

"Cousins, many times removed. Maddy's no close kin to that old buzzard in any way that's important," Bailey declared airily.

"Doctor G., you don't know all that's been goin' on," Leila

said emphatically before her employer could reply. "My friend, Ava, over at Mistah Drake's place, says the poor ol' soul's doin' mighty poorly these days, with headaches something awful. He's been worryin' 'bout payin' his doctor bills, and payin' for the medicine he's takin' night and day."

"I didn't know the old goat's been sick," Bailey admitted sheepishly.

"Well he *is*," Leila scolded, her hands on her hips. "That's why he's so anxious to sell his property to that oil company. Ava says she hasn't got her full salary in quite a while now. Mistah Drake's doin' what he's doin' with those toxic dump folks has *nothin'* to do with tryin' to pester you, or pay you back for winnin' Miz Caroline's hand all those years ago."

"Hmm," Bailey said with an embarrassed expression while he took another sip of his drink.

"Hmm y'self," Leila declared. "You two should bury the hatchet 'fore we *all* dead and in our graves, y'hear? Men of your age!"

Bailey appeared startled by her blunt declarations, then grew thoughtful. "I didn't know he was sick," he repeated.

Leila returned to her kitchen while Bailey and Daphne relived the most exciting moments of the benefit concert. The clock on the mantel struck eight. Where was Sim? she wondered.

"Maybe Sim's decided to camp out in the Trace one more night?" she suggested.

Bailey shook his head. "No… when he called he said he was on his way back here from Jackson. He's bringing somebody he wants me to meet. Says it might solve all our problems, though, believe me, I doubt anything could be that simple."

The rich aroma of Dr. Gibbs's dinner wafted from Leila's kitchen "It's getting late, Bailey," Daphne said, glancing at the clock again. "I think I'd better scoot along." Sim obviously had business with Bailey to conduct tonight, Daphne realized, disappointed.

"Won't you stay to supper?" Dr. Gibbs offered, ever the hospitable Southerner. "I'm sure there's plenty and—"

"Thanks… but no," Daphne replied quickly. "Another time, though. When we celebrate victory."

"I hope that happens," Bailey replied with a worried look. "I don't trust any of those politicians up in Jackson debating in the back rooms, and I 'specially don't trust that Jack Ebert fella and the Able Petroleum folks. We gotta watch our backs with *that* crowd after the way I saw them twist things 'round in those legislative hearings all summer."

"Keep the faith, Bailey," Daphne reassured him, rising from the brocade chair to take her leave. "No new bills are introduced before the January session next year. Now, you go on in and enjoy your supper, and I'll just show myself out the front door. Give Sim my love, will you? Tell him I said we need to get together right away. Please ask him to call tonight. Something important's on my mind."

"I 'spect so," he said with a sly wink. "Be glad to." He pointed to his leathery cheek in a demand for a kiss. Grinning, she gave him a peck and waved good-bye.

A few minutes later, as Daphne was about to nose her Jeep out of the drive into the highway, Sim's Range Rover rolled to a halt, signaling his intention to turn into Bailey's property. She slammed on the brakes, rolled down her window, and called excitedly, "Sim! Hey, Sim!"

She started to wave, then saw that beside him in the passenger seat a beautiful brunette smiled and pointed in the direction of the hand-carved sign announcing Gibbs Hall.

In shock, Daphne could only stare at the couple. At first, she simply couldn't believe that Francesca Hayes was in the company of her former husband, who had probably just driven down with her from the state capital.

Daphne saw that Francesca had suddenly recognized her. She laughed, pointed at Daphne, and then leaned close to Sim's right ear. Was she *kissing* the man?

Daphne and Sim locked glances. He appeared every bit as unnerved to see *her* as she was to see *them*. In an act of pure instinct, she floored the Jeep's accelerator and made a careening right turn toward Natchez, speeding away in a hail of gravel. She never slowed down until she reached the city limits.

The light on the veranda at Bluff House was on. It was still early enough that Madeline Whitaker was probably awake. Despite this, Daphne made straight for the stairs without even greeting her cousin. By the time she'd reached her room at the top of the house she'd shed her jacket and shoes. She immediately threw herself facedown on the bed, waiting for the tears to come.

Again… how could it happen again?

And still the expected tears didn't fill her eyes. In fact, she almost felt as if she weren't in her body at all. Her breath was ragged and her heart was pounding, but she couldn't actually stitch a coherent series of thoughts together. After a while, she flopped over on her back and stared out the window that overlooked the broad expanse of the river. It was the same body of water that had flowed past this bluff for a thousand years, lapping at the base of the cliff.

The cell phone stashed in her purse began to ring. She ignored it. It had to be Sim. He always called her at night on her cell to avoid disturbing Maddy. A barge, lights winking on deck, glided past.

The old river had seen it all, she thought, the fleeting joys and weighty sorrows of a host of people just like Daphne—gullible, fallible people like her namesake, Daphne Whitaker, and her poor, benighted mother, Susannah—betrayed by the men in their lives.

But look what kind of men they chose! Daphne thought, her throat raw with unshed tears. Charles Whitaker drank to excess to escape life's problems. Jacques René Hébèrt had been nothing but a libertine. Aaron Clayton was just plain mean and utterly narcissistic. Only Sim Hopkins the Younger truly cared for the women he loved…

Sim… Sim… how could you turn out to be such an awful rat?

And then, finally, the tears began to pour down her cheeks and she burrowed her face into the pillow and cried as if a baby had died. After an hour, spent and feeling no better, she dragged herself to the bathroom to splash water on her swollen eyes. Taped to the mirror was a note written in Maddy's bold hand.

Call Althea right away!

Bleary-eyed, Daphne peered at her watch. It was quarter to

ten, She stumbled into her office and picked up the receiver. Fortunately, Althea hadn't yet started her set at Cafe LaCroix and came to the phone immediately.

"*Finally* you call me back! Didn't Maddy tell you what's up?" Althea demanded.

"No." Daphne was afraid if she said another word, she'd burst out crying again.

"Boy, you sure sound cheerful," Althea commented. "That gig at the Eola Hotel must be putting nails in your shoes, sugar. Well, never mind 'bout that because you're goin' go *crazy* when I tell you what's happening."

"What?" Daphne said without enthusiasm.

"Jazz Fest!"

"Jazz Fest? It's not 'til April. We have plenty of time to get tickets." The annual event that brought the world's greatest musical talents to New Orleans for two consecutive weekends in the spring was too far off to get excited about, especially considering she wouldn't be taking Sim, as she'd planned.

"We're gonna be *in* it!" Althea screeched.

"What?"

"At least it looks like we are if you can just get your lil' fanny down here for a meeting tomorrow at eleven o'clock. Then you can drive me back to Natchez after lunch Friday, 'cause my car's broke and none of m'brothers can loan me any of theirs and I hate taking that ol' bus."

"Are you telling me that the Aphrodites might be asked to play at *Jazz Fest*?" Daphne demanded, stunned.

"Got a call from Chappy Barrone today," Althea declared smugly. "Remember him? He came up to hear us at the 'For the Birds' gig? Well, sugar pie, he recorded our stuff that night, made a quick CD, and got the music committee to okay asking us to be one of the openin' acts. Now, all's we gotta do is figure out how much they'll pay us."

"We ought to pay *them*!" Daphne said, her spirits raised several notches.

"Hell no," Althea scoffed. "Get y'self down here, and pronto!

Be sure to get a move on real early so you beat the traffic coming down I-10 tomorrow mornin', y'hear?"

Daphne flashed on the memory of Sim Hopkins at the wheel of his car with Francesca sitting beside him and couldn't bear to face the "Dear Jane" call she knew she'd receive on the house phone in the morning.

"Wait up for me, girlfriend," she said decisively. "I'm leaving right now and I'll be there in three hours."

"Don't you drive down here late at night like that," Althea ordered. "And besides, I'm beat. I'm goin' to bed soon as I can get outta this place."

"I'll stay with my brother. I've got a key, and I can let myself in and not even wake them up."

"That's even *worse*," Althea exclaimed. "You'll have to park your car somewhere on the street in the French Quarter and you'll risk your sweet *life* walkin' back to King's place at one a.m., girl!"

"I'll be fine," Daphne assured her. "I have to get out of here."

"Why?" Althea demanded.

"Man trouble. Big Time. Tell you later."

And with that she hung up the receiver, dashed off a note to Maddy telling her where she'd gone, grabbed her purse and some interview-worthy clothes, slipped on her shoes, and raced downstairs toward her car with only one thought in mind: her mother would keel over in a dead faint when she found out that her daughter might be an opening act at New Orleans's bacchanal of popular music and hedonistic celebration held right in Antoinette Kingsbury Duvallon's own backyard.

Screw it! Daphne thought, both angry and elated at once. *And screw Sim Hopkins and his long-lost wife!*

CHAPTER 28

"WELL, THAT WAS QUICK," Althea commented dryly, pointing to the sign that marked the turnoff to downtown Natchez. "Don't you want us to live to see Jazz Fest next year, girl?"

"Was I driving too fast?" Daphne asked vaguely. "I sort of do this route on automatic pilot. I've been coming up here since I got my driver's license when I was fifteen years old."

"That's what worried me," Althea retorted. Then her voice softened. "You okay, sugar? After we sang 'He Done Me Wrong' driving through St. Francisville, you've hardly said a word the whole trip."

"No. Okay, I mean."

"Didn't think so," she said, watching Daphne make the turn onto Clifton Avenue. "At least you got the Jazz Fest gig to look forward to. I still can't believe it," she chortled. "M'brothers are sooooo jealous. I *love* it!"

"Oh, Jesus, Mary, and Joseph," Daphne exclaimed as she wheeled her Jeep up the driveway to Bluff House. "Sim's sitting right there on the veranda with Maddy!"

"Well, you have to face him sometime, sugar, even if it's to tell him to go to hell," Althea said mildly, "though if I was you, I'd at least hear him out."

"There's nothing to hear," Daphne said, angrily stomping on the parking brake. "I saw all I needed yesterday to get the picture. I just feel like such an absolute *chump*."

"Daphne, dear," Maddy called, jumping to her feet so swiftly that the porch rocker tilted wildly behind her. "I'm so glad you're back. Sim and I were worried to death when we saw your note sayin' you'd driven down to New Orleans in the middle of the night."

Daphne marched up the four wooden stairs, gave her cousin a peck on the cheek, and glared at Sim, who said, "You turned off your cell phone, didn't you?"

"You could have just emailed me," she said to him shortly, and brushed on by, taking the sweeping staircase two steps at a time. She refrained from slamming her bedroom door, but she sure as hell felt like it.

A few seconds later she heard three raps.

"There's nothing to say, Sim. Just spare us both the humiliation."

Sim opened the door, stepped inside, and closed it behind him, turning the key in the lock. "Look," he began, "I can understand why you're upset—"

"*Upset?*" She marched to the window overlooking the river and wrapped her arms around her chest, hugging herself, her back to the intruder. "I'm way, *way* beyond upset. I was upset yesterday. Today I just want you to go away." She whirled around and said, "Go! Get out of here! I mean it, Sim. Hit the road, as you do so brilliantly!"

Sim stared at her as if she'd slapped his face.

"You really don't like to get left, do you?"

"Who does?" she shot back, furious that he should so deftly poke that particular wound. "Who the hell *does?*" Her voice had risen several decibels and she was fighting back tears. "*You* hated it, remember? Remember when your wife walked out? At least she had the decency to leave you a note!"

Sim now appeared angry. "I've been calling you for ten hours, so I want you to listen, and I want you to listen carefully. Yes, I've spent some time with Francesca—"

"I don't want to hear about it," Daphne retorted, her voice raw.

"Well, that's tough, because you're going to!" Sim took a deep breath and continued. "As you probably guessed from what I've told you before, there was a fair amount of unfinished business between Francesca and me. After ten *years*, Daphne, I had the opportunity to sit down and hash it out with her, so I grabbed it."

"Congratulations," Daphne said sarcastically. "It's just that I would have greatly appreciated it if—before you went to some cozy little motel room in Jackson—you'd have had the guts to tell the woman you were *currently* sleeping with that you were going to do the nasty while you held your little tete-a-tete!"

"Yes, as a matter of fact, we went to her motel room in Jackson. It just sort of happened."

"Oh, well... *that's* reassuring."

Sim glanced around Daphne's bedroom, and then suggested, "Why don't you and I sit down... in your office?"

"Because I really, truly don't want to hear what you're going to tell me." She abruptly turned her back on Sim again, willing herself to stay furious and keep her tears at bay.

"Well, that's too bad, I'm not leaving this room, and neither are you, until you hear what I have to say!" He grabbed her by the shoulders and propelled her into the other room, seating her on her office chair while he sat on the edge of the desk two feet away.

"Sim, really..." she pleaded.

"Francesca got hold of me on my cell phone when I was on the Trace. She called because she wants to cut a deal about the toxic dump."

"Fine," Daphne spat "That's what she does. Cuts deals. Between rats and superrats. So what?"

Sim's lips hardened into a straight line, but he continued to speak in an even voice. "So, I said, okay... I'd hear her out. Nobody wins when there's a protracted court battle after a legislature decides something. I met her at the place she was staying in Jackson and we talked about the terms of a deal, which took a long time. That's why I asked her to bring down my photographs because, by then, I was way behind schedule and had to go back and get my gear before driving to Natchez. Francesca figured she and Jack could confer on the drive down, and if everyone was on the same page, we could begin to nail the terms of the deal the following week with all the parties up in Jackson."

"Yada, yada, yada... How stupid do you really think I am, Sim?

You didn't call me to tell me this was in the works because the cell towers fell down."

"I didn't call you because... I wasn't ready to."

"Oh... so *you* get to set the schedule on my life, is that it? *You* get to decide what I'm to know or *not* know?" Daphne slammed her hand down on her desk. "This is just crap! Why am I even talking to you?"

Undeterred, Sim said, "That night in the parking lot after the show I told Francesca that, now that the settlement was in the works, I wanted to talk to her about... us."

"Who—us?"

"About Francesca and me. About what happened."

"For God's sake, Sim... excuse me, but I've heard this story before, remember? When we were supposedly falling in love out at Gibbs Hall. I was understanding. I was sympathetic. I was *empathetic*! It happened a decade ago. I'm terribly sorry your baby died, but it did. If you've decided now that all is forgiven between you and Francesca and everything is hunky-dory and you two can carry on from here... that's fine. You just should have *warned* me that a ten-ton Mack truck was heading my—"

"I wanted to ask Francesca why she took such rotten care of her health when she was pregnant," Sim interrupted with dogged determination.

"You know what? I don't really care," she snapped.

"Maybe you should, because her fury and vitriol after the baby died have haunted me, Daphne," Sim said, pleading now for her understanding. "Made me unfit to be with you or anyone else. All Francesca's accusations about my not being there for her and her predictions that I'd be an absent dad... *waylaid* me, you know what I mean? It stuck in my gut. Ever since she walked out, I go cuckoo when I'm being criticized for letting someone down."

"Well you *do* let people down," Daphne protested. "You let *me* down as my partner in the 'For the Birds' benefit! Saturday night after the show you were cold and distant and a pain in the ass, and then you dropped off the radar screen."

"And you assumed the worst, didn't you?" he shot back.

"Well, who *wouldn't!*" she yelled. "You sucked me into your grand scheme to do the benefit when I hardly know how I'm going to make enough money, some months, to pay Maddy the rent! Thanks to you, I really cared about raising money to try to stop the pollution that's giving cancer to people I know and love." Blinking back tears she whispered, "I thought you felt the same way—until you took a powder the entire week leading up to the concert and let me do all the work! What am I *supposed* to think?"

"Without knowing *all* the facts, you assumed that my absence *had* to mean I was fooling around behind your back?"

"That's exactly what I thought and that's what happened! Give it up, Sim!"

With surprising gentleness, he reached out and grasped her chin between his hands. "Don't you get it? It's the same deal for *you*," Sim said. "You go absolutely nuts when you think a guy is two-timing you or is *about* to do you wrong. It warps all your perceptions."

Daphne reached for a tissue from a box on her desk and pressed it to her eyes while Sim continued to talk in a voice that throbbed with intensity.

"You and I both suffer from a similar sort of paralysis, don't you see? And it will doom anything we've got going unless we deal with it. That's what I decided to do about my old stuff with Francesca. Deal with it."

"Frankly, Sim, from here on out, you and I've got *nothing* going here."

"You're saying that there's nothing between us?" Sim asked. "Are you sure you want to stand by that statement?"

Privately, Daphne was forced to admit that some aspects of Sim's declarations were definitely true. She *did*, in fact, go kind of nuts when she thought a guy was going to "do her wrong," as he'd so aptly phrased it. The proof? She did stupid things like drive alone to New Orleans in the middle of the night with half a tank of gas in her Jeep, and arrive at one a.m. in a city with one of the nation's highest crime rates.

"Okay…" she said, attempting to calm down. "So what happened?"

Sim paused to gather his thoughts and continued. "The question for me had become how can I be fit company for a serious relationship with *you* if I haven't put Francesca's ghost to rest?" he asked rhetorically. "And the same goes for you, my dear Ms. Daphne. I don't want to take crap from you for stuff *I* didn't do."

"Such as?" she demanded.

"Such as sleep with my ex-wife or anybody else since we met."

"Well, did you?"

"Sleep with Francesca? No, I did not."

"Come close?"

"Didn't even open the car door for her."

"She obviously slept over at Gibbs Hall last night," Daphne asserted.

"In the guest room in the main house. I was in the cottage." He shot her a crooked grin, and asked, "Far enough away for you?"

Daphne had a moment of chagrin. Then she steeled herself to listen to the outcome of Sim's rendezvous. "And after all this, did you slay the ghost?"

"It took a while," Sim acknowledged. "But something you said the night you first surprised me at the cottage had been nagging me for months."

"Something *I* said?" Daphne replied, startled.

"Yeah… remember you theorized that Francesca might be projecting all that blame onto me when, in fact, during her pregnancy she was smoking and drinking and working unbelievably late hours?"

"So, you were wondering if, after ten years, she was finally willing to take some responsibility for how her own unhealthy behavior might have contributed to a miscarriage?"

Sim paused, and then said quietly, "In fact, she took *all* the responsibility."

"What do you mean?"

"When I demanded to know why she'd been so reckless the last few months we were together, she broke down."

Ah ha! Daphne thought. Just as she'd thought, Ms. Francesca regretted cutting loose such a dishy guy after all and had come to Mississippi to make her amends in a bid to get Sim back.

"I'll just bet she cried her little eyes out."

Sim shot Daphne a warning look.

"Sorry," she said with genuine contrition. "It's just I'm having a hard time with the thought of you two in a motel, talking about such intimate stuff."

"We spent most of our time in the back rooms at the Capitol when we were negotiating the specifics on the toxic dumps with a bunch of cigar-smoking legislative assistants. Yesterday, we talked about *our* stuff... for three hours in her motel room, and another two on the drive down."

"Hmmm." Daphne shrugged, girding herself for what came next. She gazed at her hands folded in her lap to avoid looking at Sim. "Look... from what I know about these things, a woman's hormones after childbirth or miscarriage can go up and down like a yo-yo, which could account for why she—"

"Francesca didn't miscarry."

Daphne raised her eyes and stared at Sim in confusion.

"She *didn't?*"

"She waited until she knew I'd be out of town on a shoot and got a woman doctor friend of hers from college to perform an abortion."

"Oh, Sim, *no!*" Daphne said, barely above a whisper. "And she kept it from you all these years? But why did she *do* such a thing?"

Sim rose from where he'd been sitting on the desk and gazed out the window. "For the simple reason that she'd been having an affair with a colleague at work."

"Oh, my God!"

"At first she figured she'd pass the child off as mine."

"Even if it wasn't? Shades of Antoinette," Daphne murmured. Months before, she'd told Sim about her brother's true parentage. Now she was shocked that the other important man in her life, too, had been subject to such deceit. "So, when she found out she was pregnant, she told you the baby was yours, and of course you believed it." She was unable to mask her sense of outrage. "What happened after she unleashed *that* bombshell?"

"This is making Francesca sound like a callous bitch, and she's not," Sim insisted. "She's more complicated than that, but... the sad truth was, she hated being pregnant. She told me yesterday that then, as now, she really didn't want to be a mother, regardless of who was the father."

"Wow," she whispered. "That must have been hard to hear."

"It was."

"At least she was finally straight about it, though." Daphne rose from her chair and crossed to the window. "What did the father have to say about what she'd decided to do?" she asked, gently placing her hand on Sim's arm.

"The day after she broke the news to him that she was pregnant—probably with his child, given my traveling schedule around that time—*and* in love with him, the guy negotiated a transfer to the firm's Washington, D.C., office without telling her first. After he took off, Francesca was devastated."

"Who wouldn't be?" Daphne murmured in spite of herself.

"And she was scared. Once she got over being scared, she was more certain than ever that she didn't want to be a mother. She'd figured out long before I did that *our* marriage was a mess and our incompatibility manifestly obvious... and since she couldn't have *him*, she kind of went berserk. She persuaded her doctor friend to perform a second-trimester abortion—which is legal in California—and covered it up."

"But Sim," Daphne protested, aching for him and the heartbreak he'd endured, "what was she by then, five or six months pregnant?"

"Four and a half months," Sim replied hollowly.

"Another month and we start to talk about the marvels of modern science in the prenatal ward!" Daphne said, starting to feel furious in Sim's stead. "Why did she have to do such a horrible number on *your* head?"

"Given her emotional state at the time, I think she was doing exactly what you'd guessed at months ago: projecting all those negative feelings about herself onto *me*. She felt so guilty, she told me yesterday, that she actually began to believe her own made-up story—in other words, that I was the original cause of all her problems."

"I'd say that *she* was the original cause of all her problems."

Sim turned around, his face inches from hers. "That's right," he said simply. "And you cannot imagine how learning all this has made me feel."

"Well... like *how*?" Daphne asked cautiously.

"Like I've been let out of jail. Like I've had a sentence commuted. Like I'm not such a bad dude, after all. Like I shouldn't ever again accept anyone else's opinion of me if I don't believe it myself."

"And how does it make you feel about Francesca?"

Sim was silent for a moment, turning his thoughts over in his head. "That she's... trouble. Always was and always will be. Lovely to look at. Smart as a whip. A fabulous lawyer. But big trouble one-on-one. And I picked her to marry, so I have to take responsibility for that and ask myself why."

"Frankly, I'm amazed you didn't punch her lights out."

"Actually, now that I know the truth, I feel some compassion for her. She was scared she'd be a bad mother because she truly loved practicing law and didn't want to give it up or let motherhood slow down her making full partner in her firm. Kind of a guy thing, you know? Which only made her feel doubly guilty."

"But aren't you angry?" she demanded. "Why are you being so goddamned charitable to a woman who *really* did you wrong? Not to mention... maybe your child."

"I—am angry," Sim said quietly. "At her... and at myself. From the very beginning, she and I hadn't dealt straight with each other. When our marriage crashed and burned, I took it out on myself, on my family, and on all the women afterward who wanted to get close."

"Like me, by not letting me know what was going on with you this week when we'd agreed to produce the benefit together."

Sim paused. "You're absolutely right. When things got complicated I did my typical head-for-the-hills routine, which stinks."

"Definitely," she agreed. "My heading for New Orleans in the dead of night was sort of the same deal." Then she murmured, "Wow. That's a first in my life."

"But, here's the good part," he said with a bemused expression. "Now I understand what happened back then. I can see that very little of what Francesca did in those days had much to do with me. Her walking out was a major blow, but she didn't do it *to* me, if you know what I mean? If I'd known that a week ago, I'd have called you when all this started happening and explained what was going on and probably have saved us both a lot of grief."

Daphne was silent for a long moment, shaking her head from side to side. Then she sought his gaze. "I cannot tell you how sorry I am that you've had to go through all this again... and that I lost faith about... us."

Sim fell silent too. Finally he said, "Thank you. And I admit, given the context of what you saw yesterday, it looked bad."

"Especially when she leaned over in the car and kissed you," Daphne reminded him.

Sim laughed. "I told her to get her mitts the hell off me. We were right at the end of hashing all this out when we got to the turnoff at Bailey's and saw your Jeep."

"She kissed you deliberately. All along I bet she's wanted you back," Daphne said, watching him carefully.

"The subject came up."

"And?"

"I told her she can't have me," he said with his old grin. "I told her flat out that I was in love with you and that her offer, while flattering, didn't tempt me even a little."

"Good answer," Daphne said, the first smile in twenty-four hours brightening her features. "What in the world did Bailey think when you walked into Gibbs Hall with Francesca Hayes in tow? Didn't the good doctor think it was strange to have you consorting with the enemy on his turf?"

Sim laughed a second time. "He sure did. Almost didn't let Francesca in the door. Almost didn't let *me* in the door."

"Yea, Bailey!"

"He said he'd just had a nice visit with you." Sim seized her hand gently and rubbed his thumb across her palm. "He was very pointed in the way he mentioned your name in front of Francesca about every third sentence."

"I love that man!"

"And what about me?" Sim demanded, his eyes growing grave. "Are you ever going to get to a place where you'll trust a guy you don't have in your line of sight twenty-four hours a day?"

He'd asked her a direct question and Daphne felt as if she'd been punched in the stomach. Her eyes suddenly filled with tears. "That's a pretty mean thing to say."

"No," Sim insisted. "It's a fair question, and the answer is important to me. Can you learn to assume that, unless you have iron-clad evidence to the contrary, my intent toward you is always going to be *good*?"

"It *looked* pretty iron-clad, you must admit, Sim," she replied stubbornly.

"I know sweetheart," he nodded, "but I need you to someday get to the place where you truly believe that I've got your back, now and always."

Daphne nodded her assent and swiped her eyes with the back of her hand. "This trust stuff is hard for me, Sim." She was breathless now, and couldn't put into words the misery that had engulfed her when she'd spotted Sim's Range Rover about to make the turn into Gibbs Hall.

"I expect none of the last week has been fun for you," he agreed, "but still—"

"It was horrible," she interrupted in a choked voice.

"And I absolutely should have been clearer with you about what was going on."

"Yes, you *absolutely* should have." Her gaze grew troubled again. "And I want to say that I am so sorry for the way I behaved yesterday and just now on the veranda," she confessed, tears spilling down her cheeks, "but I hope you can understand, now, why I sometimes felt so... so... bereft. So betrayed."

He took her in his arms and she burrowed her head into his chest.

"I know, baby," he said soothingly. "I have an idea how hard it's been. But we've both got to show a little more moxie about this stuff," he teased, giving her shoulders a gentle squeeze. He leaned away from her and pointed both thumbs at his chest, and said, "It's *me*... Sim. I'm the only guy in the room." He glanced around, and declared with a faint smile, "No Jack. No Rafe. No rats. Just Sim."

"Oh, stop!" Daphne said tearfully. "I wasn't that bad. Admit it. Any normal person would have been *very* suspicious, given the circumstances."

Sim shook his head vehemently. "Well, sure, but you don't get off that easily. I already told you, but you don't really believe me yet. I'm like a veritable old swan. My feathers are pretty scruffy, and I don't fly very well anymore, but I plan to mate for life the next time."

"I'll give you a high-five for that one, Bird Man."

"You'll give me more than that," he said, pulling her back into the circle of his arms.

"Sim," she protested. "It's one o'clock in the afternoon! Maddy and Althea are downstairs."

"And later, you and I, Maddy, and Bailey have a big pow-wow set up with Francesca and Able Petroleum about settling the toxic dump case, but right now, you gotta show me how *much* you care."

"Get outta here," Daphne said, laughing and amazed by the emotional roller coaster she'd been on within the space of a single day.

Undeterred, Sim led her toward her own double bed. He turned to face her and expertly pulled off her "For the Birds" T-shirt. "You couldn't have hated me *that* much," he said, lean-ing forward to graze his lips against the base of her neck. "Even today, you're wearing my photograph of the chickadees next to your heart."

"Don't flatter yourself," she muttered, abandoning herself to the sensations radiating along the path of Sim's kisses as he gently nuzzled the tops of her breasts. "I got dressed in a hurry last night."

"Maybe your subconscious told you to wear it," he mumbled.

She took a step back, cast him a sidelong glance, and put her hands behind her back to unhook her bra. "Well, guess what?" she said with a provocative smile. "All of a sudden, my conscious mind is telling me to take this *off*."

Sim lent a hand in removing the rest of her garments and led her to the bed. "Pull down the covers, Harp Honey," he drawled, "and let's start playin' some of that honky-tonk jazz."

⚜

Sim and Daphne were jolted awake by sharp knocks on the bedroom door.

"Are you guys goin' loll 'round in bed all *day*?" Althea said from the hall. "You've both got 'bout twenty-five phone calls waitin' on you down here!"

Daphne pulled the top sheet over her head. "Oh, my God... I can't face Cousin Maddy."

Sim dove beneath the covers and kissed her soundly on the shoulder blade. "Don't go there," he advised solemnly. "Just tell yourself we had a long meeting up here about the toxic dump deal we're going to do tonight, and descend the stairs with your head held high. And furthermore, don't even *think* what your mother would say about your outrageous behavior today."

"How did you guess?" she said, poking her head out from the bedclothes.

"I'm getting to know you *really* well."

There was another sharp rap on the door.

"Now, personally, I don't care a hoot what you guys are doin' in there," Althea said from behind the door, "but you've been in there—*doin'* it—for about three hours. Poor Cousin Maddy's worried you're gonna be more than love-starved if you don't come down and have some supper."

"Tell her we've just finished our strategy meeting and will be right down," Sim called out gallantly.

"Oh, yeah. Right. You two are a riot. See ya downstairs. We've got a show to do tonight at ten o'clock, Miz Magnolia, in case it's slipped your mind."

"I'll get you for that, Althea!" Daphne called through the door, scooting to the edge of the bed and thrusting one leg into her jeans.

"I completely forgot to ask," she said to Sim, who was just as quickly donning his clothes, which were strewn across the floor. "With everything that's been going on, how'd you do on the Trace? Did you ever find that flycatcher?"

"Nailed the last bird on my list on Tuesday," he declared proudly.

Daphne froze, her left leg poised over her pants leg. "So your project is finished?"

"Oh, God, no," Sim said, buckling his belt. "I've got to *write* the whole thing now, with the Audubon Society looking over my shoulder, might I add."

Sim could do that anywhere, Daphne thought. "Have laptop, will travel," he'd said more than once. She watched him button his shirt and slip on his loafers. She hadn't even had time yet to tell him the good news about Jazz Fest. He opened the bedroom door and she wondered, yet again, how they would cope with the geographic "challenges"—as Sim had called them—of their separate worlds.

Before she could raise such a thorny subject, Sim patted her gently on the derriere and said, "Come on, toots, let's tuck into some red beans and rice. Believe me, we're going to need our strength tonight when we tell old Jackie boy the news that he may not get to put that dump in Bailey's backyard."

"Tonight? But what about my show?"

"The settlement meeting is *after* the show. At his funeral home. One a.m. His call," Sim said grimly, and Daphne wondered if he could be dreading any confrontation with Jack Ebert just as much as she was.

CHAPTER 29

DAPHNE PEERED THROUGH THE windshield of Sim's Range Rover. The former Livingston Funeral Home was located in a quiet business district at the edge of town. Her watch said it was five minutes to one in the morning. All was in darkness at the front of the low-slung redbrick building except for the handsome, new, hand-carved Ebert-Petrella signpost burrowed into the grass and lit by two small floodlights.

"Boy, do these places give me the creeps," she announced under her breath, shivering at the memory of her last experience playing her harp at Farrell's.

"Why do we have to meet here, of all depressin' places?" Cousin Maddy asked, nodding in agreement. "And why do *I* have to come?"

"Your name is on the trust account with Bailey's and Daphne's," Sim explained gently. "We might need you to cosign a letter of agreement at the end of the settlement conference if we're able to hammer one out."

"We're not *bribing* anyone, are we?" Maddy asked, alarmed.

Sim laughed. "Boy Scouts like Bailey and me? No way! But the good doctor has some very interesting ideas about what to do with the benefit money and he'll need you to sign off on them, too, if you agree."

"Seriously, Sim," Daphne chimed in. "Why do we have to meet on Jack's turf? I hate this." And besides, she was dead tired after getting no sleep the previous night and singing for ninety minutes at the Under-the-Hill Saloon, packed to the rafters with patrons from the visiting *Delta Queen*.

"Jack told Francesca that he doesn't want anyone to know here in Natchez or up in Jackson that a settlement is being considered. But I think the main reason we're here is exactly what you say. He feels more in control on his own turf."

"I wonder about that…" Daphne murmured, reflecting upon her firsthand observations of Jack Ebert's consistently unpleasant behavior around the family business.

Just then, Bailey Gibbs drove up in his old Ford with Francesca Hayes beside him in the passenger seat, along with an elderly gentleman sitting alone in the back.

"Shouldn't Bailey have his own lawyer with him?" Maddy asked worriedly.

"Maybe that's him," Daphne said, nodding in the direction of the stranger.

"No, that's not an attorney," Sim declared. To Maddy he said, "There wasn't time to get all the players involved, but don't worry, we're just trying to get the principal parties into one room to see if everybody's in agreement about the proposal. If we can nail down the makings of a deal, then we'll have Bailey's lawyer review the legal language. C'mon. Let's go in."

Daphne glanced apprehensively at the building. "Now that we're actually here, Sim, I've got butterflies playing hopscotch in my stomach. The two things I like least in the world combined into one: a funeral parlor *and* Jack Ebert. I can't wait for this to be over."

Bailey, Francesca, and the man Daphne didn't recognize caught up with them on the walkway leading to the front door. Francesca had come to do battle dressed in a chic navy pinstripe suit and navy suede pumps that Daphne reckoned cost as much as her own entire fall wardrobe.

"Well, hello again," Francesca greeted her smoothly, extending her hand. "And this must be your cousin, Madeline Whitaker. How do you do."

"How'd you do," Maddy echoed politely. Then she turned toward the elderly gentleman standing to Francesca's right. "Why, Cyrus Drake! I haven't seen you in the longest time. I'm Madeline

Clayton Whitaker. I doubt you remember me, but I was Marcus's wife. Clayton's mother? Our boys played baseball together... oh, years ago, it was, and I do believe our great-grandmothers—or maybe it was a bunch more 'greats' than that—were cousins."

Cyrus Drake, a rangy man with a caved-in chest and a pinched look on his face, summoned a wan smile to his thin lips. He looked to be in his late seventies, and unwell.

"Yes, of course, Miz Whitaker," he said, bowing in a courtly fashion, though the effort appeared to cause him some pain. "My boy, Avery, spoke of your son often. I was so sorry to hear of your loss."

"You're kind as can be to say so," Maddy replied with a bleak smile.

Daphne was astonished that the neighbor she understood Bailey had been feuding with over the proposed sale of the Drake property to Able Petroleum—not to mention their long-ago rivalry for the hand of Caroline Minger—was going to take part in the "summit meeting" chauffeured by his old nemesis.

The group of six entered the building. Maddy whispered in Daphne's ear, "Nothing much has changed. Looks just like it did when the Livingstons owned the place. Remember Marcus's viewin', Daphne, darlin'?"

"I sure do, Maddy." Daphne gave her cousin's hand a gentle squeeze. It couldn't be easy for her to return here, even to aid a worthy cause.

Daphne glanced at her watch. It was now just after one. The visitors passed through the foyer and proceeded down the carpeted hall toward a room at the end of the corridor.

"Oh, Lord," Maddy murmured. "Don't tell me we're meeting in *there*?"

They entered a room much like the one at Farrell's where Daphne had played at Abigail Langhorn's funeral. Jack was dressed in a dark blue suit not unlike Francesca's pinstripe. Without any pleasantries, he suggested they all take chairs that were placed around a sort of altar arrangement in front of the rows of mourners' seats. Daphne realized instantly their makeshift conference table was the bier on which the casket normally rested while family and friends came to pay their respects.

"I propose we get right down to business," Jack said brusquely. "Mr. Drake, Able Petroleum has made you a generous offer for your land—above fair-market value, I might add." He paused and heaved an audible sigh. Then he cast Francesca an irritated glance. "I was informed by Ms. Hayes here, that you may have changed your mind?"

"I might," Cyrus said with a faint wheeze. "And I might not. Depends."

"Depends on what?" Jack snapped, looking angrily around the room as if each person present were a declared enemy.

"Depends on what everybody's offerin'."

"I'm to blame for Cyrus having second thoughts," Bailey spoke up. "Now that we have twenty-five thousand dollars earned by our benefit concert, I thought, 'why spend all this on lawyers' fees?' So, I called up Cyrus this mornin', and I told him I'd put every dime toward buying twenty-five of his one hundred acres that are closest to my land as a kinda buffer zone—that is, if you still seem determined to build your toxic dump in Adams County. Cyrus was kind enough to say he'd consider it."

Jack suddenly looked like the alligator that had swallowed an angel fish. "Well I'm afraid that's not at all acceptable to us, Mr. Drake. Y'see, Able Petroleum is only interested in securing *all* one hundred acres to meet company standards for such facilities, y'see what I'm sayin'?" He shot a triumphant look at Sim and Daphne, adding, "We've offered top dollar, and if you sell off those twenty-five to Doc Bailey, here, Able Petroleum will immediately withdraw its offer."

Cyrus Drake's expression conveyed his disappointment. He glanced at his long-time neighbor and shrugged. "Sorry, Bailey. I thought maybe we could work somethin' out here, but I don't want to leave a mess for my children, y'understand? Twenty-five thousand dollars doesn't go very far these days when you don't have good insurance, and I'll probably have to go into a nursin' home at some point."

Bailey patted his former rival on the sleeve and nodded. "I understand... surely I do." The next instant, however, his expression was alight with a new thought. "Well, what about this? I pay the same amount for the *entire* one hundred acres?"

Everyone around the table exchanged puzzled glances.

"Please, Doctor Gibbs," Jack said harshly. "It's late. Let's not play stupid games."

"No... I'm serious," the doctor protested. Bailey put the palms of both hands flat on the table. "Let the sanctuary buy all your land for twenty-five thousand. That's under market value, of course, but we'll allow you to continue to *live* in your house as long as you want to—just as if it still belonged to you—till you die. That way, there'll be no toxic dump, and you can be buried on your own property with the rest of your kin. Now, if that's not a generous offer, what is?" he said, beaming. "I'll even throw in payin' your housekeeper's salary so Ava can work full-time for you and look after you real good, for as long as you need it. What do you say?"

Before Drake could respond to Bailey's newest proposal, Jack cut in icily.

"And I will sue Mr. Drake for welchin' on a deal that was all but signed, and I'll sue you too, Gibbs, for interfering with a pending legal contract."

"He's just blowing smoke," Sim declared angrily. "Pay no attention, Mr. Drake. I think that's a brilliant idea, Bailey. What do you think, Mr. Drake? Wouldn't that meet all your concerns for your future well-being?"

Jack turned to Francesca. "Oh, I think Mr. Drake should pay *strict* attention to what we might do, don't you, Ms. Hayes?" he asked sharply. "Please explain, in detail, how our lawyers can tie up Mr. Drake's property in court till he *dies*, if we have to, and then go after his heirs."

The reactions in the room to Jack's threats ran the gamut from outrage to shock to dismay. However, one person appeared totally unruffled.

"Really, Mr. Ebert," Francesca scolded mildly, "there's no need to harass these good people like that."

"Look, Miz Lawyer Lady," Jack growled, dropping all pretense of civility even toward someone ostensibly on his own side, "if you don't have the balls for this work, go back to Fog City, will you please?"

"Oh, I have the 'balls' for it, as you so indelicately phrase it," Francesca replied with a cool, appraising stare. "The problem is, neither you nor I have the authority from our employers to threaten to sue these parties. May I suggest that you pay attention to the wishes of your superiors at Able Petroleum and keep your temper under control while I work out a compromise here?"

Jack appeared speechless with indignation. Meanwhile, Sim swiftly reached beneath his chair and laid out on the table a series of photographs he'd taken of Bailey's birdhouses.

"Here's why Ms. Hayes's suggestion that we negotiate a compromise makes eminent sense, Jack," Sim said pleasantly. "As I pointed out to her yesterday, you could have a public relations disaster on your hands if you force Mr. Drake to sell to you."

Jack looked disdainfully at the photographs. "A bunch of birdhouses," he scoffed. "Big fuckin' deal."

"It'll be a big deal to my sister-in-law," Daphne blurted. "You remember Corlis McCullough, don't you, Jack? The TV reporter who covered our aborted wedding? She's back at WJAZ. I'll just bet she could persuade her station to do a story about a big, bad oil company whose products are suspected of causing cancer from Texas to Louisiana and points north."

"That's right, Jack," Sim added quickly. "How would it look if Able Petroleum held these two courtly old gentlemen hostage with threats that Mr. Drake had better sell all his land to them—or else." He shook his head solemnly. "Or that Doctor Gibbs must surrender his lifelong dream of a bird sanctuary for endangered species made famous in the area by America's most beloved naturalist, John James Audubon?"

Sim paused for breath, and Daphne added innocently, "My guess is that in no time, you'd have a producer from *Dateline* or *60 Minutes* down here photographing Bailey's adorable birdhouses and picking up on the story where Corlis McCullough left off."

"Daphne's sister-in-law has wonderful media contacts, I hear," Maddy chimed in.

"Try again," Jack retorted. "Y'all aren't the only ones who know how to work the media. Once Francesca here takes a hike, I'll get the home office back on track and they'll hire an army of lawyers and publicists who can get the job done."

"Well..." Bailey said slowly. "Neither Cyrus nor I wanted to do this, but we have one more photograph to show you, Mr. Ebert—and it isn't pretty." Bailey pulled a large manila envelope from under his folding chair.

Jack shook his head in mock resignation. "Another bird about to go extinct doesn't make a bit of difference. If you both don't want to get sued and have all your assets tied up till you croak, you'd better—"

"First of all," Bailey cut in with barely controlled fury, "Cyrus hasn't signed *anything*, and you know it. Ms. Hayes here knows it. We *all* know it." He pulled out a large X-ray and held it up to the fluorescent lights overhead.

"Oh, *no*?" Maddy swiveled her head from one old friend to the other. "Cyrus!" she cried, anguished. "Bailey! Which of you is ill?"

Daphne and Sim were as startled as Maddy by the X-ray film at which Bailey pointed the tip of his pencil. Daphne reached for her cousin's hand while everyone around the table stared at the medical photo.

Bailey addressed Cyrus. "May I tell them the sad news we discovered today, old friend?" he asked softly, his voice full of sympathy and compassion.

Cyrus nodded and stared dully at his hands in his lap.

"My housekeeper, Leila, told me that Cyrus has been suffering bad headaches and all sorts of upsets during the last year," Bailey Gibbs began. "It concerned me right away that it might be somethin' serious, y'see, because those were the first symptoms my poor, dear Caroline had. So I went over to Cyrus's this mornin' and offered to take him right down to the hospital I used to administer in town, and got the nice people there to run a bunch of tests... X-rays, an MRI... that sort of thing."

Maddy began to sniffle. Daphne reached around her shoulders and gave her a squeeze as tears welled in her own eyes.

Bailey nodded solemnly. "Mr. Drake here's got a brain tumor, Mr. Ebert. The same damned *rare* kind that killed my darlin' Caroline." He patted Cyrus's sleeve a second time. "We know much better, now, how to manage the pain, but you'll need home care, and maybe hospice at the end."

Cyrus looked up and nodded stoically. "Don't want to be a burden on my kids," was all he said.

"You see, Mr. Ebert, looks like Cyrus, here, has a glioblastoma multiforma, the same deadly and untreatable brain tumor that's killed so many people 'round the South." He nodded at Sim, and added, "Mr. Hopkins here knows as well as I do that these illnesses were probably caused by uncontrolled oil drilling and the petro-chemicals used to defoliate and fertilize the cotton fields in these parts for the last fifty years."

"No go, fellas," Jack said snidely. "You can't show me absolute proof that these chemicals are directly linked to the specific cancers you're talkin' about."

"That's what the tobacco companies used to say," Sim challenged him. "'Show us that nicotine is addictive and that smoking causes lung cancer.' Eventually the other side had its proof."

Bailey spoke up again. "Mr. Ebert, I don't think you'd like one of those network exposé programs Daphne mentioned to insinuate to the entire country that first your company gives folks 'round here cancer, and then it tries to steal their family burial grounds. I may be a simple, country doctor, but it doesn't sound like good public relations, to my way of thinkin'."

"May I say something?" Francesca intervened briskly. "Look, Jack, if I thought Able Petroleum could take these people to the mat and pull the trigger, I'd be the first one to recommend we haul them into court and make Mr. Drake, here, sell you his land." She pointed to Sim's photographs of Bailey's birdhouses. "But just *look* at these," she insisted. "I've seen Dr. Bailey's bird sanctuary. There's a very high cuteness factor at work here. If *Dateline* or someone did a segment out there, you'd be a dead duck, so to speak." She glanced at Sim and then at the rest of those present around the table. "Know when to fold your tent, Jack. It makes life a lot easier."

Jack's expression was devoid of emotion. He appeared, in fact, barely to be listening when Cyrus spoke up.

"Mr. Ebert, I think Bailey's offer is a lot more attractive than yours... so I'm gonna accept it." The taciturn old man added, with the ghost of a smile, "I hope your company isn't gonna sue me, but if they do, they'll be suing a dead man, and that'll look pretty bad for you on TV."

Jack remained silent but shot a look of loathing in the direction of Sim and Daphne.

"I promise, though," Cyrus continued with a faint twinkle in his eye, "to consider the Ebert-Petrella Funeral Home when the time comes... I surely will." He turned to address his neighbor of more than seventy years. "What do you say, Bailey? Let's us go home. I'm mighty tired."

"We can sign the lifetime tenancy agreement tomorrow, Cyrus, and we'll write out that check right along with it, won't we Maddy? Daphne?" Bailey declared. "And then I'll ask Leila to make us all a round of mint juleps to celebrate your keepin' your home."

"Mighty kind of you, Bailey."

Jack stared stonily as the two elderly gentlemen pushed back their chairs and slowly rose to leave.

"As your attorney, Jack," Francesca spoke up as she snapped shut her briefcase, "my high-priced advice is to back off from these people and save Able Petroleum a lot of money and grief. I recommended to your employers today to stop lobbying in Jackson for this particular scheme and to put the toxic dump someplace less—shall we say—environmentally sensitive. I suggested across the river in Louisiana, where you appear to have stronger... *connections* than you do in Mississippi." She cast a long, hard look at Sim and Daphne and then stood up. "So long, everybody. I'll hitch a ride with Doctor Gibbs to a motel in town, pick up a rental car tomorrow, and catch a flight out of New Orleans." To Jack she added, "I'll email you my bill, including expenses. Send the check to my firm in San Francisco."

Bailey, Cyrus, and Jack's hired gun walked out of the room. An awkward silence descended while Daphne dared to glance over at her former fiancé. Jack's anger was palpable, and the shell-shocked expression on his face reminded her of the moment she had blurted her knowledge of his affair with Cindy Lou Mallory to the assembly of five hundred wedding guests inside Saint Louis Cathedral.

"Well, let us know what your company decides to do," Sim said without rancor, rising from his chair and helping Madeline to her feet. "If Doctor Gibbs purchases Cyrus Drake's land and Able Petroleum takes its disposal problems somewhere else, I'm sure all parties will agree to sign a confidentiality statement."

Jack's thin lips had settled into a hard line. He seemed to be willing himself not to lose control of his boiling emotions. "Sure thing," he replied finally. Then he inhaled deeply and affected a shrug. Daphne hoped that if they all kept their cool he would accept his defeat with reasonably good grace. "Let me take you out the back way, okay?" he suggested. "It's the shortest route to the parking lot."

For a split second, Daphne hesitated. "We parked out front, Jack," she said.

"Well, you'll have to go out this way anyway because I told the night watchman to put on the security alarm and lock up the front of the building before he went home."

Daphne, Maddy, and Sim were halfway down the hallway following in Jack's wake before she wondered how Bailey and the others had gotten out just now. The instant they passed through the unmarked door into a room filled with steel gurneys and metal sinks, Daphne knew they'd made a horrible mistake. Jack held the door for them and then slammed it shut, turning a key in the lock and pocketing it.

"Jack, what are you doing?" Daphne demanded.

Sim didn't wait for the answer and strode to the double doors on the opposite side of the room that led to a loading bay. He tried both handles.

"They're always kept locked," Jack announced. "Neighborhood kids try to get in here, y'know? Daring each other to do nasty stuff like we all did when we were that age." He turned around to stare steadily at Daphne. "Don't you remember, Daph, when your mama used to bring you 'round all the time to the old Ebert-Petrella place in New Orleans? You didn't much like it, did you? You were always too much of a goody-two-shoes to have any fun."

Daphne averted her eyes from Jack's and glanced around the embalming room. She offered up a silent prayer of thanks that at least none of the gleaming aluminum gurneys was occupied. The room was sterile and antiseptic, with metal tanks and plastic hoses clustered around two industrial-size sinks set into a long metal table that ran along one wall. On the opposite wall stood a high set of shelves with a row of three gallon, amber glass bottles full of embalming fluids. On the lower shelf sat trays piled high with sinister-looking metal instruments rendering their surroundings ominous and surreal.

Cousin Maddy was rooted to the floor near the door they had entered, her expression filled with horror and dismay. Sim swiftly returned to her side and put a protective arm around her trembling shoulders.

"Jack, this is going to get you exactly nowhere," Sim said. "You lost this battle. I'm sure you and Able Petroleum will manage to foil the good guys the next time around."

"You're smart, lover boy. You're so smart, aren't you, you two?" Jack said caustically. "You know, of course, don't you Daphne, that lover boy, here, was schtuppin' Miz Lawyer Lady up in Jackson this week?"

"Jack…" Daphne pleaded, abject terror coming over her as she noted the wild, erratic gleam in his eye. "Look… you did the best job you could for your company, but now we've found a compromise that—"

"Compromise!" Jack spat. "Capitulation. That's what you wanted, isn't it, Daphne? To pay me back for cuttin' those stupid harp strings at your bastard brother's wedding!"

"What I want is for you to be okay, Jack," she said quickly. "If you just let us go home now, everything will be all right."

Sim stared at Daphne in amazement. She gave a faint shake of her head, silently pleading with him not to intervene, and took a step closer to their captor.

"Cut the 'sincere' shit, Daphne," Jack snarled. "I've had as much of you and your damned family messing with my life as I'm gonna take."

"I can see why you'd be angry and frustrated over the way this has turned out, Jack," she placated, "but let's just all go home and—"

"You're not goin' home tonight, so shut up about it, will you?" By this time, Sim had taken hold of Maddy's hand and moved closer to where Daphne was standing in the middle of the room. Jack, meanwhile, marched over to the bank of stainless steel shelves and seized a sharp, knifelike implement, waving it menacingly as he pointed toward a large door that looked something like a bank vault.

"But, you know what? *I'm* goin' home all right." He crossed to the heavy metal door nearby and pulled it open. "I'm leavin' for Texas tonight." Daphne could see it was a large, walk-in refrigerator with at least one shrouded occupant. "And I think I'll just let y'all spend a night in the Ebert-Petrella Hilton with a few of our other guests. I'm sure one of the staff will see to y'all when they come in tomorrow morning."

"Oh, good Lord," Maddy gasped. She turned to Jack, begging, "Please, Jack! I can't bear it." She took a step closer, and pleaded, "Please, *please*, don't make me go in there! It's so sad… my memories are so, so terribly sad. Please!"

Daphne was alarmed to see that the more Maddy begged Jack, the more he wore a pleased expression and gestured, impatient for his trio of hostages to do as he'd ordered. The fragility of Maddy's emotional state and the cruel pleasure Jack was deriving from seeing her suffer alarmed Daphne more than the man's threats.

Meanwhile, Sim had moved to put himself between the two women and their abductor. Jack whirled and brandished his knife.

"Stay right there," he shouted, his voice high-pitched and frantic. "Or y'all are goin' to get more than a bad night's sleep, y'hear?"

"Jack," Daphne cried. "This is absolutely crazy! You locked my brother into a cemetery crypt and were almost charged with a felony! Do something like this again and you'll ruin the fresh start you've made. Just let us go now, and—"

"Get *in* there!" he screeched.

For a moment, he seemed unsure of what to do next and Daphne realized, suddenly, that this entire scenario was being ad-libbed by a man who had been pushed to his breaking point by another public humiliation. Sensing this, she decided to hold her ground.

"We won't die in there, and there will be hell to pay when they let us out," she declared quietly. "It's not worth it to you, Jack. Just let us go and we'll forget about all this. Nobody here wants to humiliate or hurt you. You've got to believe that."

Jack kept the razor-sharp instrument extended toward Sim while he turned slightly to glare at her. "You've done *nothin'* but humiliate me, Daphne Duvallon," he said between clenched teeth, "Since day one."

"What do you mean?" she asked, bewildered. "*You're* the one who's—"

"Since that day you ran to your bossy mama cryin' that Jackie had tried to diddle you in the embalmin' room. Then, you had to run and blab it to everyone, didn't you, bitch?"

Confused, Daphne shifted her gaze to Sim and shook her head as a signal that she didn't understand what Jack was saying. Then an old, long-repressed memory came back with a rush.

The Ebert-Petrella Funeral Home. Her mother making another flower delivery. Young Jack Ebert taunting her and dragging her by the hand into a storeroom next to a room like this one, and then, with the crudity of an incorrigible nine-year-old, trying to fondle her pre-pubescent breasts. When she'd attempted to wiggle away, he pinched her nipple hard and pressed his knee between her legs.

She remembered, now, pushing against his thin chest with all her seven-year-old might, and when he couldn't manage to get past her protests and protective stance—he'd roughly shoved her against a wall...

"I fought you, didn't I?" she said hoarsely. "I kneed you in the groin that time and ran away and locked myself in Mama's car again," she said, almost gasping. "I was just a little kid! Of *course* I told my mother. And guess what, Jack? She refused to believe me. Your nasty little secret was safe as safe could be! She managed to convince me I'd made it up just to get attention."

A jolt of pure adrenaline was coursing through her veins, and for a second, she nearly leapt upon Jack with intent to pound him into the floor.

Her captor, however, took a step closer, and said belligerently, "You were a big crybaby and you blabbed to my mama, too, and my daddy gave me a whippin' and put me in there all night," he shouted, pointing at the refrigerator. "'Teach you a lesson, boy,' he said to me." Jack gestured again with the scalpel. "I'll teach *you* a lesson, Daphne Duvallon. I'll teach you a lesson you'll never forget!" He turned and glared at Sim, who stood not two feet away from the sharp instrument in his hand. "You first, lover boy. *Get in there! Now!*" He lifted his chin in Maddy's direction, and yelled, "And you, old lady! Go, go, *go!*"

Sheer survival instinct governed Daphne's next move. Before either Sim or Maddy could take a step, Daphne quickly moved sideways until she stood next to a wheeled gurney, placing its length between Jack and herself.

"No!" she shouted. "No, we *won't!*"

"Daphne, don't!" Sim yelled.

Jack turned, and growled, "You little cu—"

Before Jack could finish his sentence, Daphne grasped the gurney's cold metal, about to send it careening straight for her captor. Then she saw the scalpel hurling in her direction and flinched to her right, as if she were the target of a knife-throwing act at some macabre circus. Jack grabbed for the gurney, and for an insane few seconds they engaged in a tug-of-war.

Sim sprang forward and tackled Jack around the waist, and the two men crashed to the floor in a flurry of grunts and epithets.

Madeline Whitaker had flattened herself against a wall in terror while Daphne looked on, helpless to assist Sim in any way. The combatants rolled on the polished cement until Jack suddenly scrambled to his feet. He dashed back to the shelves on his side of the room and seized a strange pincerlike instrument from the tray.

Daphne was still holding on to the gurney for dear life when Jack advanced toward Sim with a murderous look. She knew what he intended to do as surely as if he'd shouted it aloud. In a lightning move, she pushed the wheeled stretcher with all her might. The force of the gurney hit Sim's attacker squarely in the stomach and sent Jack hurtling backward into the tall metal shelves laden with instruments and the soldier's row of gallon-size amber glass bottles full of chemicals.

For the rest of her days, Daphne would remember Jack's screams when several large bottles of caustic chemicals pitched off the shelf and shattered against each other, midair, raining down an acid mixture, along with the lethally sharp glass shards, directly onto Jack's head.

Sim raced forward to where Jack lay on the floor, bloody and writhing in pain.

"*Sim*," Daphne screamed. "The chemicals! Don't touch him!"

"Where'd he put the door key?" Sim demanded to know.

"In his pocket, I think, but be careful!" she cried. Sim glanced around the room and located a pair of thick, brown rubber gloves stacked neatly on the drain board and swiftly donned them. Meanwhile, Daphne spotted a wall phone and dialed 911.

The Natchez police and paramedics arrived in record time, met by Sim at the back door of the funeral home.

"I'll need statements from all of you," the police lieutenant declared loudly. Jack's howls of pain could be heard above the incessant wail of the security alarm all the way to the parking lot and the waiting ambulance.

"Cut the wires on that thing!" shouted the lieutenant.

"Please," Daphne begged Sim, "we can't just send him off like this." Tearfully, she turned to address the officers. "I've known Mr. Ebert since we were kids. He's... he was..."

Blessedly, the alarm suddenly fell silent.

Daphne had started to tremble uncontrollably and couldn't speak. Explaining the long, dark tunnel of Jack's life was too overwhelming to put into words.

"What I think Ms. Duvallon is trying to say," Sim said quietly, "is that Mr. Ebert has had a history of emotional problems. I suggest we follow you guys in my car and we can answer your questions at the hospital."

Daphne cast Sim a look of eternal gratitude.

"Let's go," the lieutenant said gruffly. "This is one story I 'spect I can't even guess at." He looked kindly at Maddy. "Miz Whitaker, I'll let one of my men drive you home and take your statement there, if that would be easier for you?"

"Oh, you are kind," she replied gratefully. She turned to Sim and Daphne. "Are you sure you two are all right?" she asked anxiously.

Sim put his arm around Daphne. His strength felt like the Rock of Gibraltar. "Speaking for myself," Sim said with a grim smile, "I've had better days, but I think we're okay... thanks to Wonder Woman, here."

Jack's cries of pain echoed across the emergency room. Daphne sat beside his bed in the curtained cubicle, awaiting the surgeon who would make the decision whether or not to operate immediately. When the ER attendants had put Jack on the bed, his face had been a red, swollen mass, as were his shoulders where the corrosive chemicals had rained down on him.

"Mr. Ebert, we're going to give you something more for the pain," the intern declared loudly over Jack's continuing screams.

Daphne bent toward Jack's ear. "Just hold on..." she said soothingly. "You'll feel much better soon." The metallic sound of the curtain being pulled back revealed Libby Girard. Jack's cousin halted and stared, slack-jawed, at his condition.

"I came as soon as I got Mr. Hopkins's call," she whispered, her expression horrified. "He told me what happened. I've called Jack's mother, and she and his father are drivin' up from New Orleans right away." She nodded in Jack's direction "How is he?"

Daphne turned her head toward Jack, whose cries had become low, ceaseless moans in the wake of the medication he'd just been given.

"Pretty bad," she murmured. She rose from her chair. "Could you sit with him for a while?" she asked, suddenly weary to the marrow of her bones. "I need a break. I'll just step outside for a minute."

"I'm amazed you'd come within a thousand yards of the guy," Libby said harshly under her breath. "From what your friend just told me, Jack could've killed you."

"He could have," Daphne said, her heart heavy with the sad futility of Jack's life. "But he didn't, and now he can't hurt anyone anymore."

Libby lowered her head and whispered into Daphne's ear. "He's gonna be blind, isn't he?"

"We won't know for a while," Daphne replied softly. "But the first people who saw him said the odds are ninety percent he'll lose all or most of his sight and he'll be badly scarred."

Libby dutifully took Daphne's seat in the chair next to Jack's hospital bed. Daphne drifted out of the cubicle to the ladies' room, then took a long, deep drink from the water fountain at the entrance to the ER. Sim was still talking to the cops when she quietly slipped back inside the enclosure and sank wearily into a second chair at the foot of the bed. Her body felt as if it were made of lead.

Jack's pitiful cries filling the curtained room began to gain intensity until Daphne wondered sleepily why Libby didn't go for help. A long, attenuated keening rent the air, and still no one rushed into the cubicle voicing alarm. Louder and louder the cries became, rising to a harrowing pitch. Such piercing shrieks couldn't possibly be Jack's, she thought groggily.

Suddenly, the atmosphere around her appeared charged by an eerie force that reverberated with the anguish of a woman's broken heart and the torment of her tragic destiny.

CHAPTER 30

MAY 7, 1840

DAPHNE WHITAKER CLAYTON—LOOKING far older than her fifty-nine years—stood in her attic room at Devon Oaks, her moans echoing the cries of the wind and rain that violently lashed the windowpanes. Outside, a ghostly green light illuminated the glowering afternoon sky. In the distance, an ominous black funnel cloud moved slowly, inexorably toward the river's edge.

Daphne hated the wind. It frightened her. And she hated the thunder and lightning even more.

An arc of electricity streaked across the sky and she screamed in terror. A clap of thunder immediately rent the air, and she shouted till her throat ached.

Tornado weather, she would have pronounced in her younger days, and then headed for cover. However, after nearly two decades confined to the top of the house, just as her mother had been, she seemed incapable of thinking logically. In some dark recess there was the thought that she had become a burden, an embarrassment to one and all.

It must be true, for no one came for her. No one climbed the stairs to comfort her or see that she was unharmed. And now, sobbing in terror, she stared through her garret window with wild, seeking eyes for a glimpse of Whitaker Creek. She hugged herself as she gazed across the flattened cotton fields and swayed from side to side in rhythm with the branches of a nearby pecan tree writhing and groaning in the mounting gale.

Another bolt of lightning illuminated the green sky. She wondered frantically where her eighteen-year-old son, Drake Clayton, had gone. Earlier, she'd seen him astride his horse, riding faster than the wind blowing outside her window, and began to call once again for the tall, handsome boy she hardly knew. Her brother, Keating, kept Drake away from her. The lad seemed to take after his uncle much more than his father, Aaron, and—

Aaron…

Daphne pushed away thoughts of the massive, blustering man who used to terrify her so.

Now *why* did he frighten her? she wondered, confused as she always was when memories of her intimidating husband crossed her mind. She could no longer clearly recall what she had done to earn Aaron Clayton's contempt those long years ago.

A third bolt of lightning, jagged as a scar and followed by a sharp crack of thunder, sheared off a branch of the pecan tree. Before Daphne knew what was happening, the enormous tree limb crashed through the roof not fifteen feet from where she stood, slicing through the shingles and joists. Now the winds were shrieking inside the attic walls and still no one came to find her. Chairs from the veranda, buckets, an old carriage wheel from behind the stable, flew across the storm-tossed landscape. Sheer instinct finally prompted Daphne to turn from the debris and destruction of her living quarters and race toward the door the wind had blown out. A loud roaring force at her back propelled her down the stairs. Down, down, she sped, past the bedroom floor. Down, down another flight, till she spied the portraits of long-dead Whitakers, Keatings, and Drakes hanging on the walls of the grand staircase that led to the entrance foyer. Down, down she raced, past frightened slaves and a butler whose name she didn't even know, though the servant had lived in this house for half her life.

She paused for an instant and stared at her golden harp, her cries of terror drowned by the sounds of trees being yanked from the earth. No one wished her to play her harp or dance anymore. She was old. Useless. Sick. Despised by one and all, she supposed. Mammy had been in her grave a decade or more. Daughter

Maddy had married and moved to New Orleans. Now, there was no one to care or remember what had transpired in this house. No one wanted to know about a lonely little girl who dreamed of being loved.

Daphne flung open the heavy front door and felt the wind catch her long skirts and whip her drab linen petticoats around her ankles as she ran toward Whitaker Creek. No one would remember that she had once worn a satin gown—its lime-green color as ugly as the glowering skies overhead—to the governor's ball at Concord so many years ago. No one would remember those singular days when she'd played an etude or cantata flawlessly on her harp. No one would remember...

No one.

Daphne felt like a young girl again as she stumbled past the slave quarters and propelled herself into the woods. She was sure she would find her father if she went down to Whitaker Creek. She was certain that Charles and her sister, Maddy, and all the little children whose headstones had been moved to the new cemetery in Natchez were still down at the stream. She had sensed them when she went for walks, though no one else remembered them. Did the dead have picnics, splash their feet in the creek, and enjoy a summer's breeze, she wondered.

Unmindful now of the roaring wind, Daphne lurched down the path strewn with broken tree limbs. The wind whipped her gray hair, its strands so matted a comb could not separate them. Twice she stumbled, but she kept on, determined to make her way toward the deep pool where she knew they waited for her. Their spirits were everywhere, guiding her steps. The many dead children and her father and the sister who'd hated her so... would all love her now. And Mammy, who had always loved her, and Willis, who had saved her from that brutal Frenchman... they all would be there to welcome her.

When she glimpsed the creek, she was startled to see how swiftly its rain-swollen waters rushed past the big rock where her family used to swim on hot summer days and where her father had set traps for the catfish near the deepest part of the pool.

Daphne's dress was soaked through with rain, and she was gasping for breath. She looked up and down the banks of the stream and wondered where everyone was.

In the pool… in the pool…

She could see them now. They were waiting for her down there, just below the rushing water. The winds of the most terrible storm she had ever seen howled across the landscape. Dwellings were swept like chaff from their foundations, the woods were uprooted, the crops beaten down and destroyed. But it would be lovely and quiet beneath the waters of Whitaker Creek, and Daphne was free to go now. All she must do was gather the stones that would surely take her to them.

And she would escape the tempest raining down on this land. For there was no one left to put a light on the veranda.

Keating Whitaker and his nephew, Drake Clayton, stood before Devon Oaks Plantation and surveyed the damage. The tremendous power of the wind had sheared off one section of the roof near the attic where Daphne had lived. The slave quarters were virtually blown away, but the plantation house still stood, and for that, the last remaining members of the Whitaker-Clayton clan sank down on their knees in gratitude.

Bluff House, in Natchez proper, had come through the terrible storm remarkably unscathed except for a few broken windows. Keating and Drake had hitched a wagon and ordered their surviving slaves to haul the finest pieces of furniture from the plantation—including Daphne's harp—to their town residence until repairs to Devon Oaks could be completed.

Keating had never forgiven himself for not assigning one of his servants to sit with Daphne when the storm first blew up. He and Drake had run frantically out of the house to help the slaves drive the workhorses and other animals to safe shelter. It had been two days before they found Drake's mother beneath the waters of the creek—a discovery that had only prompted more talk among the servants about the "Whitaker Curse."

They had buried the poor, benighted woman in the city cemetery along with all the other family members who had died before her. Amidst the horror and carnage of the killer storm, the death of an unbalanced old woman was just one more tragedy for the town to absorb.

Long lines of mourners had joined in their sorrow, for the Tornado of 1840, as it would forever be known, had taken three hundred and seventeen lives. Among them were Rachel Gibbs Hopkins and all her children, save the eldest. Trey Hopkins had been down at the barn with his father, securing the animals as best they could, when the funnel cloud cut its lethal swath across their land and sliced through Hopkins House itself, leveling it to its foundation.

The sound of horse hooves caused Keating and Drake to turn as two mounted riders appeared in the drive.

"We came to say farewell," young Simon Hopkins III announced. He gazed sorrowfully at the men of Devon Oaks as he and his father, mounted on their two surviving horses, approached the wide steps leading to the broad veranda.."We've taken what we could find 'bout the place and now, we're heading west."

Their horses were laden with bedrolls, saddlebags, and the provisions they would need for the treacherous journey along the trail that Lewis and Clark had forged some thirty-five years earlier.

Young Simon's father had aged almost beyond recognition. Overnight, his hair had turned completely white. Today, he sat slumped in his saddle, mute with grief for the wife and children he had loved and lost. He had bequeathed his plantation lands to Daphne's son, Drake, in hopes that the young man would eschew the law firm of his father and remain on the land. Aaron Clayton had never returned from Europe, and Gibbs, Senior had engaged the husband of his eldest daughter to join the legal partnership in the scoundrel's stead.

"Will you write us, Simon, when you decide where you'll be settling?" Keating asked of the older Hopkins.

"If I live to see where that is... yes, I will."

Keating was proud of his nephew when Drake spoke up, saying

"I hold the Hopkins lands in trust only, should either of you decide to return."

Hopkins's hands on the reins were trembling, and Keating wondered how long this lover of armchair botany and Sunday painting would survive the journey toward the towering redwood trees and mountains said to be so tall, their summits touched the heavens.

"No... no," Simon murmured, glancing at Trey. "We're both certain we must leave this place. There is too much sorrow... too much loss to be borne..."

"We'll miss you mightily," Keating said, his throat tightening at the thought that he was unlikely ever to see his oldest friend again. "Won't we, Drake?"

"Yes sir... that... we will," Drake replied, his voice cracking.

Trey reached into one of his saddlebags and withdrew a piece of canvas rolled tightly and tied with string. "Here," he offered, "Father and I both want you to have this."

Drake reached up and retrieved the proffered gift. "What is it?" Keating asked, touched by this gesture.

"Father found it in... in the only part of Hopkins House left standing," Trey said slowly, each word painful to utter. "In the... study. It's a sketch of a great-footed hawk. Its Latin name is *Falco peregrinus* or peregrine falcon. Mr. Audubon did it when he ventured far along the Trace. He made a present of it to Mother when he visited our plantation... when was that, Father?"

"Eighteen twenty-two," Simon murmured. "He did a much bigger version of the hawk for his folio, but he wanted Rachel to have this as a memento of his stay at Hopkins House."

Keating shook his head. "We can't accept this, Simon," he said regretfully. "*You* keep it. 'Twill remind you of this land and the birds you loved here."

"Just to look at it cuts at my heart like a knife," Simon cried, his anguish suddenly raw and displayed for all to see. Then he gathered himself and his voice softened. "And besides, Keating... you are a man of science, as was Audubon. Hang it on a wall at Bluff House, for all to see that we welcomed a genius in our midst who chronicled a world both beautiful and terrible to behold."

"I will cherish it," Keating replied humbly.

"And, one thing more, if you'd be so kind."

"Anything, Simon."

"Will you be so good as to tend the Hopkins graves at Natchez Cemetery?"

"Of course we will," Keating assured him. "And Drake will see to it after I'm gone, won't you, nephew?"

"Yes sir," Drake said, nodding furiously as if relieved there was something useful he could do amidst the devastation.

"And remember," Simon asked, his voice choked, "to put a magnolia and a pale pink rose on Rachel's grave on her birthday every year, will you? Those were the flowers she painted most often," he added wistfully.

"May twenty-eighth?" Keating asked.

"Yes," Simon murmured. "Five days from today."

And with that, the two men turned their horses and urged them down the graceful, curving drive, setting off bravely for territory unknown.

CHAPTER 31

"DAPHNE? DAPHNE?"

Daphne Duvallon could hear Sim calling her from far off as the image of two men on horseback faded slowly and disappeared. She sat bolt upright in her chair at the foot of the hospital bed in the Natchez emergency room and attempted to regain her bearings.

"Sweetheart," Sim asked, kneeling at eye level, his hands grasping both arms of her chair. "Are you all right?" he demanded, his voice filled with concern. "I practically had to shake you to get you to come around."

Daphne nodded, blinked, and stared in confusion at her surroundings. The hospital bed was empty and Jack's cousin, Libby Girard, was nowhere to be seen.

"Jack!" she cried, twisting in her chair. "Is he—"

"In surgery," Sim explained, standing. "They whisked him out of here and let you sleep. Libby's in the waiting room keeping Alice and René Ebert company. They arrived a few minutes ago." He stared at her with a puzzled frown. "You look a little pale. Are you *sure* you're all right?" He glanced at his watch. "It's four thirty in the morning. Christ, what a night!"

"When did the Hopkins family first arrive in California?" Daphne demanded.

"W-what?" Sim replied, amazed that she was asking such a non sequitur.

"It's a long story," she hastened to explain, "but I *have* to know right now—that is, if you know. What year did your family go west?"

Sim cocked his head and appeared willing to humor her.

"Well… let me think. Around the time of the Gold Rush, probably. They struck out as miners so they moved south of San Francisco and started raising those artichokes."

"That's around eighteen forty-nine, right?"

"Yep… the Forty-Niners—the pioneers, not the football team," Sim joked. "But what's that got to do with anything?"

"Do you have a flashlight in your car?"

"Daphne," Sim said, exasperated. "What in the world are you talking about?"

"Remember the sketch of the peregrine falcon, supposedly by Audubon, that's hanging in Maddy's house?" she demanded.

"Yes," Sim said, his brow knitted. "On the stairwell, right? You pointed it out to me once."

"I think *your* ancestors gave that sketch to *my* ancestors, only I'm lucky my ancestors had any descendants at all, because several of them committed suicide by stuffing their pockets with rocks and throwing themselves into Whitaker Creek," she finished breathlessly.

Sim looked at her strangely. "It's pretty late, but maybe you'd better explain what you mean while we drive to Maddy's. And yes, I have a flashlight. Two, in fact."

"It's pretty weird and I'll tell you everything," she promised. "But first we have to make a short detour to the Natchez Cemetery."

"At this time of night? Or rather, morning?" he protested. "After everything that's happened? Aren't you dead on your feet?"

"No, *they* are!" she said, laughing strangely. She clasped Sim's hand in her own. "But I just have to make sure!"

❧

They parked on the grassy verge of Cemetery Road and, despite the time, sat talking for an hour.

"What a story," Sim said as he stared out the windshield at the filigree fencing that surrounded the Natchez Cemetery. "If I hadn't had that bizarre experience myself on the bank of Whitaker Creek, I might think that you're as loony as a few of your ancestors."

"Maybe Susannah and my namesake weren't really *crazy*

crazy, but just driven nuts by prolonged emotional abuse and too many pregnancies."

"Well, it's all speculation, unless we can find the headstones of the people who supposedly are buried here. Are you ready to meet your forebears, Ms. Magnolia?" Sim asked.

"Are you ready to meet *yours*?" she replied.

Sim arched an eyebrow, nodded, and opened the car door. Flashlights in hand, they walked slowly through the wrought iron gate into the town's cemetery, established in 1822. The moon was low in the sky, casting little light as they picked their way through the thicket of gravestones. A sliver of pinkish-gold on the horizon hinted at dawn an hour away.

"The librarian told me that the old burying ground was on a hill near St. Mary's, downtown," Daphne disclosed, sweeping Sim's flashlight along the shadowy paths between clusters of headstones, angel statuary, and marble crypts. "Then, when this cemetery was established north of Natchez by the town fathers, most of the remains from the old burial ground and from family graveyards on plantations all around here were gradually moved to here."

"How're we going to locate the ones we're looking for?" Sim asked doubtfully. "This place is pretty big."

"Well, I think I can remember the general area where Maddy's husband Marcus and my cousin Clayton are buried, so that will take us to the Whitaker section," Daphne replied. "Their ancestors helped found the town, so they'd be given the best plots, right smack in the middle, is my guess."

They threaded past many a stone marker before Sim called out, "Oh, boy… here are some of Bailey's folks… the Gibbses."

"Oh!" Daphne said, startled. "And here are the Claytons." She pointed to a statue of a baby sleeping on a stone pillow. "Doesn't that just make you weep?"

"Can you find Daphne Whitaker Clayton?" Sim asked, striding to her side.

"Well… let's see… yes…" Daphne said in a stricken voice. "Here she is. See the Whitaker monument? There're Whitakers all over the place in this section." With the beam of her flashlight, she pointed to a headstone tilted to one side. "'Daphne Drake Whitaker Stimpson Clayton,'" she read aloud. "'Born 1781. Died 1840. And the Wind Wept.' That's *her*!" Daphne said in a hushed voice. "She died in the Tornado of 1840, and can you believe it? In the end, she's buried with her *sister* Maddy on one side and her *daughter*, Maddy on the other."

"I suppose when they reburied the remains from Devon Oaks, they overlooked the fact the two sisters were suicides," Sim said softly.

"It all gets lost in the mists of time." She touched the three stones and said a silent prayer for their peaceful repose. Subdued by this discovery, she wandered down a nearby path, peering at headstones as she passed. Suddenly, she exclaimed, "Oh, my God…"

"What?" Sim said, still staring at the Whitaker family plot.

"Over here, Bird Man. I think you may be about to get the shock of your life."

Sim bolted to her side and aimed the light at an impressive-looking stone mausoleum.

"Hopkins… John, James, Henry, Katherine, and *Rachel* Hopkins," he said in a low voice.

"But no 'Simon,'" Daphne said excitedly, "because of the fact that Simon the Younger, and his son, Simon III, headed *west*!"

"Wrong," Sim declared, pointing the flashlight on the weathered side of the Hopkins family crypt. "Here's Simon. In there."

"But look at the dates. This Simon died in 1820. He must be Simon the Elder. The one who didn't want his son to marry Daphne Whitaker. The younger Simon then married Rachel Gibbs—lost her to the tornado—and *that* event propelled *his* son to head for California."

"This is all pretty unbelievable," Simon said, pulling her close so that her back pressed his chest. "But you know? The more I think about it, my father *did* say that his ancestors—a father and son—followed the same route as Lewis and Clark."

"How does Mark Hopkins fit in, then?" Daphne mused.

"That branch came from New York and ended up in Sacramento, selling goods to miners setting out for the gold country. Later, the famous Hopkins became a railroad baron. The hotel was named after the spot on Nob Hill where his mansion once stood."

"Don't you find it amazing that *your* people eventually farmed out west and raised artichokes, instead of trying to make a fortune panning for gold?" Daphne asked.

"Maybe that sort of life just came to them naturally… a hold-over from the days the family raised cotton and dispensed Southern hospitality to folks like John James Audubon," Sim replied softly.

Daphne reverentially patted the elder Simon's gravestone. For a long moment, she and Sim continued to gaze at the Hopkins family plot. "I guess I'd say that Trey blazed his own trail, and yet in a way, he remained true to his roots," Daphne mused.

"Kind of like us," Sim said, nuzzling his lips against the nape of her neck. Daphne turned in Sim's arms so she could face him nose to nose.

"So… what about you, shutterbug? Where does it feel like home to you?"

"I could ask you the same question," he challenged. "Are you sure you're not going to want to go back to New York?"

"Yes, I'm sure," Daphne said promptly. "Forget the Big Apple unless you're with me. But please don't duck the question."

Sim shook his head. "The honest answer is, I don't know. I'll still have to travel some till I can figure out another way to make a decent living." He brought his eyes on a level with hers. "You going to be okay with that?"

"Honest answer? Maybe." Daphne affected a shrug. "I guess we have the best chance of keeping the good stuff between us going if we always keep the batteries on our cell phones charged." Simon nodded wryly. "And considering my budding musical career, Althea says the Aphrodite Jazz Ensemble may be doing some traveling itself."

Simon's brow furrowed briefly, and secretly, Daphne wondered if the trails west and south that began in the little town of Natchez, Mississippi, so long ago might not make it impossible for Simon Chandler Hopkins and Daphne Whitaker Duvallon to figure out where they truly belonged.

On March 20, marking the first wedding anniversary of King Duvallon and Corlis McCullough, a happy group lounged on the weatherbeaten porch furniture that dotted the veranda at Bluff House. Several champagne bottles stood empty on the table—including a bottle of Veuve Clicquot that Daphne had been saving for an entire year.

Bailey Gibbs raised his glass on high and called for attention. The commotion was enough to spook Harpo and Chico, and the two cats skittered across the porch and around the side of the house. Groucho, however, remained curled up on Daphne's lap.

"Sim and I have an announcement, but I'm goin' be the one to make it!"

Conversation ceased and all eyes came to attention as the elderly physician bowed formally in Sim's direction.

"I am mighty pleased to be the one to inform y'all that, after much thought and due consideration," Bailey said, "Doctor Sim Hopkins has decided to give up most of his wanderin' ways to become the director of the Caroline Gibbs Memorial Bird Sanctuary."

"Way to go, Bird Man!" Althea shouted over the applause.

"Oh, my God…" Daphne blurted, then flushed to the roots of her curly blond hair with embarrassment. This proved too much for Groucho, who headed off across the lawn.

Sim bowed modestly amid the clapping, and tilted his champagne glass in the direction of his well-wishers. "Thank you, thank you, thank you!" he said.

"I convinced him that since, most likely, his family originally came from Natchez," Bailey continued, "he was practically my relative. Therefore, he should reclaim his heritage and keep the sanctuary goin' in honor of all families in these parts."

Daphne merely stared at Sim in shock while everyone else continued to clap and cheer. Meanwhile, Bailey raised his glass once again, calling for order. "And I decided this mornin' that I would do something else that would *really* seal the deal!"

Now it was Sim's turn to look puzzled and surprised. The old doctor pulled a yellowed piece of paper sealed in a laminated pouch from his inside jacket pocket and handed it to Sim.

"What *is* this?" the younger man asked, mystified.

"Oh, Lord…" Daphne murmured, peering over his shoulder. She gazed at Bailey, and declared to the group in a hushed voice, "It's the original deed to Gibbs Hall Plantation."

"That's right," the doctor declared over the exclamations of everyone present.

"Oh, Bailey… are you sure?" Sim murmured.

"You bet I'm sure!" he replied emphatically. He looked directly at Maddy, and declared, "And I'm not doin' this because my cancer's flared up and I'm settlin' my affairs, or anything, darlin'. Far from it!"

Maddy burst into tears and accepted the cocktail napkin Amadora Bendhar hastily handed her to wipe her eyes.

"I—I don't know what to say…" Sim said, looking from Bailey to Daphne with astonishment.

"Say you accept!" Bailey demanded jovially.

"Well, if I do, you're welcome to live at Gibbs Hall forever," Sim declared, giving his benefactor a bear hug.

"Not a chance," Bailey announced.

"But Bailey—" Sim started to protest.

"That's because I want to move into town."

"You do?"

"How wonderful!" Maddy declared with a watery smile.

"That's right, darlin'," Bailey said, nodding. He gently hooked an arm around her shoulders, and declared, "Either you marry me, Miz Maddy Whitaker, or we'll just shack up at Bluff House, here, and let the Town That Time Forgot say whatever they want. Take your choice."

"Why, Bailey, I thought you'd never ask," Maddy's said, smiling, while wiping her eyes. "And you're most welcome at Bluff House, now that I've remembered to pay the homeowners insurance!"

After the hubbub over this announcement died down, Sim rose from his wicker chair and seized Daphne's hand, announcing, "Please excuse us, everyone, will you? I want to take the lady for a ride. We'll be back in twenty minutes."

"Where are we going?" she demanded when they were heading north of town in Sim's Range Rover.

"You'll see. Just be patient," he shushed her as they pulled up in front of the Natchez Cemetery. When they had exited the car. Sim seized her gently by the wrist and pulled her along the pathway until they reached the convergence of the Whitaker, Gibbs, and Hopkins family plots.

"For a minute, there, I was afraid Bailey was going to make another announcement and blow my surprise. Now, in order to make this really, truly official..." Sim declared, reaching into his pocket while bending down on one knee, "and in front of each and every one of our ancestors, I, Simon Chandler Hopkins, ask you, Daphne Whitaker Duvallon, to be my lawfully wedded wife at some date soon to be determined." He slipped an emerald-cut diamond up to the first knuckle of Daphne's left ring finger. "My mother told me the ring is Victorian... from Dad's side of the family. Who knows? Maybe it belonged to Rachel Hopkins. What do you say?"

Daphne gazed down at Sim, smiling and shaking her head with happiness while she blinked back the moisture rimming her eyes.

"Of *course* I will," she finally managed to reply as Sim slipped the ring onto its permanent place. Staring at the magnificent stone, she helped Sim to his feet and then wrapped her arms around his waist, tucking the top of her head under his chin. "Was there ever any doubt?"

"In a word, yes," Sim replied, dryly. "But let's don't go there."

Daphne leaned back in his arms and gazed at the headstones encircling them.

"Natchez it is, then? Home base? Are you *sure*?" she asked dubiously.

"October first through Jazz Fest in May, okay? We'll put our feathered friends in Leila's care when it gets so hot you could toast birdseed around here."

"Deal!" she said happily. "And nice, cool Fog City in June, July, August, and September?"

"Great scenery... good food... and temperatures in the sixties," he declared eagerly. "Our summer base camp for photographic safaris, agreed?"

"Yep. And fabulous music out west, right shutterbug?"

"The Aphrodites will be a huge hit there," he assured her. "All the great New Orleans acts cycle out our way during the summer months."

"It's so amazing," she murmured, scanning the cemetery. "It's all here, isn't it?"

"The proof that neither of us is crazy?" he teased with a nod to Susannah Whitaker's headstone.

"That, I suppose," she agreed quietly. "But much, much more. It's right *here*!" she emphasized, patting the top of her namesake's grave marker. "All the endings and beginnings—including us."

"Amen," Sim said, kissing her on the nose. "Plus, perhaps a few new branches on our family tree?"

"Amen," echoed his bride-to-be. "Amen—at least twice."

Author's Note and Acknowledgments

At the outset of writing a book, every novelist could use a band of guardian angels. With regard to *A Light on the Veranda*, mine arrived in flocks over nearly fifteen years.

I owe the re-introduction of this novel to a new readership to my ace agent, Celeste Fine of Folio Literary Management, and to the wonderful Deb Werksman, acquiring editor and head of Sourcebooks Landmark—my publisher's division of historical fiction. There is no finer or wiser or more courteous editor in our business, and I will be forever grateful to have landed on her desk and, through her good offices, for the opportunity to reissue five of my novels, along with a new work, *A Race to Splendor*. In fact, the entire team at Sourcebooks has my admiration and appreciation for all they have done behind the scenes for the six books of mine they have published since 2010.

The publishing history of *A Light on the Veranda* began in April of 1998, when the dogwood and roses were in full bloom. My close friend and fellow novelist, Michael Llewellyn, then based in New Orleans, urged me to consider the Town That Time Forgot as the perfect setting for the stand-alone sequel to *Midnight on Julia Street*—an earlier novel, also reissued by Sourcebooks, that takes place in the Big Easy.

"If Daphne Duvallon ever dares to show her face again down South," Archangel Michael advised, "send her to Natchez!"

He promptly arranged for the first of numerous "location scouting" trips that took me to many of the sites described in *A Light on the Veranda*. Once in Natchez, Michael opened doors to Mississippi landmarks like Monmouth Plantation, Governor

Holmes House, Cover-to-Cover Bookshop, and restaurants as wildly various as the Pig Out Inn ("Swine Dining at its Finest"), Pearl Street Pasta, Mammy's Cupboard, Fat Mama's Tamales ("Eat In or Haul-It-Home"), Club South of the Border, John Martin's, the Magnolia Grill, the Under-the-Hill Saloon, and the West Bank Eatery ("Fantastic Cookin' & Big River Lookin'").

Bookseller Mary Lou England also served as a personal tour guide through this landscape *and* as an eleventh-hour fact-checker for details a non-Natchezian might miss—although any errors in later drafts are my responsibility. Included among her gifts to me were her first-person descriptions of a tornado, a night on the *Lady Luck*, and a day spent at the ruins of Windsor picnicking amid the ghostly Corinthian columns of the mansion that burned in 1890. Between them, Michael and Mary Lou introduced me to scores of local experts who were equally generous with their time and knowledge.

Among these, Maggie Burkley invited me to experience "life on the edge" from her veranda—the prototype for "Bluff House"—perched on a cement-blanketed bluff overlooking the Mississippi River. The late Bob Pully, owner of The Governor Homes House B&B, and his staff, Thelma Matthews and Lucille Dobbins; Jeanette Feltus of Linden (where overnight guests are also welcome); Ron and Lani Riches, owners of the Monmouth Plantation Hotel (dubbed "One of the ten most romantic small hotels in America" by *Glamour* and *USA Today*); and Jerry and Betty Jo Krouse, owners of the spectacular private house, Cottage Gardens, all opened their beautiful homes to me as if I were a long-lost relative.

Also, many thanks to the Natchez Pilgrimage Tours and the selfless tour guides at Rosalie, Longwood, Dunleith, and Stanton Hall—the last mentioned a treasure trove of exquisite antique silver for sale and the best fried chicken I ever tasted. Much appreciation also goes to Lynette Tanner, who provided a private tour of Frogmore Plantation, a wonderfully preserved 1,800-acre working cotton-growing operation—open to the public—with its gins, former slave quarters, and eighteen dependencies that offer a glimpse of life when cotton was king.

At dinners hosted by the Riches and other serendipitous encounters, I met local historians Alma Carpenter, Sim Callon, Mimi Miller, Carolyn Vance Smith—along with the Armstrong Library staff and especially Donna Janky, Karen Wilkinson, and Suzanne Ellis—who were excellent sources of past and present Natchez lore. Dr. Tom Gandy, a physician and photo archivist of nineteenth-century Natchez, urged me to make use of the wonderful historic photographs on display at First Presbyterian Church. Activities director Chip Saporiti welcomed me aboard the *American Queen*, and Riverlorian Clara Christensen provided invaluable background for life on the Mississippi—past and present. The Natchez Opera Festival was truly inspiring.

Nan McGehee, the floral designer at Monmouth, served as my tutor for local flora and the magical world of the Natchez Trace Parkway. En route, she also kindly invited me to visit her planter-style house under construction. On several afternoons I enjoyed cups of tea at the Eola Hotel in historic downtown Natchez and experienced heavenly pampering at Anruss Salon, a beauty emporium in town "where all things are known..."

In the spheres of classical and jazz music, Juilliard alums Cipa Dichter and Sylvia Johns Ritchie, along with chamber orchestra maven Louis DeVries, music teacher Doris Burt, and harpist Rachel Van Voorhees introduced me to the rigorous worlds of student and professional musicians. The incomparable jazz harpist Deborah Henson-Conant traded her CDs for copies of my novels and allowed me to interview her across a continent for hours at a time. Singers Etta James, Diana Krall, and Paula West have my profound admiration, as does songwriter David Frishberg, whose "Peel Me a Grape" knocks me out each time I hear it sung.

Undying thanks also go to Dr. Clifford Tillman and his wife Sarah, who shared with me their love and knowledge of birds along the Mississippi flyway and their concerns regarding the health of citizens in the region. Special appreciation to my cousin Alison Thayer Harris, an R.N. in the pediatric oncology field, and currently co-owner of Peas and Harmony Organic Food Gardens in Folsom, California. She was the first to alert me to GBM, a deadly brain tumor that, in fact, has been linked in some studies to contaminated groundwater in a swath that runs from Texas, north along the Mississippi River Valley. I am grateful, too, for the nonfiction work *A Civil Action* by Jonathan Harr for sounding the alarm regarding water contamination in America.

Among the finest photographers of birds is Tupper Ansel Blake. His magnificent pictures can be seen in *Tracks in the Sky*, *Wild California*, and *Two Eagles*. These large-format books poignantly alert us to the dire effects of "civilization" on the natural world of plants, animals—and especially birds. Tupper and his wife Madeleine Graham Blake (a wonderful photographer in her own right) devoted a precious day in Mendocino, north of San Francisco, where they explained the intricacies of telephoto lenses, and the peculiar habits of the world's fastest animal, the peregrine falcon.

The books, manuscripts, letters, and contemporary news-papers I consulted are too numerous to list here, but my research included: *Classic Natchez* by Randolph Delehanty and Van Jones Martin (Martin-St.Martin); *Natchez: An Illustrated History* by David G. Sansing, Sim C. Callon, and Carolyn Vance Smith (Plantation Publishing Company); *Antebellum Natchez* by D. Clayton James (Louisiana State University Press); *Lost Mansions of Mississippi* by Mary Carol Miller (University of Mississippi Press); *The House of Percy: Honor, Melancholy and Imagination in a Southern Family* by Bertram Wyatt-Brown (Oxford University Press); *Daily Life on a Southern Plantation* by Paul Erickson (Lodestar); *Sweet Revenge* by Regina Barreca (Berkley Books); *Post-Traumatic Stress Disorder* by Raymond B. Flannery Jr., PhD (Crossroad Publishing Co.); *Treatment of the Borderline Adolescent: A Developmental Approach* by James F. Masterson (Wiley-Interscience); *Concise Birdfeeder Handbook* by Robert Burton (National Audubon Society); *A Natural History of the Senses* by Diane Ackerman (Vintage Books); *Molecules of Emotion* by Candace B. Pert, PhD (Scribner); *Toxic Parents: Overcoming Their Hurtful Legacy and Reclaiming Your Life* by Dr. Susan Forward (Bantam Books); *A Harp Full of Stars: The Journey of a Music Healer* by Joel Andrews; *Healing Music: Four*

Pioneers Explore The Healing Power of Music (Acoustic Research CD Series).

I am grateful for the friendship and professional skill of my critique partner, fellow Harvardian and broadcaster-writer, Diana Dempsey. I've also been blessed by the varied talents of friends and family who traveled to Natchez with me, where on one memorable trip, one visitor claimed there was even a ghostly visitation.

And then there is editor Shauna Summers who, during the writing and publishing of the first edition of this novel, kept the Ballantine battleship afloat amid shifting seas and changing management. Likewise, West Coast publicist Marie Coolman and agent Jane Chelius were always alert and on deck, helping to achieve bestselling status for this novel in several national newspapers.

Other angels encountered on this novelist's journey include Diane Barr and Ken Young. Doctors Gary and Diana Arsham, Michi Blake, Betsy Booth, Ellie Cabot, Jayne Cantor, Cindy Challed (aka novelist Cynthia Wright), John and Linda Grenner, Jan Gough and Seamus Malin, Kay Hall, David Harris, Anthony and Susanna Jennens, Dennis Koenig, Wendy Kout, Suzanne LaCock-Browning, Ed "Sleuth" Kelly, Lynne and John Mangan, Terry Cagney Morrison, Mary Murphy, Paul Nevski and Bill Coble—then owners of the Le Monde Creole shop in New Orleans, Bill and Fiona Orde, Jack Reardon, Meryl Sawyer, Dan and the Rev. Diana Phillips, Samara Poché, Mary Jo Putney, Martha and Ricardo Segovia, Russel Thompson, Andy and Barbara Thornburg, Susan Wintersteen, the Ware, Cook, Thayer, and McCullough clans, Andrew Ware Volmensky, Susan Wintersteen, Joanne Woods, Diane and Michael Worthington, Dr. Hal and Betsey Urschel, Deb Wehmeier, and "Katering Kate" of Nob Hill.

Among four-footed guardians, the feline trio of Yankee Doodle, Dandy, and Catmandu bear remarkable similarity to Chico, Harpo, and Groucho.

And, as always, I offer deepest thanks for to my sister, Joy McCullough Ware, for her copy-editing skills on the home front;

my son Jamie, and his wife, Teal; and my husband Tony Cook, whose love, kindness, and understanding of the writer's life are among life's most precious gifts.

Ciji Ware
Sausalito, California

Ciji Ware enjoys hearing from readers at www.cijiware.com.

ABOUT THE AUTHOR

Ciji Ware has been an Emmy award-winning television producer, reporter, writer and radio host. A Harvard graduate, she has written numerous fiction and nonfiction books, including the award-winning *Island of the Swans*. When she's not writing, Ciji serves as Chair of the Sausalito Woman's Club Preservation Society and is a Cavalier King Charles Spaniel fancier. She and her husband live in the San Francisco Bay Area.